ALL THE BROKEN PIECES

MIA HAYES

FINNSTAR

Kintsugi: The Japanese art of repairing broken pieces of pottery with gold and creating something more unique, beautiful, and resilient.

1

CRY IT OUT

One stray sock and a toothbrush.

That's all that remained of Ellison's ex-husband. The furniture, sheets, and paintings were new. The townhouse, too.

She hadn't wanted the divorce – didn't see it coming – but it was there lurking, waiting for her to let her guard down. And when she felt comfortable in her life, with the comings and goings of her husband, with the money and the children, he declared he no longer loved her and had fallen in love with someone else.

Someone else.

Not her.

The thought still left her breathless, but she no longer curled into a sobbing ball.

The demise of her marriage wasn't a series of mini-announcements the way many of her friends' divorces had been. There was no arguing over housework or finances. There was sex, albeit a bit mundane, but she made an effort to sleep with her husband at least three nights a week. She worked out regularly and kept her weight down. Botox was a close friend. She was attentive and interested in his work. She kept a neat house and made dinner more often than not.

All this, and she had been a kick-ass real estate agent in between raising her kids and caring for her husband.

No. Ellison did everything right, or so she thought.

A sock and a toothbrush.

With a swift movement, Ellison gathered the offensive objects and tossed them in the garbage. Then, she picked up her cell phone and called the first person she thought of, her best friend Andrea.

"Hello?"

Ellison shifted the phone to hear better. "Hey, Andi, it's me."

"Ellison! I was just thinking of you. What's up?" Andi had a way of speaking fast and running her words together, so if you didn't listen closely, she was nearly incomprehensible.

"Drinks tonight? Josh is picking up the kids, and Mom needs a night out." Since the divorce, Ellison had taken to drinking bottles of wine at home alone after the boys went to bed. But even she knew that kind of behavior was pathetic.

"Sure. What time?" Andi was always ready for something. Having never married nor having had kids, it made her the perfect partner in crime – that is, when she was in town.

Ellison tucked a piece of her shoulder-length, ash blond hair behind her ear. "Seven-thirty?"

"Perfect. I say we try out the new bar. What's it called?" Andi rattled.

"Whiskey Blu."

"Right. I'll pick you up, okay?"

Ellison nodded before answering. "So I can get sloshed?"

"So you can have fun!"

Fun. What is that? Ellison thought before saying, "Okay, see you at seven-thirty."

After hanging up, she glanced at the time. Five-eighteen. Josh was late picking up the boys. As usual.

"Mom?" Dash yelled up the stairs. At ten years old, he was already as tall as her. But he looked like a mini-Josh: tan skin, brown eyes, brown hair. "When's Dad getting here?"

"Soon," she yelled back, having no idea. When the judge ordered joint custody of the boys, she hadn't understood how hard it would be sharing them. That and the gossip that went with it. In a small town like Waterford, everyone knew everyone else's business. Didn't help that Josh put it up on Facebook the day he left.

Status update: Josh Brooks is single.

Followed shortly by:

Status update: Josh Brooks is in a relationship with Jennifer Cartwright.

The messages and questions began pouring in almost instantly, and her humiliation was complete. Everyone in Waterford knew she'd been cheated on and tossed away. There was nowhere she could hide, except maybe somewhere new. So that day, she started looking for a new house, in another small town not too far away. It distracted her from the reality of what was happening. That Josh had been having an affair with his work subordinate for nine months. That he really was leaving her.

How did she never pick up on it? Well, that was the easy part. His mistress traveled with him on business, and Ellison was too trusting. Her Josh would never stray. He was the ideal husband and a great dad, for the most part. They'd been together since college and had basically grown into adulthood together.

But somehow, the judge declared her cheating husband an equally-fit parent, even though throughout their marriage, all he'd done is play the role of "Big Kid," while she handled all the administrative stuff like homework, dentist appointments, and discipline. The divorce had only been final for a month, and to be honest, Ellison was still spinning.

Cheating on your spouse, it seemed, didn't really matter to the courts. Or anyone else. How many girlfriends told her it was no big deal, everyone does it? How many times did she listen to her mom tell her she didn't try hard enough? That her marriage failure was her fault?

Well, here she was now. Newly-divorced, mom to two rambunctious boys, and sexless for months.

Not a good place to be. Even her vibrators remained packed away. She couldn't bring herself to use them, knowing how much Josh used to enjoy the show.

Ellison walked into the bathroom and swiped on some lipstick before running her fingers through her hair. Tousling it in a sexy bedhead way. There was no point in letting Josh see her look frumpy. In fact, she hoped he saw her and wanted her.

When will that go away?

The doorbell sounded with a tinny dong, and the boys were at the door before Ellison made it halfway down the stairs. She paused on the landing, where Josh could see her, knowing the window behind her backlit her nicely.

"Hey, Ellison," her ex-husband said in his slow, drawn-out way. To think she once found his southern accent sexy. He didn't apologize for being late.

"Hi."

He ruffled the boys' heads. "Why don't you two run out to the truck?"

Dash and Alex needed no further instruction. They left without so much as a good-bye.

"Love you!" Ellison called after them and finished her descent down the stairs. *One foot in front of the other. Steady. Don't let Josh see you as weak.*

Josh didn't move from the doorway. "I need to talk to you. About the wedding."

"I don't have time for this now. I need to get ready. I'm going out." Ellison stood with her hands on her hips, trying to seem firm.

"C'mon, Elle." She cringed at the use of her nickname, but Josh either didn't care or notice. "We're going to have to discuss it at some point."

"I have plans, and you're going to make me late." She prayed it sounded like she had a date.

Josh persisted. "The wedding is in two weeks."

Vomit sat in the back of Ellison's throat, wanting to spew out all over her ex-husband. "Your wedding is not my concern. Your love life means nothing to me." It was lies, lies she told herself over-and-over again. Of course, she cared that *her* Josh, the man she'd been married to for fourteen years, chose a woman five years younger. It hurt. Strike that. It burned. At thirty-eight, she felt washed up and discarded.

"I want the boys there, but it's your weekend."

"I know. We can work something out. Just not now."

Josh gave her one of his looks, the kind that she'd grown to know too well over the years. He was going to devastate her again. She held up her hands as if to stop what was coming next.

It didn't work.

"Jenn is pregnant."

Whoosh. Gut kick.

Breathe, Ellison, breathe.

"How nice," she squeaked before turning away and closing the door on Josh.

"Ellison!" Josh hammered the door with his fist. "We have to talk."

No, no we don't. It took all her strength to pull herself to the staircase. Tears rolled down her smooth cheeks as she balled into her defeated position. Why did Josh have to do these things? Why tell her now? Couldn't he at least let her have one night out without ruining it?

No, of course not. He was selfish, as evident from the affair to his wedding requests.

And right now, it seemed like he existed only to make her life hell.

She cried it all out, marveling at how many tears she could still cry over Josh. While drying her eyes on the bottom of her fitted orange t-shirt, Ellison walked to the kitchen. The green glare of the clock stopped her. Six-thirty. She had exactly an hour to pull herself together. Not that she was ever together anymore. The slightest things sent her into either a rage or a quivering mess.

What is my life? she thought as she willed herself back upstairs to her bedroom and stripped off her clothes.

She cranked up the shower, allowing it to get steamy before entering. Her tense muscles relaxed as she massaged her neck and shoulders. Once upon a time Josh would have done this for her, but he--

Stop it, Ellison. Stop giving Josh so much power over you.

Maybe what she needed was a one-night stand. Andi had mentioned it before, but Ellison dismissed it. Partly because she was a mom, and partly because who would want to be with a hot mess like her?

Still, she made sure to shave all the possibly important parts and lotioned her legs. She left the towel wrapped around her head as she stood in her closet naked, not knowing what to wear.

Ellison ran her fingers on the row of dresses before her. She felt like wearing purple. Josh always said it brought out the green in her hazel eyes, and that made her feel pretty.

To think she'll never hear him say it again almost drove Ellison to tears, but she blinked them away. "Fuck Josh," she said reciting her new favorite motto while grabbing skinny jeans and a loose, olive green blouse.

Andi arrived exactly on time, just like she always did. She was never one minute early or late. Always exactly punctual, which to be honest, drove Ellison nuts sometimes.

"Whoa. Have you been crying?" Andi asked when Ellison opened the door.

"Damn it. I thought I'd de-puffed." Ellison had chopped up a cucumber and rested two circles against her eyes before applying her make-up. She'd gone for a dark, smoky eye, hoping to hide some of the redness. And Visine. Lots and lots of Visine.

Andi flung her purse down on the kitchen island. "What did dumb ass do this time?"

This is why Andi was her best friend. She got Ellison and didn't judge her. Didn't tell her the affair and divorce were her fault, but she also didn't badmouth Josh unless there was a reason. And clearly there was a reason.

"He knocked her up."

Andi let out a low whistle before laughing. "Guess who's going to be all bloated and pukey during her wedding?"

That was exactly what Ellison needed to hear, and she grinned. "And how will she make it through all those nights without alcohol when he's traveling?" Ellison had heard Jenn had quit her job. Presumably because of the work conflict, but most likely because she wanted to be a stay-at-home mom. Ellison had also heard – from her other friend Eve – that Jenn liked her wine.

"May hellish morning sickness rain down on Jennifer Cartwright," Andi said, taking the cap off a bottle of vodka and swigging from it before passing it to Ellison. Ellison declined. "What, no pre-game?"

"I thought you were my driver tonight?"

Andi put the cap back on. "Right. I get to be reliable Andrea tonight. How boring."

Ellison wrapped her arm around her best friend. "Tell me I look hot."

"You look hot. I love the boots," Andi said. Ellison lifted a leg in the air ,so her friend could get a better look at her olive green, suede boots. Andi whistled. "Definitely hot."

"C'mon," Ellison answered. "Let's go before we end up here all night having a love fest with my vodka bottle."

2

TEQUILA, I FEEL YA

The line outside Whiskey Blu wrapped around the corner, just past the entrance to the W Hotel. It was a short block, but still, to have to wait to get in was a serious pain-in-the-ass. Luckily, the line of amped up twenty-somethings moved fast.

"ID?"

Andi looked at the bouncer and flashed her prettiest, don't fuck with me smile. "Do I look underage? Do either of us look underage?" She pointed to Ellison. Only Andi would get upset over being carded.

Ellison rustled around in her bag, before producing her wallet. "Here you go," she said, handing over her driver's license.

"Go on." He waved both ladies through without Andi showing her ID.

"I fought the law, and the law did not win," Andi said with a smile.

"Last time I checked, you are the law," Ellison countered.

Andi laughed. "Only when I'm working, and right now, the CIA is the farthest thing from my mind."

The two women pushed back the heavy velvet curtain, revealing a two-story room with a large bar running down one side of the room and wrapping along the back. Blue underlights gave the whole room a coolish vibe.

"What is this place?" Ellison yelled over the thumping bass. She felt old and out-of-place. Not hip enough to be there.

Andi flashed a giant smile. "A good time!" She pushed a hesitant Ellison into the room. "When have I steered you wrong?"

"Paintball," Ellison said. "My bruises have finally gone away." Two weeks earlier, Andi had bullied Ellison into trying paintball. It would be fun, she had said. They'd met guys, she had promised. It wasn't fun, and all the "guys" were under the age of eighteen.

"Okay, so paintball wasn't a winner, but what about when we did the Renaissance Faire? That was fun, right?"

"Guys eating mutton legs while wearing tights is hardly fun," Ellison answered. Since the divorce, Andi had become Ellison's personal fun concierge. She was always getting Groupons and making Ellison join in whatever the kooky idea du jour was. Ellison both appreciated and hated it. Still, it got her out of the house and that was something she struggled with on her own.

They bellied up to the bar. Music pulsed around them, and Andi jumped up and down. "I love this song! C'mon dance!"

Ellison scanned the crowded bar. Apparently, someone sent out a memo to every person between twenty-one and thirty in DC, and the joke was on Ellison. She and Andi were by far, well maybe by just a few years, the oldest people in the room. This was quickly going down as another fun fail.

"Andi, I can't dance in these boots."

"Hmmm." Andi leaned closer to Ellison and shouted over the music. "Take them off."

"Somebody could steal them." Ellison scrunched up her nose. "Plus, nightclub floors are disgusting."

"Quit bitching and have some fun." Andi waved at the bartender who beelined for them. "I know you're depressed. I would be too, but seriously, you need to try."

The bartender slapped the countertop. "What can I get you ladies?"

Andi tossed her riot of curls over her shoulder. "What's the bitchiest bitch drink you can make?"

Ellison raised her eyebrows and gave a little smile. Andi was a fire-cracker, and this bartender didn't know what he was in for.

"A Cosmo or a vodka cranberry." He winked at them. "That's what most ladies like."

"Tequila shots it is!" Andi said with a laugh. "I was just kidding about the bitch drink. I want to grow hair on my chest."

This time, Ellison did roll her eyes. "Andi," she shouted over the music. "I don't want to do shots, and if you're the designated driver, you shouldn't either."

Andi stuck out her tongue. "Buzz kill." She pushed her credit card toward the bartender. "If we drink too much, we'll get a room. No big deal."

"Maybe for you, but I can't afford a room." Ellison watched the bartender fill shot glasses with tequila. There was no way she was getting out of this.

"We'll share," Andi said. "Besides, I want to have fun."

There was an understanding, one Ellison didn't like, that Andi paid for everything. She paid for their Groupon adventures, their dinners, and usually their drinks, and whenever Ellison protested, Andi would act offended. But they both knew, if Andi didn't pay, Ellison probably couldn't afford it. She was living off alimony and child support, and it barely covered the bills.

The bartender placed the glasses in front of the two women. "Bottoms up, ladies."

All around her, people ogled each other, sizing one another up and posturing to catch the most attention. She'd never been into the bar scene, and she definitely wasn't now. Still, she took her glass, clinked it against Andi's and swallowed the burning drink in one gulp. The fire spread from her throat to her gut. She was so going to regret this.

"Good, right?" Andi yelled. She motioned to the bartender who came right over. "How about two of those bitchy vodka cranberries?"

He nodded, turned his back, and grabbed two glasses from the shelf behind the bar.

Andi pulled Ellison's head down so that her ears met Andi's lips. "He's cute! You should flirt with him."

"Are you serious?" Ellison said. "I don't know how to flirt anymore." And she didn't. A sexy night, pre-divorce, was watching Netflix in bed and wearing a shorter nightgown then normal. Hmmm…maybe that's why she was divorced.

"Ellison, you have to try. Just a little." Andi pushed her back toward the counter. "Try."

That was the problem. Ellison didn't want to try. She didn't want to meet random guys or party with twenty-one-year-olds. She wanted a relationship with someone she could grow old with. And you didn't find that type of man in a hotel bar.

Thundering bass filled Ellison's ears. She was going to have a headache if nothing else after this adventure. The bartender had returned with their drinks, and Ellison took a sip of hers. The vodka clashed with the residual tequila taste in her mouth, and she puckered her lips.

"You're not going to attract anyone making that face," Andi teased.

Ellison sighed, but she felt relaxed now that the alcohol had entered her bloodstream. Maybe the tequila had been a good idea after all.

"Well, if you're not going to flirt, let's dance!" Andi declared, grabbing Ellison's arm. "Get your drink, and let's show these kids how to party!"

Andi led Ellison into the middle of the crowed floor. Despite her initial hesitation, Ellison tossed back her drink and let herself meld with the wild, pulsating music. It was nothing she'd ever heard before, but that didn't matter, she wanted to dance for the first time in ages. Maybe it was the alcohol, but maybe, it was also her loosening up a little. She could be fun Ellison. All she had to do was try.

Sweaty bodies swayed around her, and Ellison kept dancing. Her buzz was in full effect now, and she didn't care who saw her flailing around like a crazy woman. She swung her hips side to side and shimmied her shoulders. Andi was right, she needed this.

"You have an admirer," Andi yelled. They were both going to be hoarse after tonight.

"He's probably looking at you." Ellison wiped away the beads of sweat dotting the back of her neck. "Every guy always looks at you. You're all cute curls and wide eyes."

Andi shook her head. "Nope. I smiled at him, but he pointed at you."

"What?" Ellison didn't know if she should be flattered or creeped out. "Why would he do that?"

Andi laughed. "Look at him. The tall guy next to the bar. He's hot."

Ellison turned her head slightly to the left and pretended to be looking elsewhere, but it wasn't her smoothest move. A man at the bar lifted a glass of amber liquid toward her, and chills ran down Ellison's spine. He was tall, broad-shouldered, and without a doubt, the best-looking guy in the place. He was near forty, making him probably the oldest, too.

Could this guy really be reaching out to her?

Some girls next to them screamed and grabbed at each other. Their drinks sloshed, and Ellison was positive they were going to spill on her.

"Oh. My. God. He's like, totally your dad's age!"

Ellison blushed. How could she be so stupid? Of course he was looking at the younger, fitter models. She was a middle-aged mom of two. Men wanted young and supple, not saggy and old.

"He isn't looking at me, Andi." Ellison turned so that she faced him directly. He smiled, and Ellison looked over her shoulder to see if the girls where gone. They were.

"Yes, he is."

"Are you sure?" Ellison didn't want to make an ass of herself. He'd already watched her dance, no need to embarrass herself more.

"Go," Andi ordered, pushing her toward the bar and the guy. Ellison was keenly aware that she seemed neither confident nor sexy as she stood there uncertain about what to do.

Just do it, she thought. *Just walk over to him and say hi. It isn't that hard.*

The alcohol gave her a boost of confidence, but her legs shook a little even though all she had to do was make it over to the bar and order a drink. If she did everything right, the guy would pay for it, and they'd start a conversation. It was easy.

Or so Andi had told her a thousand times on the car ride over.

He smiled at her again, and Ellison's heart pounded wildly.

Oh, Ellison, what are you waiting for? You don't need Mister Right. You need Mister Right Now. Go.

She lifted her free hand and gave a wave. The guy waved back, and Ellison impulsively wiggled her shoulders at him. He laughed.

And that, plus the tequila, was all she needed to cross the dancefloor.

3

LIKE RIDING A BIKE

"Hi," he yelled over the music in a deep baritone. "I'm Luke."

He offered his hand, and Ellison stared at it for a moment before taking it. His handshake was firm and solid, and she tried to match it. No limp, sissy handshakes for her.

"Ellison," she said, keeping her voice light and bubbly. Unlike Andi, Ellison couldn't be the cute, impulsive, wild girl, but she could play a sassy cheerleader-type.

"Allison?"

"No, Ellison. With an 'e'." She drew a looping, cursive "e" in the air with her finger.

"Well, Ellison with an 'e,' can I get you a drink?" Luke had a faint stubble on his jaw, short-but-not-too-short dark hair, and maybe it was the strobing lights, but Ellison swore his dark eyes twinkled.

"Sure," she said, trying to make her eyes large the way she'd seen Andi do. Guys seemed to love that. She ran her thumb over the bare spot on her ring finger, a reminder that she was not married; that she was untethered, and strange men could buy her drinks. "I'll have a vodka cranberry."

He cocked his eyebrows in amusement. "Really. I thought you'd be a martini drinker."

Since she didn't know if that was an insult or compliment, Ellison let it slide. "I've already had a tequila shot and a drink."

Luke laughed. "Okay, then. We'll stick to the simpler things."

Ellison liked the way he said that. Simpler things. Not messy. *She* could be simple and unmessy for the night.

Luke bellied up to the bar. *Nice ass,* Ellison thought before turning her head to see where Andi was. As expected, she was in the middle of a group of guys - mostly about ten years younger than her.

"Ellison?" Luke called and jerked his head toward the wall lined with booths. "Want to sit?"

She nodded and followed him toward a semi-circle booth. The leather was a deep navy color, and the table had gold accents around the edge. It was elegant in an understated way.

"It's quieter over here," Luke said as he slid into the center of the booth. His biceps bulged through his simple, white t-shirt, and Ellison had a hard time pulling her gaze away from them. "Are you going to sit?"

"Oh! Right!" Ellison blushed. She scooted around the booth the best she could while trying to not look too awkward. She stopped when she was nearly side by side with Luke.

"So Ellison, tell me about yourself," he said as he pushed her drink toward her.

What was something fun to say? Definitely not that she was a depressed divorcée who was still pining for her ex-husband. That would make Luke run for the door.

"I'm a real estate agent," she said and immediately regretted it. There was nothing sexy about her job.

"That's interesting. Do you like it?" He leaned closer to her, and the corner of his mouth ticked up. He smelled like an earthy aftershave, and Ellison fought the urge to inhale deeply.

"I'm very, very good at what I do," she said. There was no need to brag that she cleared ten million dollars in transactions last year. That is, before Josh devastated her life, and she took a leave of absence.

Luke swigged from his scotch. "I like your confidence."

Confidence? That wasn't something anyone accused Ellison of

having anymore. Maybe it was his line – the one he used to flatter lonely women.

She felt she needed to return his compliment, but didn't think telling him about her obsession with his biceps was a good idea. "I like your aftershave," she blurted. "You smell like a forest after a rainstorm."

Luke laughed. "A forest, huh? That's a new one."

Ellison nodded and sipped her drink. It barely tasted of vodka, but vodka cranberries were sneaky. "Not a pine forest, just a normal forest."

"You've spent a lot of time in forests?"

She giggled. "No, but if you're not a lumberjack, what do you do?"

"I work in education." Luke leaned back against the booth, and his broad chest puffed out as he stretched.

"So you're a teacher?" A damn, hot sexy teacher. Ellison shook her head in disbelief. What was she doing here with this gorgeous man?

Luke grinned, showing off all his dazzling, white teeth. Good God, how did he make his smile so brilliant? "Yes."

Ellison set her empty glass down. In her nervousness, she chugged the whole thing, and now her head was a little foggy.

"Another?" Luke asked, pointing to the glass.

What am I doing? I'm already buzzed.

"Are you buying?" Ellison laid her arm on the table, and Luke gently rested his hand on it. Heat rushed down Ellison's spine as her heart sped up. And when she locked eyes with him, she could barely breathe. *Don't act weird.*

"Of course." Luke lifted his hand and motioned the waitress over. "Another scotch and a vodka cranberry, please."

He could be Mister Right Now, Ellison thought. I could be like Andi and have a fling with him.

"Are you here on business?" Luke asked. It was a logical question given that they were in a hotel bar.

"No, I used to live in Waterford which is nearby, but we recently moved to Lodi."

Luke scrunched up his brow and glanced at her ring finger. It still had the indent of where her wedding band used to sit. "We?"

Way to go, Ellison. "My boys and me. I'm divorced."

"Hello!" Andi pushed her way into the booth, her riot of curls bouncing around her face. "I'm Andi," she said as if Luke should already know.

He looked confused.

"Andi is my best friend," Ellison offered. The waitress came up to their table and set down the drinks. Ellison couldn't remember if she was on drink three or four. Or was it five if she counted the tequila? Her memory was hazy. "Luke, where do you live?"

Andi leaned forward like she was eavesdropping on the most riveting conversation.

"Nowhere yet," Luke said. "I'm in town for an interview. I'm staying here at the W for a few days."

Under the table, Andi kicked Ellison in the shins. "Maybe Ellison can help you, if you get the job. She's great at finding the perfect place for her clients.'"

"Andi!" Ellison knew exactly what her friend was trying to do: set-up date number two. If this could be considered date number one. Which Ellison wasn't sure it was.

"Gotta go! So many boys, so little time." Andi tossed her car keys at Ellison. "We're Ubering home."

"I thought you wanted to get a room?" Ellison shouted after her, but Andi shook her head as she walked away. "This isn't going to turn out well."

"She seems…interesting?" Luke said. Concern crept into the corners of his eyes, and Ellison wished it wasn't so dark in the bar so that she could see what color they really were. "Are you going to be able to get home?" he asked.

"Yeah, but I should probably have a water."

Luke moved so that there was barely a sliver of air between their bare arms. He radiated heat. "Do you want to dance?"

"Ummm…" She did, but the room was spinning a little, and she didn't want to look more spastic than she normally was.

"Or we could sit here and talk," Luke offered.

Ellison turned so that she faced him square on. She bit her lower lip before smiling and touching Luke's hand. He didn't flinch. In fact, he gasped, which made Ellison shiver in excitement. If she was going to do this, now was the time to make her move. "So you're staying here at the hotel?"

"Uh huh." Even in the dim light, Ellison could see Luke blush, which made her braver.

"Care to show me your room?" *Oh my God, I did not just say that.*

Luke stared into his glass, and for a moment, Ellison thought she had misread his vibes. Was she being too forward? Wasn't this why guys hung out in hotel bars and struck up conversations with random women?

Did Luke not get that memo?

"Do you want to see it?" He said as his hungry eyes devoured her.

For the first time in ages, Ellison felt desired and that fueled her bravery. "Yes."

"Do you want to go now?" Luke leaned into her, and his warm breath tickled Ellison's ear. "Should you tell your friend?"

Bouncy balls piled up in her stomach, and Ellison was getting more nervous the longer they waited. "I think she knows."

Luke pointed toward the dancefloor where admiring men surrounded a laughing Andi. "Is she okay alone?"

"She'll be fine," Ellison answered.

"Okay. Well, there's an elevator to the hotel over there." Luke slid out of the booth, but didn't offer Ellison his hand. In fact, they didn't touch at all as they made their way across the crowded room. When they reached the elevator, Luke punched the up button, and the doors opened.

He waited for her to enter first.

Then the doors shut, and their eyes locked. Ellison's heart raced as she nodded slightly, granting him permission to close the small space between them. His hand, strong and warm wrapped around the back of her neck, pulling her closer. And when their lips touched, he kissed her hungrily.

I'm kissing someone who is not my husband. New lips, new tongue.

She yielded into him and let her hands wander down his back and up to the base of his neck. He sucked her bottom lip into his mouth, and she gasped.

The door dinged open, and he stepped away from her. "My room is this way," his voice shook a little.

Good, so he doesn't do this all the time.

Ellison's head spun, and she hesitated. "I've never done this before. I--"

"I don't do this either. It's okay, if you want to stop." But Luke's hand skimmed the back of hers, like he needed to touch her. Ellison turned and smiled up at him, and her breath hitched.

Luke leaned down and pulled her into another kiss. Then another, longer, more devouring one. Everything about Luke – his biceps, his eyes, his kisses – turned Ellison on.

Outside his room, he playfully pinned her against the wall and nibbled her neck while tapping the key card against the lock. Ellison's heart stopped, skipped, and went into overdrive. Her stomach was a wild mess of jitters. It had been years since she'd done anything so public, let alone make out with someone in a hotel hallway.

But it was like they say – once you know how to ride a bike, you never forget.

Luke shoved the door open and pulled Ellison in after him. His kisses became soft, torturously soft, and she found herself tingling in all the right places.

With shaking hands, Ellison pulled Luke's t-shirt over his head. His chest had nicely cropped hair and she kissed his warm skin. Luke moaned and pulled her closer.

"That felt nice," he whispered before knibbling her neck. Each little bite was followed by a lick and a kiss.

He pushed her gently backward on the couch and lifted up her legs. "Nice boots."

"Thank you."

"Too bad you can't leave them on." He grasped one of her olive green suede boots in his hand and pulled it off before moving on to the next one. "And these have got to go," he said unfastening her tight, skinny jeans.

For having never done this before, Luke certainly knew exactly what to say and do.

A thrill ran through Ellison as she reached for Luke and pressed hard against the outside of his pants. Nice and solid, just like the rest of him. No surprises there.

I'm really going to do this. I'm going to sleep with this stranger and never see him again.

Luke knelt in front of her and slowly pulled Ellison's jeans down, revealing her sky blue, lacy underwear. "Pretty," he said, hooking one finger just under the waistband. "What's up here?"

With courage Ellison didn't know she possessed, she lifted her arms above her head and let Luke take off her top. "Gorgeous," Luke said as he bent to kiss the tops of her breasts.

He took his time, lingering, before planting a trail of kisses to her collarbone and up to her mouth. Her ragged breath betrayed her. She wanted him. All of him. And she didn't care if he knew it.

I'm standing in just my bra and panties before a man I don't know.

Before she could register what he was doing, Luke scooped her up in his arms and carried her to the bed. His hand reached around her and flicked her bra loose. Ellison gasped, but Luke's lips were on hers, swallowing her sounds. "Is this okay?" he asked.

"Yes." More than yes. Definitely, yes. "But you're overdressed," she said. It hardly seemed fair that here she was nearly naked, and Luke still wore his pants.

"Do something about it."

Ellison sat up on the bed. She pulled away and flicked the button of his jeans open. Luke shoved them down until they reached the floor, and he stepped out of them.

When he was standing in just his boxer briefs, Ellison gingerly reached out to touch him. He felt warm, strong, and firm beneath her touch. All the things Ellison liked in a man.

Unexpectedly, Luke broke away and wandered over to the mini-bar. "Condom," he explained, taking a small box from the top of the mini-bar. "This hotel thinks of everything."

Ellison nodded. She hadn't even thought of that. It wasn't even on her radar.

With the smile of a self-assured man, Luke asked, "Is this okay, Ellison?"

"Yes." Ellison moaned in pleasure when his fingertips danced over her stomach. *So this is sex,* she thought. *God, how I've missed it.* "It's more than okay."

He tugged off her underwear and pressed between her thighs as he leaned over her. Luke covered the side of Ellison's face with soft kisses.

"Now?" he whispered.

Every single nerve in Ellison's body tingled. There was no going back. "Now."

Ellison's body was about to explode. She shuddered against Luke and his warm, gentle touch.

Waves of golden heat washed over Ellison, and she lifted her hips higher, pulling Luke deeper into her.

If this was a one-night stand, she was going to do it right.

4

WITH BITCHES LIKE THESE, WHO NEEDS FRIENDS

As they lay in a sweaty heap, Ellison pulled a pillow to her chest and covered herself from the sight of the man she had just slept with. What if he wasn't used to stretch marks and slightly saggy breasts? Now that the heat of the moment – and what a moment it had been – was gone, she was painfully aware of her physical shortcomings.

"I have to go," she said, rolling off the bed in a not-at-all glamorous way and landing on her knees. Her clothes were across the room, but her panties and bra near the bed. She scooped them up and considered her options. Was there anything more embarrassing than getting redressed in front of a guy you slept with, but don't know? She could run to the bathroom to dress, or she could stuff herself back into her clothes in front of Luke. Neither thought appealed to her.

In all her life, Ellison had only slept with people she loved: her high school boyfriend, her first college boyfriend, and of course, Josh. Now she had to add Luke...what was Luke's last name?

"Do you have to go so soon?" Luke asked from his position on the bed. He couldn't be serious, could he? Why would he want the awkwardness of her staying?

Ellison kept her back to him as she dressed. "'Fraid so."

"Can I get your number?"

Ellison slipped on her blouse and turned around. "I don't think that's a good idea."

And with that, Ellison Brooks left her first, and hopefully only, one-night stand waiting in bed wanting more.

"Tell me all about it!" Andi squealed from her perch at the kitchen island. "Did you blow him? I know you did."

Heat rushed across Ellison's face. "Andi!" she cried. "You're horrible."

"So you did." Andi wore the look of a person hungry for more details. "Was he good?" she prodded. "Tell me it was worth it."

Ellison sighed. When she got home (with the help of Andi's car keys), she didn't shower right away and instead let Luke's scent linger on her body. He had been amazing, and he knew exactly what to do to make her tremble.

"Let's just say I'm no longer going to think of Josh as my sex savior." Ellison leaned against the counter and took a swig of hot, green tea. She had spent the rest of the night remembering the way Luke had kissed her, and the way her body had responded. There was no denying they had fit together perfectly.

Andi laughed. "I didn't know you did." Then she crinkled her forehead. "Tell me you used protection."

"Of course!"

"So?" Andi asked with her eyebrows raised.

"So what?" Ellison replied, knowing full well what her friend was asking.

Andi blew into her Starbucks cup and wisps of steam curled away. "If he was so incredible, are you going to see him again?"

Ellison shook her head, and a wave of regret rolled through her. "I can't. First, he was only in town for an interview. Second, I didn't get his contact info and didn't give him mine. He's gone. Out of my life."

"Fwww," Andi whistled. "A true one-nighter. Welcome to my life."

Ellison wondered how Andi did it. Dating in the real world was hard and a little terrifying. But if she learned anything from the night before, it was that getting a man into bed was not challenging at all. A man will sleep with anything with a pulse.

Which made Ellison feel even cheaper.

Her emotions were all over the place. Relief that there was life after Josh, and that a very attractive, seemingly-sane man, wanted her. Remorse she didn't get Luke's info, if only to make up her mind about him later. Embarrassment over what she had done. Delight over what she had done.

"Hey, are you beating yourself up?"

"What if he was married?" Ellison said. "I never checked for a ring."

"A ring wouldn't have stopped him, if he was determined." Andi scooted away from the table. "Trust me, I know."

Ellison pretended she didn't hear the last part. "How horrible would it be for me to sleep with a guy who was married? Me? After all I've been through with Josh and his mistress." Speaking Jenn's name aloud was still too painful. Who plans a wedding two months after your lover's divorce is final? A knocked-up whore, that's who.

"Elle, I doubt he was married. I didn't see a ring or a tan line." She opened the fridge door and took out a cartoon of eggs. "Scrambled or sunny side up?"

"Scrambled." Ellison answered. Even though it was Ellison's house, Andi acted like it was her own. They had known each other for thirty years, since the age of eight, and were closer than sisters. "After we eat, we should head over to the pool. Soak up some sun and sweat out some of the alcohol."

"Sounds like a plan," Andi said as she cracked the eggs.

Ellison followed Andi past the overcrowded adult pool to the family pool. It wasn't where she wanted to sit since she was childless, but there were no other seats, and she comforted herself with the promise of being served some sort of frozen drink. It was weird being back in

Waterford, but part of the perks of the divorce was that she got to keep the country club membership, and Josh had to pay for it.

"Triple trouble straight ahead," Andi said under her breath. "In the shallow end." She raised her hand and waved at Ellison's friends. "Are we sitting with them today?"

Ellison shrugged. "I don't think we can avoid them. It would seem weird."

Kate, Julia, and Eve lounged near the zero-entry part of the pool. Kate half-heartedly watched her youngest son splash in the water while Julia, mother of three, rested her head against the back of the chair with closed eyes. Eve, well, Eve did what she did best – ignored her kids and played on her phone.

"Hey, ladies," Ellison said nervously as she and Andi approached. Other than Andi, these were her closest friends. Or they had been. Ellison wasn't sure where she fell on the social pecking order anymore.

"Oh my God, Ellison! Where have you been?" Eve dropped her phone and jumped up, nearly falling out of her tiny bikini top in the process. Her hug was like a death grip. Before the affair, before the divorce really, Eve had been one of Ellison's fiercest friends. Their kids were the same age and went to the same school. Post-affair and post-divorce, Eve seemingly avoided Ellison as if Ellison's divorce may rub off on her. "I've missed you!"

Ellison stiffened, remembering all the unreturned texts. All the nights she spent alone, wishing someone would reach out to her. All the times she cried because she was clearly being forced out of the inner circle – the one she once ran.

"I've missed you too!" Ellison said, forcing her voice to be chipper and dropping her pool bag on the ground next to a chair. "I've got a killer hangover that I need to sweat out."

Andi rolled out a towel on a lounge chair next to Kate who held her baby in her lap.

"You look so cute, Andi!" Eve said in her friendliest-bitch-in-the-East voice. "I wish I still had my pre-baby body. You're so lucky!"

Andi's bathing suit was no more skimpy than anyone else's. The only difference was that she hadn't had plastic surgery to achieve her toned, flat stomach. Eve was being a bitch. She had never really liked Andi – something Ellison never understood.

"Good thing I don't want kids," Andi said dryly. She rummaged in her bag and pulled out a book. "They seem like a terrible time suck."

"Oh, Andi," Julia said. "Being a mother is so rewarding. You don't know what you're missing."

"Don't care to know," Andi said, opening her book.

Had they always been so nasty to Andi? Ellison wracked her brain, trying to remember. Mostly, her friends had avoided each other, and Andi was gone so often that it hadn't ever been a huge problem.

"Oh, God," Kate said. "The Bitch Brigade is across the pool. I think they see us."

Ellison turned her head. Sure enough, Veronica White and Alexis Frond posed in barely-there bikinis with hands on their hips. They'd never sit down because, you know, stomach wrinkles were gross.

"They're so old," Eve snorted. "Like over forty old."

Julia nodded. "Their time has passed."

In her former life, Ellison would have joined conversation, but she didn't really care about those women anymore. At least not enough to gossip about them. Yes, like every other woman in Waterford, she had been obsessed with the "Surviving the Suburbs" blog that dissected their lives, but Ellison didn't have the time for that ridiculousness now.

"So what's new?" Ellison asked, hoping to change the direction of the conversation.

Before anyone could answer, Andi blurted, "Ellison had a one night stand last night."

All three jaws dropped open. Only Julia had the good sense to shut it.

"Andi," Ellison chastised, but it was too late. Her friend had already launched into details. Ellison sat there, listening to all of Luke's wonderful attributes, and she wanted to disappear. Andi didn't say anything too sensitive, but she gave the ladies just enough to get their tongues wagging. What was she doing?

Julia sighed dramatically. "What I wouldn't do to be with a new person for just one night. That's all I'm asking. One night." She checked her friends' reactions. "Just to spice things up, you know?"

Eve bobbed her head. "Was he good? Would you do it again?"

Ellison reclined on the lounge chair and somehow managed to not blush. Just thinking about last night and Luke had her heart racing. "Yes, he was good. No, I wouldn't do it again."

"What?" All four of her friends said.

With closed eyes, Ellison said, "It was embarrassing after. I mean what do you say? Thanks for banging me?"

Kate clamped her hands over her toddlers' ears, which Ellison found silly.

From her bag, Andi fished out an apple and took a bite. "That's exactly what you say," she said with a full mouth, making it harder than normal to understand her. "Thank you for showing my lady parts some action."

Eve laughed. "If you don't want him, I'll take him."

"You don't even know what he looks like."

"Hot," Andi answered with a grin.

"Then I'll double take him. I need some spice in my life," Eve, with her fake boobs, flat stomach, and platinum blond hair was the ultimate guy's wet dream. She'd have no problem picking up a stranger in a bar. Well, if she wasn't married to the most decent guy in the world, that is. Still, as Ellison knew all too well, affairs happen. Not even Eve was immune.

Ellison positioned her lounge chair so that it lay flat. "Too bad. I didn't get his info." Wanting to change the subject, she asked, "Julia, are the girls ready for school?"

Her friend shook her head. "I have so much to buy still. How about you?"

"Done. With the boys gone during the week, it gives me a lot of free-time to get stuff done." *Plus, it fills the void in my heart.* It wasn't unusual for Ellison to leave the house at ten in the morning and return well after dinner so that she didn't have to be in an empty house all day long. She tried to convince herself she did her best work out in public (the local Starbucks), but the truth was that she was lonely. And being in her house, alone, reminded her of it.

A sheepish look crossed Kate's face.

"What?" Ellison asked her. Kate had always been Ellison's favorite because unlike the other women, she couldn't lie. She wore her thoughts and emotions on the outside. Eve liked to make fun of Kate behind her back, calling her 'sensitive,' but Ellison had always found Kate refreshing. She wasn't fake the way so many of the women in Waterford were – the way Eve and Julia were.

"I got the invitation."

Ellison's heart dropped into her gut, and her eyes burned. She knew it wasn't the Junior Committee invitation. She knew, but had to ask. "What invitation?"

"To Josh's wedding." Kate looked like she was on the verge of tears.

"I got it, too," Eve said.

"Me three," echoed Julia.

Ellison stood there for a moment, not moving, not breathing. Just trying to find her inner happy place. The one her therapist told her to focus on during moments like this. Breathe in, breathe out. Five, four, three, two, one.

"Are you going?" she asked.

All three women started speaking at once.

"It's Dave, he's still friends with Josh," Kate said. "I don't want to go, but Dave is making me."

"Mike and James are the same," said Eve answering for both herself and Julia. "You know how they all get together and golf every week."

Of course she knew. She was the one who used to host Thirsty Thursdays for the women while their husbands played a round or two. Until Jenn came along, Ellison was the Queen Bee. She had been the one driving the gossip, organizing the fundraisers, and hosting the parties. She was the head bitch in charge, not Eve. And certainly not Jenn.

"So you're all going?" she asked in disbelief. She knew they had distanced themselves from her, but hearing them say they were going to the wedding still shocked Ellison.

More sheepish looks.

"Just tell me you're not going to be friends with her. Please." There was a pathetic quality to Ellison's voice, but she didn't care. Right now, she was on the verge of losing to the whore. Again.

"Never!" Kate said. "I may have to go to that awful wedding, but I won't be her friend."

Eve slid her fingers over her phone. "You know I wouldn't. She's so trashy. I mean, who hooks up with their boss and wrecks a family?" If only Ellison believed her. Eve was now the leader of the other two, and whatever she did, they followed. Funny how so little changes from high school. Eve was the wild card, willing to do whatever it took to climb the social ladder. If that meant stabbing Ellison in the back, she would do it.

"Excuse me." Ellison leapt to her feet and fled toward the bathroom. Her eyes burned, and her vision blurred. These were her friends. Hers. Not Jenn's. And yet that bitch was taking something else from her. It wasn't fair.

Ellison barricaded herself in a bathroom stall and let the tears fall. When the main door swung open, she closed her eyes, but that didn't stop the crying.

"Ellison?" Andi asked. "Are you in here?"

"Yes," Ellison gasped between sobs. She tore off a piece of toilet paper and dabbed her eyes.

"Come out."

Ellison opened the stall door. Andi stood there with her arms outstretched. "Oh, man. I'm so sorry."

"Why is this happening?" Ellison sagged against Andi who held her up. "What did I do to deserve this?"

"I don't know." Andi rubbed her back. "But what I do know is that you have to walk out there with your head high and not give those bitches anything to gossip about."

"I can't."

"Yes, you can. Just keep breathing. You can do it."

5

PLAYING GAMES

The last week of summer dragged by until Friday night when Josh magically appeared in the driveway on time with the boys. Magically, because he'd never been on time once in the seventeen years Ellison had known him.

He didn't get out of the car today, just dumped the boys out and sped off. Maybe the conversation he needed to have with her wasn't so pressing after all.

"Mom!" Alex, her youngest, cried, wrapping himself around her leg. At eight years old, he passed for five, and most people assumed he was a kindergartener. It didn't seem to faze him though. At least not yet.

"Hey, baby," Ellison said, mussing his hair. Of the two boys, Alex favored her in looks – ash blond with hazel eyes. And short. She crouched down and kissed both his cheeks before finding Dash and fist-bumping him. At ten, he thought he was too big for hugs and kisses.

The boys dropped their bags at the front door, kicked off their shoes in wildly different directions, and ran for the computer room. "Dibs," Alex yelled.

Despite the mess, Ellison smiled. Her boys were home. Right

where they belonged. In her former life, she would call them back out and make them pick up after themselves, but now, now she stooped down and gathered the belongings like litter. A stray shoe here, a backpack there. If you'd asked her two years ago if she'd be happy washing the boys' laundry and picking up after them, she would have laughed, but the truth was, she loved it now. It gave her life purpose.

"What game are you playing?" She popped her head into the den.

"Minecraft," the boys said in unison.

"Dad got us our own server," Dash said.

Click. So that's what they did all week. Nice. "Did you have fun at Dad's? Go to the pool a lot?"

Alex shook his head while keeping his eyes trained on the computer. "No. Jenn wasn't feeling well. She kept puking. So we mostly played Minecraft until Dad got home."

Ha! The morning sickness gods had heard Ellison's prayers. Everything aside, Ellison couldn't help but worry about what was going to happen when the baby came. Would Josh forget about the boys? Could he? It would destroy them. Josh had to know that.

The clock caught her eye. Sigh. Why'd Josh get to bring them home so late on Fridays? "Bath time in five minutes," she said, eyeing the two boys. Neither looked like they had bathed all week – which if Jenn had hellish morning sickness, didn't surprise her. Still, Dash's hair was greasy and food – chocolate by the look of it – rimmed Alex's mouth.

"Mooom," Dash moaned. "It's not fair. We get to stay up until ten at Dad's."

Ellison choked on her spit. Ten PM? No freaking way. She'd have to check with Josh on that one. "Well in this house, bedtime is eight-thirty."

"Mom!" Dash started to protest, but Ellison flashed him one of her 'mom' looks, and he stopped.

"You're losing time by arguing with me." She turned and headed upstairs to draw a bath for Alex. Once the jetted tub was full, she called to the boys, and to her surprise, they didn't fight back. Dash headed off to the shower while Ellison oversaw Alex.

After Alex had been soaped and scrubbed, Ellison wrapped her youngest in a fluffy towel and carried him into his bedroom. She buried her nose in his hair. This is what she lived for now. Not gossip. Not hot hook-ups. Just precious moments with her boys.

"Get your jammies on," she said, setting Alex down. "I need to check on Dash."

"Okay."

Dash's lights were turned off. "Dash? Where are you buddy."

There was no answer.

"Buddy?" She walked across Dash's bedroom and knocked on the bathroom door. "Are you done?"

A long wail erupted from the other side of the door. Ellison didn't wait for permission to enter. She flung the door open.

Dash was huddled on the floor with a towel over his head, sobbing.

"What's wrong, baby?" With an aching heart, she sat down next to him and pulled Dash onto her lap. She wrapped the white, fluffy towel over him.

Dash crumpled into her. "Why'd you and Dad have to get divorced?"

The therapist they'd been working with said to expect questions like this and had given her some responses, but nothing could prepare her for the pain in her son's voice.

"Daddy fell in love with Jenn." Since Ellison had no idea if Josh had told the boys about the baby, she kept that information to herself.

Dash wiped his snotty nose on the towel. "But didn't he love you, too? Doesn't he want us to be a family?"

Deep breath. "Families can look all different ways. Ours looks like this. Dad will always be your dad no matter what, and I'll always be Mom. Okay?"

Her son sniffed and nodded. "Mom?"

"Yeah?"

"I don't really like Jenn."

That makes two of us.

"Once you get to know her, that may change."

Dash shook his head violently. "No. She's the reason you and Dad got divorced."

Another deep breath. *I bet Josh doesn't have to deal with any of this crap.* "Don't be hard on Jenn. Dad made his decision, and I made mine. We couldn't be married any more. It's just how things are."

Ellison kissed the top of his damp head. "No matter what, I love you. And Alex. Both of you very much."

That seemed to appease her sweet son. Before the divorce, Dash had always been such a good boy. Very much a pleaser. After the divorce, he started acting out and pushing her away. But the therapist said it was to be expected. Children funnel their anger in different ways than adults.

She walked Dash into his room. "I'll be right back. Going to tuck Alex in, but then we can talk more if you want."

"Okay."

Alex was curled up asleep on his bed. Probably because of his late nights this past week. Ellison pulled the covers over him and kissed his head. *Please let my boys be okay*, she thought. *Please don't let them be damaged from all this.*

She walked back down the hallway and pulled up short outside Dash's door. He was on his knees, praying. They weren't a religious family, going to church only on Easter and Christmas, so the sight of Dash talking to God stopped her dead still. She couldn't hear what he was mumbling, but she could guess.

Tears welled in her eyes. Her family was broken, and she didn't know how to piece it back together.

Oh Josh, what did you do to our family?

After Dash was tucked in, and she was alone, Ellison stripped off her jeans and t-shirt and replaced them with a sexy nighty she'd bought on one of her spending sprees. One of the things she was doing post-divorce was wearing lingerie to feel pretty. For herself. Not for any man.

She curled up on her bed and flipped on the TV. When nothing caught her attention, she opened her laptop and pulled up Facebook.

She'd never taken the time to de-friend Josh, so she searched through his timeline looking for pictures of the kids.

Nada.

Her own timeline was filled with silly pictures of the boys. Pictures of them at the playground, at an amusement park, passed out in the back of the car. Ellison was obsessed with documenting the boys' summer with her. Andi insisted she suffered from "Mom of the Year" disease, but Ellison just really wanted her boys to have a good first summer post-divorce.

She wanted them to feel wanted, and not like cast-offs and second thoughts.

Ellison scrolled through the status updates of her friends, all with seemingly perfect lives. Eve, Kate, and Julia had all posted pictures of themselves at the pool with their kids and each other. Eve, of course, updated the world with the fabulous dinner she had prepared: roasted salmon with dill aoli, sautéed chard with balsamic glaze, and red potatoes. Ellison had eaten a Lean Cuisine that tasted like cardboard.

Her fingers hovered over the search bar. She typed in Jenn's name, something she hadn't done in weeks. When everything first went down, Ellison was obsessed with Jenn. She scoured the Internet for any picture, post, or website that Jenn may have posted to. She wanted to know who this woman was that stole her husband. This went on for months, and no amount of therapy made it stop. Only time. Slowly, Ellison went from searching hourly, to daily, to weekly, to occasionally. It was progress.

Sure enough, Jenn's Facebook page was full of pictures of her and Josh, and a few of the boys. But seeing her boys on Jenn's page isn't what made Ellison's blood boil. No, what really got her revved up was the selfie of Jenn and Josh at a party. It was posted on Wednesday – during Josh's week.

Had he farmed the boys out to a babysitter, so he could go to a party? Ellison exhaled heavily. The boys hadn't mentioned it, but she'd bring it up to Josh the next time she saw him.

She tapped the search bar again. For a brief moment – okay, more like a few minutes – she fantasized about finding Luke. Or maybe having him reach out to her. She did tell him her job, after all. And Ellison wasn't exactly a common name.

Was it weird she was still thinking about Luke a week later? About the way his hands knew exactly where and how to touch her? About the sweet way he had pushed her hair out of her face and said, "That's my girl," when she came?

Andi was wrong. Sleeping with a stranger didn't help her get over Josh, it just turned her into a crazy woman who wanted to be stalked.

Excellent.

It had been a long week.

Maybe what she needed was to prowl as Andi did. Find a new guy every so often and sleep with him with little concern of whether it's going to be a relationship or not. She could go all crazy divorcée and have the time of her life.

Or not.

Ellison slid beneath the covers. She tossed and turned, worried about her boys and angry with Josh over his lack of responsibility.

After nearly an hour, she got up and found a Xanax in the back of her bathroom drawer. Immediately after Josh had left her, Ellison's doctor had given her a prescription, but she had rarely taken the pills. Today was different, though. Maybe because she had a tendency to take on her kids' pain, or maybe because despite what she wanted to believe, she was still insanely hurt. Either way, her anxiety was through the roof.

As the medicine took effect, she closed her heavy eyes and saw Luke's smiling face. It was as if she could feel his warm hands and his soft kisses. She hadn't fantasized about anyone in ages, and a content smile formed on Ellison's lips. She rolled over, pulled the covers to her chin, and dozed off thinking of Luke.

6

FIRST DAY JITTERS

"Don't forget your backpack," Ellison said, handing Dash his overstuffed-with-school-supplies bag. He slipped it on and stood there looking as if he may topple over. Alex's was just as packed, and he bent forward to compensate for the weight.

"Mom, it's too heavy," Alex moaned.

"Just carry it to the car." Ellison had her own hands full with her handbag, computer bag, and coffee mug full of green tea.

The boys lumbered past her, full of excitement and nerves about the first day at their new school. All weekend, she'd tried to pump the boys up about today, but last night had been a long one. The boys were scared to start a new school and needed reassurance that they would indeed make new friends. But despite all that, this morning had gone off without a hitch.

She pulled the door shut and dug around her purse to find the keys. Holding the fob over her shoulder, she unlocked the car door before sliding the key into the front door and bolting it shut.

The Suburban was huge, probably bigger than she needed now that it was just her and the two boys, but she couldn't bear to part with it. Plus, it came in handy when she was on carpool duty.

After the boys were buckled in, she backed the behemoth out of the driveway and onto the street. The new school was only ten blocks away – walking distance – but since she was going out to work, she thought it would be nice to drive the kids on their first day. Small, well-maintained yards with two-story attached homes whizzed past. She lived in the townhouse section of Lodi, which was completely fine, but it wasn't what she'd grown accustomed to living in Waterford. Lodi had solid schools, and more importantly, affordable homes. It was a starter community. A place where people busted their asses to one day afford moving to Waterford. Ellison couldn't help but feel that she'd gone a little backwards in life, but then again, she had bought her townhouse herself with no help from Josh. It was all hers.

"Are you excited?" Ellison asked as she rolled to a stop. The car behind her honked, and she hit the accelerator. People were so impatient.

From the backseat, Alex answered. "What's my teacher's name again?"

"Mrs. Hamlin."

"I hope Mrs. Hamlin is nice." He paused. "Is third grade hard?" Alex asked his brother.

"No, but I heard fifth grade is. You have to take all kinds of tests, and the teachers are meaner because they're getting you ready for middle school."

Ellison resisted laughing. "I'm sure Mr. Peterson is an excellent teacher."

"He's probably a troll."

"Dashiel! That's not a good attitude." But inwardly she laughed. Dash reminded her of herself at that age.

A remorseful, "Sorry," came from the middle row.

Ellison drove carefully down the crowded street, making sure to watch for kids darting out between cars. This close to the school it was a possibility.

Good thing she had nowhere urgent to be because the line to turn into the school was ridiculously long. She glanced at the parking lot and frowned. Apparently, ever other parent decided to drop off their kids today, too. Not wanting the boys to be late, Ellison found a spot down the street, and the three of them walked up the hill to the school together.

Her stomach rolled like a nervous new kid. What if the boys don't like their new school? What if they don't make friends? Alex could be terribly shy at first.

In her hand, she held the boys' teachers' names and room numbers. Alex was in room eighteen, Dash in room seven. She scanned the hall for directions on where to go, but finding nothing, decided to turn left. The rooms were descending in number, and they found Alex's room first. He hesitated at the door.

"It's okay, sweetheart. I'm sure you're not the only new kid," Ellison said to calm him.

A woman about Ellison's age with long, brown hair and a pleasant smile walked over to them. "Who do we have here?"

"Alex Brooks," Ellison answered. "We're new to the school."

The woman crouched down to Alex's level. "Hi Alex, I'm Mrs. Hamlin. Why don't I introduce you to some of my friends?"

Alex nodded tentatively. His backpack bobbled, and for a moment, Ellison was sure he was going to fall over. But he didn't, and he turned around and gave Ellison a brave smile.

"Have a great day, baby. I'll see you this afternoon. Remember, I'm picking you up today."

Alex nodded. Ellison could tell he wanted to hug her, but was too self-conscious.

After Alex walked off with Mrs. Hamlin, Ellison turned to Dash. "Do you want me to walk you to your classroom, too?" She half-expected Dash to shrug her off, but instead, he grabbed her hand and clasped his fingers tightly around hers.

"Yeah," he whispered.

He still needs me, Ellison thought, as they wound their way through the halls looking for room seven. Dash stayed right at her side as if afraid he may get swallowed up in the chaos of the hallway. Parents and kids were everywhere, making it hard to walk without nearly tripping over someone.

Outside door seven, though, Dash dropped her hand and adjusted his backpack. He lifted his chin a little and puffed out his chest. She'd seen Josh do this whenever he felt unsure. Now, their son was doing the same.

Ah, she thought, *I hope he doesn't pick up any of Josh's other habits.*

Dash looked up at her and hesitated in the doorway, and for a moment, Ellison didn't know if she should follow him or not. Would it be social suicide to be seen with your mom?

"Can you come with me, Mom?" Dash asked, his voice a little shaky.

Ellison smiled, trying to ease some of Dash's fears. Maybe she could meet some of the parents. After all, she was new also. "Of course I can."

She gently prodded Dash through the door, took one step into the classroom, and froze.

Luke stood near a window with a girl Dash's age. He was helping her get her backpack onto a hook.

A cold sweat sent shivers down Ellison's spine, and she huffed. *Damn it. I knew it. He was married. And he has kids! He was probably only at the bar trying to pick someone up, and I fell for it.*

What an asshole.

But then Ellison's body betrayed her, and a warmth spread through her core. She wasn't going to let him off easily.

She fussed over Dash while waiting for Luke to turn around. She waited patiently, but she didn't know what she would do. Talk to him? Yell at him? Whatever it was, Ellison wanted him to see her. She scanned the room for his wife, and there she was, at the girl's side, kissing her good-bye. Rather frumpy, in Ellison's opinion, in her yoga pants and t-shirt. She was happy she took the time to blowout her hair and put on an easy wrap dress this morning.

Stop it, she yelled to herself. *That's his wife.*

Then it happened. Luke's gray eyes met hers, and his face lit up. He waved, and her breathing sped up. He said something to his wife and little girl, before walking toward Ellison with a broad smile.

Despite herself, Ellison grinned, and she mentally began undressing him, taking off the pale blue shirt, tie, and dress pants.

What was wrong with her? He was a lying, cheating asshole. Not to mention someone else's husband. She shouldn't entertain the idea of taking off his clothes.

Ellison's hands trembled at the thought of a confrontation. Surely, his wife would notice the way he was acting. How could she not?

Way to go, Ellison, she thought. Here she was, the 'new' parent, and she was already causing drama.

She scurried toward the door, anxious to get away before Luke's wife saw her.

"Ellison!"

What the hell was he doing calling her by name? Didn't he have a shred of self-preservation? And why didn't his wife look up at her?

Ellison took a deep breath and turned around slowly. She wasn't going to let him see her rattled. "Yes," she said coldly. "Do you need something?"

Luke's face fell, and with it, Ellison's heart sunk into her gut. Despite everything, she had good memories of him. She wanted to maintain them. Especially the ones of his magic kisses.

"I thought I'd introduce myself." His dazzling smile pulled her in, and she couldn't help but smile in return. "Luke Peterson, fifth grade teacher."

Oh my God. He's the teacher! If she weren't standing in a room full of parents and kids, she would have laughed. Instead, she stuck out her hand.

Luke looked at her quizzically before gently lifting her hand to shake it. His touch was like fire, and Ellison sucked in her breath. "I'm Ellison Brooks. My son, Dash, is in this class." She pointed to her son across the room. He was already talking to some kid wearing a Minecraft t-shirt.

Good, he's making friends.

Luke leaned in closer to her so that no one else could hear him. "I looked you up, but chickened out. I thought, after the way you left, you didn't want to see me again."

Heat flared across Ellison's cheeks. In her fantasies, she'd done all kinds of bad things with Luke, which made standing here, fully clothed, talking to him all the more awkward. Especially since she knew there was a fit body hidden underneath his dress shirt and tie. And damn if he didn't look amazing dressed up.

"I have to go. I have work." But she knew she'd barely, if at all, get work done today. Her mind was stuck on Luke. Luke Peterson.

"And I have to wrangle this motley crew." He jabbed his thumb back over his shoulder. "I'll talk to you soon," he said, but it sounded more like a question.

"Okay." Ellison nodded before turning around. Without waiting for him to say anymore, she left Luke again.

It was becoming a habit.

"He's what?" Andi squeaked into the phone. Ellison had managed to catch her before she disappeared into the CIA building for work. Andi wasn't allowed to have her private cellphone inside, so Ellison was thankful she didn't have to wait all day to tell her the news.

"He's Dash's teacher. My hot, one-night stand, is Dash's teacher. Meaning I'm going to have to see him all year long." Ellison sat in her Suburban, waiting for her tea to cool down.

"Hot damn."

"Andi, I need advice. I'm mortified."

"I'll bring the wine over tonight, and we can brainstorm, but let's just assume Mr. One-Time may be interested. After all, he looked you up."

"Only because I put out!"

Andi sighed. "Seriously, he's just as big a slut as you. Get over yourself."

Ellison knew rationally her friend was right, but still. She could only imagine what Luke thought of her. Of the way she invited herself to his room, of her hurried exit. What if he thought she made weird noises? Was he as impressed with her as she was with him? Sure he had lit up in the classroom, but what did that mean?

And what did she think of Luke? Mostly that he was super attractive, amazing in bed, and maybe interested in her. No one had been interested in her in years.

"So tonight?" Andi said, breaking the silence.

"Come over around seven," Ellison said. "You can help me with the boys, and then we can drink."

"Sounds like a plan," Andi answered.

Ellison hung up and rested her head against the steering wheel. What was she going to do? Lust after Dash's teacher all year? And how would that impact Dash? The poor boy was already having a hard enough time wrapping his mind around Josh and Jenn. And once he found out about the baby, who knew how Dash would react. Right now, he didn't need Ellison also trying to date his teacher. It would be too much for his little heart to handle.

And even if Luke did want to date her, could he? Would it break his contract with the school district?

On the seat next to her, the phone vibrated, and the screen flashed. Ellison picked it up.

Josh.

Oh hell, what did he want now?

"Hello?" Ellison said in her best annoyed voice.

"Hey Elle, it's Josh."

"I know. What do you want?"

"Are you working at Starbucks in Waterford today or your office? I thought I could swing by for a talk."

The last thing she needed today was a visit from Josh, but what choice did she have? They needed to finalize the details of the wedding, and doing it in public made it seem less likely Ellison would have a breakdown.

"Starbucks," she answered. "I'm headed over there now."

"See you in ten?"

"Sure." She clicked off the phone. Breathe, Ellison. Breathe.

"Jenn is having everything repainted. All new carpet too - for the baby, you know." Hearing Josh talk about his mistress remodeling the house she and Josh had had custom built made Ellison fight back tears. Add the baby to the mix, and she wanted to scream. "So it'll be hard having them there."

Ellison pursed her lips. "Have you told the boys about the baby?"

Josh shook his head. "Not yet. I want to wait until after the wedding."

So the boys don't think you knocked her up and had to marry her? Or so they don't feel like you're replacing them?

"I'll keep my lips sealed," Ellison said.

Josh fidgeted in his chair. "About the wedding, do you think you could drop the boys off around eight-thirty in the morning and pick them up around midnight?"

Ellison reeled back. He wasn't serious. "You want me to come to your wedding and retrieve the boys? No. We're switching weekends. Have your parents watch them."

"C'mon, Elle. Help a guy out."

He'd gone too far. "Help out the whore who stole my husband?" Ellison hissed. "Help out the man who decided I wasn't good enough? Hell, no. You're lucky I'm even letting the boys go."

She knew she was being nasty, but didn't care. How dare Josh ask for her help. It was his wedding and his problem. If he couldn't figure it out, then the boys would stay with her, the way they were supposed to.

"Don't make me call my lawyer," Josh said and pulled his lips tight. Like he was ready to snarl at her. "I'll fight you for custody again."

Ellison tossed up her hands. "Don't threaten me, Josh. We both know you don't have a leg to stand on. Besides, your bride-to-be seems a little too sick to be dealing with your bullshit right now."

A dark shadow flashed across Josh's face before he relaxed and changed the subject. "How'd the boys do with the new school this morning?"

She wanted to say, *You mean the new school they're forced to go to because your mistress wouldn't let their mailing address be your house?* But instead, she muttered, "Fine."

"That's all I'm going to get?" Josh asked. "What are their teachers like?"

Thoughts of Luke in his blue dress shirt and tie flooded back to her. "They were nice. The boys seemed to like them."

But not as much as I did.

"Well, let's hope they don't like piling on the homework," Josh said. "I can't stand the amount of homework they give kids nowadays."

Ellison had a feeling that Josh would never see them doing homework because he never came home until dinner time. At least, that's how it had been in their marriage. "I'm sure Jenn will manage just fine."

"Stop harping on Jenn, Ellison. She's going to be the boys' stepmother, and you need to get used to it." Josh had stood and now glared down at Ellison.

"I'll do it for the boys' sake. Not yours, and definitely not Jenn's." Ellison's heart beat wildly as she tried to keep her voice calm. "And I suggest, if you're worried about homework, you should come home earlier to help with it, so Jenn doesn't get overwhelmed."

Josh narrowed his eyes. "You are such a bitch." He spun and stormed off.

Ellison took a deep breath in. Maybe she was. Maybe that had been the problem with their marriage, but she was 100 percent sure, Josh was a jerk. And like it or not, she had to co-parent with him.

For her boys, she had to do better.

STALKING IS THE NEW DATING

Ellison and Andi sat in Ellison's microscopic kitchen sharing a bottle of Malbec. While her new townhouse was nowhere near the size of her old single family home – the one Jenn now occupied – Ellison loved the coziness of it. Sometimes, in her old house, a sense of emptiness would overwhelm her. There was never enough furniture or paintings or knickknacks to make her old house feel cozy. But in this house, every nook and cranny was filled, and it finally felt like home.

She sighed. The boys were tucked in, and her best friend was here. All was good. Even if the kitchen could barely fit a table for four.

"Let me get this straight," Andi said, tearing off a piece of baguette and dipping it olive oil. "You don't want to date him because he's Dash's teacher. But you do want to date him because he's hot and makes your toes curl."

"That about sums it up," Ellison said, breaking off her own piece of bread. "Well that, and he probably thinks I'm a total whore. I mean who has a one night stand with a guy she met in a club?"

"Ummm, he did," Andi said raising her hand and laughing. "And if I didn't, I'd never get laid. My life isn't exactly conducive to having a relationship."

Ellison watched her friend closely. In all the years they've known each other, they've told each other everything. But all this time, she'd assumed Andi didn't settle down because she was a free spirit, not because of her job.

"What do you mean?" Ellison asked.

Andi shrugged. "You know what I mean. I travel too much. I can be gone for a month or more, and I'm overseas more than I'm home sometimes. That's why I don't have plants or pets."

Ellison knew all this, but for some reason, she'd never given the impact it had on Andi's dating life much thought.

"But enough about me and my wild sex life, let's talk about you." Andi chomped down on the bread and spoke with her mouth full. "Would you do Mr. Sexy Teacher again if given the chance?"

Ellison tilted her head and studied the bowl of olive oil between her and her friend. Would she? And if she did would it hurt Dash somehow?

"I don't know," she said. "The carnal part of me screams 'yes,' but the motherly side of me thinks it's a very, very bad idea. I don't think Dash can handle anymore right now." The memory of her son, kneeling by his bed, hit Ellison hard. She needed to protect Dash even if it meant forgoing her own happiness.

"Let your hair down, Ellison. Live a little."

"I would if Jenn wasn't pregnant. Now, I have to play the stable, loving parent role while Josh gets a whole replacement family."

"You think that's how Dash will see it?" Andi asked

"Yup. And if things go wrong between Luke and me, what then?"

"You're adults. You deal with it." Andi drained the rest of her wine and refilled both of their glasses.

Ellison shook her head. "No. I can't do that to Dash." She flipped her phone over. "Besides, this is all hypothetical. We have no idea if Luke wants to date me."

Ding.

Ellison picked up her phone and tapped the 'mail' button.

Inbox.

Peterson, Luke.

Her heart sped up, and with shaking hands, she tapped the message.

Hi Parents,

Thank you so much for all the offers to help in the classroom this year. Attached you'll find a link to a sign-up sheet. Please take a minute to fill it out and send back to me if you'd like to volunteer.

Luke Peterson

That's it? A call for volunteers. Ellison hated to admit it, but she'd hoped he was reaching out to her. She frowned. Maybe he realized he needed to keep things professional between them?

Andi pushed Ellison's Malbec toward her. "What is it?"

"Nothing," Ellison lied. She didn't want Andi to see her disappointment. Didn't want her best friend to know that she was more than a little interested in Luke.

"Are you worried he may punish Dash if you guys don't work out?" Andi asked.

Ellison swigged from the glass and shook her head. "None of this matters. I'm sure the school board has rules about that kind of thing."

"There are ways around rules," Andi said, her lips pursed into a playful smile. "Luke will figure it out if he's interested."

Ellison sighed. "I don't think he's interested."

Andi raised her eyebrows. "You said he lit up when he saw you. That the fireworks were there."

"Maybe I read the situation wrong. Maybe he was just being friendly."

Andi wrinkled her nose. "What was in that email?"

Ellison tapped her phone on and spun it across the table toward Andi. Luke's email filled the screen. "What do you think of this?"

A smile danced across Andi's face as she read. "You know, Elle, I think you'd be the perfect writing workshop volunteer. What do you have going on Wednesdays at ten-thirty?"

"Absolutely nothing." Ellison took a huge gulp of wine. "But I know nothing about writing. I'm a real estate agent."

"So," Andi said. " All that matters is if you can you get your embarrassment in check."

Ellison sighed. "Maybe. I guess it will get less awkward with time."

"I'm confused," Andi said. "Do you want to try to date this guy, or do you want to hide from him? Because you're throwing off all kinds of mixed signals."

Ellison chugged her wine and set the empty glass down on the table. Liquid courage pulsed through her veins. She snatched the phone from Andi, and before she could change her mind, hit reply. She'd volunteer in the classroom on Wednesdays.

"What are you doing?" Andi asked, hurrying around the table and reading over Ellison's shoulder. "You're really doing it? You're going to be in his business every Wednesday?"

"Yes." *What am I doing? I can't try to date my son's teacher. I can't.* Ellison looked over her shoulder at her best friend who grinned. "What are you smiling about?"

Andi walked back around the table. "I could work some of my research magic--"

"No. I want to get to know him in a normal, sane way." Ellison still held her phone. She kept glancing at it, expecting Luke to respond immediately, which was completely asinine.

"Pre-date stalking is the norm now," Andi teased. "Trust me, he's already looked you up."

Ellison's mind flitted back to earlier in the classroom. Luke had admitted to finding her, but being too nervous to reach out. "Are you sure that's what normal, sane people do?"

Andi nodded. "Absolutely."

"I can't believe I'm going to ask this," Ellison said. "But can you help me find out more about Luke?"

"Where's your laptop?" Andi sat down in her chair and held out her hand.

Ellison got up and retrieved it from the adjoining family room and gave the laptop to Andi.

As she typed, Andi's normally cheerful face took on a more serious look. Ellison always wanted to see Andi at work, to see her goofy best friend in action, but Andi never really discussed what she did for the CIA. Over the years, Ellison had learned not to ask, but she was intrigued, and the more Andi clicked away at the keyboard, the more Ellison wondered who her best friend really was.

"Here," Andi said after a few minutes. "Luke Peterson, age forty, previously resided in San Francisco." Andi looked up from the keyboard. "I can't find a marriage record. So no ex-wife drama to worry about." She winked and spun the computer around so Ellison could see. "That's good."

Ellison's heart jumped. With the exception of Luke being Dash's teacher, there was no reason they couldn't date...except for the fact that he *was* Dash's teacher. It would look bad. It could hurt her son. There were probably rules.

"You should try to seduce him. Wear tight little outfits and stilettos when you volunteer." Andi smiled and wiggled her eyebrows. "Flirt with him a little bit. Tell him you write erotica on the side or something like that. I bet guys would go crazy for that." She paused and snorted. "Hey, I'm going to use that!"

Ellison rolled her eyes. "There will be no stilettos and no erotica. Besides, I already told him I'm a real estate agent." Andi was being ridiculous. "I'm just going to be myself and see where that gets me." Ellison pointed at the computer. She was curious. "What else can you tell me about Luke Peterson?"

Andi smirked. "Welcome to the dark side, my friend."

"It's not the dark side. It's how dating works now. You said so yourself." Ellison crossed her arms, pushed the laptop back toward Andi. "Do some more of your magic."

Andi shook her head. "Nope. That's as far as I'm taking it. You need to leave some mystery, or it won't be any fun." She gave Ellison a sly look. "Speaking of fun..."

"What?" Ellison asked. She had a suspicion that whatever Andi was about to call fun was anything but.

Andi grinned. "Two words: goat yoga."

"One word: No." Ellison shook her head.

"Oh, c'mon Elle. I have Groupon already, and I need to use it."

Ellison sighed. Andi had taken Ellison's pathetic social life on as a challenge and was determined to drag her out of her rut. "You need to stop buying those. The sweat lodge was freaky, and no, I did not have a spiritual awakening, or whatever was supposed to happen."

"But this is different," Andi said. "It's baby goats. Who doesn't like baby goats?"

Ellison raised her hand. "I like yoga just fine, but the thought of doing it with goat poo everywhere is gross."

"Baby goats are cute," Andi badgered.

Ellison blew out a breath. "Doing yoga in a barnyard can't be hygienic. I mean, think about petting zoos. You have to disinfect after visiting one of those."

"Fine, no goat yoga, but you have to promise that you'll let Mr. Luke Peterson know you're interested." Andi nibbled on a piece of bread dipped in olive oil. "If you don't, it's goat yoga for you."

With a groan, Ellison said, "I'm never doing goat yoga."

"Well then, there you go," Andi said. "Talking to Luke it is."

8

NEVER SAY NEVER

"The wedding," Josh said, yelling into the phone. Ellison could just imagine the veins popping out of his neck. "It's in a week, and the boys still don't have their tuxes."

Ellison picked fuzz off her shirt with her free hand. "That's not on me. You had them all week. You could have easily taken them." She kept her voice low, so the other patrons of Starbucks wouldn't hear. At least this time they weren't fighting in public.

"I've been busy Elle, and Jenn hasn't been feeling well. The boys, well, you know how the boys can be. They wear her out."

"Not my problem."

"Why are you being such a bitch?"

Ellison recoiled. Throughout the divorce proceedings, things had been tense, but somewhat civil. That is, until it came to alimony and child support – then things got personal and mean. Josh refused to be a weekend dad, which was great, except it meant shuttling the boys every week between their homes. And her alimony was limited to two years, which meant Ellison needed to step up her listings or get a nine-to-five job.

Still, all of that paled next to Josh's behavior about the wedding. Every time the wedding came up, he became nastier and nastier.

"Look," Ellison said into her hands-free microphone. "I'm not being a bitch. I am no longer your errand runner, meal maker, or babysitter. This is your wedding, the one you couldn't wait to have. You need to act like a grown-up and make decisions."

Silence.

Then, "Well, fuck it," Josh snapped. "If you won't help me, I need to pick the boys up after school one day and take them."

"That's fine."

There was some rustling on the other end of the phone. "How does Tuesday look?" he asked.

Ellison did a quick search through her calendar. "They're free. Do you want to pick them up from school?"

"Yeah, that works." A long pause on Josh's end. "What about the wedding? Can you bring them like I asked?"

Ellison's blood boiled. No. No she wouldn't bring them. "Like I said before, I won't be doing that. In fact, I have plans for that day. If you want them, you're going to have to get them Friday night. And my plans Saturday are overnight, so you can't drop them off until Sunday lunchtime at the earliest." She didn't tell him her plans consisted of drowning herself in vats of ice cream, watching bad romantic comedies, and listening to Andi try to cheer her up – all with a few bottles of wine.

"Wonderful. Thanks for fucking over my wedding," Josh hissed.

Ellison dropped her voice to a whisper. "You fucked over my life."

Josh hung up on her. It wasn't the first time.

For the most part, Ellison tried not to let it bother her. After all, Josh's bad attitude was someone else's problem now. But still, that slightly sick feeling in her gut wouldn't go away, so she got up from her table and headed toward the counter. "Can I have a green tea?" she asked the barista.

"Sure. Will that be all?"

"And these," she said, tossing some salted caramel candies onto the counter. Nothing like tea and candy to turn her mood around.

After she paid and got her drink, Ellison sat back down and opened her computer. Working, like most things that required concentration, had become difficult in the days after the affair discovery, or D-Day as it was called on the online chat sites she used to frequent. She'd stopped working for several months and lived off her savings until the alimony payments kicked in. But now she needed money, clients, and some self-esteem – all of which she lacked.

Ellison stared at the listing on her screen. It was a pretty two-story colonial in Waterford with a price tag of $784,000. If she sold it, she and the boys would be comfortable for a few months, and other listings would surely follow. But she was drawing blanks on whom to market it to. So, instead of doing what she should, she decided to journal. Her therapist had encouraged it, and Ellison had to admit that it was a great way to unload some of her stress.

Why ex-husbands suck. She began typing and didn't finish for thirty minutes. When she was done, she felt unblocked and energized. It was amazing how much better she felt once she put her feelings down on paper. Now, she was ready to develop a marketing plan for the listing.

I'm going to sell this house, and then I'm going to sell twenty more houses this year. Ellison's fingers flew over her laptop's keyboard. She finalized her photo choices and began writing the copy.

Maybe it was her focus, or maybe it was the oversized headphones she wore to block out the noise, but she didn't see or hear Andi until she tapped her on the arm.

Ellison slid the ratty old headphones off. "Hey," she said. "I didn't see you sneak up."

Andi dropped into the seat across from Ellison while holding her full, lidless coffee. Ellison was positive the whole thing was going to spill across the table. And yet, like everything Andi did, the liquid stayed exactly where it was supposed to.

"What are you working on?" her best friend said, leaning forward in her seat and pulling Ellison's computer toward her. "Anything juicy?"

"A new marketing plan for a listing I miraculously landed. Seems someone out there still believes in me." Ellison tried closing her journal window before Andi could see.

"What's that?" Andi's eyebrows shot up. "Something you don't want me to see?"

Ellison shrugged. "Just a journal entry about sucky ex-husbands."

"What did Josh do now?" Andi asked before blowing into her coffee. She lifted the cup to her lips. "Damn. Still too hot."

Ellison tried not to laugh because Andi did this every time – her impatience got the better of her.

"Don't you have to be at work or off saving the world or something?" Ellison teased.

"I don't need to be in until nine-thirty." She checked her watch. "That means I have fifteen minutes to hear all about sucky ex-husbands." Andi smiled and stuck her finger in her coffee.

With a huff, Ellison said, "Josh wants me to take the boys to get tuxes. This is after he asked if I could drop them off and pick them up from the wedding."

Andi's eyes grew large. "Wow. He has balls." She tried sipping her drink again and gave up. "Please tell me you castrated him."

"I calmly arranged for him to pick the boys up on Tuesday from school." Andi opened her mouth to speak, but Ellison cut her off. "And no. I'm not playing taxi service for his wedding either."

This made Andi smile. "It's about time you stood up to him." She started laughing. "See? Your one-nighter paid off. It gave you lady balls."

"I don't need lady balls, thank-you-very-much."

"Maybe not, but I know what you do need. A Match profile. You need to get out there and start dating. Especially if you're not going to pursue Mr. Hot Teacher."

So far, she hadn't approached Luke, and he hadn't reached out to her. Which meant the electricity she had felt was probably just her imagination.

"He's not interested," Ellison said sullenly.

Andi frowned. "You know, this is the twenty-first century. You can pursue him."

A faint blush crept into Ellison's cheeks. Luke was hot. That was for sure. She loved his slightly messy dark hair. And that smile! Oh how it lit up his face. Then she thought of Dash and frowned. "I don't think it's a good idea."

"Then give me this." Andi grabbed Ellison's computer and turned it around, nearly knocking her drink over.

"What are you doing?" Ellison sputtered.

"We're going to make you an online dating profile." Andi's fingers were already tapping against the keys. "The first questions are easy - your hair and eye color. Religion?"

Ellison waved her hand. "I don't want to do this. I'm not ready to date."

"Says the chick who bedded Mr. Hot Teacher."

"Will you quit calling him that? His name is Luke," Ellison said.

"Whatever. You were ready that night. Why not now?"

Ellison sighed. "Fine. What else is there?"

"It's the 'About Him' section. What color eyes and hair?" Andi asked.

"I don't care."

Andi clicked and clacked for a bit before saying, "Okay, Ms. Picky. Now I need you to get creative. You need a tag line. Mine is 'Good girls break the rules too.'"

Ellison nearly choked. "Are you serious?"

"Absolutely. You need to stand out."

"Write 'hi'," Ellison offered.

"You have to be more creative than that." Andi typed some more. "How about, 'I'll never say never to trying something new?'"

"No!" Ellison exclaimed. "That makes me sound kinky," she whispered so that the other customers couldn't hear her.

Andi raised her eyebrows. "Aren't you? I mean, you said-"

"Give me that." Ellison scooped the computer away from Andi and deleted what she had typed. "Full of fun; full of life."

"Yawn." Andi patted her mouth with her hand. "But if that's what you want."

"It is." Ellison hit enter.

"What's next?" Andi asked.

Ellison studied the screen. "A two hundred character essay on me or my match."

"Easy," Andi said. "Type this." Ellison held her hands at the ready. "I'm easy to talk to and enjoy great conversations, full of spark and life. I'm looking for a person who can keep me on my toes and put a smile on my face. I'd prefer more of a type-A, take charge personality."

"Are you sure?" Ellison asked, re-reading the screen. Josh had been a type-A and that hadn't worked out well. "Maybe I need a sensitive man-bun wearing guy to start off with?"

"Um. No." Andi said. "Although, I will say, I did have a thing for man-buns a few months ago."

Ellison stared at her. "Do I even want to know?"

"Probably not," Andi said with a sly grin. "What's next?"

Ellison read the screen. "It wants a picture."

"Oh! Use the one of you in the purple dress. You look hot in that one."

Ellison scrolled through her Facebook photos until she found the one Andi liked. Once the photo was in place, she hit 'continue.'

"Do you see your matches?" Andi asked excitedly. "You should have your twelve daily matches."

Ellison blinked at the screen. There they were. Twelve potential dates. Her heart raced. "What do I do with these?"

"X out the ones you don't like," Andi said. "And we'll email the others."

Ellison had to admit, reading through the guys was exciting. She found one, "Bennydate," to be promising, and at Andi's prompting, sent him an email.

"What do I do now?" Ellison asked. This whole new way of dating confused her. It was way more complicated than she remembered.

"You wait," Andi said. "Guys are going to eat you up."

Ellison blanched. "I don't want to be anyone's tasty, little morsel."

Andi laughed in her musical way. "Oh, Ellison. Never say never."

9

CIRCLING LIKE SHARKS

Ding.
    Ding.
Ding.

Ellison turned her phone to the side and slid the mute button down. Ever since Andi put up a profile for her on Match, Ellison's phone had been blowing up. And not in a good way.

Andi had been right. The men were eating her up. Or circling like sharks. She wasn't sure which was more apt.

It had been a long weekend without the boys, but now they were home, snug in bed after a day at school, and she was going to unwind with a mug of green tea. And maybe, just maybe, she'd look at all the Match emails she'd received and been avoiding.

Butterflies flitted around her stomach, and Ellison couldn't tell if it was because there were men out there interested in dating her or because Wednesday was fast approaching. Wednesday, the day she'd see Luke again. Albeit in a classroom surrounded by twenty-four students, but still, she'd see Luke. She would talk to him and flirt with him in a class-room appropriate way. But would he reciprocate?

In her mind, Ellison ran through outfits. Nothing too sexy, nothing to frumpy. Maybe jeans and a nice top? Luke seemed like the kind of guy who would appreciate a woman in a fine gown as much as he would in a pair of form-fitted jeans. Oh hell, what did she know? She'd seen him exactly twice in her life, and one of those times, she'd been naked.

Too bad Andi was out of town on business again and unreachable. Ellison wanted to call her and run through the list of clothing options. Andi never truly steered her wrong when it came to dressing – her jokes about stilettos aside.

Her phone dinged again, and Ellison reached for it. *This could be good*, she told herself. *This could be the beginning of a whole new chapter in my life.* She opened her email. Forty-three emails stared back at her – most of them from Match, but one of them was from her boss. She opened that one first.

Hi Ellison,

Hope this finds you well. We need to discuss your plans to continue on with the agency.

Best,

Laura

Ellison groaned. The last thing she needed was to lose her job. Sure she went to Starbucks and tried to work, but it almost always ended with her staring at a listing before writing a couple of hundred words in her journal. Or being yelled at by Josh.

She really needed to get her shit together.

Ellison took a long drink of her tea. How do you tell your boss you need more time because your life is still falling apart?

After a long sigh, Ellison typed on her phone keypad. Not ideal, but she was too lazy to get her laptop.

Hi Laura,

I've recently contracted a new listing and have developed a marketing plan. I'd love to meet to discuss next steps.
Ellison

Before she hit send, she re-read the email. It sounded sane enough. So far, she'd hidden from Laura how badly the divorce had affected her. It was work, after all. But Ellison knew a point was coming where she'd have to be honest with her boss – the drive she once had wasn't there anymore.

Part of it was psychological. Josh had told her that he had felt her work took precedence over him and their marriage. That's why he cheated. After that accusation, which Ellison found totally offensive, her drive evaporated. What if she spent more time working on listings than she did with her husband and boys? What if Josh had been right?

Ellison pushed those thoughts from her brain. After a year, she was still shaky, but determined to stand on her own two feet. Besides, she had two amazing boys to raise. She needed to set a good example. There was no time to second guess what went wrong in her marriage. Josh was a dick and liked to stick his where it didn't belong. It was as easy as that.

But for Christ's sake, they had had sex the day before he dropped his bombshell on her. Passionate, love-making sex.

Enough, Ellison told herself. *Enough wallowing. You need to earn some money fast, and that's only going to happen if you sell a house.* She rested her head on her hand. If only she hadn't gone on that shopping spree, decorating her empty townhouse. Truth was, the shopping had been therapeutic, but now she was literally paying for it. The bills were piling up, and her alimony and savings barely covered her mortgage and food. What she needed was a two-year plan to get out of this mess.

So far, she'd kept her dire financial situation a secret from everyone – even her parents. But, if she didn't sell something soon, the time was coming when she was going to need to ask for help because attorney fees don't pay themselves.

Her phone dinged again, and Ellison scrolled to the top of her inbox and began reading. More Match results. Too bad they all started the same: *Hi! I see we are a match.* Or some variation of that. She kept scrolling until one stood out.

Hey there,

I'm a forty-two-year-old white male who is looking for that special someone to share friendship and more with. I would love to take you out for a drink sometime this week, if you are free. I've attached my info and links to my pictures (nothing racy!). I hope to hear back from you soon.

-K

Ellison read the message over a few times. K, whoever he was, could at least string a paragraph together without spelling mistakes. That was more than most guys on the site. Still, she hesitated before responding. She flipped through his pictures. Most of them were outdoors – hiking, biking, boating – but one stood out: K and a blurry faced little girl in front of a Christmas tree.

So he has kids, she thought. *That could be a plus.*

If Andi were around, she'd know exactly what to say, but she wasn't. Which meant Ellison was flying solo.

Before she lost her nerve, she replied.

Hi K,

I'm available this Friday, after seven, for drinks if you are free.

E

She pushed 'send' and held her breath. Either this was going to go well, or extremely bad. She picked Friday because that was the night Josh had to pick the boys up for the wedding, and she didn't want to think about it. *That* honor she was reserving for Saturday, when Andi was home, and the actual wedding was happening. Because try as she did, she still wasn't over Josh, despite his affair and his nasty attitude with her lately.

Ellison wasted another hour scrolling through her matches, and finding no one else she liked, decided to work on her marketing plan. She trekked across the living room to where her laptop sat plugged in, and after retrieving it, settled into her favorite chair, legs crossed beneath her.

Real estate may sound like a fun life, but it wasn't. Sure, she got to see the insides of some fabulous houses, but her three-percent commission meant she had to go after the bigger, more expensive houses, and the competition for those listings was fierce. Once Ellison loved the dog-eat-dog world of high-end real estate. Now, it had her doubting herself. What if Laura was gently letting her go? What if she could never convince a homeowner to choose her again?

She hated the feelings of self-doubt that coursed through her veins.

Before opening her laptop, she took one last glance at her phone. Sure enough there was a message from "K." Her heart hammered, and she couldn't believe how nervous she was.

She clicked it open.

E,

Sorry but Friday night is out for me. Maybe next week?
-K

Disappointment she wasn't expecting settled into her gut. He hadn't rejected her outright, but she couldn't go out next week as she had the boys. Unless Andi babysat, something she'd done a few times for Ellison over the course of the past year. She'd probably do it, if asked, but right now, Ellison had no way of reaching her.

Ellison typed back:

· · ·

Next week won't work. How about the following Friday?

E.

She pushed send and waited a few minutes. When nothing came, Ellison turned her attention to her computer.

"Alright," she said. "Time to get serious."

She opened her file and re-read some of the plan she'd written at Starbucks. She'd spent all day there until it was time for her to meet the boys. The barista had joked that they were going to put a "Reserved for Ellison" sign on her favorite chair.

The plan she had managed to eke out was okay. Not stellar, but not God awful either. She knew she could do better and began highlighting the weak spots.

Ding.

Ellison's grabbed at her phone. Sure enough there was a message from K, but once she opened it, she wished she hadn't.

If you don't want to go out with me, just say so. No need to be a passive aggressive bitch about it.

Whoa. That wasn't what she was expecting at all. Her face flushed, and her lips fell slightly apart. Was this how people spoke to each other online?

With one flick of her finger, she deleted the message and K from her life. *Wouldn't it be nice if I could do that with Josh*, she mused? *Just swipe my finger, and he'd be gone.*

Ellison settled back into her chair and took a sip of tea. It was almost cold now, but she was too lazy to reheat it. Instead she gulped it down and turned her attention back to her computer.

She turned her full concentration on to her marketing plan. She needed to get more listings and end her dependency on Josh. The sooner, the better. She was laser focused, and it was nearly midnight when she stopped.

As she read back the plan, a soft smile came over her face. Maybe she couldn't erase Josh from her life, but she certainly could show him how strong she was. How she didn't need him anymore. How the divorce hadn't ruined her.

The smile turned into a grin.

She was going to get back at the bastard one way or another.

10

YOU CAN'T GO HOME AGAIN

It turned out Josh was incapable of dropping the boys off at Ellison's Tuesday night, so she pulled herself together, put on her cutest outfit, and drove to her old home. The one she and Josh had built especially to her liking.

Driving down Cherrywood Street, past the perfectly manicured lawns and soaring rooflines, a flood of memories hit Ellison: her boys learning to ride bikes around the cul-de-sac; decorating the house for the holidays; neighborhood parties. That part of her life was completely over, and she fought back tears.

I can do this.

As she pulled into the driveway, another more horrible thought hit her. Jenn was inside her old home, happy and pregnant. Just like she'd once been.

Let it go. Just let it go.

The grand two-story house loomed over her. It was three times the size of her townhouse. And yeah, she was a little bitter. To go from 6,000 square feet to just under 2,000 was tough. Maybe that made her spoiled, but there it was. Ellison missed her big, custom-designed house and all the little touches she had put into it.

During the divorce, Josh had bought out Ellison's portion of the house, and she often believed he did it just to spite her. He never loved the house the way she did.

Ellison jumped out of the Suburban and walked slowly up the cobblestone walkway. They had upgraded from simple cement and spent a fortune on landscaping – something Josh had always complained about. But, she knew the value of great curb appeal, and the house still looked great.

Her insides trembled, as did her hands, but she could hold herself together enough to get through this. It would be over in under five minutes.

Ellison climbed the stone porch stairs one-at-a-time and paused before the--

Red?

The front door was a deep crimson. Ellison's gut rolled. The brick front colonial had always had a dark gray door while she lived there.

But now it was red. Jenn was certainly putting her stamp on things.

Ellison rang the doorbell and prayed she didn't answer.

No such luck.

"Hello, Ellison." Jenn was tall - almost as tall as Josh - with sharp cheekbones, dark brown hair and tan skin. She was the physical opposite of Ellison in every way.

"Hi. Are the boys ready?" *Let's not make this more painful than it already is*, she thought.

Jenn shook her ponytailed head. "No. They wouldn't listen to me to put their shoes on."

Ellison resisted a satisfied smile. As much as she wanted to raise good, well-behaved boys, she got secret pleasure from hearing they disobeyed Jenn.

The TV blared from the family room. Jenn moved slightly and exposed a glimpse of the formal dining room. It's once pale green walls were now a vibrant red that matched the front door.

Does Jenn not have Instagram? Ellison thought. Red dining rooms are so ten years ago and not making a comeback anytime soon.

"Are they back there?" Ellison asked motioning toward the rear of the house.

"They're watching TV." Jenn opened the door even wider, but kept herself wedged between the edge and the jam, as if she didn't want Ellison to see inside her old home.

"Can you get them?" Ellison asked civilly even though she wanted to pull Jenn's perky ponytail and kick her in the shins.

Jenn smirked. "You can go get them if you want."

That was the last thing Ellison wanted. No, she was better off staying outside. "Boys," Ellison yelled over Jenn's shoulder. "Get your shoes, and let's go!" She looked at Jenn. "Where's Josh?"

"That's none of your business." Jenn sounded agitated.

Ellison gritted her teeth. Arguing with Josh was one thing; arguing with his mistress slash soon-to-be wife was another. No she wouldn't bite. Not today.

The boys came tumbling out of the house, but not before Jenn ruffled Alex's hair. "Hey buddy, see you next week. We're making cupcakes. Don't forget."

Alex paused and gave Jenn a hug around the thighs. Ellison wanted to rip her son away, but she knew she had to act responsibly.

Being an adult sucked.

The boys pushed past Ellison and out onto the porch. It had only been a few hours since she'd dropped them off at school, but it felt like years. "Get in the car," she said, patting Dash on the head.

They obeyed and shouted their good-byes to Jenn, who waved at them.

"Those boys have a lot of energy," Jenn said, laughing.

"They're boys," Ellison answered. "They don't stay babies forever."

Jenn wrapped her arm around her stomach. "I suppose they don't."

"So, *is* Josh working?" It was a dig – during the affair, he'd often come home for dinner before heading back to work, i.e. Jenn.

"He had to leave work early to take the boys to get their tuxes." She pouted out her bottom lip.

As if that's my fault.

"So, yes, he's back at work," Jenn answered and smiled tightly.

"Uh huh. I'm sure he is. He always goes back to work." Ellison turned and walked down the front stairs. She hoped she planted just enough doubt in Jenn's mind to drive her crazy.

Wednesday morning's routine went smoothly. The boys got up, got dressed, didn't lose any articles of clothing or homework, and they made it out the door on time. Ellison was in great spirits until she saw the school.

Shit.

She had to volunteer today at ten-thirty. In Luke's class. She looked down at what she was wearing and made an immediate decision to go home and change. Yoga pants weren't going to cut it.

On the drive back to the house, she called Andi, who had returned from whatever mysterious place she'd been. Ellison had stopped asking her about her travels years ago. "Quick, what should I wear today? I have to work in Luke's classroom."

"Something slutty." Andi crunched into her ear.

"Are you eating?"

"Granola. Want some?" She crunched some more.

Ellison caught her phone between her shoulder and ear as she drove back to her house. "C'mon Andi. I need help. I don't want to look like I'm trying too hard, but I don't want to look like a slacker either."

"Jeans," Andi said.

"And what on top?"

"What about your cute pink tunic, ballet flats, and some interesting earrings? Dress like it's a casual date."

At the word 'date,' Ellison's stomach flip-flopped. "You know, Match might not be working for me."

"Oh?" Andi said.

"Yeah, I had some guy call me a passive-aggressive bitch because I wasn't available on his time."

"Ouch," said Andi. "We'll keep looking. There has to be one good match for you, unless you're ready to date Mr. Hot Teacher."

Ellison's cheeks flared hot. "No. I told you, I can't. It would be too hard on Dash. Probably Alex, too."

"So there's no one else on the site you'd consider?"

She turned into her driveway. "There is one – Bennydate – who sounds interesting, but I haven't responded."

"What makes him interesting?" Andi asked, still crunching on her granola.

Ellison hopped out of the Suburban and strolled into the house, still holding her phone to her ear.

"He likes hiking and wine."

"Maybe Mr. Hot Teacher does too. You should ask him when you see him on your date today."

"It's not a date. It's just me volunteering," Ellison said.

"And getting in Luke's face." Pause. "I don't understand why you just don't ask him out."

"Andi, haven't you been listening to me? He's Dash's teacher. It would be disastrous for Dash. Not to mention awkward."

"No. Awkward is having slept with the teacher, not dating him."

"Andi!"

"Hey, I'm just calling it like I see it. Speaking of which, I ran into Eve last night. Guess who she was with?"

Ellison was pulling the pink tunic off the hanger. "I don't know. Who?"

"Jenn."

A prickling heat ran through Ellison's body. She must have run out the door as soon as Ellison picked up the boys. Bitch.

As for Eve, even when they were friends, Ellison didn't trust her, but now? After her declaration of friendship at the pool just a few weeks ago, Ellison definitely didn't trust her.

"Elle, you okay?"

"I'm fine." It was a lie, but she needed to keep going. No time to wallow.

"Have fun on your non-date date, okay? And wear your hair up. It shows off your eyes."

"Okay. Thanks. See you soon?"

"I'm flying to Seattle tomorrow and get back Friday."

"Just in time for Drunkfest," Ellison said, referring to her and Andi's plans for Josh's wedding.

"I wouldn't miss it."

And Ellison knew her best friend meant it.

———

After being rung into the school and printing off her ID in the office, Ellison made her way to Luke's class. With each step, her pulse sped up until her heart was hammering against her ribcage. Good God, what if he could hear it? What if Luke Peterson could tell the effect he had on her? How mortifying.

Outside the classroom door, Ellison paused, fussed over her shirt – the pink tunic, just as Andi suggested – and prepared to spend the next hour in the presence of a man who had seen her naked, and who was the object of her nighttime fantasies.

Not awkward at all.

Ellison kept staring at the door. Was she supposed to knock or walk right in?

When the door flung open, Ellison gasped. She hadn't meant to, didn't want to, but she did. Luke stood before her in dark, fitted jeans and a crisp, white button-up shirt. The top two buttons were undone exposing just a hint of his bare chest. Ellison's breath slowed to deep inhales, like she was trying to breathe Luke in. Oh God, did he smell good.

"Hi, Ms. Brooks. Welcome to Room Seven."

Her mouth went cotton dry, and all Ellison could squeak out was a weak, "Hello." She waved to Dash, who waved back and didn't seem at all embarrassed to have her there.

"Class, this is Ms. Brooks, Dash's mom. She's going to help us with our small moment stories today." Twenty-four pairs of eyes were trained on her, so Ellison waved.

"Ms. Brooks? You can sit over here." Luke gestured to a crescent shaped table.

He approached her and whispered, "Just help the kids brainstorm ideas today. We're pre-writing."

She nodded, too afraid her words would come out like a jumbled mess. Her brain was fuzzy with Luke. His smell, his deep voice, his washboard abs...

"Ms. Brooks?"

Ellison snapped her head around.

"Are you ready?" Luke asked.

"Yes. I can't wait." She forced enthusiasm into her voice. Better be peppy when working with kids.

"Who would like to work with Ms. Brooks?"

Hands shot into the air like she was a rock star or something. Luke called out five kids' names, and they jumped up from their seats and raced toward her.

"Hi, Ms. Brooks," said a little girl with glasses.

"Hi, Ms. Brooks," said a very tall, lanky boy.

"Jjdjlj" mumbled some kid looking down at his feet.

She glanced over at Luke, and he flashed his brilliant white smile at her, causing her to rock off balance a little. His grin grew.

"Alright," she said, taking her place inside the crescent table. The kids filled in around her. "Who would like to start?"

A small girl with braids raised her hand first, so Ellison called on her. "What's your name?"

"Kenzie."

"What is your small moment about, Kenzie?"

"My small moment is about when my brother was born."

"That's good. Do you have any more details?"

The girl shook her head.

"Do you remember how you felt, or what he looked like?"

"No."

"Hmmm...is there something else you'd like to write about?"

Kenzie looked up at Ellison as if she just heard the worst news ever. "No. I want to write about this."

Ellison forced a smile. How Luke does this all day long was beyond her. She looked over to him for guidance, but he was lost in conversation with a boy sitting near Dash.

"Okay," Ellison said. "Let's start with how old you were."

"I was two."

Good Lord. This was going to take all hour.

Luke caught her eye and smiled again. If this is what she needed to do to keep seeing that smile, she was going to do it.

The man was sexy, no denying it.

11

MIDDLE SCHOOL PART 2

"Ellison, it's Eve. How are you?"

"I'm well, and you?" All the blood in Ellison's body rushed to her head, and she felt like it might explode. She flicked off the TV and dropped the remote next to her. She'd been fighting a headache all day, and hearing Eve's voice wasn't helping.

A faint clink of a glass against something hard made Ellison think Eve was already drinking – at two-thirty. But why was she surprised? When Ellison had been part of the group – when she'd hosted the meetings and ran the show – she and the other women often started drinking at lunch.

Day drinking was a Waterford habit.

"I've been better," Eve said slowly. "But let me tell you, the Junior Committee could use your touch this year. We really miss you."

Ellison tried not to choke on her spit. No one missed her. If they did, they would call or text or come by. In fact, neither Eve nor Kate nor Julia had even stepped foot into her new home despite promises of girls' nights and happy hours. No, they did not miss her in the least.

"You want me to work on the Gala?" Ellison said. Granted Ellison had years of experience chairing it, but why reach out now? Why so close to the event? Was Jenn not available?

"Of course!" Eve said in her annoying perky way. "We've all wondered why you're not involved this year. I mean, you do still have membership, don't you?"

"I do." Ellison shifted on the couch and kicked her feet up onto the coffee table. "I didn't think you needed me this year." In reality, she had wanted to get involved, but after learning that Jenn had joined the committee, Ellison surrendered that part of her life too.

"Oh, Ellison! You're always needed!"

"What's the catch?" Ellison asked before she could stop herself.

"There isn't one," Eve purred. "We just need that special Ellison touch."

At this, Ellison actually did choke. In all the years she had worked on the Junior Committee, never once did Eve ever say she was vital. In fact, Eve often bitched about the way Ellison ran things. Not to her face of course, but Kate would tell her about it later.

Ellison was torn. Working on the Gala meant getting out of the house – even if it was with some of her old friends who had abandoned her. Anything, Ellison thought, was better than sitting around doing nothing but eating ice cream and moping. Maybe this is what she needed to reclaim some of her former self.

"When is it?" Ellison asked.

"How do you not know? It's October 6th." Eve sounded slightly irritated.

"What do you need me to do?" Ellison had a feeling she was going to regret this.

"We need help with everything." Eve paused as if she got caught saying the wrong thing. "Well, we're down a committee member and could use help wherever you can give it."

"Is Jenn on the committee?" Ellison asked as her neck hairs pricked up. No amount of cajoling would convince her to work with Jenn.

"Well, not exactly," Eve said. "She took a leave of absence."

"So you need me to fill her spot."

Eve sighed loudly.

So freakin' dramatic, Ellison thought.

"If you put it that way, it sounds terrible," Eve whined.

"But it's the truth, isn't it?" Ellison said. Something stirred in her, something she had thought was long gone.

"Do you want to help or not? You're still a member of the Club, so you should care about our projects." Eve was guilting Ellison. Or at least trying to. This particular fundraiser was for early childhood literacy.

"Fine. What do you need me to do?"

"Excellent!" Eve squealed. "Can you come by my house around seven tonight?"

"I have the boys tonight."

"Oh."

Oh geeze, I can't believe I'm going to say this, Ellison thought. "Can you Skype me in?"

Long pause. "Well, if you can't make the meetings, maybe I need to reconsider."

"That's fine," Ellison said. Eve was making this out to sound like Ellison's idea. "I have other things to do." *Like working on my listings and taking care of my kids.*

"Don't say I didn't try to include you, Ellison." Eve paused. "You know, if you just tried to get along with Jenn, this wouldn't be so awkward."

That was too much. "Are you listening to yourself?" Ellison shouted. "You want me to get along with the woman who stole my husband? What the hell is wrong with you?"

"God, Ellison. Chill. I'm only trying to help you socially."

Ellison pursed her lips. If Eve were in the room with her, she'd be tempted to shake her, but she wasn't. So Ellison said, "If that's all you need, I have to run."

"Bye!" Eve said in her bitch-cheerleader voice.

Ellison clicked off and threw her phone to the other end of her navy blue sofa. What the hell? What the actual hell? Is that how all her former friends felt? That she needed to make more of an effort to get along with a homewrecker?

Tears streamed down her face. Fuck that. Yes, she missed her old life, but were Eve, Kate, and Julia her real friends? Not even close. She had learned that the hard way when they all suddenly stopped returning her texts.

She pulled a tissue from the box sitting on the end table, blew her nose, and tossed the tissue back on the table. Her life was a disaster even though she wanted to believe otherwise. She had barely worked despite having had a meeting with her boss Laura earlier in the week to discuss when she'd be back full-time. Ellison had, perhaps foolishly, promised to go all-in starting that moment, but her heart wasn't completely in it. She had one listing. One. Laura wanted her to have three more clients by the end of the month.

Ellison didn't know if that were possible. After all, she had just ex-communicated herself from the club by pissing off Eve. Which was a problem because Ellison had always relied on member referrals for the majority of her clients.

What was she going to do?

Someone banged on her front door and rang the bell over and over again. Ellison glanced at her watch. Damn it. She'd forgotten about the boys.

She definitely wasn't winning mother of the year.

When Ellison unbolted the front door, her sons dropped their bags on the hard wood floor and darted past her and into the kitchen.

"Is there anything to eat?" Dash asked.

"Crackers, cheese, and apples," Ellison replied. Neither boy bothered to say 'hi,' and the gloom hanging over Ellison settled a little deeper into her soul.

"Yum!" Alex flung the fridge door open and dove into the cheese drawer. He emerged with a chunk of cheddar. "Can I have this?"

"Of course," Ellison said, getting a knife from the drawer. She sliced the cheese while Dash grabbed the crackers from the pantry. "How was school today, boys?"

"Great!" Alex said with a mouthful of food.

Dash looked at the ground.

"What is it?" Ellison demanded. Dash avoided her gaze. "Dashiel, what do you need to tell me?"

He hung his head. "I got a note sent home."

This was so unlike Dash. Normally, his teachers praised him. Was Luke punishing him because Dash was her son?

"Let me see," Ellison said.

Dash handed Ellison an envelope and left the room. She tore it open and found a neatly-folded piece of lined paper sitting inside. She unfolded it and began reading.

Ellison –

I hope this isn't too weird, but I'd like to take you out to dinner. As a thank you for helping in the classroom.

Luke

P.S. Dash is doing great!

Why didn't he email her? It was weird that he sent a written note, wasn't it? Or was it? She'd have to ask Andi.

"What does it say?" Dash asked.

"Mr. Peterson said you're doing great in school." Ellison ruffled Dash's hair and shoved the note into the pocket of her jeans. "I'm so proud of you!"

The letter burned against her thigh, and she felt like a middle schooler again. A silly little girl with a note from her crush – that's what Ellison was. She pressed her hand against her pocket feeling the outline of the note. Dinner with Luke was a temptation. But did she dare? What if someone saw them? Would Josh find out? After all, gossip moved fast around Waterford.

She hummed as she swiped cracker crumbs into her hand and dumped them into the sink. Luke was interested, that was clear. But, was she ready to take the leap into the dating world? Playing around on Match was one thing, going to dinner was a whole other level – one she wasn't sure she could make.

It took her over an hour to write a response back. The whole thing reminded her of being thirteen and passing notes back and forth during class changes.

There must be a reason for the paper note – namely he didn't want an electronic trail – one that could get him in trouble with the school board. It was the only explanation Ellison could come up with that made any sense. He did, after all, have her email and phone number.

Ellison stared at the blank sheet of paper before her. She'd start to scribble something, found it too abrasive, too passive, too something. and crumpled it up. Finally, after ten or so drafts, she was satisfied.

Luke,

While I'm flattered by your offer of dinner, I would be more comfortable if the whole group of parent volunteers went out together. In this small town, people talk, and I'd rather not be the subject of it.

Ellison

She hoped it sent the right message – that she was interested, but worried about public opinion. Ellison hoped, really hoped, Luke picked up on that. Because she felt dating while he was Dash's teacher was off limits, there was always next year – if he could wait that long.

A horrifying thought hit her. What if she had read the letter wrong, and Luke was just trying to be nice, and there were no romantic overtones. Or worse, what if he was only looking for a hook-up buddy? Andi had told her this was normal in the singles world and to expect it on Match. But would her son's teacher really be interested in her like that?

Argh. Why did this have to be so hard? But then again, maybe she was making assumptions. And what if Dash was okay with it? How would she find out without asking him and risk causing him more pain and confusion?

Ellison shook her head. No. Talking to Dash was not an option. Her note was the right way to handle it. Politely decline, but open the door to have a group dinner. That way she could still see Luke, but without the drama that goes along with being seen alone with him.

Heaven forbid Eve saw them together or found out about the dinner date. She'd spread rumors faster than a hummingbird beats its wings – especially now that Ellison was on her bad side.

She walked over to her desk, retrieved an envelope, and slid the letter in. In her loopy cursive, Ellison wrote Mr. Peterson across the front and stuck it in Dash's backpack.

All there was to do now was wait. If he wanted to see her, he'd agree to the group outing.

At least, she hoped he would.

12

HUSTLIN'

Her client was late. Not in a 'oh, I made a wrong turn late,' but in an 'oh crap where are they?' late. Ellison checked her watch again. One fifteen. They were supposed to meet at twelve thirty, and she'd been waiting in her car, calling them but getting no answer.

Well, this wasn't going as planned.

She tried calling the cell number Marsha had given her one more time, and it went straight to voicemail.

Well, shit. There goes that lead.

As Ellison stuck the key in the ignition, disappointment reared its ugly head. Marsha, her potential client, had reached out to her earlier in the morning about the Lodi listing and insisted she see the house that day. Ellison had been positive, based on Marsha's sense of urgency, that this was going to be her first success in ages.

It made absolutely no sense why Marsha wouldn't show up.

Just as Ellison pulled away from the curb, she spotted a black Mercedes sedan creeping down the street like it was looking at house numbers. Ellison re-parked and waited until the Mercedes pulled up behind her before killing her engine.

"Marsha, hi!" Ellison said in her best, professional voice. "Is everything okay?"

The petite blond gave Ellison a confused look. Yes. Why do you ask?"

Now it was Ellison's turn to be confused. "I thought we were meeting at twelve thirty."

"One thirty, and I'm early." Marsha wore a look that said, 'don't contradict me,' so Ellison let it slide.

The two women knew each other casually from the country club, but they didn't run in the same circles. In fact, Ellison had always treated Marsha and her friends as cast-offs. Marsha was the kind of person that Ellison said hi to, but never took the conversation farther.

"I must have messed up my calendar," Ellison said, walking down the sidewalk toward the house. She pointed at the landscaping. "Isn't it cute? And it's easy to maintain. A lawn service could take care of it in half-an-hour, easily."

"Uh huh." Marsha glanced around the yard and kept her face expressionless.

A sense of unease grew in Ellison's stomach. Something about their interaction seemed off. Most people got excited about seeing a new home, but Marsha appeared pained.

Ellison, however, was a professional, and she'd keep trying. "How have you been?" she asked. "The kids keeping you busy?"

Marsha kept pace with Ellison. "Everything is fine. They love their teachers. Olivia has Mrs. Haggarty, and James is with Ms. Garrett." She smiled in that way someone does when breaking bad news. "It's too bad Dash and Alex aren't at Greenbriar this year. We have so many fun activities planned."

Ellison's stomach flopped. Was Marsha on a fishing expedition, or did she truly want to look at a house?

"The boys do miss it and all their old friends," Ellison tried to remain calm. Not only had she been kicked out of the Waterford social circle, but her boys had been too. At least when it was her week with them. "The court decided to have them use my address even though Josh and I share custody," It was a lie, but no need to bad mouth Josh to a near stranger. "So a new school it was."

"Do you like living in Lodi? I mean, I'm sure it's fine, but it isn't exactly Waterford." Marsha didn't hide the amusement in her voice. In fact, she chuckled. "The schools are only rated a seven on Niche," she said naming the website that ranked schools for real estate purposes.

"Lodi is actually lovely. The boys and I have a townhouse close to school – which, so far seems excellent – and they can walk, unlike in Waterford. Plus, it's an up-and-coming neighborhood. Lots of young families moving in, and higher-end retail is going up along Barclay Street. It's the perfect time and place to buy an investment property."

They had paused on the front porch, and Marsha waved her hand around as she appraised the front of the house. "It's a lot smaller than I expected. Cute, but smaller."

Ellison opened the lockbox and stuck the key in the door. "The homes *are* smaller than Waterford, but you don't want something that size for an investment property. Just think of the cost of maintaining it."

She swung the door open, revealing a sunlit foyer and curved staircase. A hallway leading to the back of the house revealed a great room and kitchen.

"I'll let you look around," Ellison said, positioning herself at the kitchen island.

"Tell me the price again?"

Ellison handed Marsha a brochure. "It's listed at five ninety-five, but I think you could get it for five seventy-five. It's a bargain."

"Three bedrooms? Three-and-a-half baths?" Marsha said, not bothering to look at the brochure she held at her side.

"Four, if you count the bedroom in the fully finished basement. And it's legal."

Marsha walked to the stairs and disappeared upstairs.

This isn't going well, but I can salvage it, Ellison thought. *All I have to do is play up the growth potential. It's a solid house on a good street not far from the school.*

She glanced at her email. The little red number said she had fourteen unread messages. Since Ellison hated getting behind on email, she swiped it open.

Nothing but spam. Her heart sank a little. A small – okay, maybe a large part – had hoped Luke had gotten back to her. But so far, he hadn't responded to her letter, and Ellison was driving herself crazy imaging why.

It didn't matter. Right now, she needed to focus on selling this house. If Marsha was truly interested, they could do a thirty-day close since the place was vacant.

"Ellison?"

She jerked her head up and smiled. "What do you think?"

Marsha tapped her finger to her lips. "It's small, but in good shape. I don't like the colors, but I'm not going to be living here, so what does it matter?"

Small. It was 3,000 square feet – larger than Ellison's townhouse. Perspective, she guessed. She would have thought this was small too when she lived in Waterford.

"The area is very safe, and you'll draw a high quality tenant." Ellison felt she knew what Marsha's brain was thinking. "Rent could easily be $3,000."

That perked Marsha up. "You think so?"

"I do. And my office handles rentals too, so we could take care of everything for you."

Marsha tilted her head, opened her mouth, and snapped it shut.

"Is something wrong?" Ellison asked.

Marsha shrugged. "I'm surprised by how nice and professional you are. I always had the impression you were – forgive me – a bit of a bitch."

Ellison didn't flinch even though Marsha's words stung. "My divorce taught me many things. One of them was how to be a better person."

"Guess so." Marsha tucked a blond lock behind her ear and looked around the room. "Let me talk to Derrick. I really like it and think it could work, but I want to run it by him first. He's the numbers guy."

"Absolutely." Ellison escorted Marsha to the front door. "Call if you need anything or have questions."

"I will. I'm sure we'll talk soon."

When Marsha was gone, Ellison leaned against the door and hung her head. What kind of person was she pre-divorce? A shallow, mean-girl just like Eve, Kate, and Julia?

Two years ago, she would have called Eve right away and made fun of Marsha wanting an investment property in Lodi. But here she was, selling homes – and living – in Lodi.

She'd fallen hard, but she wasn't going to let that stop her from climbing back to the top – although in a nicer, more compassionate way.

She would be Ellison 2.0, and she'd be happy doing it.

Ellison sat across from her boss, Laurie, and softly tapped her foot under the glass and metal desk. She felt as if she'd been called into the principal's office and was waiting to hear her punishment. Granted, Ellison hadn't done anything wrong. She just hadn't been productive for the past year, and unfortunately, she hadn't heard back from Marsha despite several texts and phone calls.

It had been two days, and Ellison wished she had great news to share with Laurie.

As she waited, she studied the sparse décor of Laurie's office. Steel cabinets, a laptop, a few pictures of her kids, and an inspirational picture saying, "Everyone starts at the bottom. Be the one who isn't afraid of the climb."

How appropriate, Ellison thought.

The office was a lot like Laurie – straight forward and no nonsense.

Laurie clicked through the Power Point of the marketing plan Ellison had sent her and scribbled on a notepad every once in a while. Why hadn't she done this before they met?

"This is good," Laurie finally said, closing her laptop and looking directly at Ellison. Laurie had been Ellison's boss for five years, and they were friends. But not good enough friends for Ellison to confide in how the divorce had devastated her.

Some things needed to stay out of the professional realm.

"Only good?" Ellison asked, raising her eyebrows. She had spent hours on the plan and had reached out to other agents about showing the house. In fact, she was having lunch with another agent the following day to discuss working together.

"Only good," Laurie said. She folded her hands on top of the desk. "You were my best agent. You still could be, but I see nothing in this plan on how you're going to find new clients." She shoved the laptop to the side. "Part of the reason you were number one were your Waterford connections. How do those look now?"

Damn. Laurie was right. Aside from Marsha, the divorce had all but dried up her Waterford clientele. "Well, I'm living in Lodi now, and I'm involved at the boys' school, which as we both know, is a great place to mine for business." Ellison paused. "My goal is to establish my reputation there as well as rebuild my business in Waterford. And so many Lodi parents aspire to get their kids into Waterford schools. I could help them move out of their starter homes and into something grander."

"Ellison, we both know Lodi is down market. You'll have to sell two houses for every one Waterford home. Are you really up for it?"

With a flash of a smile, Ellison answered, "Yes. I know I can do this. This past year has been rough, but there is a reason I was number one, and I plan to do it again. In fact, I'm having lunch with an interested agent tomorrow. She has a buyer lined up already."

Laurie nodded her head. "That's what I needed to hear." She stuck her hand out across the table, and Ellison shook it. "It's good to have you back."

"It's great to be back." Ellison stood up. "Now, I have some hustling to do, so I need to run."

"Go, get 'em, Elle," Laurie said, giving Ellison a thumbs up.

Ellison grinned, but worry overwhelmed her. If she didn't find a buyer fast, would Laurie be so understanding? She prayed her lunch tomorrow panned out because Marsha certainly didn't seem like a prospect anymore, but she couldn't tell Laurie that. Not yet, anyway.

She needed to prove herself quickly. She had to be Top Dog Ellison, not crying, miserable Ellison.

If she didn't, she might need to find a new job.

13

FLYING SOLO

Ellison had become a pro at eating dinner alone. Lean Cuisine when she was at home and a table for one when she could afford to go out. She loved eating out, if only to be around other people and not stuck at home shoveling food into her mouth while watching *The Real Housewives*. That was the problem with working from home. She was at risk of becoming a pajama-wearing, cat-crazy recluse.

Today, however, had been particularly bad, and she needed a pick me up. Not only had she still not heard from Marsha, but her lunch with the other agent was a bust. He had only wanted her connections, which was hilarious, because she no longer had any.

But the absolute worst part was when Josh had picked the boys up at seven, acting chipper and excited for tomorrow's wedding. Alex had asked if she was coming to see "Daddy marry his new friend," and Dash had forgotten to give her a good-bye hug.

It all around sucked.

And unfortunately, Andi wasn't back from her work trip yet to kick off Drunkfest, so Ellison had only a book and her laptop to keep her company when she bellied up to the hostess station. Merrick's was her favorite place to eat solo. The food was well-priced and delicious, and people from Waterford generally didn't come here. Merrick's dim interior and leather booths gave it a slight old-school feel that Ellison loved. It was, in her opinion, a great place to have a martini and recharge.

But tonight, it was nearly empty and didn't have its normal vibrant energy. Is the whole world depressed, Ellison thought. Or is it that I am so sad that everything looks that way?

The cute hostess perked up when she saw her. "Hi, Ellison! Table for one? Or is your friend joining you?"

Ellison sighed. She'd been here so many Friday nights with Andi that the staff knew her. "Just me tonight."

The young girl grabbed a menu and motioned for Ellison to follow her. The hostess' skirt was so short, Ellison wondered if she had to use tape to keep it in place. *Must be nice not to have cellulite.*

"Is this table okay?" It was a cozy booth for two overlooking the main dining room.

"It's perfect," Ellison said as she slid in. From here, she could sit back and watch the world pass by uninterrupted. And since it wasn't too busy, she wouldn't feel the need to hurry her meal along.

The hostess handed Ellison a menu. "Jamie will be your server today. Have you met her before?"

"Can't say I have," Ellison answered.

"Well, she'll be over in a minute." The hostess, whose name Ellison didn't know despite their familiarity, walked away.

Ellison didn't bother looking at the menu. She ordered the same thing every time she came in: A Southwest Chicken Salad and a bread basket. She absolutely loved Merrick's bread and butter.

A glass of water thunked down before her. "I'm Jamie, I'll be your server today." Ellison looked up. Jamie had a short sassy hairdo, the kind Ellison often dreamed of wearing but was too afraid to try. She thought it would make her facial features look too large – especially her nose. Not that there was anything wrong with her nose, it just wasn't as delicate as it could be.

"Are you ready to order?" Jamie was brash and to the point, which was unlike the other servers.

Ellison glanced at the menu out of habit. "I'll have the Southwest Chicken Salad."

Jamie scribbled down her order. "Okay, I'll get right on it."

"No rush, but I'd like to start with a dirty martini." Alcohol would make the meal more expensive, but she really needed a stiff drink after the day she'd had.

"Okay," Jamie said. "One dirty martini it is."

When she was gone, Ellison took her laptop from her bag and began going over comps to send to Marsha. It was her last ditch effort to get Marsh to see what a bargain the house was as an investment property.

However, even work couldn't keep her mind occupied, and she shut her laptop after sending Marsha an email.

Josh was getting married tomorrow, and all the pain of the past year sat heavy in Ellison's heart. He was over her. Moved on. Ready to marry someone else.

Will I ever get over it?

Admittedly, not much had changed since she discovered Josh's affair. In the days after, everything was a blur, but she remembered not wanting to hear music or read because every song seemed to be about affairs and reading required too much concentration.

It was as if her life had screeched to a standstill.

Just thinking about D-Day made her stomach roll. It was the morning her whole life changed. Josh had forgotten his phone on the kitchen counter in his rush to get to work, and she...

No. I can't think about this. I need to focus on more positive things.

Ellison picked up her book and turned to the dog-eared page. She read slowly, letting the fantasy world take over. She didn't even acknowledge Jamie when she delivered the martini.

"Hi."

The deep, rumbling voice sent waves of heat rushing through Ellison. She glanced up, very aware that her top scooped a little low and gave off more than a hint of her cleavage. Luke stood before her, next to the empty booth seat. He flashed his brilliant smile, and Ellison's pulse sped up.

"Thanks for helping out the other day," he said before she could speak. "The kids loved you."

Her voice had gotten lost somewhere, so she nodded.

"Is this not a good time to talk?" Luke asked. God, he looked amazing. Jeans and a fitted light green t-shirt. His dark hair messy in a good way. His gray eyes held her attention and seemed to see right through her.

Ellison swallowed hard. "No, it's fine. I'm alone."

"Me too."

Ellison eyed the empty seat across from her. Bravery surged. "You could join me."

What was she doing? Inviting gossip, that's what. But then again, she was in Lodi. It wasn't exactly a hotbed of Waterford activity.

Luke smiled so that his perfectly white teeth practically reflected light back at her. "I'd like that." He tucked himself into the seat. "Have you ordered?"

"I did." She set the book next to her on the bench. "Have you?"

"Yeah. I need to see if they'll bring it over here." He turned around to flag down his waiter who came rushing over. "Can I get my food delivered here?"

"No problem, sir," the waiter, who Ellison vaguely recognized, said with a knowing look that made Ellison blush. Did he think she was on a date? Or desperate enough to get picked up in a restaurant? Did it even matter?

"I hate solo dining, but here I am," Luke said.

"And here I am," Ellison retorted. Sitting here like this was reminiscent of when they met at the bar. Maybe it was reminding Luke of it too because he had a goofy smile plastered on his face.

"What?" Ellison demanded.

"You look gorgeous."

Ellison tried not to laugh. Her ash blond hair was pinned up in a messy bun, and she wore only mascara. *It must be the slutty shirt*, she thought. *He must be enjoying the view.* "You're not getting me into bed again," she blurted a little louder than she meant to. The elderly couple next to them glanced over, and Ellison about died. *Why can't I keep my mouth shut around this man?*

"I'm not trying to bed you, Ellison. I just thought you should know how gorgeous you look right now."

Who was this guy? Sure she'd been intimate with him, but she knew nothing about him. And damn, he had good lines.

Jamie returned with a huge plate of salad and placed it before Ellison. She was a little self-conscious to eat in front of Luke, but she was starving. "Tell me about yourself," she said, hoping to distract him while she ate.

"My name is Luke Peterson. I'm forty. Never been married."

She already knew all that. "Why?"

He hesitated. "I haven't met the right woman."

"Go on," Ellison said.

Luke folded his strong hands on the tabletop. "I moved here from San Francisco."

"Why?" She didn't want to sound like an interrogator, but she couldn't help herself.

"Cost of living is cheaper," Luke said. "Better schools. More chance for advancement."

Ellison pushed her salad around the plate. "Do you like it here?"

"So far, the scenery isn't bad." He winked at her.

Ellison blushed hard and spun her martini glass around. Luke's waiter arrived at the table and put a sizzling steak down before him. It smelled delicious.

"What about you? I see you're drinking martini's now," he teased.

"The dirtier the better." She pressed her tongue against the back of her mouth and smiled. Luke brought out the flirty, forward side of her, and she kind of liked it.

He chuckled. "Tell me about Ellison Brooks."

She settled back against her seat and cocked her head. What to tell him? That she was a recent divorcée and fantasized about him often?

"I went to Stanford."

"So you know the Bay Area." He gave her a weird look, like he was expecting something.

"Not really. I didn't leave Palo Alto much."

"That's a shame," Luke said, as he cut off a piece of meat.

She shrugged. "After Stanford, I moved here – well to DC – to work as a staffer."

"How'd you end up in Waterford?"

"I met my ex-husband." The word stuck to her tongue. "He's a government contractor, and we thought Waterford would be a great place to raise kids."

Her body relaxed, and Luke flashed more of that giant grin. She felt her lips twitch up and smiled back.

"Am I wrong, Ellison, or is there chemistry between us?"

Chemistry? Full-on fireworks were more like it. Ellison's entire body was calling out to his. "I can't date my son's teacher."

"Why not?"

"Because...because it would look bad." She didn't know if the school district had a policy or not, but Ellison knew that the court of public opinion wouldn't be kind if they dated. And how would it affect Dash? He was having a hard enough time adjusting to Jenn and Josh. If he had to see his mom's boyfriend every day, it could be disastrous.

"How long have you been divorced, Ellison?"

Her stomach dropped. She had to tell him the truth. "Six weeks, but he's getting remarried tomorrow."

Luke shook his head slowly. "I'm sorry."

She wasn't sure if he was apologizing for the divorce, the wedding, or for not being able to date her. "It's okay. We've been separated for a year. He found his soul-mate in a cubicle at work."

Luke cut off another piece of meat and chewed.

"It's all okay, though, because I'm over him." She was rambling and probably sounded desperate, but Ellison didn't care. All she wanted was for Luke not to think she was a weak, still-hung-up-on-her-ex, sad, depressed woman. She wanted him to see her the way he made her feel: alive and vibrant.

Jamie came over to the table, and eying their near empty plates, asked, "Would you like to see a dessert menu?"

"Not tonight," Luke said. "I'll take both checks."

Ellison bristled. What if she had wanted dessert? "I'd like to see the dessert menu."

Luke touched the back of her hand and fire coursed through Ellison's veins. Andi was right. This man was walking sex. Everything about him made her want to scream, "Do dirty things to me. And then do them again."

"I thought," he hesitated. "I'm sorry if that was a bit presumptuous, but I wondered if you'd like to walk with me to get frozen yogurt."

Now it was her turn to hesitate. If she said yes, did that mean they were on a date? If she said no, did it mean she wasn't interested, because she was. Very.

What would Andi do? Ellison studied her empty plate. *She'd beat me if I didn't go.*

"Okay."

"Awesome." Luke leaned back in his chair and smiled like he just won the lottery.

They sat there quietly while they waited for Jaime to bring the bills. When she handed them both to Luke, Ellison said, "I can pay for my own, thank you very much."

"I'm sure you can, but this is my treat. After all, you're doing me a favor volunteering in my classroom."

She could accept that. Except it made it seem like less than a date. Which was fine.

Problem was, she kind of hoped it was a date.

The yogurt shop was nearby, and it took less than a two-minute walk to reach it. During that time, Ellison managed to work herself into a state. What if someone saw her walking with Luke? What if people thought they were dating?

So what, she thought at one point. So freaking what.

But then her thoughts would turn, and she'd start worrying again.

Still, here she was walking alongside the sexiest teacher at Eagle's Landing Elementary School – hell, probably in the entire state of Virginia – and not relaxing enough to enjoy it.

You're too uptight, Ellison, relax.

When they reached the yogurt shop, Luke held the door for her, and she walked through, making sure to put more swing into her hips than normal.

After they took turns ordering, Luke pointed Ellison over to a table. "You okay?" He asked in his gravely bass voice.

No. She wasn't. She wanted so badly for tomorrow to be over. And she wanted Luke to find her attractive – which, if she believed the earlier conversation, he did.

What she needed was some comfort. Either in liquid form or carnal.

She blinked up at Luke. He was the best thing to happen to her in months. "Do you want to come over?"

Luke dug into his yogurt, but didn't eat it. He stirred the concoction over and over, as if mulling her question. "And what would we do? Play charades?"

Embarrassed, Ellison hung her head. "Well, there's that chemistry between us, and I thought–"

"I'm not going to sleep with you, Ellison. Not tonight." He reached across the table and touched her cheek with the back of his hand. Electricity trilled along her skin. "You're too vulnerable."

Who was this guy? All Ellison wanted was an easy lay and a good time, and here Luke was saying no. Did he not enjoy himself last time? Was she that terrible in bed?

"Here's my number." He took Ellison's phone and tapped it out. Then he stood up from the table. "Call me if you need anything. I'm a good listener."

A sense of helplessness washed over her. "Stay," she whispered.

Luke shook his head. "I should go before I agree to something stupid."

Without asking, he planted a kiss on the top of Ellison's head. She shuddered. "You're going to be okay, Ellison. Tomorrow will be done before you know it."

She watched him disappear through the doors before letting the tears come.

14

I'VE GOT YOU

Ellison hadn't slept all night. She had tossed and turned, replaying the scene with Luke over and over again. But when she would doze off, images of Josh marrying Jenn haunted her.

Luckily, at seven, Ellison's phone began to ping with texts from Andi.

Andi: If you're up, I'm ready to go.

Me: Come over now?

Andi: Sure. See you in twenty with my good friend Vodka.

Maybe seven in the morning was too early to start drinking, but Ellison didn't care. Right about now Josh would be up, trying to get the boys ready. The wedding was at noon.

Why did she know these details?

Ellison pulled herself from bed, groggy from crying herself to sleep, and entered her bathroom. Two swollen, red eyes peered back at her. A rat's nest of hair sat on her head, and she wore a torn robe over her nighty. Definitely not sexy.

Maybe this is what Luke imagined waking up to, and that's why he turned her down?

Speaking of Luke, did she make the biggest ass of herself, or what? Inviting him over only to have him say no? What was she thinking?

Oh right. She was hurting, and it seemed like a way to pass the time. Maybe she *was* going all slutty divorcée the way Andi suggested.

Ellison ran a brush through her hair and pulled it back into a messy bun. Since today was a stay-in-the-house-and-wallow day, she didn't do her make-up. For clothes, Ellison chose sweatpants and a navy tank top with no bra. Yup. She looked like the hot mess she was.

The doorbell rang, and she ran down the stairs to answer it.

"Holy hell," Andi said, upon looking at Ellison. "What happened to you?"

"I don't look that bad."

"Worse. You look like you were run over by a truck."

Ellison sighed. "Gee, thanks. I tried to make myself look like a fashion plate for you."

Andi pushed past Ellison and walked into the kitchen. "Bloody Mary's for everyone," Andi announced, reaching into a shopping bag and pulling the ingredients out. "Do you want to talk or just drink?"

Ellison perched on a barstool. "I had dinner and yogurt with Luke last night."

"Nice! Was it planned?"

"No. We bumped into one another. I asked him to join me," Ellison said.

"Does this mean you're giving up on the whole, 'I can't date my son's teacher thing?'"

Ellison took her drink from Andi and shook her head. "No. But I did invite him over last night, and he turned me down."

Andi didn't have a punchy line for that.

"What?" Ellison said, raising her eyebrows.

"Smart call," Andi said, sipping her drink. "You're not in a place to be making those kind of decisions, but you are in a good place to casually date guys." She slammed her drink down, and miraculously, it didn't spill. "Speaking of which, have you gotten any hits back on Match?"

To be honest, Ellison had given the site very little thought after being called a passive aggressive bitch. "I don't know."

"Where's your laptop?" Andi asked.

"In the family room."

Andi grabbed her drink and motioned for Ellison to follow.

"We've become alcoholics, you know," Ellison said. Since the affair, she and Andi had been drinking more than normal. They drank to celebrate, and they drank to commiserate.

"So what? We deserve it. Especially today."

The laptop was on the couch, and Andi opened it and began typing. "Look!" she cried. "You have a message from Bennydate and twelve other interested guys. That's great!"

It didn't feel great. It felt, well, a little lame. "Shouldn't there be more? It's been a few days."

"Greedy, greedy," Andi said. "Let's just focus on what we have to work with."

For the next three hours, the two women went through the list of men, carefully crafting individual email messages and doing sleuth work on each one. Bennydate was the most promising – emailing back-and-forth with them all morning until he eventually asked to see Ellison on Tuesday at The Bar.

"What should I do?" she asked Andi. "I don't have the boys this week." Even with his wedding taking place today, Josh wasn't taking his honeymoon until Thanksgiving – to give Jenn time to get over her morning sickness – may it never end.

"You say, 'Yes.'"

"How's this sound?" Ellison asked. "I'd love to meet up Tuesday at seven-thirty. Thanks for inviting me out. I look forward to meeting you."

"Sterile, but totally appropriate."

Ellison clicked send before she could change her mind. "So," she said coolly as she dropped her voice. "Luke and last night. What do I do? I basically propositioned him. Again. Only this time he turned me down."

"You either acknowledge it and thank him for having the good sense to not come over, or you ignore it and pretend you aren't hot for him."

"Easier said than done." Ellison typed Luke's name into Facebook and pulled up a picture of him. "I mean look at him, Andi. He's gorgeous. He works with kids; you should see him in the classroom. Totally heart melting. And he's thoughtful." She sighed. "He's damn near perfect."

Andi shook her head so that her chestnut brown curls bobbed. "The two of you are ridiculous."

"Did I tell you he said we had chemistry?"

Now Andi stood up. "I'm all but ordering you to date this man. Please, so I don't have to listen to any more angst."

"I can't. He knows it too - that's why he didn't come home with me last night. Plus, I have to think about how it would impact Dash."

"Dash wouldn't have to know. Keep it secret. It's not like the kid is here all the time."

"But what if-"

Ding.

Ellison looked at her computer. Someone posted on Facebook and tagged her. She clicked through.

Status update: Josh Brooks is married to Jennifer Brooks.

Picture after picture began zooming by. Ellison paled, and vomit rose in her throat. But no matter how hard she tried, she couldn't stop looking.

"What is it?" Andi asked, peering over Ellison's shoulder. "Okay, someone needs to step away from the computer," Andi said, slamming the laptop closed. "This isn't healthy."

"Why would he do that?" Ellison cried. "Why would he tag me in pictures of his wedding?"

"Because he's a dick."

Ellison fought back the tears. She wasn't going to let him win again. Not today.

"How's work coming along?" Andi asked, changing the subject.

"It's…well, it could be better. I have one listing and did a showing the other day, but the woman isn't returning my texts or calls, so I'm going to back off."

"It's only going sort of okay?" Andi asked with concern. "You aren't close to closing any deals, are you?"

Ellison sighed. "I'm just getting back in the game. It takes time."

Andi tilted her head. "Ellison, I know you know this, but you've got to be financially independent of Josh. At some point soon, he's not going to be paying your electricity bill. The alimony is going to stop."

"I know."

"Maybe you should consider getting a steadier job. Something to supplement your real estate career since you seem to be starting over." Andi paused. "So many companies are looking for hard workers. Hell, even the CIA requires us to be able to hustle and write coherently – both of which I know you can do."

"I don't want to work for the CIA," Ellison said. "The hours are terrible, and I'd never see the boys. Real estate gives me flexibility."

"The CIA was just an example. I'm sure you could find something that worked with the boys' schedule. Something part-time, maybe?"

Ellison buried her head in her hands. "I don't even know how to be independent anymore. I've spent fourteen years as Josh's wife, and then I became the boys' mom. I used to be good at real estate, but even that's questionable these days."

"You've lost sight of who you are," Andi said, refilling their near-empty glasses. "Do something for yourself for once."

"The boys don't need two irresponsible parents."

Andi glared at her. "No, what they need is a happy mom who loves them to pieces. Not a woman who is a broken shadow of herself."

Ellison held up her hands. "That's not fair."

"It's true."

Andi was right, but that didn't make her words sting less.

"Look," Andi said, pointing at the pile of bills sitting on the corner of the counter. "I know you're struggling to pay all those and your divorce lawyer's fees. You never say it, but I know."

Heat crept into Ellison's cheeks. "I've got it under control."

"What if I gave you a gift, something to help you get back on your feet."

Tears welled in Ellison's eyes. How could she accept Andi's overly generous offer?

"I've known you almost my whole life, Ellison. Let me do this for you. At least let me pay off the lawyer fees."

Ellison nodded, because words wouldn't come to her. How did she get so lucky as to have a real friend like Andi?

"And if you're interested, I'll put out a few feelers for jobs for you."

"I don't know if I'm ready for that.," Ellison said.

"You're going to have to at least entertain the idea."

Andi had a point. Once the alimony dried up, Ellison would be struggling to support herself and the boys if she couldn't close a deal. And even then, she may not get paid for months. It hardly seemed fair. But unless her real estate career picked up fast, she'd be living on food stamps in two year's time.

Andi dug through the pile of bills and plucked one out. "I'll take this with me." It was the overdue attorney bill.

"Thank you." Ellison said, her voice shaking.

"Hey," Andi said, wrapping her arms around Ellison. "This is what friends do."

"What movie are we watching first?" Ellison asked, forcing her words out and changing the subject. She knew Andi would always be there for her, but this was beyond generous.

"*First Kiss*. I thought it was appropriate." The two women walked into the living room.

Ellison pulled her feet up onto the couch and tossed a throw over her legs. Tears still sat heavy and hot behind her lids.

"Hey," Andi said, pulling Ellison into a hug. "It's okay to cry."

And with that, Ellison let loose the sobs she'd been holding in.

15

DRUNKFEST

A round four, Andi declared they'd run out of liquor and needed salted caramel ice cream. Since neither of them could drive, Andi did the unthinkable. She texted Luke.

Behind Ellison's back.

So when Ellison answered the door in her sweat pants, messy hair, and puffy eyes, she came face-to-face with Luke holding a bag of what appeared to be groceries.

"What in the world?" she gasped. "How the hell do you know where I live?" Andi had said stalking was the new dating norm, but this was beyond that. Luke was on her porch.

"She didn't tell you?" Luke shifted the groceries and looked uncomfortable. "Andi said you needed this." He held out the bag. "It's ice cream and vodka."

Ellison turned around. "Andi!" she yelled. "Where are you?"

Andi, of course, was nowhere to be found. Ellison turned back toward Luke. Should she take the groceries, thank him, and send him on his way, or should she invite him in? And where the hell had Andi gone?

She took the bag from him. "Thanks. I didn't know Andi had texted. She's-"

"Trying to set us up?" Luke answered.

"Would that be awful?" Ellison blushed, and the world tilted. Was it the booze or did Luke make her woozy?

"Not at all." Luke looked her up and down, but not in a creepy way. More like he was trying to assess the situation. "I should go."

Maybe it was the wine, but Ellison decided to risk the humiliation of Luke turning her down again. "Want to come in? We're watching rom-coms and drinking." She shook the bag. "And apparently, eating ice cream. I have the large bowls out."

Luke laughed. It was a soothing balm on her torn heart. "How can I resist?"

Ellison moved over so he could enter the house and miraculously avoided stumbling over her own feet. She reeked like a saloon while Luke's familiar, foresty scent followed him. Ellison inhaled. Damn, if he didn't smell yummy.

"How are you?" he said, once he was in the small foyer. It wasn't a foyer, really, just a small space between the front door and the staircase. There was a coat closet to the right and a hallway to the side of the staircase that led to the family room.

"Holing – no, that's not right - holding up." She'd been drinking since the early morning and slurred her words accordingly.

Luke took the groceries from her and carried them to the kitchen. He put the ice cream in the freezer before turning around. "I'm going to guess you're not eating the ice cream with the vodka."

Ellison shook her head, and a smile formed on her lips. "You came to see me."

"I did. Andi said you needed help, and I was available. So I thought I'd join your party." He quickly glanced at her. "I mean, you are okay with it, right? I'm not intruding?"

"I'm not sure where Andi disappeared to, so you're not intruding on anything except my pity party." She pouted out her lower lip. "And that's really a party of one situation."

Luke caught her by the arm. "Ellison, if you want to be alone, just say so."

She eyed his hand on her arm. "We're just hanging out, no sex,"

Ellison said. "At least not until you're as drunk as me." She giggled. "But then the equipment might not work, right?"

Luke blushed. "I'm going to mark this up to you being drunk."

Ellison threw her arms around his neck and snuggled into him. "Damn. You always smell so yummy."

Luke untangled himself, grabbed the vodka, and started toward the family room. Ellison tried to walk normally, but instead, stumbled into the room.

"You're a grown woman," Luke said as he helped Ellison regain her balance. "So I'm not going to tell you that you can't drink more, but I will say that you're going to hate life later if you keep drinking."

"Trust me, I can't hate life any more than I already do," Ellison slurred. Her brain was fuzzy, so maybe she was imagining Luke. She reached out and pinched him.

"Ow!"

She recoiled. "Oh, you are real! I thought maybe I had invented the perfect man to come to my DrunkFest."

Luke shook his head. Andi was passed out on the family room floor, snoring lightly. Laughter bubbled up in Ellison, and she doubled over. "Drunk," she said, pointing, and laughed some more. "At least I'm still awake."

"I have no idea how that is even possible," Luke said.

Empty bottles of wine, vodka, and tequila littered the coffee table. There were open boxes of cookies spilled onto the floor and a half-eaten bagel rested on the couch. Ellison tried tidying up, but she tipped over onto the couch, and the world spun.

"Give me a minute," Luke said. Like a gentleman, he took a light blue throw blanket from the back of the couch and arranged it over Andi. When he looked at Ellison, who was sprawled on the couch, it was with the kindest eyes she'd ever seen. "Want to watch a movie? I heard that was part of Drunkfest."

"Sure. Andi and I were about to watch The Outsiders. Not a Rom-Com, though." She clicked on the TV and tried to sit up, but the movement made her dizzy. "I'm just gonna lie here, okay."

"If that's what you need to do." Luke sat at the other end. "Wait here," he said suddenly and jumped up. "I'm going to get you some water."

"Oh! Yes, please," Ellison said. "I need lots and lots of water."

"Yes, you do."

Ellison closed her eyes, but it didn't stop the spinning. She was going to be so sick later. And Luke was here. Seeing her in all her drunk glory. If he didn't run off after this...

"Here. Drink." Luke lifted Ellison up and held a glass to her lips. She slurped off the top. "You have to hydrate, or you're going to end up in the ER for alcohol poisoning."

After she had taken a few sips, Luke took the glass away and sat down so that her head was in his lap. "Is this okay?"

"Uh huh." It felt so good to be next to Luke. To be held by a kind-hearted man who found her attractive. Or did. After seeing the shit show of DrunkFest, he would probably lose interest. She rolled onto her side, and a tear slid from her eye.

"What's wrong," Luke asked, stroking her hair. "Did I do something wrong?"

Ellison sighed. "I'm so sorry," she sobbed. "I'm broken. I'm trying not to be, but I am. You don't need to see this."

"It's fine, Ellison," Luke said. "Today is a rough day for you. I get it."

Snot bubbled in her nose. How completely unsexy. "What is wrong with me? Why did Josh have to fall in love with someone else? We had a solid life. I loved him."

Luke didn't say a word.

"And I've probably ruined things with you after this mess." She braced against the back of the sofa and sat up. Her stomach was sour. Ugh.

"You haven't ruined anything," Luke said gently. "In fact, I'm happy we got this awkwardness out of the way. I mean, there had to be a first time to see you with snot running down your face, right?" He handed her a tissue and chuckled.

"Do you still like me even though I'm a broken mess?" She held her breath, not wanting to hear the answer, but needing to know at the same time.

"Not all broken things are ruined, Ellison." Luke squeezed her hand. "Sometimes, they're even more beautiful than when they were whole."

She sighed. *He's just being a friend*, she told herself, but in the back of her mind, she knew it wasn't true. Luke wanted something more, and so did she.

At some point in the night, she awoke to gentle jostling. It took Ellison a moment to place where she was – in Luke's arms.

"Shhh," he said. "Go back to sleep."

Ellison nuzzled Luke's chest as he carried her upstairs. For the first time in months – years, maybe – she felt safe. When he arrived at her bed, he set her down and pulled back the covers. Ellison flopped underneath and smiled coyly at him, hoping Luke would join her. But he pulled the covers over her and walked out of the room.

She waited patiently as he rustled around the kitchen. What was he was up to? She'd usually go find out, but the room was spinning, and her teeth were numb. In fact, she could barely form sentences.

Luke re-appeared a few minutes later, and Ellison peered at him through half-closed eyes. He set an extra-large bottle of water and a glass bowl on the bedside table. Even though she couldn't talk, she grunted her thanks.

He hesitated next to the bed as if he didn't know what to do next.

Ellison lolled her head to the side and rested her hand on the other side of the bed. "Here," she slurred. "Sleep here."

Luke leaned down and tucked the covers around her. "Andi is all taken care of. She's on the sofa. She didn't wake up when I moved her."

"Thank you," Ellison said. "For everything."

Luke walked around the bed and laid down next to her, on top of the covers. "You're going to be okay, Ellison." He rolled onto his side. "And if not, I'll be here in the morning to help you out."

"You're the best," she whispered and closed her eyes.

16

WALK OF SHAME

The morning came too soon and too viciously. Ellison heaved into the glass bowl again. She'd been up puking since three, and the room was still dancing around her.

"Oh, God. I'm so sorry. You really don't have to stay for this." Inside she was dying. Luke had already emptied the bowl twice. Plus, she probably smelled and looked terrible.

"Ellison," Luke said, holding her hair back. "It's okay. I knew what I was getting into."

She wiped her mouth with a tissue. "How's Andi?"

"Not much better."

"Wonderful," she moaned. What was she thinking drinking that much?

"Don't worry, I've got you ladies covered." Luke said. "When you're both doing a little better, I'll set you up with my famous hangover breakfast."

Ellison waved her hand. "No food talk. Too soon."

Luke laughed and collected her bowl. "Be back in a minute."

When he disappeared from view, Ellison groaned. First, she had a one-night stand with Luke. Now he was dumping out her puke. Mortifying, both situations.

After last night – when she may or may not have come on to Luke, and he turned her down, AGAIN – she was confused about where they stood.

"Hey, Ellison? You okay?" Luke stood at the foot of her bed, watching her. He set the bowl on the bed.

This was the time to ask him what was going on, before things got any weirder between them. "What's going on here? With us?"

Luke ran a hand through his hair. It was already tousled, but was now more so. "I like you, Ellison. A lot. More than I should, and it's making me not use my best judgement."

Her heart pitter-pattered against her ribcage. "What are you worried about?"

"There are rules about fraternizing with parents." He looked around the room. "What I'm doing right now could get me in trouble."

"But you're here?" she said softly.

"Because I like you, Ellison. There's something about you-" He broke off and turned away.

Ellison sat up in the bed. "Luke, I like you too, but-"

"Sentences that start with 'but' are my least favorite sentences followed closely by 'we need to talk,'" Luke said. His gray eyes searched her face as if pleading with her to change her mind.

"But," she said again. "Rules aside, I need to think of Dash and his feelings. He's still having a hard time with the divorce and Josh's new marriage."

Luke nodded. "You don't want him to see you dating."

"Exactly." She felt utterly ridiculous for what she was about to say, but it had to be acknowledged. "Plus, there's the gossip factor. I don't need it getting back to my ex that I'm dating. If he found out, he'll make my life hell."

"Why? He's the one who got remarried when the ink had barely dried on your divorce decree."

Ellison had revealed too many messy things about her life already and didn't want to get into more right now. She said, "Child custody. Alimony. The works. I'm kind of dependent on Josh still."

Luke's eyebrows shot up, and his lips parted. "Ah. I see. You're having money problems."

Her cheeks flamed hot. It was bad enough to share that information with Andi. There was no way she'd tell Luke the truth. "No. I'm working. It's just that real estate can take a while to pay off." She rested her head on a pillow. "But what about you? Aren't you worried about losing your job?"

"I am, but as long as I'm doing my job in a professional manner, and we keep this between us, how would anyone know?"

Her heart flopped, and she felt sick – not from the hangover either. "I don't want you to lose your job."

Luke nodded. "We can be discreet."

Ellison shook her head. "I can't ask you to risk your job for a date with me."

"And I'm not going to ask you to upset Dash or Alex any more than they already have been."

Ellison let out a long sigh. "Just to be clear, you would date me if you could?"

"Absolutely." Luke's eyes seared into her heart. Was she crazy letting this sane, attractive, caring man walk away?

Yes.

This was going to be a long school year.

"Breakfast is served," Luke said, standing proudly in the middle of the family room.

The smell of grease hit Ellison, and she wretched. "McDonald's? That's your famous hangover breakfast? I thought you went to the store so you could cook."

"It is, and no, you never want me to cook for you. Trust me."

"McDonald's is terrible." Ellison grabbed at her stomach and doubled over from the smell. "Are you trying to kill me?"

Andi snatched a bag from Luke's hand. "I, for one, think this is fabulous. Thanks, Luke." She tore open the bag and began gobbling

down hash browns. "Nothing better than grease to cure a hangover."
She swallowed. "Except for maybe a Bloody Mary."

Ellison gagged. "Water. That's all I'm drinking today."

Luke held out a bag to Ellison. "Just try it. I swear it will make you
feel better. Right, Andi?"

Andi bobbed her head. "Like I said, excellent meal choice."

Ellison reluctantly took the greasy breakfast sandwich from the
paper bag and tried not to dry heave. Just the thought of food made
her stomach roll. Still, it tasted fabulous when she nibbled at the
corner.

"Eat the hash browns. They're so greasy and yummy," Andi said,
inhaling her food.

Ellison took a few more bites before tossing the sandwich into the
paper bag. Her stomach wasn't liking the food very much.

Luke picked up the disaster that was the living room. Empty
glasses, bottles, and throw pillows were strewn everywhere.

"Hey," Ellison said. "You don't have to do that."

"You don't seem like you're in any position to do it yourself." Luke
held an armful of wine bottles. "Where's the recycling?"

"By the patio door," Ellison said. She tried not to think about how
much he'd already done for her.

"Hey, Luke," Andi said when he returned with a garbage bag. "How
much do we owe you for the Mickey D's? I'm marking the babysitting
up to you being a generous guy."

Luke laughed. "Don't worry about it. I got it covered."

"Are you sure?" Ellison said, reaching for her handbag. Teachers
didn't make very much money, and she didn't want to impose on him.

"Ellison, put your wallet away," Luke said. "It's fine. I promise."

"Sure?" she asked again, not wanting Luke to think she was
freeloader.

"Positive."

She dropped her wallet back into her bag and began helping Luke
pick up. The damage she and Andi had done was a bit unbelievable.
Even with the small bit Luke had already carried to the kitchen, there
were still bottles, pillows, and cushions everywhere. Ellison stooped

to gather up the mess of blankets in front of the TV. She tried not to think about the scene in her bedroom where her puke bowl sat next to the bed.

How embarrassing.

In the course of one night, she'd told two people of her money woes, been generously helped out by Andi, and taken care of by Luke.

It was mortifying. She needed to get her drinking under control. At least around Luke. How many more times could she proposition him before he begins to think she's either desperate or slutty.

Slutty. What a funny word. She'd heard Eve use it when talking about Andi, and Ellison had quickly put that to rest. So what if Andi had a bevy of men? Who was she hurting?

And what was slutty anyway? A too-low cut shirt? Dry humping someone's leg? Puking in a bowl while your crush holds your hair? Eve's scanty bikinis? Who was Ellison to say?

Suddenly, Ellison didn't feel well again. She laid down on the sofa, and the room began spinning. "Ugh," she said. "I think I'm still drunk."

"You probably are," Luke said. "Look at how much you drank. It's amazing neither of you have alcohol poisoning." He'd finished picking up the living room and took one of the folded blankets and placed it over her. "Do you need your bowl?"

Ellison felt her cheeks go warm. "Probably."

"Be right back."

Andi plopped down on the floor next to Ellison's head. "He's a keeper, Ellison. Don't let him get away because you're afraid."

"I'm not afraid. We discussed it last night, and we agreed it's not the best time."

Andi frowned. "You're hiding behind Dash, and it isn't right."

"I'm not hiding." Ellison said. "I'm being the responsible parent."

"You need to live a little, Elle. The boys will be okay."

"I'm not discussing this right now." Ellison turned onto her back, and that made the room spin harder. "How are you not sick and miserable?" she asked Andi.

"It's one of the qualifications for joining the CIA – can you hold your liquor and not give away State secrets?"

Ellison rolled her eyes. "You and that job. One day, you're going to tell me what you do."

"I'm in intelligence. That's all I can say."

From the doorway, Luke said, "You're in intelligence. For the CIA?"

"Yes."

He burst out laughing.

"What's so funny?" Andi asked.

"I don't know. I just kind of imagined you as a ball buster at some *Fortune* 500 company or something."

"Well, I'm not. I'm a lowly civil servant, and if you have a problem with that, you can suck my balls." Andi raised her eyebrows as if challenging Luke.

Luke shook his head. "A lot of people are more than they seem, Andi. You're one of them."

That seemed to appease Ellison's best friend. It was hard, after all, for Andi to stay mad. She just couldn't do it – unless the person messed with Ellison. Then Ellison had seen Andi's inner momma bear come out.

"Look, I have to go," Luke said. "But if you ladies need anything else, just call."

Ellison tried to sit up, but gravity pushed her back into the couch cushions. "Thanks, Luke."

"Yeah, thanks for everything," Andi said.

Luke dipped his head and grabbed his car keys from the table.

"See you Wednesday?" he asked Ellison.

"If I survive today, you will."

Luke laughed. "Good luck."

17

DODGEBALL

A ball whizzed past Ellison's head, and she ducked. But that knocked her off balance, and she fell onto her backside in the grass. She was still woozy from her hangover, but Andi had ordered her out of the house.

"You're supposed to catch it!" some guy yelled at her.

She stood and brushed herself off. For some reason, she allowed Andi to drag her to a dodgeball game. An adult dodgeball game. That the other participants – including Andi – were all a little too into. The whole thing gave Ellison bad flashbacks to middle school.

Another ball zoomed toward her, and this time, she reached out and grabbed it.

"Dude!" a thin, scruffy looking guy said. "I thought you were an easy target!"

"Think again." Ellison whipped the ball at a woman on the other side and missed. A ball whacked Ellison in the thigh. "Ow!"

"Get over here!" Andi yelled. She was already out and sat on the sideline happily chatting to a guy.

Ellison trotted over as the man handed Andi back her phone. "Text me later," he said. "We can grab a drink or something."

Andi smiled coyly. "Sounds great!" The two women didn't talk until he was out of earshot, and then Andi said, "At least one of us got something out of this."

"I got a bruise. And my hangover feels worse." Ellison retorted. Out of all of Andi's ideas, this had to be the worst. Who plays dodgeball let alone when they're hungover. Still, Ellison appreciated her friend's effort. "He seemed nice."

Andi screwed up her face as she stood. "Who?"

"The guy you were talking to just now," Ellison answered.

Andi waved her hand. "He was fine. A bit forgettable, but fine."

Behind Ellison, the game played on with lots of shouting on both sides. Andi hadn't told her that all the cool girls wore knee-high athletic socks, booty shorts, and crop tops. Ellison, unlike Andi, had on yoga pants and a ill-fitting t-shirt. "I so don't fit in here. Everyone is under thirty, trim, and fun."

Andi shrugged. "It's a mindset, and you've got to change yours. You'll never meet a guy if you don't try."

"I—"

"Don't try," Andi said. "You wallow. You feel bad for yourself. But you do nothing to change things."

Ellison flinched. Andi never spoke to her this harshly. "What would you like me to do?"

Andi softened her face. "Ellison, I'm worried about you. You're depressed. I get it, but look," she dropped her voice as a group of younger women set up next to them. "Luke wants to date you. He told me. And you're saying no."

"He told me he could get in trouble with work."

"Okay, but let him make that decision," Andi unscrewed her water bottle and sipped.

"You, meanwhile, are a grown up, and you can date people without it majorly screwing up your kids."

The game ended, and her team rushed the field. "We won?"

Andi laughed. "I guess so. Want to go?"

"Oh, God yes!" Ellison couldn't grab her backpack fast enough. Even though her nausea was gone, she still felt shaky. "Never make me do this again."

As they walked toward Andi's car, Ellison was torn. Her best friend was right. She needed to try, but Dash and Alex's therapist told her she needed to provide a steady, secure home life with routine. Which she was doing. But what about the weeks when the boys weren't with her? Why couldn't she date then? She didn't have to introduce her dates to her sons.

"I should date," Ellison said out loud.

"Yes! That's what I've been saying." Andi unlocked the car doors. "It doesn't have to be Luke – although I think he'd be good for you. What's going on with that Bennydate guy?"

Ellison got in the passenger seat. "I honestly forgot about that. He wants to have dinner on Tuesday, but I haven't confirmed."

"Do it," Andi said.

"Right." They had exchanged a few texts, and their conversations had been playful and flirty. They'd even exchanged photos – nothing racy, just something to pique the imagination. "He does sound promising."

Problem was, she wanted Luke. His breakfast choice aside, he was still the best guy she'd met in months – years, even. She wanted to be open to the possibility of liking Ben, but didn't know if it was possible – not with the way Luke had gotten under her skin.

"Right. So go for it! Go all in," Andi ordered. "Confirm that date!"

Andi sped down the street, past the perfect homes with perfect kids playing outside. Everything about her old neighborhood was idyllic, but Ellison had learned too well over the past year that much of it was an illusion. There was no such thing as perfection. In fact, the more perfect something looked outwardly, the more messed up it probably was behind the scenes.

"How are you feeling? Okay?" Ellison asked. She felt green while Andi was full of energy.

"Me? I'm an old pro. My job lends itself to a shit ton of drinking." Andi often said things like this. Sometimes, it felt like while her best friend knew everything about her, Ellison didn't really know Andi.

They pulled into Ellison's driveway. "I'm going to need your help picking out what to wear on my date with Ben. Can you come over tomorrow?"

Andi checked her calendar. "Sure. Around seven?"

"Perfect." Ellison climbed out of Andi's two-door sports car. "See you then."

"Okay," said Andi.

Ellison unlocked the front door and was greeted by silence. She dropped her backpack near the coat closet and headed toward the kitchen. Dinner tonight would be chips and salsa because that's all she could muster on her shaky stomach.

Andi was right. She needed to try in all areas of her life. She had spent the past year waiting for others to do things for her. Even though Eve and Julia hadn't exactly been there for her during the divorce or after, she hadn't really reached out to them either. Kate had tried, coming by once in a while and checking up on Ellison, but somewhere along the way, her visits had stopped. Ellison had to take a little responsibility for the situation.

And then there was Luke who was more-or-less off limits. *Because,* she thought, *let's be real. We can't be friends.*

With one hand, Ellison pulled her laptop from under the couch and flipped it open.

After dipping a chip in delicious salsa, Ellison re-read the messages between her and Bennydate. Before she could lose her nerve, she accepted his offer of dinner. Her heart pounded wildly. Hopefully, he hadn't changed his mind.

And then, in a fit of madness, she decided to call Kate. Out of all her former friends, Kate seemed like she'd be the most receptive to Ellison's overtures.

"Hello?"

"Hi Kate! It's Ellison."

No answer.

"Kate?"

There was a ruffling on the other side. "I'm sorry. I was just going over the Junior Committee Gala RSVPs. How are you?"

"I'm great!" Ellison screwed up her face. What should she say? "I...I wanted to see what you've been up to. We haven't talked in ages."

"No, we haven't." Kate sounded a bit reserved, which was so unlike her.

Ellison dug deep to find something to say. "Oh, hey! I completely forgot to send in my RSVP!" As much as Ellison didn't want to go, she knew she needed to – if just to retain her dignity and show that she hadn't become a recluse hiding away from Josh and Jenn.

"You're coming?" Kate sounded surprised.

"Yes, I wouldn't miss it." Ellison's mind tumbled over itself. She couldn't show up stag. That would look bad. And it would make her feel uncomfortable – like all eyes would be watching her.

"Great!" Kate said. "I'll put you down for one. That is unless you have a date?"

Ellison's breath stuck. She hadn't thought this out well enough. If she showed up solo, it would look like she was spying on Josh and Jenn.

"Put me down for two," Ellison said, coolly like she already had a date. Maybe Ben would work out, and he'd go with her

She twirled a piece of hair around her finger and stared blankly at the television. She'd get Andi to RSVP, too. After all, she'd have no problem finding a date.

"Ellison?" Kate's voice cut through Ellison's wandering mind. "Are you still there?"

"I am. Sorry, I got distracted by something."

"It's okay. Happens to me all the time." Out of the terrible three-some – as Andi had started calling Eve, Kate, and Julia – Kate was the one with the most compassion. She'd always seemed more generous and caring than the other two.

"So put me down for two, and please make sure I'm seated with Andi and her date."

"Will do. Anything else?" Kate asked.

"Nope."

"Have a good night, Ellison."

"You too."

After she'd hung up the phone, Ellison curled onto the couch, knees to chest, and rocked back-and-forth. Would being single ever get easier? Josh didn't have to go through the whole 'plus one' or 'table for one' questions, and it seemed unfair. In fact, the whole, entire divorce and affair and all the crap that came after was unfair. Fat tears sat in the corners of Ellison's eyes, and no matter how hard she tried, she couldn't blink them away. Instead, they ran hot and heavy down her cheeks and onto her shirt. Her nose was snotty, and she sniffed loudly.

God, I'm a hot mess.

The tears kept rolling, and the snot flowing, and Ellison didn't know how to stop it. Sitting on the coffee table, she stared down at her computer and contemplated throwing the damn thing across the room. During the divorce, Josh had fought to keep the computer – Ellison's personal laptop – not because he needed it, but rather, he didn't want her to have it.

How she had forgotten about that until just now escaped her. She hated moments like this, when rage and memories collided. What an asshole.

Ellison rolled off the couch and onto the shag rug. She laid there for a few moments, drying her tears, before sitting up and taking a deep breath.

"I have a lot to be thankful for," she said aloud, as her therapist had instructed. In moments like this, find the small joys. "My boys are healthy and relatively happy. Jenn, by all reports, was miserable with morning sickness. I have a best friend who would do anything for me. And I have a date tomorrow night. With a guy who is available."

She could live without Josh, and it was time she started trying.

18

DINNER DATE

The restaurant was near empty when Ellison walked in. A lone man sat at the bar with his back toward her. He had dark hair that was slightly graying at the temples and was dressed in slacks and a button-up shirt. *Okay,* thought Ellison, trying to pump herself up, *so he's a little older than his pictures showed. Doesn't mean it has to be a bad date.*

She smoothed the front of her yellow dress and took a few tentative steps in his direction. About halfway across the room, she froze. What was she doing meeting a strange man at a restaurant? Andi said she'd call in an hour to check on her, but what if the date was going beyond badly? What if it was just plain awkward? What then? Did she excuse herself for the bathroom and never return? No. That seemed bitchy. Did she say an emergency came up and leave?

Would dating ever be easy?

"Ellison?"

She turned around and was greeted by a large smile and a dimple. *A dimple! How cute is that?* Ben was exactly what she imagined. Great smile, sandy blond hair, and hazel eyes.

"Hi," she managed to say, and held out her hand. "I'm Ellison. You must be Ben."

"I am indeed." He kept smiling at her while shaking her hand, and all her worries about awkwardness vanished.

"Should we sit?" Ellison asked, taking a step toward the bar. "I think there are plenty of seats."

Ben laughed, and Ellison found herself being wrapped up in the sound. "I guess it's not a normal night to go out on," he said. "But it'll be easier to hear you."

The restaurant Ben had chosen was ultra-modern with steel beams, hard edges, and a cool gray color scheme. It wasn't exactly inviting, but she was willing to give it a try.

Ben grinned, and he lightly touched Ellison's arm. She didn't pull away, despite it being a bit forward. "I hope you don't mind me saying this, but you really surprised me, Ellison."

"Oh?"

"You look just like your pictures."

"Don't most people?" She walked over to a bar stool, a few over from the graying man. Several minutes ago, she believed him to be Ben.

"Hardly. Most use old pictures. Sometimes pictures of their friends." Ben towered over Ellison, even in her three-inch heels.

"So I surprised you?" she said in a flirty voice.

Ben nodded while pulling out a bar stool for her. The stool was taller than normal, and she had to hoist herself up. Ben offered her his hand.

He can't be real, she thought. *He's almost too perfect. Like Luke. Or maybe I've become used to being treated like shit by Josh.*

She cringed and immediately hoped Ben didn't see it. Memories of Josh were like annoying gnats. She wanted to swat them all away and focus on her date.

"You're new to this aren't you?" Ben asked while flagging the bartender.

"Relatively. And you?"

"Unfortunately, no. You're my sixth date this month."

Ellison's heart dropped. She knew something had to be wrong

with him, but she couldn't make it out. Not yet anyway. "Always first dates?" she asked.

"Yes." At least he was honest.

"What can I get you?" The bartender asked. He stood in front of a wall of up-lit bottles of brightly colored alcohol.

"A gin and tonic for me and..."

"Maker's and Coke, please," Ellison said, naming a drink she'd sip and not guzzle.

The bartender nodded and walked away.

"You were saying," Ellison prompted, wanting to know more about why this seemingly attentive, attractive guy couldn't get past round one.

"Oh, the first dates. I've had a string of bad ones. From women looking nothing like their photos, to being years older than they claim, to having one woman tell me over drinks how good looking our kids will be. Things like that."

A laugh tumbled out of Ellison, and she found she enjoyed Ben's company very much. It didn't hurt that he was handsome, too. Almost made her forget about Luke. Almost.

The bartender slid the drinks across the bar. "Tab, or do you want the bill?"

Ben reached into his wallet and pulled out a black – BLACK – American Express. "Keep it open."

So he has money. That's always nice, Ellison thought. Not that she was superficial, but she didn't want to date down. Between her income and Josh's, she'd become accustomed to a certain lifestyle.

"What about you? How have your dates been?"

Ellison stirred her drink and looked up at Ben with her lids half-lowered. A sexy look, or so Andi told her. She'd made Ellison practice it over and over again. "I'll let you know later tonight."

"So I'm your first?"

A blush crept into Ellison's cheeks. "I'm a virgin." She blushed harder. "Not technically, but-"

"I know what you mean. You're new to the single world, I take it?"

She held up her naked ring finger. "It's been final for a little over a month."

"Ah. Well, it gets better. The loneliness – that's the worst." He swirled his drink. "Do you have kids?"

"Two boys. They're eight and ten."

"And they're with your ex tonight?"

"For the week."

Ben sipped slowly from his drink. "My ex gets the girls the majority of the time. I'm a weekend dad." He put his drink down and turned so his body faced Ellison's more squarely. "Enough of this depressing talk. Tell me about yourself."

Ellison withheld her sigh. This was the part she hated. She really had nothing going on in her life. "I played dodgeball with a bunch of twenty-somethings yesterday."

Ben's face lit up. "That's not what I expected you to say."

"Well," Ellison said with a laugh, "I could tell you about my exciting career as a real estate agent, but dodgeball makes me sound more adventurous. How about you?"

"My job is as dry as they come. I'm a government contractor specializing in data harvesting." She must of made a weird face, because Ben added, "See? I told you it was dry."

Ellison tasted her drink. She didn't really sip, more like pressed it against her lips and pretended. She wasn't in a hurry to finish or rush the conversation.

Their banter was playful, and Ben seemed to be enjoying her company as much as she enjoyed his. In fact, it wasn't until her phone rang that Ellison had realized how much time had slipped away.

"I'm sorry," she said. "I have to take this."

Ben tapped his finger on the bartop. "Friend check?"

"Something like that." She slid off her stool and walked a few feet away.

"Hey, Andi."

"Everything good?"

"It's going great," Ellison didn't fight the giddiness in her voice. "He's cute, engaging, and easy to talk to."

"Okay, then. Do everything I would." Andi chuckled. "Unless, of course he turns out to be crazy."

"I've got this," Ellison said. "No need to worry."

She clicked off and walked back to where Ben waited. He had been looking at his phone and immediately put it away when Ellison sat down. "All good?"

Ellison nodded. "Yes. Where were we?"

The conversation flowed easily. Andi was right. Maybe she just needed to try harder. She shifted so that her arm lay on the bar. Ben reached out and touched her hand. "Do you want some water?"

After Drunkfest, she learned her lesson. She wouldn't get buzzed with a stranger. Granted a very hot, nice stranger, but still a stranger. "Water would be great."

Ben motioned to the bartender. "Two waters, please."

Ellison downed hers. She'd barely touched her drink, but Ben either didn't notice or didn't care. It was nice that she didn't feel like she had to get buzzed to keep Ben entertained.

She checked her phone for the time. Ten-thirty. "Oh! I have to go," she said with a hint of disappointment. She hadn't had this much fun...well, since the night she met Luke. "I have a showing tomorrow."

"Can I walk you to your car? Or maybe call you an Uber?"

"I'm fine to drive. But you can walk with me if you'd like. Where did you park?"

"In the garage," Ben said, tilting his head in that direction. "How about you?"

"The same."

"Good, I'll walk with you." Surely a kiss was coming, and to her surprise, Ellison looked forward to it.

She waited while Ben signed for the drinks. Watching him and his strong shoulders made the butterflies in Ellison's stomach all worked up. She was a ball of nervous energy as they walked out of the restaurant and to the parking garage.

"I'm over here," she said, pointing to her car. Ben followed her. *He's going to kiss me,* she thought. *And I'm so not prepared.*

At her car Ben pinned her against the side, taking care not to touch her. He stared into her eyes for a long moment. Ellison's heartbeat sped up, and she began to tingle in all the right places. Maybe Andi was right, and there was more than one guy out there for her.

Ben slowly reached behind her and gathered her hair with one hand and pulled. Roughly. A little too rough, but she didn't complain. His mouth was on hers in an instant, his tongue chasing after hers. Ellison yielded and kissed him back harder.

Until...

He wrapped his free hand around her throat and squeezed.

Whoa.

Ellison couldn't breathe, let alone kiss. This is not what she had planned. Sure she liked a little kink as much as the next girl, but not on the first date. She broke away from the kiss, and Ben dropped his hands. "Did you like that?" he growled in her ear. "Do you want more?"

Suddenly, what was so sexy five minutes earlier seemed threatening now.

"Ummm...I really have to go," she gasped and pulled away from her. Thankfully, Ben moved aside.

Undeterred, Ben asked, "Can I follow you home?"

No wonder this guy only went on first dates. Damn it. She knew there had to be something wrong with him. "No." She rubbed her aching throat. "I have an early morning, remember? I have a showing."

Ben went in for another kiss before Ellison could stop him. This time she broke it off before it got to the choking part. "I really have to go." And with that, she yanked the driver's side door open, slid in, and locked the door before putting the key in the ignition. She maneuvered the Suburban around Ben and out into the street.

Once she was sure he wasn't following her, she bashed her hand against the steering wheel. Why did dating have to be so hard?

19

FRIENDS...WITHOUT BENEFITS?

E llison ran her hand over the sore spot on her neck. Flashes of Monday's date gone wrong came back to her. Had Ben really choked her? She had to be imagining that, and yet, her neck ached. Slowly, she rolled out of bed, found her favorite fluffy slippers, and crossed the hardwood floor to her bathroom.

When she looked in the mirror, she gasped. Her red eyes and wild hair aside, she looked horrible. The worst part was three slightly purple bruises on her neck. They were worse than yesterday when she somehow convinced herself that she misunderstood the situation.

Ben had to have grabbed her harder than she thought. Or, she was a little too delicate. She studied the bruises more carefully.

He absolutely was too rough with her. Part of her felt that she had a duty to report it, but what would she say? That while kissing he got too rough and stopped when she told him to? How is that against the law?

Ellison gently touched the bruises. They were going to require a lot of concealer or a turtleneck – neither of which she owned. She sighed before taking one last look at herself.

They were bad, and everyone would notice them. More importantly, Luke would notice them when she volunteered later that morning. And then she'd feel compelled to tell him the story of how she went out on a date with someone else.

Ugh. Why did everything come back to Luke? She had bigger problems, like hiding these bruises from her client this afternoon.

She cranked the handle on the shower to the hottest position and waited for the room to fill with steam before stepping inside. The water was scalding hot, so she adjusted it until it was perfect. As the water ran over her naked body, Ellison replayed the date in her head. Everything seemed so promising until the very end. Ben's charming smile, the easy banter between them, the gentle touch of hands. Everything Andi told her to do, she did. And it worked.

Until Ben went crazy and choked her.

Ellison stood under the steady stream of water and let it wash away all the bad feelings. Now that more time had passed, she began to see the whole date through very different eyes. Ben could have killed her, and no one other than Andi would have known.

In fact, how was she supposed to tell if the guys on the website were normal or not? How could you tell with anyone? It's one thing, taking a leap of faith. It's a whole other when the man tries to choke you and pull your hair.

When she climbed out of the shower, her phone began to buzz. Out of habit, Ellison picked it up. A text from Ben.

Awesome.

Would love to see you again. Is tomorrow too soon?

Ellison debated whether or not to text him back. On one hand, it would encourage him – even if she were firm. On the other, not answering left things in limbo, and she'd probably get more texts from him until he gave up.

She stared at her phone. The problem was she couldn't reconcile the charming man with whom she had drinks with the guy who went all kinky on her in the parking lot. Who was she kidding? It was more than kinky. It was downright assault.

Bravery surged through her, and Ellison typed out a quick text.

Sorry, but I don't think it's going to work between us.

Quick and to the point. She hit send and set the phone down on the countertop before getting her make-up out. Ellison found old foundation in her make-up drawer and began dabbing it onto her bruises. Once they were covered, she dusted powder over them. They were still there, but much less visible. If she wore a collared shirt and the one scarf she owned, she should be fine.

With a sigh, she stared in the mirror. This hadn't been her luckiest year. But things were bound to get better. After all, how much bad luck can one person have?

Still, she thought while touching the tender spots on her neck. *Dating, it seemed, wanted to kill her.*

Ellison glanced at her phone. So far, no more texts from Ben. She shuddered. Maybe what he did wasn't against the law, but Match should know. It was unlikely she was his first…Ellison didn't know what to call it. Victim seemed too harsh, but that's how she felt. She picked up her phone, opened her Match account, found their contact info, and typed out an email to them. Then she blocked Ben from her phone and Match account.

She'd had enough of assholes.

A riot of noise greeted Ellison when she entered the classroom. She hadn't seen Luke since Drunkfest, and she was more than just a little embarrassed. She had, after all, thrown up several times, and each time Luke would clean up after her.

She owed him. What, she wasn't sure, but she owed him.

As Ellison surveyed the room, Dash ran up and wrapped his arms around her. They hadn't seen each other since last Friday – the day before the wedding. It was moments like this that reminded her that she only got the boys part-time.

"Mom!" Dash exclaimed, clearly excited to see her. Her heart swelled a little, and she hugged her son back.

"Where's Mr. Peterson?" Ellison asked. She fidgeted with her scarf. She generally, didn't like wearing them, but before leaving the house, she had wrapped it around her neck, hoping to hide the bruises.

"He had a meeting, so Ms. Morales is watching us." On the floor near the windows sat a pretty woman about Ellison's age with dark hair and bronzed skin. She was working on something with a small group of kids.

"Oh," Ellison said, hoping she didn't sound too disappointed.

"I think he's coming back soon."

"That's nice," Ellison said, trying to ignore the butterflies in her gut. She walked over to where Luke kept her volunteer folder. On the outside was a post-it note.

Ellison,

Take this group of four and work on the sentence structure of their small moments story.

Luke.

She looked around the room and called out the four names listed on her sheet. Ms. Morales didn't even look up. Some substitute.

When Ellison had the kids gathered around her, she asked the little girl to her left to read her paragraph. When she was done, Ellison took the paper and looked it over for capitalization and grammar errors. Finding none, she handed it back. As she was taking a look at the next student's paper, the door swung open. Ellison lifted her head, and there was Luke framed by the doorway. The light from the hallway glowed around him, and he looked amazing: pink dress shirt with the sleeves rolled up, fitted jeans, and boots.

Yum.

Ellison had to remind herself to look away – no easy task.

"Hi, Ms. Brooks," Luke called from across the room. Ellison immediately felt heat flush across her face.

"Hi," she mumbled back and tried her best to focus on the kids before her.

Ms. Morales stopped whatever it was she was doing on the floor and stood up.

"How were they?" Luke asked as he walked toward his desk. Not that Ellison was paying attention. She just happened to notice in a not noticing kind of way.

"Just fine," Ms. Morales said. "They were relatively quiet."

Ellison screwed up her face. If that's what Ms. Morales thought quiet sounded like, Ellison would hate to see her definition of noisy. Maybe the woman was hard of hearing?

Not wanting to seem anxious or like she was wanting Luke's attention, Ellison tried to focus on her group of children. She successfully blocked him out until he splayed his hand on the crescent shaped table and said, "How's everything going over here?"

Ellison swallowed hard. Her stomach was a mess of excitement. At the same time, she was embarrassed over the whole Drunkfest incident. Her memory was fuzzy, but she vaguely recalled asking Luke to climb into bed with her. And she definitely remembered him holding her hair as she puked.

Oh good heavens. Did she make an ass of herself or what?

"We're doing great!" Her voice did a weird uptick thing, and she wanted to slump under the table. Why couldn't she be normal around this man?

"Let me know if you need anything." Luke walked away, and Ellison admired his broad shoulders. His biceps were equally nice. And his—

"Ms. Brooks?" a little boy asked. "Is it my turn?"

"Ah, yes." Ellison had to focus on her job, but it was so damn hard with Luke in the room. Still, the kids had to come before her hormones.

The hour zipped by, and before she knew it, Luke called for the kids to gather their lunches. Ellison began packing her stuff.

"Ellison, if you don't mind, can you wait here for a minute?" Luke said, standing near her, so the kids couldn't hear. "I need to talk to you."

"Sure," she answered, curious about what he could possibly want to discuss. Did she say anything really stupid during Drunkfest? Did she come on to him? Dread rolled through her. Oh. God. She had. She totally had. What if he was now going to let her down gently after telling her he'd date her? Was he just trying to be nice to the drunk woman?

All these thoughts raced through Ellison's head as Luke led the kids out the door and to the lunchroom.

With nothing to do, she meandered around the classroom, stopping by Dash's desk. It was a mess – papers shoved into every corner, pencils and erasers spilling out of his pencil box, and used tissues everywhere. Gross.

Ever the mom, Ellison began cleaning out some of the mess, tossing the tissues into the garbage can and putting his pencils and erasers away. There were still papers shoved everywhere, but Ellison didn't touch those. She'd probably end up throwing out something important.

When Luke walked back in, she was buried deep in the desk.

"Hey, Ellison," he said in his velvety voice.

She popped her head up and dropped a ball of paper on the ground. "Tell me none of this is Dash's homework," she said, hoping to keep the conversation light.

Luke shook his head. "Despite that mess, your son has turned in every assignment on time."

Ellison settled back onto her heels before straightening up. Luke was just on the other side of the desk. From where she stood, she could see the faint stubble lining his jaw. It was sexy as hell.

"So," Luke said, placing both hands on the top of the desk and leaning into her. "What are we doing?"

"Cleaning desks?" she said, hoping he'd laugh. When he didn't, she averted her eyes to the ground.

"I've been thinking about you. A lot." He held her gaze, and Ellison's took a long breath. "I know you have concerns over us dating – I do, too – but can we at least talk about it more?"

Why did everything have to be so complicated? "I don't know," Ellison said. "There's Dash and your job and…"

"Public opinion?" Luke asked.

Ellison hesitated. Why did she care so much what everyone else thought? "There's that."

"Did Drunkfest feel too much like a date to you?" Luke asked, lowering his voice.

Ellison shrugged. "Honestly, the night is a blur."

Luke let out a whoosh of air. "I should never have come over, but I wanted to see you."

Without thinking, Ellison jutted out her hand and rested it on Luke's forearm. "As much as I like you, I think it's better if we keep things platonic for now. Besides, doesn't your contract prevent you from dating parents? I remember talking about that."

Luke shook his head. "It's not encouraged, that's what Principal Sylvian said when I asked her about it the other day. And if it's thought to interfere with my objectivity, I can be removed from the classroom."

"You outright asked?" Ellison's mouth gaped open.

"I never mentioned you."

Ellison sighed and dropped his arm. "So, if you weren't Dash's teacher, and I didn't have my hang-ups, we would date?"

"I'd like to." Luke looked down at her. "If you'd have me."

She flashed her prettiest smile at him. "Of course I would. As long as it was okay with my kids, but they're not ready for me to have a relationship yet." Her face fell. "Where does that leave us?"

"As friends who really, really like each other?" Luke said.

"I think it's for the best," Ellison said with regret in her voice. "You're a new teacher and don't need the gossip. I don't need it, either."

Luke stuck out his hand. "Friends?"

Ellison took his hand and electric bolts coursed through her. How was she ever supposed to be friends with Luke? Still, she answered, "Friends."

It was like a knife being shoved into her chest. She didn't want to be friends with this man. She didn't. And her heart knew it. She wanted to spend chilly evenings wrapped up in his arms before a roaring fire. She wanted to hold his body close to her and feel the rise and fall of his chest.

She wanted to see where things could go with him.

20

LOW BLOWS

"Hi, Ellison!" Eve stood a little too close to Ellison's table. She had on the latest Lululemon pants with a cozy sweatshirt wrap. And of course, her hair looked perfectly imperfect in a messy ponytail. It was like she had just come from yoga, but had barely broken a sweat. "Can I sit with you?"

There were a dozen open tables in Starbucks, and Eve wanted to sit with her? Interesting. Kate must have said something to her. Ellison moved her things around so Eve could sit. "What's going on?"

"I heard, through the grapevine of course, that you have a date for the Gala tomorrow night." Eve's eyes danced with curiosity, and she gave Ellison a sly smile. "Anyone special?"

Ellison pressed her lips together. She hadn't given much thought to the Gala and honestly had forgotten she was supposed to be a 'plus one.' She had no idea where she'd find a guy to be her date? Maybe an Andi cast-off? "I do have a date, but unfortunately, he may have to go out of town on business."

"Who is this mystery man?" Eve said, leaning forward on her elbows. She wasn't even trying to be subtle. "Do tell."

Ellison quickly ran through names, and could only come with Ben and Luke. "Ben, she blurted. "His name is Ben."

Eve batted her eyes. "Ben who? Does he live in Lodi?"

Shit. Ellison had no idea what Ben's last name was, and even if she did, she wouldn't want Eve looking him up. Especially since Ellison had no desire to ever see him again. "He does. We met...at the grocery store."

Eve laughed. "Love on aisle two?"

Ellison wasn't sure if Eve was trying to be funny or bitchy, but she laughed while adjusting the scarf she still wore wrapped around her neck.

"Whoa." Eve's eyes grew wide, and she jutted out her hand and touched Ellison's neck. "What the hell happened here? Did someone hurt you?"

"It's nothing." Ellison tightened the scarf. Wonderful. Now Eve wasn't just going to gossip about Ben, she had a story about Ellison's reckless sex life. Or whatever she was going to spin.

"Ellison, what happened?" There was real concern in Eve's voice, but Ellison knew from experience that anything she said would become public information within the hour.

"It's really okay. Not a big deal," Ellison said.

Eve sat back in her chair. "It looks awful. You should have it looked at."

"Thank you for your concern," Ellison answered. She had to get Eve to talk about something else. "But, if you don't mind, I have to prep for a showing this afternoon."

"Oh? You're back in real estate?" Eve smiled coldly. "I swore Jenn said-"

"Jenn knows nothing about my life," Ellison snapped.

"Of course not. She only babysits your kids fifty percent of the time while you run around and get bruises all over your neck."

"It's not what you think it is," Ellison said.

Eve raised her eyebrows. "Right. Because if you had been assaulted, you would have said something, but you didn't, so obviously, you're bruised because of something you did." She smirked. "Way to keep it classy."

Eve's words were daggers, but Ellison knew how to play this game.

134

She'd perfected it over the course of their friendship. "As classy as your new BFF Jenn sleeping with a married man? I'll try to take that under advisement."

"You need to let that go, Ellison. It's been, like, a year. Time to move on." Eve dropped her voice. "And by the look of things, you certainly have."

Something inside Ellison cracked. "You know nothing. Nothing. Jenn ruined my life, and all of you think it's perfectly okay. Well, it's not. What she did was a horrible, awful thing, and my kids and I are paying for it."

Eve shook her head. "Josh did that to you, not Jenn. Jenn simply fell in love with the wrong person."

Ellison gritted her teeth. "Is that really how you see it?" People were staring, but Ellison didn't care. She didn't care that her voice had hit a hysterical pitch, or that she may possibly appear unhinged. "Because just you wait. When it happens to you, I'll be the first in line to tell you how everything is your fault."

"You know, Ellison. I used to envy you. You had it all together: the house, the family, the career. But now I see what a bitch you are. No wonder Josh left you."

Without thinking, Ellison grabbed her green tea and threw it at Eve, but missed. The paper cup hit the floor, and the contents spilled everywhere.

"Oh my God! You are fucking crazy!" Eve yelled. "What is wrong with you?"

Ellison trembled. What had she done? "Eve, I'm sorry. I'm just—"

"Out of control and psycho!" In a swish of platinum hair, Eve spun around, stepped over the mess, and headed for the door. "You're a hot mess. Try pulling yourself together before the Gala, okay?"

Ellison was keenly aware of all the eyes staring at her as she stooped to wipe up the floor. She couldn't cry. Not here. Not in public. And definitely not right before her client meeting. She needed to do like Eve said and pull herself together. There would be plenty of time to wallow later.

She dumped the empty cup and napkins in the garbage and

checked her watch. She was meeting new clients at two, and it was now one thirty.

"Ellison?" the day shift manager stood behind her. She was a round-cheeked cheerful young woman.

"Yes?"

"Ummm…is everything okay?" she asked.

"It is. Thank you for asking." Ellison walked back to her table, and the manager followed.

"Look," she said. "I can't have you fighting in here. Maybe you should go leave for today?"

Ellison blanched and looked around the room. People were openly listening, and she couldn't stand the attention. "Okay."

"Please don't do that again, or I'll have to ask you not to come in anymore," the manager said.

"I understand. Can I just finish up here before leaving?" Ellison asked.

The manager nodded. "Sure, but not too long, okay?"

"Twenty minutes, tops," Ellison answered.

The papers she had moved for Eve were in a neat pile, and Ellison thumbed through them looking for the right one. When she found it, she pulled it out and studied it while pretending nothing had happened. Thankfully, most of the people who had been in Starbucks when she threw the cup had already left. But she was still shaking and needed to calm down. She needed to distract herself, so she opened her email. She still hadn't heard from Marsha, so she made a meeting reminder to call her after the showing.

Despite her outburst, it felt good to be busy again. One house for sale, two clients who were looking. That was a potential of three sales. If she could close on all of them, she'd be financially solvent for another six to nine months. She could pay Andi back and catch up on her bills.

Ellison needed this. All she had to do was focus.

"Troy, Amy. So nice to meet you in person." Ellison held out her hand to the man, before shaking the woman's.

Troy studied the front of the house. "It looks a little old."

Amy gently nudged him. "Old as in twelve years. Nothing we buy in Waterford is going to be new construction."

"That's right," Ellison added. "The development is about twelve years old. It has mature trees and great schools."

Amy rubbed her bulging belly. "Schools are important. I heard Waterford has some of the best."

"Is this your first?" Ellison asked.

Amy beamed. "Yes. We're having a girl in January, so I really want to find a home quickly."

Now it was Ellison's turn to smile, despite her throat constricting. This woman was so happy and unaware of how horrible marriage could be. Ellison wanted to wrap her up in her arms and protect her.

Hell, she wished someone had done that for her when she was newly pregnant and building her home in Waterford.

But then again, she wouldn't have listened. What would that person have known? Her Josh was perfect and excited about being a dad.

"A girl!" Ellison exclaimed. "Congratulations! I have two boys, myself. And Waterford's schools are top-notch."

Ellison unlocked the front door and waited for Amy and Troy to enter. Amy gasped.

"Is everything okay?" Ellison asked. She'd seen and heard all kinds of things as a realtor, but gasps were something she still couldn't read.

Amy turned around, taking in the grand entry, the second story balcony, and the light filled dining room. "It's beautiful."

A smile formed on Ellison's lips. "It does show well. The owners have done a beautiful job with it."

"It's pretty, but what about the systems?" Troy asked. "HVAC and stuff?"

Ellison flipped through her folder. "New as of last year, as is the roof."

Amy waited half-way up the stairs. "Troy, c'mon. I want to see where the baby's room could be."

As Ellison watched them disappear, sadness overwhelmed her. Amy's belly reminded her of Jenn, and Jenn reminded her of what she'd lost. Ellison leaned against the wall, trying to compose herself before the couple came back downstairs. One breath, two breaths, three breaths, four.

What the hell? Why did everything have to come back to Jenn?

"Ellison!" Amy called from somewhere upstairs. "We love it!"

Five breaths. "Then come down here so we can discuss numbers."

Troy jogged down the backstairs while Amy waddled behind and into the kitchen where Ellison waited.

"It's perfect. Five bedrooms. More than enough bathrooms. And that master suite is to die for." Ellison wasn't sure if Amy was out of breath from excitement or physical activity.

Troy nodded. "It's close to my office, too." He stared at Ellison. "What do you think a reasonable price is?"

Ellison pulled out a few brochures and comps. "Well, as you know, they want eight fifty. I think we can get them down to at least eight twenty-five."

The couple eyed each other.

A soft, "Oh," escaped Amy's lips.

"Is something wrong?" Ellison asked.

Troy frowned. "We thought a more fair price would be seven ninety-nine."

Ellison retained her composure. "This house is on a cul-de-sac in a highly desirable part of Waterford. If you look at the comps, you'll see nothing has gone for less than eight fifteen in the past two years. We could try starting at seven ninety-nine, but I'm positive the owners will counter higher."

"We're going to have to think about it, then. Going that high will be a stretch for us – especially with the baby coming." Troy took the papers Ellison held out to him.

With a plastered smile, Ellison led them to the door. They knew the price going in, so the fact that they were lowballing was irritating.

"Okay, think about it. We can always put an offer in, and the worst that can happen is that the seller's turn it down."

Amy grasped Troy's arm. "Let's do that."

"Let's talk about this at home," he said.

Ellison didn't want them to walk away without knowing their options. "We could also look at other homes. There are a few smaller houses coming onto the market in Waterford and Lodi. I could arrange showings."

"We'll consider it," Troy answered.

As Ellison watched them drive away, her heart sunk. The chance of them buying this house was slim, and she knew it. Maybe they'd be interested in the Lodi house – the one Marsha was stalling on. Her commission wouldn't be as big, but Ellison was determined to find the perfect house for them, and she wouldn't give up.

Her independence, and maybe her sanity, depended upon it.

21

ELLISON 2.0

ere goes nothing, Ellison thought, as she pulled the heavy glass door to the Club open. The hum of the party floated down the richly appointed hallway. In years past, when Ellison was part of the Junior Committee, this was the party she most looked forward to. She loved getting dressed in black tie attire and feeling fancy for the night. She had bought a new hot pink, chiffon dress for the occasion, and her hair fell in loose waves. She looked good. But as she entered the Club, a ball of anxiety formed in her gut.

It was her first big outing as a single person, and it didn't help that she had had that blow up with Eve. Or that she didn't have a date. Or that Jenn and Josh would be there.

No, she really shouldn't be there. She should be home, with the boys. Josh had returned them the night before, and, trying to be the best mom ever, she had taken them to the pumpkin patch for the day. But Ellison had no doubt Josh was surely going to question her mothering for getting a babysitter. She was prepared for his onslaught. Or, so she told herself.

Outside the ballroom, she paused and collected herself. A few people she vaguely recognized said hello, but no one lingered. She only got the precursory drive-by treatment. She had never given much thought to how people catered to her before, but it hit her now. She was no longer someone to impress, so no one tried.

At least Andi was coming. Albeit with some random guy from what Ellison could tell. But maybe it wouldn't be bad, and people would talk to her. Maybe her shunning was all in her head.

Then again, there was no way Eve was going to let her outburst at Starbucks pass, which meant Ellison had to enter with her head held higher than normal and a springier bounce in her step. She had to look sane and not like the tea-cup-throwing maniac Eve was probably making her out to be.

"Hey, Ellison!" Veronica White had come up behind her. "You look pretty."

Ellison smiled. Veronica was on the Junior Committee and had surely heard about her meltdown, but here she was talking to Ellison and exchanging air kisses. "Thank you. You look gorgeous."

"Picture?" Veronica whipped out her phone and positioned herself next to Ellison.

At least I'm still photo-worthy, Ellison thought. She flashed a grin as Veronica snapped away. Ellison knew that Veronica would plaster the picture all over social media, and it made her feel a little better. Like she mattered again.

"Catch you later?" Veronica asked.

"Of course!" Ellison put on her bubbly façade and hoped it was convincing. When Veronica was gone, she stood in the doorway of the ballroom and surveyed the room, hoping to spot Andi, but instead, her eyes landed on Josh and Jenn. Jenn stood close to Josh with one hand resting on her stomach and the other on Josh's arm. She was laughing.

Ugh.

What Ellison needed was a drink. Something to take the edge off her nerves, but not so strong that she was buzzed. She couldn't chance not being completely in control.

She made her way through the crowd of elegantly dressed party-goers, past white-draped tables with simple centerpieces, and bellied up to the well-stocked bar. She rose her hand to flag the bartender and froze.

Luke stood at the far end of the bar. But he wasn't alone. Oh no. There was a leggy blond, dressed in red, dripping off his arm. Someone Ellison had never seen before.

"Ellison. You came." Eve wedged herself next to Ellison. Her platinum hair cascaded over one shoulder and down the front of her silver dress, and she had on a plummy lipstick. She looked untouchable. "After the other day, I didn't think you'd be brave enough. I mean, you did have those bruises and all."

This wasn't about the bruises, and they both knew it. Despite the sick feeling in her stomach, Ellison decided to eat crow. Eve was baiting her, but Ellison had to ignore it if she wanted to move forward. "Eve, I'm sorry about the tea thing. I lost my temper."

Eve surveyed her. "I suppose you have to say that don't you?"

"Actually, I don't." Ellison glanced over Eve's shoulder for Andi, but couldn't spot her. "I'm trying to be nice."

Eve tossed her head back dramatically and laughed. "You? Nice?" She gave a tight smile. "You've never been nice to anyone unless there was something in it for you. So, what is it you want?"

Heat built in Ellison's cheeks. There was some truth to what Eve said. Before her divorce, she wasn't always the nicest person. Okay. So she was a gossip and slightly bitchy. But they all were. It was, like, a rule of their group or something.

"I want to be friends again," Ellison found herself saying, even though deep down, she didn't. Sure, she was lonely, but she didn't need Eve. Or Julia. Or Kate. And yet, she couldn't stop herself from groveling. "I don't know what happened between us."

Eve waved her hand. "Ellison, really? You're the one who stopped being our friend. You moved away. You stopped hanging out. This is all on you." She licked her upper lip. "Frankly, I'm surprised you came. You have balls."

"Of course I'd come," Ellison said icily. "I've never missed a Junior Committee Gala. Besides, childhood literacy is close to my heart."

"Of course it is." Eve's head swiveled around. "By the way, where's the mystery guy Kate said you were bringing? Did he have to go out of town?"

Eve was digging for gossip, and Ellison wasn't going to give her any, but she was thankful for the change of conversation. She eyed Luke at the end of the bar, and her heart sunk. He found a date, so why couldn't she? "I'm flying solo tonight. My date couldn't make it."

"Oh, That's too bad." Eve said, not sounding sad at all. More like a catty bitch. "But you know, almost everyone here is married."

It was a warning: don't talk to our husbands. Because that's exactly what Ellison wanted to do – stoop to Jenn's level. Not.

"Where are Kate and Julia?" Ellison asked. "You three never go anywhere without each other."

Eve huffed. "Still not here. We were supposed to pre-game, but Kate's sitter was late, and Julia wasn't ready on time."

"Ah." Pre-gaming was an essential part of any Waterford outing, and who you pre-gamed with was a huge deal.

"Did you show up alone?" Eve asked.

"I did. Andi's meeting me." Ellison looked around the room. "Have you seen her?"

"I did earlier." Eve held her hand against the side of her mouth and said in a stage whisper, "Her date is dreadfully young. But h-o-t hot."

Of course he was. Andi didn't do anything half-assed and that included finding a date for herself. The other day, Ellison had asked Andi to set her up with a few of her castoffs, but Andi had said, "No. There's a reason they're not my boyfriend, and I wouldn't do that to you, no matter how desperate you are."

Which made Ellison wonder where Andi had found this new guy, and just how long she'd known him.

"Do you need a drink?" Ellison asked Eve, trying to be somewhat civil since Eve didn't seem in a hurry to move on to another victim. Going up to the bar would also give her better look at Luke's date.

"No, I'm good, but don't let me stop you," Eve said.

Ellison went back to trying to catch the bartender's attention. That's when it happened. Luke turned, and he gaped when he noticed her. But he didn't wave or make any other acknowledgement.

"What a jerk," Ellison mumbled to herself. How could Luke not acknowledge her? Maybe he was too enraptured by the blond to pay any attention to Ellison. And where did he find her? Ellison was positive she wasn't a club member.

"Did you say something?" Eve asked.

"Just commenting on how pretty it all looks." And it did. White flowers covered every surface of the room, and gold accents finished off the look.

"The committee really out did itself this year, didn't we?" Eve asked. While it was pretty, this Junior Committee Gala looked like all the past ones. The ones Ellison had chaired. They were kind of unimaginative, to be honest.

Ellison resisted an eye roll. "You did indeed." Her gaze fluttered back over to Luke and the leggy blond. Why did he have to show up at this event? He couldn't possibly be a member of the Club on a teacher's salary, could he?

"There are a lot of new people here tonight, aren't there?" Ellison said, knowing Eve would have the latest gossip.

The corners of Eve's mouth twitched up in excitement. "We have some new members. So nice to see them here, enjoying themselves." She clapped her hands together. "One of them is a single guy about our age. I should play matchmaker, but he has a date."

After their earlier exchange, this seemed positively insane. Eve coupld flip the charm on and off. But Ellison knew better. This was when Eve was most dangerous.

"I don't know," Ellison said, turning her back to Luke. "I'm not exactly ready for dating."

Pity flashed across Eve's face. "Well, maybe next time. But I'm telling you, he's really attractive. You'd like him."

Ellison nodded absent-mindedly.

"What are you bidding on tonight?" Eve asked, peaking at Ellison's blank bid form.

"I don't know yet." The truth was there was nothing she needed, and the things she wanted, she couldn't afford. Ellison turned slightly and flashed another glance at Luke. He and the blond were lost in conversation with Josh and Jenn.

Ellison fought the urge to walk over and insert herself. But what would that accomplish other than making her look like a jealous ex-wife and fuel the gossip about her?

"Okay, Elle. I need to mingle." Eve melted into the crowd, leaving Ellison alone in a sea of people. She was a loser standing by the bar alone and waiting for what? Someone to talk to her? Be her friend? For Luke to break away from evil Jenn and the Blond Bitch to come rescue her...again?

No, she thought. *I've got this.* She finally caught the bartender's attention. "Whiskey Sour," she ordered.

She leaned against the counter, faced out into the crowd, and scanned for Andi. When she didn't see her, Ellison began running through the different couples, remembering the gossip she, Eve, Kate, and Julia used to spew. God, had she really been that awful? Is that why no one other than Veronica White and Eve wanted to talk to her? Did everyone think she was getting what she deserved?

She pressed her lips tightly together. Okay. Maybe that's how she used to be, but she had changed. She wasn't that woman anymore, and she wasn't all about lunches, day drinking, and girls' nights out. The problem was that she was still figuring out Ellison 2.0.

"One whiskey sour," the bartender said, sliding the glass toward Ellison.

"Thank you." She shoved a bill into the tip jar.

Ellison 2.0. There was a ring to it, and tonight could be her launch. She could show everyone that she'd changed, but more importantly, she'd show herself.

22

DANCING FOOLS

"Hey, Ellison."

She recognized the voice immediately: Luke.

Holding onto her glass, Ellison turned slowly. She'd been talking to the Midels – Sam and Tracey – about their college-aged son. Ellison hadn't always been kind to Tracey; in fact, she had on more than occasion suggested Tracey lose weight. But she had approached them, pulled Tracey aside, and apologized. Tracey had graciously accepted.

"Hi, Luke," she said as levelly as she could. Her insides were rolling, but she didn't want him to know that. "Do you know the Midels?"

"Sam, right? We met a few weeks ago at the member meeting."

"That's right!" Sam clasped Luke's hand. "How are you?"

"Good," Luke said. He completely ignored the leggy blond that was just inches from him. He shook Tracey's hand. "Nice to meet you."

"Luke," Ellison said." What brings you to the Gala?" What she really wanted to know was who was the woman he was parading around, and how the hell he afforded membership to the Club, but she wasn't going to bring it up.

"Well, as a new member, I thought I should come out and support the cause. Besides, early childhood literacy is close to my heart."

Was he for real? Did he overhear her conversation with Eve?

Ellison sized him up. In his tux, Luke looked like a gorgeous James Bond. Faint stubble on his jaw, tousled hair, and those gray eyes that just about did Ellison in.

The blond laughed in a deep, throaty way. "Luke has such bad manners." She extended her hand. "It's nice to meet you, Tracey. I'm Monica." She turned. "And you must be the famous Ellison."

Ellison face grew hot under Monica's gaze. "I don't know about famous, but I am Ellison."

The blond linked her arm through Ellison's. Ellison tensed. *Who is this woman and why was she buddying up to me?* But she was Ellison 2.0. Kind Ellison. Happy Ellison. Not a drink throwing, gossiping back-stabber. Whomever Monica was, Ellison would treat her graciously.

After a few minutes, Sam and Tracey excused themselves, and Monica turned her full attention on Ellison. "All my brother does is talk about, 'Ellison this,' and 'Ellison that.'" Luke shook his head, and Monica stared at him. "What?" she asked, as Luke tried pulling the two women apart. "It's true!"

Luke turned beet red. "Maybe so, but you don't need to tell Ellison."

It took her a minute to sort everything out, but when she did, Ellison squeaked, "Your brother?"

Monica giggled. "Why brother dear, did you not tell Ellison about your fabulous twin sister?"

"There was a reason for that," Luke answered. His coloring was returning to normal, and he no longer looked as if he might throttle Monica.

"Your sister?" Ellison sputtered. How did she end up in a bad Hall-mark movie?

"Twin sister," Monica corrected. Ellison studied the siblings. There definitely was a family resemblance. Monica had the same eyes as Luke – only hers had more mischief in them. "Sometimes," Monica said. "I feel like Luke wants to keep me hidden."

"Monica is in town for the night, and I thought I could take her out, but it turns out I was wrong. She has no manners."

"Oh, stop. You know I'm just teasing."

Luke leaned against the bar. "How's your drink, Ellison? Do you need another?"

Ellison hadn't noticed how quickly she'd downed the whisky, but her head was feeling it. "No. Maybe a water. I don't need a repeat of last weekend."

"What happened last weekend?" Josh stood behind Ellison, and she turned slightly so that she could see him. His chest was puffed out, and Jenn was planted firmly at his side.

"Nothing," Ellison said, calmly. "And if it did, it's not your concern." Ellison pressed her lips together. "Monica, this is my ex-husband Josh and his new wife Jennifer. They got married last weekend, so why he cares what I was doing is a mystery to me."

Monica cocked her head. "Didn't you just get divorced?"

It was unnerving how much Monica knew about her, but she wasn't going to let an opportunity pass to make Josh squirm. Even if it made her look bad. "It was finalized last month, but you see, Jenn's pregnant, so they had to hurry the wedding along."

Monica snickered. "Nice."

"Ellison, I won't let you talk that way about my wife," Josh boomed. "Everyone knows you're jealous. Look at you. Single and without a date. It's pathetic."

You're Ellison 2.0. You don't lose control in public.

Luke stepped forward and stuck out his hand. "I'm sorry, I don't think we've meet. I'm Luke Peterson, Ellison's date for the evening."

Ellison's mouth dropped open as did Josh's. What was Luke doing?

"Your date?" Josh sputtered. "But Eve said-"

"I had to come late," Luke said. "My sister's flight was delayed." He gestured at Monica who raised her eyebrows. "But I wouldn't miss this for anything."

"We just love Ellison," Monica offered, linking her arm through Ellison's and pulling her close.

Ellison glanced around the room. Eve, Kate, and Julia stood in a tight knot, whispering and watching the scene unfold. Wonderful.

The vein in Josh's neck bulged. "How do you know Ellison?"

Luke shook his head. "I really don't think that's your business." He held out his hand to Ellison. "Want to dance?"

For being upset, she was surprisingly calm. "I'd love to."

The band was playing an 80's hit which wasn't meant for slow dancing, so Luke and Ellison jumped around on the dancefloor like two teenagers. When the music changed to 90's rap, Luke grabbed her around the waist. "This one is my favorite."

Ellison laughed. She wouldn't in a million years have pegged him for a Dr. Dre fan, but why not? She bopped along to the music, genuinely enjoying herself.

"You know," Luke shouted over the bass. "The first time I saw you, you were dancing. You looked so happy that I couldn't take my eyes off you."

Ellison stopped dancing and looked up at him. "Really?"

"Absolutely."

She grinned and tugged at his hand. "I'm sweating, and in this dress, that isn't a good thing. Plus, my feet are killing."

As they exited the dance floor, Eve and Julia rushed over. "Ellison," Eve squealed. "This is the guy I wanted you to meet. Cute, right?"

Ellison nodded and smiled. "Absolutely, but we already knew each other."

"How did you meet?" Julia asked. "You haven't been up here in ages."

"We meet at a club." She immediately regretted her words. She scrambled to make up a lie. "For...for early childhood literacy."

Amusement flickered across Eve's face. She had connected the dots, and she was going to let everyone else know, too. Before Ellison could yank Luke away, Eve blurted loudly, "Oh, is he the tall, dark and handsome guy you met at Whiskey Blu?"

Surprise flitted across Julia's face, then laughter. "Oh my God. It is! You're one night stand is your date! How hilarious!"

Ellison wanted to disappear into the floor, but Monica laughed and gripped her arm. "Oh, Luke! You didn't tell me that part!" She wiggled a finger at Julia and Eve. "Now, ladies, if you'll excuse us, I have to pry information from my brother and Ellison."

As her former friends walked away, Ellison knew it would only be a few minutes before everyone around her heard the tawdry story of how she met Luke. "I need to leave."

Monica shook her head. "Nonsense. Leaving means they won, and you absolutely can't let them think that."

"But-" Ellison began.

"But nothing," Monica answered. "It doesn't matter how the two of you met. What matters is how you behave right now. And right now, you're holding your head up."

Ellison glanced at Luke, and he shrugged. "I defer to Monica in this situation."

"Okay," Ellison said. Maybe she was crazy, but everyone was staring. And not in a good way. "Do we just have a normal conversation?"

"We do," Monica answered. "Luke, I could use another drink. Ellison?"

A drink was exactly what she needed. "Yes, please."

As Luke flagged the bartender, Monica said, "Don't worry about them, Ellison. I know a bitch when I see one, and those two top my list." She winked. "Jenn is up there, too."

"They used to be my best friends."

The corner of Monica's lip twitched up. "Really? You were like them? I didn't get the impression that you were a mean girl."

"I was, but I'm Ellison 2.0 now. Nicer and kinder." She paused. "It's amazing how divorce will humble you."

"Well, I like Ellison 2.0." Monica threw an arm over Ellison's shoulder. "And we're going to have a blast together!"

"That's enough, Mo," Luke said, handing his sister a drink. "I'm sorry, Ellison. Monica can be a handful."

"She's fine." Ellison smiled at Monica. "But it's not fair that you know all about me, and I know nothing about you."

Monica eyes grew wide. "I'm sorry. I can't tell you anything about me due to the fact that my brother wants to live out his dream of being a fabulous, hard-working, poor teacher."

What did Luke being a teacher have to do with anything?

"Monica," Luke begged. "Don't mess this up for me."

His sister placed her empty glass down on the bar top and frowned. "Someday, Luke, you're going to want people to like you for who you are and what you have. No cover stories, no turning your back on your family."

Ellison shifted uncomfortably. She hated family drama. Monica seemed sweet enough, but knowing Luke talked to his twin sister about her made Ellison feel weird. Like maybe he liked her more than he was letting on.

Nearby, Andi danced with a tall, slim man who looked vaguely familiar. Her hair was a riot of curls, and she wore a skin-tight black dress that flared around her feet. She always impressed Ellison by how she could easily move between sporty and sexy.

"Andi!" Ellison yelled over the music. "Come here!" She and Andi had briefly exchanged hellos in the bathroom, but Ellison had been too busy begging for forgiveness from others and arguing with Josh and Eve that they hadn't really talked.

"Hey, babe," Andi said to Ellison. Her date stood just behind her as if unsure about what to do. Ellison squinted at him. Ah ha! He was the guy from the ill-fated dodgeball game. Andi jerked her thumb over her shoulder. "This is my date, Tim."

"Tom," the date corrected. He was good looking in that All-American guy way. Maybe a little too preppy, but cute. And young. Much younger than Ellison remembered. Maybe twenty-five at most.

"Right, Tom." Ellison knew full well that Andi hadn't forgotten his name. She played this game with her dates when she didn't like them.

Andi took a step back and studied Monica. "I don't think we've met."

"I'm Monica, Luke's twin sister." She stared at the small group. With this she flashed Luke a hurt look. "Clearly, my brother really doesn't love me anymore."

Luke shook his head. "It's not that, and you know it."

"I'm Andi." Ellison's best friend extended her hand. "It's nice to meet you. Luke actually told me about you the other day."

Monica perked up. "Really?" It sounded more suspicious than happy.

"Uh huh. He probably thought I wouldn't remember because I'd been drinking, but I never forget anything," Andi answered.

Concern crept into Luke's features, making him seem like he might rip Monica away at any moment.

"What did he say?" Monica asked.

"He told me you live in San Francisco and that you handle PR for the largest winery in Sonoma."

Luke's mouth dropped open. Clearly, Andi's knowledge was a product of her sleuthing and not of Luke's telling. Which made Ellison a little angry. Why hadn't Andi shared this info with her?

A smile danced across Monica's lips, and her eyes twinkled. "Is that all he said?"

"That's it." Andi took a sip of her drink and smiled slyly at Luke. Like she knew something, and he knew she knew, but wouldn't say it.

Luke set his glass down on a nearby table and hooked his arm around Monica's waist. "That's our cue to leave."

"But you like her, Luke! Don't you want another dance?" Monica giggled, and Ellison wasn't sure if she were teasing him or being sincere.

A faint pink tinted Luke's face. "Thank you, Mo, for humiliating me." He turned toward Ellison. "I'll see you Wednesday. Andi as always, it's been a blast. Tim, Tom," he waited for affirmation, "It was nice meeting you, also."

Luke guided Monica across the room toward the door.

When they were out of earshot, Ellison said, "What was that?"

"What?" Andi answered.

"That whole story about Monica and the winery – how did you know that? Better yet, when? And what else do you know?"

Tim-Tom was busy staring into space. It was just Andi and Ellison.

Andi wiggled her eyebrows, but didn't answer.

After taking a sip of water, Ellison said, "What exactly do you do for the CIA? You're scaring me."

Andi laughed. "I'm in intelligence. That's all you need to know." She shifted her weight, so she leaned closer to Ellison. "Text him. Tell him to meet you after this thing is done."

Ellison shook her head. Something felt off to her. She couldn't name it, but there was more to Monica's story than any of them were letting on.

What, was the question.

23

CORNERED

"**M**s. Brooks! I need help." It was one of the children. Again. So far, all she'd done this morning is run between tables, helping kids spell words correctly and reminding them to use proper punctuation. They were working on Thanksgiving stories, and some of them were really good. It was clear Luke was doing a great job teaching these kids.

She leaned over the table to help Jessica, and her head throbbed. Like she was getting a sinus headache, but worse. The end of this hour couldn't come fast enough.

And not only because of her impending headache.

Since the Junior Committee Gala, Luke and Ellison hadn't seen each other except for in the classroom. And then, Luke kept everything professional. It was growing increasingly awkward. Before the Gala, they had always exchanged friendly banter, but now it was gone, and Ellison found herself longing for it more and more. Luke had cut her off except for at work. No more friendly visits, no more jokes. Just business.

It sucked, and she didn't understand what had happened. Was it how messy her life was? Between Drunkfest and her interaction with Josh, she hadn't exactly made the best impression. But Luke had stepped in and defended her. Did he just do it because he was chivalrous?

Or maybe she hadn't made a good impression on Monica. Maybe that was it?

She surveyed the room. Luke crouched next to a desk and spoke quietly with a student. She loved watching him do his job and the way the kids responded to his gentle, yet stern personality. It was definitely an approach that worked well with Dash, and her son often gushed about Mr. Peterson.

Thank God Dash has one positive male role model in his life.

She sighed. Luke was too good to be true, and she had somehow messed things up between them.

"Ms. Brooks?" Jessica, a little girl with too-large glasses, asked. "Why are you staring at Mr. Peterson?"

Ellison shuffled some papers together and fought the heat rising in her cheeks. "I wasn't. I was just-"

She had no answer, and everyone in the class turned toward her. Including Luke. An amused smile danced on his lips. Oh hell. Now she had to say something.

"I was just thinking about how we should have a reader's corner over there," she improvised, pointing across the room and over Luke's shoulder. "A comfy place where you could read during free time."

Luke walked over to her, passing within inches. His body radiated heat, and his familiar foresty smell hit her nose. He was so close, but he felt a million miles away. How was she going to fix this?

Luke pointed to an area full of filling cabinets. "Right here?"

"Yes," Ellison answered. "I thought some bean bags or something cozy to sit on would be nice." She honestly hadn't given the idea any thought until just now, but the more she said, the more she liked the idea.

Luke stroked his chin. "I like how you think, Ms. Brooks. We could move the bookcases over here, and the kids could decorate." He turned toward the kids. "What do you say class, should we have a reader's corner?"

The room broke into cheers, and Dash beamed at her. Ellison's heart swelled. She'd done something right.

Luke sauntered toward her, his eyes locked on hers. *This man,* she thought. *What is he doing?*

"Class, it's time to go to lunch," Luke said. "Close your work and get your lunch boxes."

The kids scrambled toward the coat hooks and lined up orderly in front of the door. Luke held up his hand, and the kids stopped talking. "Dash, you can be the line leader today."

Ellison's son raced to the head of the line with a huge smile plastered on his face. Ellison knew, from her previous days in the classroom, that being line leader was a huge deal to the kids. Luke held the door open and stepped into the hallway. "This way, young scholars!"

The kids and Luke quietly left, and Ellison gathered up her supplies and papers. Lately, she'd run out as fast as possible to avoid the weirdness between her and Luke, but today, she lingered, hoping Luke would come back. After all, he hadn't grabbed his lunch.

She spent a few minutes filing her learning folders while checking the door. Eventually, she gave up, grabbed her jacket and bag, and left the room. Luke clearly was avoiding her.

Ellison walked toward the office to check out. She wore heeled, knee boots, and they clicked against the floor with each step she took in the empty hallway. The raucous noise from the lunchroom drifted toward her. *God bless the staff that ventured in there.*

"Ellison?" Luke called.

She turned around with her heart fluttering against her ribs. "Yes?"

Luke hurried toward her. It was just the two of them in the hallway, and it felt a little like an illicit rendezvous. Okay, so it was a school hallway and not a hotel hallway, but they were alone for the first time in weeks, and Ellison's mind buzzed, anticipating what Luke would say.

"Hey," he said, stopping in front of her. "How are you?"

Ellison tilted her head. "I'm fine," she said slowly. "How are you?"

"I'm good." Luke shifted his weight. "Look, I know I've been a little distant since the Gala, but it has nothing to do with you."

"Okay," Ellison wasn't sure where this conversation was going, and she wasn't sure she liked the tone of his voice. "We're just friends. You owe me nothing."

"But I do," Luke said, touching her arm before dropping his hand. "You're a great woman Ellison-"

She didn't wait for the 'but' that was going to follow. "I have to run."

"Ellison, wait a minute."

She didn't want to wait. "I have work. My real estate listings have picked up, not to where they were, but I'm doing better." She didn't mention that she hadn't closed on anything. "So, work. I've gotta run."

Luke raked a hand through his hair. "I'm free after school if you want to go shopping with me. For the reader's corner. Since it was your idea, I thought you'd like to give me some input." He paused. "That is, if you're free."

What was this? He was talking to her again *and* wanted to go out after school? "The boys are with Josh today, and I should be able to get through my work before 3:30."

"So, it's a date?" Luke asked.

"Yes," she answered. "It's a date."

There was no point in calling Andi – she had to turn in her phone to the front desk each morning before going to work. Which made it damn near impossible to get ahold of her during the day.

Stupid CIA.

So instead of plotting with her best friend, Ellison sat in her car outside Starbucks and sorted her email into categories: work, fun, and Josh. The fun category was woefully small. Just three messages, and all from Andi. Five messages from Josh – probably about mundane things or perceived slights – those she'd read later. And nine emails from work – some inquiring about the house she had listed, and one from Marsha.

She opened Marsha's first.

. . .

Hi Ellison,

I don't know how to say this, but after much consideration, I'd feel more comfortable using someone else as my agent. Given our past history, I don't believe you'd have my best interests in mind when negotiating a deal.

Sincerely,

Marsha Thornton

"Damn!" Ellison smacked her hand against the steering wheel. This was not fair. So not fair. Marsha was using her old life against her. Couldn't she see how much Ellison had changed?

Not willing to give up, Ellison typed out a response:

Marsha - I understand completely. I wasn't the nicest person to you, but I believe if you give me a chance, you'll see that I've changed. As your realtor, your best interests will always come first. In fact, I have a new listing I'd love to show you on the Waterford-Lodi border. I think it would be perfect for your needs. - Ellison

She waited, sorting through the other work emails. None of them were nearly as bad, but oh my God, how she needed some painkillers. Her head was about to explode. She dug around in her purse until she found a bottle of pills, dumped out two, and chased them with a swig from her Skinny Latté.

Her phone dinged.

Sorry, Ellison. I've already contracted another realtor. Marsha

. . .

There wasn't much more she could do, so she scrolled through the rest of her non-Josh emails and stopped at one inquiring about the house she had newly listed. So far, she'd had no nibbles despite the house being immaculate and well-located. Not even with two open houses. But this email sounded promising, and she quickly called the number listed.

"This is Susan." The woman's voice was brisk.

"Hi, Susan. Ellison Brooks, you sent me an inquiry about a home." Ellison relaxed her tense fingers and stretched out her jaw. She probably looked ridiculous, but she didn't care. She had another lead.

"Right, thanks for calling me back. I'd like to see that house. Maybe in the next hour? I could squeeze you in."

Ellison tried not to gasp. Who operates like that? "I'm free until three," she said sweetly. "Would you like me to meet you there?"

"That would be perfect." Susan's words were fast and clipped.

"Do you need directions?" Ellison asked.

"No. I have everything here. Comps. Numbers. I have it all."

Ellison furrowed her brow. "Are you an agent?"

Susan laughed. "No. I just do my homework. See you at one."

She clicked off, and Ellison stared at her phone in confusion. Whatever that was, this sounded promising, if a little rushed.

And even though Susan said she didn't need to bring anything, Ellison knew better. She couldn't show up to her own listing with no materials – which were all at home.

So much for a leisurely afternoon dreaming about Luke. She had a house to sell.

24

HIDE AND SEEK

Ellison spotted Jenn's SUV in the pick-up line, and her heart sunk. Even with the buzz from her fantastic showing, seeing Jenn with her boys caused Ellison's stomach to churn. She hated that she couldn't go over and hug them first, because if she did, how would she explain her being there? She didn't want the boys to know she was hanging out with Dash's teacher. Plus, she didn't need Jenn drawing conclusions and gossiping about it. It was bad enough that everyone thought she'd hooked up with a new Club member. They didn't need to know about her other connection to Luke.

A knock on the window caused Ellison to jump. Luke stood on the other side, and she rolled it down.

"Sorry," Luke said. "Didn't mean to startle you."

Ellison shrugged. "It's okay. Just thinking about a showing I had today."

"Really? Because you seemed to be staring at your boys," Luke said.

"Well, there was a little of that too."

Luke smiled. "No shame in being a mom."

Ellison sighed. "How about wishing awful morning sickness on their new step-mother?"

A hearty laugh tumbled out of Luke. "Back there again, are we? I have an idea. Let's change the subject. Tell me about your showing."

"It was great! The best one I've had. She was pre-qualified, loved the neighborhood, and seemed okay with the price."

Luke smiled and leaned against the car. "When do you think you'll hear from her?"

Ellison glanced over at the Kiss and Ride lane. The boys were long gone. "I get the impression Susan makes decisions quickly."

"Well, I hope you hear soon." Luke tapped the Suburban's window ledge. "Should we drive together or take separate cars?"

Ellison hadn't thought of that. If they were seen together, it wouldn't look good, but it would look better if they didn't arrive together. Wouldn't it? "Separate cars. It will make for less rumors," Ellison said, "But would you mind if we swing by my house? I can't find my wallet, and think I've left it there."

Luke knitted his brows together. "I'll follow you?"

Ellison scribbled down her address just in case he forgot how to get there. Highly unlikely, but still...appearances. She didn't want to assume anything.

When they arrived at her home, Luke pulled up beside her in the driveway. He rolled down his truck's window. "Would you mind if I came in for a glass of water?"

Mind? Of course she didn't. But what if he thought the house was a mess? She mentally ran through all the offending things – like laundry laying on the dining room table and dishes in the sink. It couldn't possibly be worse than Drunkfest, could it? Embarrassed by the possibility of Luke seeing how slovenly she was, Ellison said, "I'll grab you a bottle of water."

She ran into the house, very cognizant that Luke was watching her, and retrieved the water. She turned to leave when she remembered she needed her wallet. Normally, she left it on the counter, but it wasn't there.

Shit.

Frantic, Ellison flew upstairs to her closet and began tearing it apart. She didn't need this today. Not now. Not with Luke waiting for her outside.

"Ellison?" Luke's voice boomed from downstairs.

"I can't find my wallet," she yelled back.

"That's because it's on your passenger seat." There was a hint of a laugh in Luke's voice.

Ellison stood at the top of the stairs. "Are you serious?"

"Yes," his smile grew wider. "Was this all an elaborate plot to get me here?"

"Full of yourself much?" Ellison countered with a grin.

"Very."

She slinked down the stairs to where Luke stood, stopping on the second step. Like this, she was almost his height.

Shyness crept over Ellison. Luke was here, in her house, alone with no kids. Not awkward at all.

Except that it was extremely awkward. They hadn't spoken outside the classroom in weeks. They stood there facing each other. Luke's gray eyes probing hers. Neither of them moved, and she felt the weight of society's disapproval, Dash's mental health, and Luke's contract bearing down on her.

Suddenly, Luke reached out and took her by both the arms, pulling her into him. "I've wanted to do this for the longest time," he whispered before giving her a hard, fierce kiss. Ellison's brain swam, and she kissed him back with more passion, as if it were a contest to see who could devour the other first. Her arms crept up to his neck, and she wound herself around him. Luke grabbed each of her legs, wrapped them around his waist and carried her upstairs.

When they entered her bedroom, Ellison was keenly aware of the mess she'd left behind this morning. Of her panties lying on the floor next to her nighty. The tea mug on the bedside table. At least the puke bowl was long gone. How embarrassing was it that he saw her like that?

And yet, in some way it wasn't. It was just Luke being a nice guy – something she wasn't used to. It had been years since Josh had done anything that caring for her. Years that all ran together.

Luke didn't seem to notice the panties or teacup as he dropped her on the bed and began nibbling her ear. Ellison moaned and let go of overthinking everything. Her hands pulled his tucked-in shirt out of his pants and slid beneath and across his chest. She played with his chest hair, remembering the last time they were together. The way they intuitively knew each other's bodies.

"I don't know," she whispered. "This might not be the best idea."

"Because of Dash?"

Ellison's heart sunk. "Because of everything. People are already gossiping about us after the Gala. If anyone found out you're Dash's teacher...if Josh found out. He knows what you look like now and your first name."

"Ellison, you're overthinking." Luke said between kisses. "Besides, I'm not going to sleep with you, and no one else is here. How would anyone know what's going on between us?"

"They wouldn't." Ellison said, suddenly feeling challenged. "But why won't you sleep with me?" She pulled him closer, inhaling his scent, and kissed his neck. Luke moaned softly, and she smiled.

"I think what you need is a good old fashioned make-out session," Luke said. "Or at least, that's what I need. There's no need to rush anything."

Relieved that she hadn't read the situation wrong, and Luke wasn't rejecting her, Ellison climbed on top of him. "Are you sure about that?"

"Positive," he said laughing. "I'm made of sturdy resolve."

She leaned over him, letting her ash blond hair fall across Luke's face. He pushed it away, holding it back with one hand. Not pulling it. Just holding it. "I like you Ellison, and I want to do this right."

With a sigh, Ellison rolled off Luke and onto the bed. "What does right look like to you?"

"Dinners, getting to know each other, a trip to Target. Things that take time. Not just hopping into bed." He propped up on one arm. "Don't get me wrong, I like hopping into bed with you, and you look damn sexy right now." Luke's lips grazed her so softly that she wanted to cling to him and beg him to take her clothes off. Beg him to do all the bad things she imagined when she was alone in bed fantasizing about him.

His lips hovered over hers for a moment. Ellison quivered, waiting to be touched. Luke's tongue darted between her parted mouth, past her teeth and tangled with her tongue.

Drowning, Ellison thought. *I'm drowning in this man. And I don't mind at all.*

Luke pressed against her harder, his groin throbbing against Ellison's leg. He moaned and tugged at Ellison's shirt.

She pulled back. "Maybe we should get to Target, so we can get this – this whatever it is we're doing – off on the right foot?"

Luke wrapped his arms around her, cradling her head in the crook of his arm. "Maybe in a little bit."

Without warning, he tugged off her shirt. A chill of cold air ran along Ellison's spine.

"I thought we were just going to make out?" Ellison said with a hint of deviousness. She wanted more, and she wanted Luke to want more also.

He ran his hand over Ellison's stomach and across her ribs just beneath her breasts.

If this was making out, she was way behind the times.

"What are you doing?" she asked.

"Treating you. Just lean back and relax."

Luke kissed the tops of her full breasts. When she began to protest with her words and hands, Luke said, "I like pleasing you, Ellison. I like making you happy."

That, she could live with.

His tongue ran along her collarbone. Deliriously soft licks that made her moan. Ellison gently grabbed at both sides of Luke's head, drawing him closer, and pressed her lips to his.

"Let go, Ellison," Luke mumbled. "Let yourself go."

A long, low moan escaped her lips, and she shuddered.

Luke pulled away and kissed her cheek. "That's my girl," he said, stroking her hair.

Ellison liked the sound of that and smiled. In that moment, there was nothing but her and Luke, and she wasn't going to fight her feelings anymore.

Target was a mad house, but for once, Ellison didn't mind. Not when she had Luke by her side. She wanted to hold his hand, but worried about running into people even though they had gone to the Lodi Target and not the one closer to Waterford. She was very aware that they may run into parents or students, so she shoved her hands into her jacket pockets.

You're not dating, she kept repeating in her mind. *Don't think you are. The two of you were blowing off steam, nothing more.*

But they were. Or were starting too. Or were coming close to maybe dating. She wasn't entirely sure how it worked in today's world.

"So what were you thinking? Beanbag chairs? Anything else?" Luke asked as she steered her way through the throng of people clogging the central aisle.

"Maybe some of those big cushions?" Ellison said, pointing at a stack of circular floor cushions stacked in the central aisle. "They're on sale."

Luke slid next to her and placed his hand on the small of her back. Her whole body tingled, wanting more. He had been true to his word and hadn't tried to sleep with her – no matter how much she begged for it.

"$49.99 each?" Luke said. "That's a little expensive. Don't forget, I'm financing this endeavor with my meager classroom budget."

Ellison rubbed her fingers together inside her jacket pockets, and the sensation soothed her. "I'll help out," she offered. "If my kid benefits from it, why not?"

Luke raised his eyebrows. "Dash isn't much of a reader though, is he?"

"Not really," Ellison answered. "He was a delayed writer and speller, too."

They managed to survive the crowded middle aisle and arrived at the home decor section. "He's a good kid, Ellison. A normal ten-year-old boy. You're doing a great job."

She sighed and tossed two beanbags into the cart – one red and one green. Nice gender-neutral colors and only $19.99.

"What was that sigh for?" Luke asked.

Since the divorce, it was hard to know if she was still a good parent. The boys were gone so much that she felt like she was treading water, just trying to keep on top of things.

"It's hard to tell sometimes. Dash doesn't talk to me like he used to, and Alex has regressed to bedwetting."

She leaned forward to grab another green bean bag chair, and felt two strong hands on her back.

"Hey," Luke said. "I should have said something earlier, but I wouldn't worry about the meeting tomorrow."

Ellison snapped her head up. "What meeting?"

"You don't know?" Luke said, his mouth agape.

"No." She dropped the beanbag into the second shopping cart, and her stomach churned. Whatever it was, it wasn't going to be good.

"Dash's disciplinary meeting," Luke said. "For throwing paper airplanes in the lunch room?"

"What? No?" Son-of-a-bitch. Not only did she not know, but why was Josh hiding it from her? Her brain flitted back to earlier, and the dozen emails from Josh she had ignored. Shit.

Luke took her face between his palms. "It's okay. It's a formality." His gray eyes probed hers.

"I'm not sure what you're-"

"Ellison? Is that you?"

Eve stood a few feet away with a scandalous smile stretched across her face. "Who's this?" She elongated her words in her annoying Eve way. "Oh," she purred when Luke turned around. "I think we were introduced at the Gala, but I've forgotten your name."

This was exactly what Ellison had wanted to avoid. She swallowed down the expletives sitting on her tongue and forced a smile.

"Luke Peterson, Eve Strella."

"Oh, you are yummy," Eve said as she shook Luke's hand. Ellison was surprised she hadn't gone in for the hug, since that was Eve's M.O. "Ellison, is it serious?"

Ellison ignored her. "What brings you to Lodi? I thought we were too down market for you."

Eve smirked. "Our Target is out of La Croix. Can you believe that?" She dramatically shook her head and huffed. "So, I'm here, and I caught the two of you!" She pointed at them and scrunched up her nose.

"You didn't see anything, Eve," Ellison said.

"If you say so." Eve eyed the cart full of beanbags and cushions. She batted – seriously, batted – her lashes at Luke before saying to Ellison, "Interesting. Are you remodeling?"

It was a jab, Ellison knew it was a jab, but she smiled. "School project."

"Oh! How cute of your boyfriend to help with the school chores," Eve said in her upbeat bitchy voice.

"Actually," Luke said. "Ellison is helping me. I owe her."

Eve darted her gaze between Luke and Ellison and pursed her lips like she was trying to figure something out. Ellison's heart pounded. She absolutely did not want Eve to know Luke was Dash's teacher.

"Well, it was awfully nice to have met you, Luke Peterson. Don't let Ellison keep you hidden." Eve tossed her long, platinum hair over her shoulder and sashayed away.

"What was that?" Luke said, jabbing his chin toward Eve's retreating figure.

"She's searching for gossip. Probably something to report back to my ex's new wife."

"Awesome." Luke piled another beanbag onto of the cart to bring their total to five.

"Right? I mean, she all but drooled over seeing us together. She probably can't wait to run home and tell." Ellison rubbed her eyebrows.

"What's wrong?" Luke asked.

"She's going to tell Jenn. Then Josh will know."

"Your ex-husband?" Luke asked.

"Yes," Ellison stepped back. Eve had caught her off guard, and she had forgotten about Dash's disciplinary meeting. "Do both parents have to be at this hearing?"

"It would be best," Luke said.

"And you'll be there?" Panic welled inside her.

Luke nodded and glanced to the side. Was he plotting his escape, or was he worried? After all, they weren't in a committed relationship. He owed her nothing, and his job seemed to be his life.

"Josh won't make any trouble for us," Luke said. "Don't worry about it. He probably doesn't even remember me. We'll keep everything professional."

Oh, Luke, Ellison thought. *If only it were that easy.*

25

IT FINALLY HAPPENS

There was a crispness in the air that only comes with the shortening of days. Hazy, golden sunlight filtered through the trees, and Ellison sighed with anxiety. She sat on a bench outside of the school waiting for Josh to show up, so they could attend Dash's disciplinary meeting. Everything in her life felt off. She had to hear about the meeting from Luke, the night before it was to take place and worry about the rumors Eve was probably spreading around town. But mostly, she was concerned about Dash. His therapist said acting out should be expected, but to have a disciplinary meeting went beyond that. Her boy must be hurting.

"Ellison?"

Josh had caught her lost in her thoughts.

"Oh, hey." She moved over on the bench, making room for her ex-husband. No need to be nasty when they were both wanted what was best for Dash.

"I had hoped you'd be here early," Josh said. "I need to talk to you."

Ellison's heart dropped, and the hairs at the base of her neck pricked up. Josh was acting too calm to know about Luke, so what was his deal? "Is this about Dash, or can it wait? I want to focus on him right now."

"We really need to talk." Josh's face took on a look of desperation. Ellison recognized it at once. He was going to tell her something she didn't want to hear.

Not again. The wedding was just a few short months ago. What more was there to say? Did he need a lift to the airport for his honeymoon?

She held up her hands, but not before Josh opened his mouth and said the words she had longed to hear for the past year. "I miss you."

A general numbness filled Ellison's body. She had envisioned this scene so many times. She had thought of how it would play out, and all scenarios ended with her forgiving Josh. Despite the fact that she no longer wanted to be with him and her acceptance that her old life was over, she wanted to win. She wanted him to understand how he hurt her and maybe suffer a little too.

"You...you...miss me?" she sputtered. Memories of Josh yelling at her and telling her he'd get custody of the boys one way or another filled her mind along with his angry texts and emails. Josh had made every part of their divorce miserable, and now this?

How in the world could he miss her when he hated her?

Josh nodded. "Things with Jenn are...well, complicated. Not at all like with you. You have your shit together."

Ellison tried not to laugh. No one thought she had her shit together, especially not her. "You didn't want me, remember?" She spat out the words, but her heart ping-ponged between anger and delight. "You wanted a newer, younger model. Better eye candy or whatever. Jenn, according to you, is your soulmate."

Josh hung his head and looked up at her like a pathetic puppy dog. "I was a fool. Will you forgive me?"

In disbelief. Ellison glanced at her phone. "We have to go in. But really, Josh, *your wife* is pregnant, and you're telling me you miss me. That's messed up."

It felt good to leave him slack jawed for once. Did he think he could say a few sweet words, and all was forgiven?

How wrong he was.

She rang the school door and held up her ID, very aware that Josh was watching her every move. The door buzzed open, and Josh followed her through. Her heels clacked down the long hallway echoing off the hard, sterile surfaces of the school. She felt trapped between two hard places – Josh's confession and Luke's looming presence. Once Josh saw Luke, she had no doubt he'd recognize him as her Gala "date." Things would surely disintegrate from there.

The office was at the end of the hallway, and through the glass window, she could make out Luke's broad shoulders. He had his back to her, which was good. It gave her a few more seconds to formulate a plan.

"If we could just talk Elle-bear," Josh said, using his nickname for her.

Ellison froze just outside the office door. "What is it you want? A divorce from your wife of less than six months? An affair with me? What?"

Josh's face pinked up. "I just wanted us to spend time together as a family. The way we used to."

"This so isn't the time or place for this conversation." Ellison said in the snippy voice she found herself using more and more around Josh.

"My timing sucks."

Ellison spun around. "No. You suck." And with that she entered the office.

Luke was in the middle of a conversation with the secretary, but he turned toward Ellison as soon as she entered the room. His words trailed off.

"Ms. Brooks," he said, extending his hand. "Thanks for coming in."

Ellison grasped Luke's hand, and memories of yesterday stirred in her. Good Lord. How was she ever going to get through this meeting when she kept imagining his demanding kisses?

When their hands parted, he said, "Mr. Brooks," and gave Josh a quick nod of the head because Josh refused to take his hand.

Josh drew his brows together. "Have we met?"

Josh had never been good at placing people and could never

remember names or faces. So why was did he have any memory of Luke?

Luke slid his gaze over toward Ellison, who subtly shook her head. "I don't think so. You haven't been into my classroom yet this year, have you?"

"No," Josh said. "But I swear we've met."

Ellison's heart pounded. Right now was the absolute worst time for Josh's memory to improve.

"Hmmm," Luke said. "We're short on time. If you'll follow me." He led them down a carpeted hallway to an office. Dash and the principal, Ms. Sylvian, were already inside. The three of them arranged themselves around the small circular table with Luke on her one side and Josh on the other.

"As you know," Ms. Sylvian began. There were no niceties, no hellos. Just business. "Dashiel has been reminded repeatedly not to throw projectiles while in school."

Projectiles? Really, wasn't this was about making paper airplanes?

"What has he thrown?" Josh asked. Clearly, Jenn was the one handling the school's correspondence.

If you paid attention to more than your dick, you would know, Ellison thought.

"Paper airplanes," Ms. Sylvian answered.

Josh laughed, but tried to cover it with a cough. The effect came out sounding like a man choking. "I'm sorry, you called us in here because my son has been throwing paper airplanes?"

"They are more dangerous than you think, Mr. Brooks. The pointed tip could injure a student."

Now it was Ellison's turn to be incredulous. "Really? Is there something in the student handbook about this?"

Ms. Sylvian pressed her lips together before saying, "No, but to be clear, this type of behavior – of creating weapons – is not tolerated."

"Weapons?" Oh. My. God. They've lost their minds. She looked at her son who had his head hung toward his chest, and tears fell from his eyes. Clearly, he was repentant, so why this meeting?

Ellison pivoted so that she was facing Luke. "Is this what you think, Lu -- Mr. Peterson? That my son is creating weapons out of paper? Should we rubberize all the paper so that it can't cut the poor, precious students?"

Luke kept his strong, large hands on the table. "He was written up by the cafeteria staff. I had nothing to do with it."

Unbelievable. "Then why are you here?"

"Ms. Brooks," Ms. Sylvian said harshly. "Please don't question my staff. Mr. Peterson is here as Dashiel's teacher, and he's given Dashiel a warning in the past."

"You gave him a warning?" Ellison shouted. Her blood boiled. Luke said Dash was doing great, but clearly he wasn't. She was pissed he'd kept this information from her. "Why didn't you tell me? Or us? Why did you not say anything?"

"Elle, calm down. There's no need to go ballistic." Josh reached out and patted her hand, a gesture that caught Luke's attention, and he frowned.

Josh focused back on Ms. Sylvian. "Ellison can get worked up easily, but it is a surprise to hear that our son has been disciplined previously, and we haven't heard about it."

"It isn't a surprise. It's ridiculous." Ellison glared at Luke. Was he keeping this information from her so that she'd think Dash was doing great, and she'd date him? Was Luke really that duplicitous?

"Ms. Brooks," Luke said. "My warnings to Dash were easily handled in the classroom and was nothing out to the realm of normal fifth-grade-boy behavior. He lost weekly points. That's all."

Ellison gritted her teeth. "You still could have informed me."

"Us, Elle," Josh said. "I want to know too."

Luke softened his posture. "I understand that now, and going forward, I will email both of you anytime Dash needs redirection."

Still angry, Ellison nodded. "I think that would be best."

Josh shifted in his seat. "Now that we have that sorted, what are you recommending as punishment?" he asked Ms. Sylvian.

"Are you serious, Josh? Dash played with a paper airplane." Ellison's voice raised a notch again. "Punishment for what? Being a boy? This should be taken care of at home."

"Dash was told not to do it anymore," Josh said, while silent sobs wracked Dash's small body.

So that's how it was. Josh was going to side with the school and make her look all momma-bear. Great.

"Dashiel, please step outside," Ms. Sylvian said.

Ellison's visibly-upset son stood and scurried for the door, but not before saying, "Don't fight. I hate when you fight."

Ellison's heart sunk. How many times would he be witness to arguing between her and Josh? Why couldn't they get themselves under control? And now he saw her arguing with his principal and his teacher. The whole situation sucked.

"We're not fighting, sweetheart," Ellison said. "It's going to be okay."

Dash nodded and closed the door behind him. Ms. Sylvian waited for a second before saying, "I'm recommending a three-day suspension with no chance to make up missed tests."

Now Josh roared to life. "You've got to be kidding. Are you serious?"

"I am," Ms. Sylvian said. "He violated school rules and refused to obey his previous warnings."

The vein in Josh's neck popped out. "I'm going to take this to the school board."

"Very well. Do as you wish." Ms. Sylvian stood. "Dashiel's suspension begins now. Please have him gather his belongings. If you'll excuse me." She exited and Luke exited the room, leaving Ellison alone with Josh.

Josh stood, and panic lined the creases around his eyes. "You'll take him, right, Elle? I have to work this week and can't stay home to babysit."

As much as she wanted to wrap Dash up in her arms, she was more frustrated with Josh. "It's your week with the boys. Have Jenn watch him." Josh paled at his wife's name.

"You're being a shitty mother. He needs you." Josh loomed over her, and despite her best effort, Ellison cowered.

Pangs of guilt hit Ellison, but Josh was being unfair. Dash needed both of them. But in this moment, he needed her more. "Fine, I'll take him until you get home from work, but like you, I have a job that requires attention so that I can pay my mortgage and feed our children."

Josh huffed. "You're a real estate agent. You make your own hours."

Ellison fought to remain calm. "Like I said, Dash can spend the afternoon with me, but then he's going to your house. He needs both of us."

Josh yanked the office door open. "You should take him all week."

Ellison gritted her teeth. The thought of Jenn spending so much time with her son made her skin crawl. "Fine. I'll watch him until Alex gets out of school. I'll meet Jenn at the school for the drop-off."

Josh stormed out of the room. "Dash," his voice boomed. "Get your things. You're going with Mom."

Her son stood against the wall, and his eyes were red. "Buddy, go get your stuff. We'll grab lunch, okay?"

Dash nodded and hurried down the hallway toward his classroom. When he was gone, Josh said. "Work on the teacher, okay? See if he'll give Dash a pass on his tests and stuff."

The last person Ellison wanted to see in that moment was Luke, but Ellison nodded. She had to do it for her son. "I'll take care of it."

Josh nodded. "Good." He smiled at her in a way she once found charming. "And Elle, think about what I said earlier. If anything, Dash needs us to act like a family more than ever."

Ellison gritted her teeth, but smiled and nodded. She didn't want to confuse her boys any more than they already were.

26

COME AT ME BRO

Ellison had just come from dropping Dash off with Jenn when she caught Kate slinking down the aisle of the grocery store, hurrying away from her.

"Kate!" Ellison shouted, freezing her former friend in place. Kate turned around slowly, her eyes large and round, like she'd been caught doing something wrong.

Ellison composed herself. No doubt Kate felt guilty over attending the wedding and gossiping about her at the Gala. Or maybe Eve had told her about the Target debacle.

It didn't really matter. Ellison had every right to speak to her old friend.

"How are you?" Ellison asked as she pushed her cart closer to Kate's. The two women hadn't properly spoken since the day Ellison had called about purchasing Gala tickets, and even then, it wasn't an in-depth conversation. To say they had drifted apart was an understatement. They were nearly strangers now, but that didn't stop Ellison.

"Great!" Kate said, sounding as fake as a plastic tree.

"No baby today?" Ellison asked, motioning toward the shopping cart seat that Kate's massive Louis Vuitton occupied.

"I have a sitter on Thursdays." Kate voice was brisk and full of not-wanting-to-be-there.

"That's right, I forgot," Ellison said. They were talking around the subject, trying to making small talk. Or at least Ellison was. To think Kate had once been one of her closest friends. She would have been the first on the phone telling her about Jenn's tacky wedding dress or the horrible food. She would have at least called after the wedding to make sure Ellison was okay. But she had done none of that. She hadn't even talked to her at the Gala.

"We've missed you at Thirsty Thursdays," Kate said, mentioning the weekly ladies' night at the country club. "You should come back. In fact, just the other day Eve was saying that we should reach out to you. We're worried that you're alone too much, even if you do have a hot, new man."

Ellison gripped her cart tighter. Was Kate referring to the Gala or the Target outing? "Is that what Eve said?"

"Uh huh."

No doubt there had been discussions about poor, poor Ellison. All alone. No husband. Can't invite her out to dinner anymore because she's single. A threat to their own marriages. Divorce, after all, was something you could catch.

"She also said she saw you at Target the other day with the guy from the Gala, and the two of you looked cozy." Kate's eyebrows went up.

Wonderful.

"He's a friend. I was helping him with a project. No coziness there," Ellison lied, and she could feel a blush creeping into her cheeks.

Kate tilted her head like she was trying to think of what to say. She never was the brightest of Ellison's friends.

"Well it was nice to see you. I was just picking up a few things." Ellison nodded toward her nearly empty cart. Well, empty except for the twenty Lean Cuisine boxes and a bag of grapes. She realized how pathetic it must look.

"On a diet?" Kate asked.

Ellison ran a hand down her side. She didn't feel fat. In fact, she'd lost twenty pounds since this whole thing with Josh started. "No. I just really love Lean Cuisine." Another lie, but one she had to tell because the truth was too depressing: she was re-stocking for her next week alone. During the day, she'd had Dash around, but in the evenings, Ellison was all alone. And she hadn't spoken to Luke since the hearing.

"Don't be a stranger, okay." Kate patted Ellison's arm. "We all miss you."

"Maybe I'll come to Thirsty Thursday tonight," Ellison offered. She didn't have anything else going on, so why not?

Kate blinked. "Oh! Well...sure! We'd love to have you."

"I didn't realize it was an invite only thing," Ellison said.

"It's totally not, you know that." Kate fidgeted with her grocery list. "It's just, well, Jenn comes."

Ellison spit out her next words. "She's pregnant. She can't drink."

"I know, but it's a social hour and..."

"You don't really want me to come." Ellison said the words as the realization hit her hard.

Kate shrugged. "It probably for the best if you don't."

Ellison struggled not to snap at Kate. "I understand. Maybe I'll see you around."

"I'd love that!" Kate exclaimed.

But Ellison knew the truth. They had picked Jenn over her despite Eve's insistence that their distance was Ellison's fault.

Ellison was 100% not welcome anymore, and it sucked.

Once she arrived home and put away the groceries, Ellison flopped down on the couch and let the tears come. When she lost Josh, she lost so much more. Half of her boys lives, her friends, her home. It was like he didn't care about the damage he did; he only cared about himself and his "soulmate." However, if their conversation the other day was true, Josh doubted his choices.

Well too bad for that.

That morning – the morning her world changed – came rushing back again. The same fiery pricks ran up her back and neck. The same sense of nausea. All those emails from Jenn telling Josh how much she loved him. And his responses back, echoing the same sentiments. When Ellison had composed herself enough, she crept back down the hallway to their bedroom. She had flicked on the light, startling Josh awake. He had paled when he saw her with his phone.

Everything felt like it was in slow motion, Josh's jumping out of bed, her throwing and shattering the phone against the wall. His falling to his knees pleading with her, telling her it was just three times. That Jenn meant nothing.

It hadn't mattered. He had betrayed her.

After Josh went to work, Ellison went about rebuilding her life – starting with finding a new house. At the time, it seemed like the best thing to do. Let Josh sit alone in their home and think about what he was losing. But that day, after he found out she was moving out, he chose Jenn. Or did he? Ellison often wondered if she had pushed him into Jenn's very willing and open arms. Never mind they were both married. Never mind that Josh had kids. Jenn was willing to give up everything to be with the man Ellison would have sworn was the most loyal and dedicated of all the husbands she knew. Her Josh would never cheat.

Except he did.

And look where it left her. Living in Lodi, trying for a career comeback, and dating but not really dating. Oh, and that didn't even include the problems with Dash.

Why did life have to be so hard? Why couldn't someone wave a magic wand and make the last year-and-a-half disappear.

Would she ever be happy again? Luke seemed promising, but the whole thing with Dash getting in trouble left her questioning their whatever-it-was relationship.

Just when she thought her life was finally getting back on track, it became messy again.

Out of tears, Ellison wiped her face with the throw blanket. She felt cleansed, ready to move on. She had to focus on what she could control. Isn't that what her therapist had told her back in the early days of her marriage imploding?

First, she had control over her career. She needed to follow-up with Susan and the couple having a baby. She could do that.

Next, she had to stay on top of Dash and Alex. Acting out wasn't acceptable behavior.

Last, she needed to clear up her dating life by talking to Luke and figuring things out with him.

She stared at Luke's number on her phone. She was still upset about his lack of communication regarding Dash, but maybe she was being too hard on him. After all, she'd been in the classroom, and if he had to send notes home every time a child misbehaved, he'd never get any teaching done.

She was being too hard on him.

Her phone rang, and she answered it without looking, thinking it was Andi.

How wrong she was.

"Are you dating our son's teacher?" Josh bellowed.

"What?" Ellison said, flustered. "No. Where did you get that idea?"

"I remembered how I knew him. He was your date at the Gala, and I have it on good authority you were kissing in Target."

Damn it. She had hoped Josh had completely forgotten, but she should have known better.

"No, we weren't kissing. Not in Target." Which was true, they hadn't actually kissed. She paused. "Who do you think I am, some little teenager?"

"I swear Ellison if I find out you've been fooling around with Dash's teacher, I'll have his head. I'll go straight to the school board, and I'll have the judge reopen the custody case."

All the conclusions Ellison had come to over the past year came crashing down on her: Josh would never leave her alone; and he wasn't a very nice person. Strike that. He was an ass. Plain and simple.

"You have no right to dictate who I can and can't date, Josh."

"Maybe not, but I have the right to decide who teaches my child."

Venom dripped from his words. "I also have the right to have my children brought up in a suitable home."

"You call your home-wrecking lifestyle more suitable than me possibly dating someone?" Ellison shouted. "You're fucking twisted."

"I'm not putting my son at risk for your sexual whims," Josh hissed.

With more bravado than she had, Ellison said, "Get over yourself, Josh."

She hung up on him and stood there with trembling hands. She couldn't tell if Josh was bluffing or not, but she needed to give Luke a heads-up.

Ellison carefully tapped her iPhone. Her body was going crazy – shaking hands, sinking heart, and dread racing through her.

"Hello?"

"Luke, it's Ellison. We need to talk ASAP. Can you come over?"

"Ellison," he said huskily. "Is this a plot to see me?"

"It's my attempt to keep you out of trouble."

Ellison swung the front door open before Luke could knock. She'd been waiting by the window. "Hey," she said. "Thanks for coming."

"Hey, yourself," Luke answered.

Ellison reached out and pulled him through the door, slamming it shut behind him.

"What's going on 007? What's with all the secrecy?" He looked around the foyer. "Are the boys here?" he whispered. "Should I not be here?"

"They're with Josh until tomorrow night. I dropped Dash off a little while ago."

Luke playfully grabbed her and pushed her up against the door. Ellison's breath hitched, and her bones seemed to disintegrate.

"No," she said pushing away from him. "I'm still upset with you."

Luke's face fell. "I understand."

Ellison crossed her arms. "I don't like finding out about Dash's behavior the way I did. It's one thing if it's a simple correction, but Ms. Sylvian made it seem like he'd been warned numerous times."

"I thought I handled it," Luke said. "But fair enough. It won't happen again."

He caught her arm and pulled at it like he was trying to coax her closer.

Her sanity was slipping away. That was the only explanation for her current behavior. Old Ellison would have shoved him away and held a grudge. Ellison 2.0 turned her face toward Luke's and paused.

His kiss was soft and gentle, but his hands grasped at her, pulling her shirt away from her skin. "Ellison," he whispered. "What have you done to me?"

She tilted her head back so he could kiss her throat, and she groaned. "I need-"

"Me," Luke answered.

And she did. She knew she did. Not just carnally, either. She needed him as a friend. As a confidant. As a lover.

"Please don't keep things concerning my child from me," Ellison said.

"I swear," Luke said. "You'll know everything about Dash that I do. My goal was never to deceive you."

With trembling hands, she unbuttoned Luke's jeans and slid her hand just along the top of his boxer briefs. He gasped.

"No fair," he said, pulling her shirt over her head, exposing her yellow polka-dot bra. "I like this." He softly stroked the outside of her bra. "Your breasts look amazing." And then, with a quick flick of his hand, he undid her bra. She shrugged it off. "And now you look even better." His fingers trailed along the ridge of her breasts and around one nipple.

Good Lord.

He bent to kiss each of her breasts, then, without warning, scooped her up and carried her to the living room. He laid her down on the couch and began undressing the rest of her. When she was naked, Luke stripped off his own clothes and settled in next to her.

Ellison tangled her arms around him, allowing the sweet, warm feeling to consume her.

Making love was so much better than mechanical sex, and that's what they did: made love. Luke's fingers meshed with hers and he took his time entering her. When he did, Ellison clasped her arms around him.

"You're so beautiful, Ellison."

She opened her eyes and found Luke staring down at her. Ellison's breath deepened, and she found herself disappearing into Luke's endless gaze.

He caught one of her legs and wrapped it around the back of his thigh. "Ellison, Ellison, Ellison," he groaned.

Ellison arched her back, closing the small gap between her body and Luke's. She wanted to touch every part of him. She wanted to feel devoured.

He leaned forward and kissed her neck. Trembles rumbled through Ellison's body.

It was the closest thing to love that she'd felt in years.

Luke kissed the top of her head, and Ellison nuzzled deeper into his arms. Laying here she felt safe, as if the rest of the world didn't matter. No worries about the boys, no back-stabbing-ex-friends, no jealous ex-husbands. No one in the world existed in this moment other than Ellison and Luke.

It was amazing.

"Is this why you called me over?" Luke asked, tracing a fingertip along Ellison's collarbone.

"No. It's Josh." All the post-coital bliss evaporated. "He's making threats and saying that if he finds out we're...doing whatever it is we're doing, he's going to make trouble for you."

"Empty threats from a jealous man."

"You don't know Josh the way I do," Ellison said. "He...before the meeting, he told me he wanted us to be a family again."

"What?" Luke untangled himself from Ellison and propped up on his arm. "Isn't he married to someone else?"

Ellison wrapped a throw blanket over her bare shoulders. "Exactly."

"So he wants what he can't have. Nice." Luke rested back on the cushion with his hands tucked behind his head and stared at the ceiling.

"He doesn't want me to be happy," Ellison said. She stood and pulled the teal blanket completely around her naked body. "And he remembered you from the Gala. He knows you were my date."

"Oh."

Ellison knelt next to the couch. "What are we going to do?"

Luke's eyes met hers. "Exactly what we have been."

"He could ruin your career," Ellison said.

Luke hardened his jaw. "Let him try."

27

CLOSE THE DEAL

Susan sat across the table from Ellison. She oozed confidence, and Ellison found herself wishing she could be more like her. More, I-don't-have-a-care than I'm-an-injured-bunny. Ellison really needed to let go of the bunny. She was starting to, but still had a ways to go.

"I think your offer is fair as are the contingencies," Ellison shuffled through the papers before her. "I'll present this offer today, and we should hear something tomorrow. But first I need you to sign here and here."

"Thanks for putting this together so quickly. When you called to tell me there had been another offer, I knew I couldn't lose it." Susan scrawled her name where Ellison had indicated. "We'll get this done. I'm sure of it."

Ellison wasn't so sure. In the past, she liked competing offers because it often drove up the amount of commission she made, but this deal made her nervous. It was, after all, her first deal since deciding to throw herself back into the real estate world. She needed it to close.

"So why Waterford?" Ellison asked. She was enjoying chatting with Susan, and a good agent always got to know their clients. "What drew you here?"

"Everything. The lifestyle. The schools. The value." Susan was a direct woman, and Ellison appreciated it.

"I never asked about your kids," Ellison said. "Boys or girls?"

Susan dropped her copy of the papers into her bag. "Two boys. They keep me busy."

"I had no idea!" Ellison said. "I have two boys also. We used to be at Greenbriar, but we live in Lodi now" Ellison quickly checked Susan's ring finger and found it bare. "My husband and I finalized our divorce a few months ago, so I moved out of district."

"The first months are the hardest," Susan said. "But it gets better. I'm on year three, and I no longer want to throat punch my ex." She laughed. "Besides, I'm – no we're – better off without him."

Ellison smiled. Susan reminded her a little of Andi. "How old are your boys?"

"Nine and eleven. Yours?"

"Eight and almost eleven. My oldest, Dash, is in fifth grade."

Susan perked up. "So is mine."

"Then I should tell you all the families, well actually mothers, you want to steer clear of, and which kids to encourage your son to hang out with." Ellison was overstepping, but it felt okay with Susan. Like she would appreciate the inside info.

"That would be great," Susan said. "I'm finding the schools here to be more political than the one we went to in Arizona."

Ellison tapped her pen. "They're their own beast." She laughed. "Before my divorce, I was the PTA president for two years and chaired the country club's junior committee for three years." She paused before confessing, "I wasn't a very nice person."

"Divorce changes us, doesn't it?" Susan asked.

"It does."

After Susan left, Ellison felt slightly euphoric. Finally, she met another woman who got it. Who understood the pain and consequences of a divorce. And if Ellison was right, needed a friend as much as she did.

With a bounce in her step, she scanned the documents and headed back to her cubicle. It was so sterile in the office that Ellison tried to avoid it as much as possible.

"Ellison? A word?" Laurie hung her head out of her office doorway.

"Sure, what is it?"

"Have a seat." Laurie positioned herself behind her desk.

Ellison's heart flipped. Had she done something wrong? "Is everything okay?"

Laurie nodded. "Are those the Jacob papers?"

With a tap on the desk, Ellison answered. "They are. Why?"

"Is she pre-approved?"

Ellison scrunched her brows together. "Yes. Why?"

Laurie squirmed in her seat. "It just, she's a single woman making a very large home purchase. It's unusual."

A tightness spread across Ellison's chest. Was Laurie implying single women couldn't afford to buy a grand home. Granted she couldn't, but that didn't mean no other woman could. The more she thought about it, the more upset Ellison became. But she kept it in check. Laurie was her boss after all.

"I think she did well in her divorce, plus she's an attorney with a large DC firm. She's self-sufficient."

This seemed to appease Laurie. "I don't mean any of this in the wrong way. I just want to protect you from chasing dead leads."

"I understand," Ellison said. But what she really meant was she understood all too well the assumptions others made about divorced woman. She held out the papers to Laurie. "She's offering $800,000. That's ten over asking."

"How bad does she want it?"

"Badly."

Laurie smiled slyly. "Then let's hope this goes to a bidding war."

In the past, Ellison would have said the same, but now it made her stomach roll. She wanted Susan to get the house for a fair price just as much as she wanted her twenty-four-thousand-dollar commission.

"Let's hope," she answered flatly.

Rule number three-hundred and twenty-one: Don't screw over the people you want to be friends with. Not that a price war was screwing Susan over, but if Ellison could get it for her offer price, she was going to do so.

"I need to send these over to the sellers'. Hopefully, they'll like this offer better than yours."

Laurie laughed. "I'll keep that in mind when I tell my clients about your offer."

This was going to be a messy transaction. Ellison represented the sellers *and* Susan while Laurie represented the other potential buyer. The upside was more money for the agency, and potentially more money for Ellison.

"Nothing like a little friendly competition to make things interesting," Ellison said.

"Exactly."

The answer from the sellers' came quickly – within fifteen minutes. Normally, she would hear back within a day – like she had told Susan she would. So when her inbox dinged, Ellison was caught off guard.

Hi Ellison,

First, thank you for all your work! We're pleased with the offer you brought us. However, we want to counter-offer. How do we do this?"

Regards,

Nick and Meghan

Argh. She knew they only wanted to counter because they wanted to see if Laurie's client would too. Everyone, except Ellison and Susan, wanted a higher price. And who could blame them? It meant more money in their pockets.

With a sinking heart, she picked up her phone and dialed Meghan's number.

"Hello?"

"Hi, Meghan. It's Ellison Brooks. Do you have a moment?"

"Of course." There was some commotion in the background, and a child cried.

"I can call back."

"No. It's fine. My daughter just doesn't want to take a nap, so I'm giving up."

Ellison laughed in sympathy. "Ahhh. I remember those days."

"You were saying," Meghan said. She clearly didn't have time for a friendly chat.

"Right," Ellison said. "What we need to do is draw up a formal counter offer. Do you have an idea of what you want to ask?"

There was a long silence. "Well, the other offer was for eight-twenty, but we don't like the contingencies as much."

"If my buyer can come in at eight-twenty with the current contingencies, would we have a deal?"

Meghan sighed. "I don't want to commit to anything verbally."

"I understand that. Let me draw up your letter. I'll send it to you for approval before it's sent to the potential buyer. Does that sound okay?"

"Perfect," Meghan answered.

"All right. Let me get to work."

"Bye." Meghan clicked off.

Ellison began clacking away on her keyboard. Eight-twenty. Shit. How was Susan going to take it? Would she be able to pony up the extra cash? Was this deal going to fall apart?

So much for an easy comeback.

Josh held the scarlet red door open, inviting Ellison inside. Since it was pouring, she didn't decline. Plus, after the day she'd had, she didn't feel like fighting.

Ellison hadn't been inside her old home since the day she moved out and going in brought back a flood of memories. Of Josh holding Dash in his arms after arriving home from the hospital. Of laughter around the dining room table when they'd have family game nights. Of that horrible day when she discovered her perfect life wasn't so perfect after all.

Everything had changed – literally. A gigantic portrait of Jenn hung in the stairwell. Or boudoir photo, to be more correct. She wore a breezy looking white nighty and stared out at the viewer with sultry eyes.

Somehow, knowing her boys had to see that every time they were at their dad's house made bile rise in her throat. It was so inappropriate.

But it wasn't just the picture that was new. Every surface had been painted. Good-bye old gray, blue, and yellow color scheme. Hello, red and cream.

Truth is, it didn't feel like Ellison's home anymore. And that was a good thing.

"The boys are just getting their things together," Josh said. His body was tense, wound tight like he was ready to pounce.

Ellison wanted to avoid all conversation about Luke, so she said, "Okay." She turned her head this way and that. "The house looks good."

"Jenn's always buying something new. We live at Restoration Hardware these days." Josh sounded upset, but Ellison didn't press him. Besides, his moods were Jenn's problem now.

Still, it took all she had for Ellison to refrain from making a snarky comment. Josh had never let her shop there. He always claimed it was overpriced.

"Where's Jenn?" she asked. Not that she cared, but she had a sneaking suspicion she wouldn't have been asked in if Jenn were around.

"Girls' night out." Josh glanced at his watch, his nervous tick. "She's been trying to get out more now before the baby comes." He paused and looked at his watch again. "Oh, and now that she's showing, Jenn and I decided to tell the boys about the baby."

Ellison realized she had no idea when the baby was due, and to be honest, she really didn't care to find out. Huh. Maybe she was letting go.

A small missile hit her in the thighs. "Mom!" Alex cried, wrapping himself around her waist. "I missed you!"

"Missed you, too, Buddy." She rubbed his head, and his hair stood up.

Dash just hung back, not looking particularly happy. "What's up, Dash?"

Her son's eyes flashed. "Did Dad tell you? About the baby?"

Ellison nodded.

"Let's go," Dash said, pushing past Josh and toward the door.

"He didn't take it well," Josh said. "But this guy." He bear-squeezed Alex. "Is excited about being a big brother, aren't you?"

Alex smiled broadly. "I won't be the baby anymore. Dash can't call me that."

Ellison's insides were churning, but she put on a good face for Josh and the boys. "That's wonderful." She turned toward Dash and the door. "Let's go before it gets too late."

Honestly, all she wanted to do was run from the house. From Jenn's domineering portrait to the ugly throw rug she put down in the dining room. Ellison didn't want to talk about the baby – conceived while she was still technically married to Josh.

"Ellison, wait."

She turned slowly, anxiety building inside her. "What?"

"Boys, go to the car," Josh ordered, and they complied. He took a step closer to Ellison. "We never had a chance to talk the other day."

"Josh," she held up her hand. "Stop. What goes on in my private life is my business. And if you miss me, that's too bad. We really have nothing to talk about."

"Are you dating him?"

Ellison gritted her teeth. "Again, not your business."

"So you are."

"We're friends. I work in the classroom on Wednesdays." She was terrified to tell Josh anything more despite Luke's posturing.

"And that's why you were at Target?" Josh said.

"Yes. We were buying things for the new reader's corner in the classroom."

"But Eve said-"

"Since when do you trust anything Eve says? You know she likes to stir the pot."

Josh dipped his head. "Good point."

Ellison stepped on to the porch. The rain drizzled behind her. "Good-bye, Josh." For some reason, saying this sounded so final. Like she was closing a chapter on her life.

Maybe she was.

Maybe she was ready for something new.

The boys were rambunctious. No doubt hopped up on sugar. Just to confirm her suspicion, she asked Alex, "What did you eat at Dad's house tonight?"

Alex grinned at her in the rearview mirror. "Pizza, Coke, and cookies."

"Don't forget the candy," Dash added, as if he wanted Josh to get in trouble. Which he probably did given his reaction to the baby news. "We had Snickers and Sour Patch Kids."

Josh had to know what he was doing. Even he couldn't be so clueless as to mistakenly load them up with sugar so close to bedtime. Good thing tomorrow was Saturday, and their only plans were sleeping in and maybe Xbox. She glanced at the boys. They were never going to sleep.

From the backseat came bits and pieces about Minecraft. Alex jabbered on, but Dash seemed less enthusiastic than normal. Probably the baby news had him feeling a little lost. Ellison needed to speak to him and call his therapist if necessary.

"What did you do this week?" Alex, her inquisitive child, asked. "Dash said you ate out a lot."

Ellison frowned. What had she done that was kid appropriate? "Laundry, worked a little, helped Dash's teacher."

"Why don't you ever work in my classroom?"

Ellison glanced at her youngest son in the rearview mirror. "I helped with the Thanksgiving Feast, and I'm coming in for the Holiday Party."

That seemed to appease Alex, and he stopped asking questions. Dash sat quietly, sullenly almost, and Ellison cursed Josh under her breath. Did he not realize the damage he was doing to their boys?

"When the baby comes, I'll be a big brother!" Alex said out of nowhere. Ellison kept her eyes on the road.

"Shut up," Dash yelled. "Just shut up about the baby."

"Alex," Ellison said. "Let's not talk about the baby tonight."

"But I'm excited," her son said. "Dad said I could hold it and help give it baths and play with it."

Great. Like a giant, living doll.

"I understand you're excited, but Dash's feelings are hurt." She checked her eldest son's reflection in the mirror. He seemed on the verge of tears.

If she were right, Josh told the boys right before she was to pick them up, so she'd have to deal with the fallout. She clenched her jaw.

"Fine," Alex said, falling back against the seat. "Fine. Fine. Fine."

Ellison turned the Suburban down their street and into her driveway. She let out a surprised gasp. Luke's truck was parked in front of her house.

What was he doing here?

Ellison jumped out of her SUV before either of the boys had a chance to ask why Mr. Peterson was at their house. She scurried around his truck to the driver's side.

Luke rolled down the window. "Hey there, Ms. Ellison," he said, his eyes lingering on her lips. "I thought maybe you'd like Dash's homework because Josh never picked it up this week."

Red-hot rage boiled inside Ellison. "What do you mean?"

"He never contacted me about picking it up, so I brought it by for you. Plus, I thought if Dash were up for it, I could review some of the stuff with him. That way he doesn't fall behind."

Who was this man? Josh would never do something like this. In fact, his son's academic success seemed like second fiddle to blowing up his world with baby news.

"Mom?" Dash said. He stood next to her, his head already to her shoulder. "Oh. Hi, Mr. Peterson."

"Hey, Dash. I brought your homework."

Dash groaned.

"Seriously, buddy, you didn't think you were taking a week vacation, did you?" Ellison asked.

Dash shook his head. "No, but Dad said it was bull- BS, and I didn't need to do it."

"Is that what Dad said?" Ellison asked and waited for Dash to nod. "Well, he was wrong. Very wrong."

"Don't be mad at him," Dash said. "Jenn wasn't feeling well when we picked up Alex from school."

"Every day?" Ellison asked with a little satisfaction. Jenn's morning sickness must have been bad. "She was sick every day?"

"Not every day." Dash hung his head. "Dad told her not to get it."

So there it was. Once again, Josh's stubbornness resulted in the boys being penalized.

Nice.

Ellison held out her hands, and Luke dropped the papers into them. "It's getting close to bedtime, but maybe, if you're free tomorrow, you could come by. I'm sure Dash could benefit from your help."

"Tomorrow works. I'm open from eleven on," Luke said.

Ellison tossed the house keys to Dash. "Go ahead and start getting ready for bed."

"Mooom," Dash and Alex moaned in unison.

"Bed. Now," she said using her snappy mom voice. She hated bringing it out, but sometimes the boys needed to be reminded that they were not her equal. Since the divorce, she found herself growing lax with the boys' attitudes, and they were all paying for it.

After the boys had disappeared into the house and closed the door, Ellison said, "Thank you for doing this. I really appreciate it."

Luke hopped out of the car and crept closer to her until there were only millimeters between them. "Ellison, don't you know I would do anything for the kids in my class?"

"And not just my kid?" She smiled and poked him in the ribs.

"Well," Luke looked down at her with his gray eyes. "I might be willing to go the extra mile for Dash. After all, his mom is pretty hot."

Heat swept across Ellison's cheeks. Through the fringe of her eyelashes, she glanced up at Luke. "Do you say that to all the moms?"

Luke wrapped a strong hand around her waist and pulled her into him. "Only you."

Ellison's heart banged against her ribs. Just as she was preparing for a kiss, Luke released her. Ellison stumbled backward.

"What," she sputtered. "Was that?"

"Why Ms. Brooks, were you expecting something else?"

She pushed lightly on his chest. "Were you?" she teased. "Isn't that why you're here?"

"I'm here to help Dash with his homework. Bonus is that I get to see you."

He swaggered back to his truck, and Ellison admired his tight backside. After getting in the truck, he rolled down the window. "I'll see you tomorrow, Ms. Brooks. At eleven. We'll make a day of it."

Before she could answer, he kicked the truck into reverse and sped off.

Spending the day with Luke sounded perfectly lovely.

It also sounded like flirting with danger.

28

FIGHT CLUB

Ellison was in a frenzy. She'd been cleaning the house since seven – before the sun was even out, and the boys were still tucked into bed. When she had checked on them, Dash's fuzzy head barely peeked over the covers while Alex slept with no blankets at all. How could two boys with the same parents be so different, she often wondered. Granted, Dash had been an only child for two-and-a-half years before Alex came along. Maybe that's where the difference came from?

She worked a broom into the crevices under the cabinets, making sure to get all the neglected crumbs and dirt. Luke had never seen her house spotless, and for some reason, it was important to her that he did. At least once. Just so he knew she wasn't a complete slob.

When she and Josh had been married, she was always wound so tightly. She'd snap at the kids for leaving their socks lying around and was always up before the boys making lunches, prepping for the day. Now, her house often looked like a cyclone had hit it, and she didn't care. It wasn't unusual, when the boys were with Josh, for Ellison to sleep until noon, and God knows, she'd become lax with Dash and Alex. She no longer punished them for things like forgetting to bus their dinner dishes or keeping messy rooms.

In short, her divorce had mellowed Ellison out.

And to be honest, she liked this version of herself better. A more relaxed, laid-back Ellison.

Except now. Why did she have to be such a slob? She wanted Luke to see she had her shit together.

Ellison glanced at the clock. It was nine. Still too early to have heard back from Susan. Intense fear gnawed at Ellison. What if Susan can't pony up the extra twenty-thousand dollars? What if she walked away from the whole deal?

Ellison had forgotten how frustrating, frightening, and exhilarating real estate could be. Still, she needed to close this deal. If not for the commission, then for the self-esteem boost. And despite herself, she feared it was going to be one of those days. When bad news comes in threes, and all that.

Sigh.

The boys were now playing Xbox, and she still needed to get herself ready. Since it was Saturday, Ellison decided on wearing jeans, but she had no idea what shoes and what shirt. Or maybe a sweater? And jewelry, something small. She didn't want to go too over-the-top, but she wanted to look pulled together.

She put the broom and dustpan back in the mudroom and returned to the kitchen. Cereal would be the easiest breakfast. Old Ellison kept a pantry stocked with Raisin Bran, corn flakes, and other healthy options, but Ellison 2.0 allowed some sugary cereals like Cinnamon Toast Crunch. She poured two generous bowls, before calling the boys to the table.

Alex burst into the room full of energy while Dash stumbled along behind his brother. "What's for breakfast?" Dash asked.

"Cereal."

Dash screwed up his face. "I wanted pancakes."

"Well we don't have time for pancakes this morning because Mr. Peterson is coming over to help you catch up on your school work."

"This is so unfair," Dash yelled. "Why do I have to do work on a Saturday?"

Ellison – Old Ellison – answered. "First, don't talk to me like that. I don't speak to you like that, so you should afford me the same respect. Second, you should be thankful Mr. Peterson cares enough to take time out of his weekend to make sure you don't fail."

With a scowl on his face, Dash hung his head. "Still sucks."

"No," Ellison said, retaining her cool. "What sucks is that you got suspended. If you had followed the rules, we wouldn't be in this position." She dropped the two bowls of cereal on the table, and said, "Now eat. And when you are finished, put your bowls in the dishwasher. Understand?"

"Yes, Mommy," Alex answered.

"Yes," Dash mumbled.

"I'm going to take a shower. When I come back, you better have a more grateful attitude, Dashiel."

As she climbed the stairs, she realized she had no idea where Luke lived, which was weird considering her job. She knew where everyone lived. But Luke had never invited her over.

Why was that?

The doorbell rang at five past eleven. Ellison tucked a piece of her ash blond hair behind her ear and smoothed out her cashmere wrap sweater. When she threw the door open, she swallowed a gasp.

It was Josh.

No. No. No. This was very, terribly bad.

"You look nice, Ellison," Josh said.

"What do you need, Josh?" She couldn't help but keep looking over his shoulder, watching the street in case Luke arrived.

Ugh. This would be a very bad time for Luke to show up. How would she explain it? With the truth – which Josh would likely not believe because he'd heard about the Target non-incident.

"I need to talk to you," he said.

Ellison closed her eyes and exhaled loudly. "About what now? Anything concerning the boys' visitation needs to go through the lawyers."

"That's not why I'm here. I just wanted-"

"Dad!" Alex ran out from behind Ellison and leg-hugged Josh. His little face turned up toward Ellison. "It's not Dad's day, is it? We just got here."

"No, sweetheart, it isn't." She patted Alex on the head. "Why don't you go play while Dad and I talk." She turned around and steered Alex toward the living room where she spotted Dash scowling against the wall. *Once again, Josh is fucking things up.*

Nervous that Luke was going to show up at any moment, Ellison didn't ask Josh in. Instead, she stepped outside where Luke could better see them if he drove by. Hopefully, Ellison prayed, he'll keep going and come back later.

"What do you want?" she said in her snippiest voice – the one she reserved just for Josh.

Josh bristled. "Why are you being such a bitch? I came here to tell you I made a mistake, and this is what I get." He reached out for her hand, but she took a step back, away from Josh.

"Mistake about what?" Ellison asked.

"You and me. Jenn. All of it. I really fucked up, Elle."

She tried not to choke on her spit. "You're just now realizing this?"

"I knew the day of the wedding, but I couldn't call it off. I don't know why, but I couldn't."

Ellison thought back to Drunkfest and wondered what she would have done if Josh had shown up remorseful and asking for a second chance.

She may have considered it. Or, she would have laughed in his face and maybe puked on his shoes.

Yup. It was official. Ellison no longer cared what Josh did, where he went, or whom he did it with.

Out of the corner of her eye she spied Luke's truck crawling past her house. *Keep going. Keep going*, she begged silently. But he didn't. Luke pulled up to the curb and jumped out of the truck. He carried a satchel across his body and looked damn good doing it too.

"Hey, Ellison," Luke called. "Is this not a good time?" His steely gaze landed on Josh.

Josh's gaze ping ponged between the two of them. "What's this?"

"Mr. Peterson is dropping off Dash's homework since you and Jenn never picked it up. Plus, he offered to review everything Dash missed this week."

Anger flashed in Josh's eyes. "Are you sure that's all this is?" He scanned Ellison from head-to-toe, and she was thankful she wasn't overdressed. "After all, people are talking about the two of you."

Ellison pursed her lips. "I told you, Eve was pot stirring. Luke is our son's teacher. Nothing more."

"He was your date at the Gala." Josh crossed his eyes and glared. "Explain that."

"I don't have to," Ellison said calmly. She wasn't going to let Josh rattle her.

Luke stepped between Josh and Ellison. "Is Dash inside? I have work to do while the two of you figure this out."

"Excuse me, that's my son," Josh hissed. "And I don't think this is appropriate at all."

"Josh," Ellison snapped. "Get a grip. Some teachers go above and beyond. Luke is one of them."

"Luke? So we're on a first name basis?" Josh's agitation was growing quickly. If Ellison didn't do something, they'd be locked in a screaming match in seconds.

She took a deep breath. "Go on in, *Mr. Peterson*. Dash is waiting for you in the kitchen." As soon as she said the words, she realized her mistake.

"How the hell does he know where the kitchen is? Has he been here before, Ellison? What exactly is going on between the two of you?"

"Yes, he's been here before. And as for the rest, it's none of your business."

"I think it is." Josh clenched his jaw. "He's our son's teacher. If you're dating, that's a conflict of interest."

"Josh, don't. Just don't."

"So it's true?" he said. "You're dating."

Ellison looked him square in the eye. "No." And it was true.

Neither Luke nor she had ever discussed making their whatever-it-was official.

"You know what, Ellison? I think you and your boyfriend just earned a trip to the school board."

"Josh, no." Desperation crept into her words. "You have no evidence. You have nothing. Plus, like I said, we aren't dating."

"So you're just sleeping with him."

Normally, Ellison would have exploded, and anger did percolate inside her, but she kept calm. "How is that any of your business?"

"You are my wife. I have the right to know what's going on."

Ellison inhaled and shook her head on the exhale. "Ex-wife, Josh, ex-wife. Your *wife* is at home, pregnant and probably waiting for you to return home with bagels and coffee."

Josh reached out like he was going to strike her, and Ellison jumped backward. "Don't," she said. Not that Josh had ever hit her, but then again, there were many sides of Josh that Ellison hadn't seen until the divorce. "Do not come near me. And do not come to my house again uninvited. If you do, we'll have to revisit the custody drop-off/pick-up. Do you understand?"

"That man will never be able to support you the way you're used to. Not on a teacher's salary."

"That isn't an issue. Like I said, we're not dating. And if we were, I wouldn't have to inform you. My private life is just that. Private."

Josh's face softened. "Elle, you've got to understand. I'm…I haven't been making the best decisions."

"And what? You want me back? You know you'd have to pay alimony and child support to Jenn, don't you? Besides, I don't want you anymore. I'm done."

She turned the doorknob and stepped inside.

"Elle. Wait. I'm sorry."

It was a little too late for that. Sorry is what she wanted to hear the day she found out about the affair. Sorry is what she'd been waiting for all those months leading up to the wedding.

Sorry had been all she wanted to hear.

But not anymore.

Now she wanted to be as far away from her disgusting ex-husband. He was nothing more than a man-child who had lost interest in his newest toy. No doubt he'd cheat again.

Then the unthinkable happened: she actually felt bad for Jenn.

She felt bad for the woman who had ruined her life.

A laugh tumbled out of Ellison.

"What's so funny?" Josh demanded.

Ellison cocked her head and studied the man who was once the center of her universe.

"Nothing," she said before slamming the door in Josh's face.

———

Dash and Luke sat at the table when Ellison entered the room. Luke raised his eyebrows, and concern filled the crinkles around his eyes. "Everything okay?" he asked.

Ellison nodded and made her way over to the cooktop. She picked up the teakettle and filled it with water before turning on the flame. When stressed, she either drank wine or tea. While she could go for a glass of her favorite Malbac, tea was more appropriate for this time of day. Plus, she didn't want Luke to think she was a lush.

"Tea?" she asked.

Luke still looked at her with those concerned eyes. "Dash, you keep working on this sheet. I need to talk to your mom."

Ellison followed him into the front room – away from Dash and Alex.

"What happened?"

Ellison began recounting the story. She stopped short. "Why did you show up? Couldn't you have waited?"

"You looked stressed."

"Well, now I'm more stressed because Josh definitely thinks something is going on between us, and he's threatening me."

To her surprise, Luke looked nonplussed. "So? What's the worst that can happen?"

"You could lose your job."

He shrugged. "Not the end of the world."

"But," Ellison said. "How would you support yourself? You need to have a job, and wouldn't being fired hurt your chances of future employment?" If anyone knew about money problems, it was Ellison. She didn't want Luke to have the anxiety she had.

Luke nodded his head. "I have savings that would get me through."

"Still, those kids need a teacher like you," she grabbed his hand. "They need *you*."

Luke smiled at Ellison. "Thank you for saying that. I love my job, but if I had to choose between that and, well, you, I think my answer may surprise you."

Ellison's breath caught. Was he being serious? Would he toss away his job and financial security just to be with her?

"Luke," she said. "Don't do that. Don't draw lines in the sand when there needn't be any. What we have is-"

"Special." His fingertips skimmed her arm. "I don't want to lose this. Teaching jobs are plentiful, but a woman like you is a rare find."

She swallowed hard, and her heartbeat skipped. She wanted to kiss him, but not here. Not with the boys around.

"Can I ask you something random?" Ellison asked.

"Sure."

"Where do you live? I've never visited your home, and well, I'm curious."

Luke laughed. "And here I was thinking you were going to ask me something tough." He squeezed Ellison's hand. "I have a garden home in Waterford. On Weller near Crimson."

"Renting?"

"Purchased."

Ellison tilted her head. "When did you buy it?"

"Right after we met, and I got my job offer. Like I mentioned before, I looked you up but was too nervous to reach out."

"I hope you got a good deal." Garden homes over there started at about $650,000. How in the world did he afford that and a club membership on a teacher's salary? If she wanted, she could look it up in the public records and see what he paid, but that seemed rude and invasive.

"It's just the right size for me," Luke said. "I can show it to you some time, if you want."

"That would be nice." Ellison's hands began to shake – the adrenaline from her argument with Josh was finally leaving her body.

"Hey, are you okay?" Luke said, clasping his hands around hers.

"I'll be fine, just some left-over pent up energy from my fight with Josh." She wiggled her hands away. "I think you have a student who needs you right now more than I do."

"Are you sure? You seem incredibly upset."

"I'll be fine," Ellison repeated. "I'm used to him, remember? Having been married for fourteen years and all."

Luke softened his face and stroked her cheek. "You should never get used to someone treating you like a jerk."

Tears she didn't know she had escaped the corners of her eyes and streamed down her face. "Thank you."

"For making you cry?" Luke looked confused.

"For being here for me – when I need you. For just being wonderful."

From behind them, Dash cleared his throat. "Are you dating my teacher now, Mom?" There was an edge to his voice, and Ellison quickly composed herself.

"No. I was thanking Mr. Peterson for being such a good friend. That's all."

Dash scoffed. "Because you know it's fine with me if you were. After all, Dad has Jenn." He spit out his stepmother's name like it tasted bad. "You shouldn't be alone."

"I'm not alone. I have you and Alex."

Dash raised his eyebrows as if he weren't buying it. He kept his arms crossed against his chest, and his eyes trained on Luke.

Luke walked over to Dash. "I'll tell you what, buddy. When your mom and I have news, you'll be the first one we tell, okay?"

That seemed to appease Dash. He smiled – smiled! – at Luke.

Maybe dating his teacher wouldn't be scarring after all. Still, they needed to take things slow. Let the boys get used to him being around.

"Okay." Dash eyed the pile of homework and frowned. "I guess we should get back to science?"

"That we should," Luke answered.

The teakettle whistled wildly, and Ellison pulled it off the flame. She poured three mugs and gave one to Dash and the other to Luke, while keeping one for herself. She poked her head into the living room, and Alex laid on his stomach, engrossed in a cartoon.

She glanced back at Luke and Dash and sighed.

This is what life should be.

29

HERE'S TO NEW FRIENDS

"Ellison? It's Susan. How are you?"

"I'm fine." Ellison cradled the phone against her shoulder as she carried groceries into the house, and the boys darted past. "How are you?"

"Good. I wanted to let you know that I got the seller's counter and it looks fine. But I need to know, how hard and fast are they on eight-twenty? Do you think we could drop to eight-fifteen and still be competitive?"

Ellison set the bag of groceries down on the counter and adjusted the phone. "Honestly, I think this is their firm offer. You're matching what they know they can get from the other party."

"I see."

"If this house doesn't work, I will find you something. Something in the Greenbriar School District. I promise."

"It's not that. It's just, you know, I hoped to get a better deal and all." Susan laughed. "Okay, let's write up our new offer and send it over."

A smile formed on Ellison's lips. After her altercation with Josh the day before, she was sure bad news was coming, but if Meghan and her husband accepted Susan's offer, she stood to make commission as both the listing and selling agent. And that was no small amount of money.

"I'll do it right now, but I can't guarantee an answer until Monday morning. Most people don't like to do business on the weekend."

"Speaking of weekends," Susan said. "Would you and your boys like to meet me and mine at Sparky's this afternoon? I promised them some arcade time."

Ellison had spent many hours at Sparky's back when she was married. Josh drank beer and watched sports while she ran after the boys.

But this was different. This was another woman reaching out to her, asking to be her friend.

"What time?"

"I was thinking around four. An early dinner," Susan said. "My boys love it there, and I thought we could have a drink and chat while they played."

"Sounds perfect," Ellison said, hoping her voice didn't give away her excitement. "Gives me enough time to get the offer in."

"Okay, great! I'll see you and the boys at four. Bye."

"Bye."

When she hung up the phone. Ellison fist punched the air. If everything went right, she'd have an accepted offer by tomorrow and maybe a new friend.

Life was getting better.

"This is Max," Susan said tapping the taller of her two boys on the head. "And this is Sam. We just moved here from Arizona."

Both of Ellison's boys mumbled hello while she introduced them. When she was finished, she handed them each a bucket of tokens and said, "Now go have fun."

As the four boys disappeared into the arcade, Susan and Ellison climbed into a jumbo booth. A pitcher of beer sat between them.

Ellison wasn't a huge beer drinker, but it was either that or soda, and she felt like an adult drink.

"I hope they get along," Susan said, staring off toward the arcade.

Ellison nodded and poured herself a glass of beer. "Do your boys like Minecraft and Pokémon?"

"That's all they talk about," Susan answered.

Ellison laughed. "Then they'll get on fine. My boys are obsessed."

Susan poured a glass of beer and took a sip. "I guess I'm a little bit worried. They haven't found their niche at school, and honestly, neither have I."

"Greenbriar can be tough," Ellison frowned. "At least amongst the moms."

"Cliquey?"

"There's that." Ellison sucked the foam from the top of her beer. "Whom have you met?"

Susan pursed her lips. "Well, Eve Strella and her friends. Do you know them?"

"Unfortunately, yes." Ellison's heart threatened to bang against her ribs. If they knew Ellison and Susan knew each other, would they try to turn Susan against her? She sighed. "They used to be my close friends."

"Let me guess, they were worried about catching the Divorce Flu and dropped you?"

Ellison's gaze roamed around the room. "That, and they befriended my ex-husband's mistress as soon as the divorce decree was finalized."

"What?" Susan's mouth dropped open. "No way in hell. No way. What did you say? Please tell me you said something."

"Not exactly." She didn't know how much to confess to her new friend. Ellison didn't want to scare Susan off. But she felt honesty was the best way to go. "Before my divorce, I was Eve. I mean, I ran Greenbriar, and I wasn't that nice to people outside my group." She sipped from her beer. "In fact, I lost a listing recently because of my past behavior."

"So you were a bitch?"

Ellison hung her head. "HBIC is more like it."

"HBIC?"

"Head bitch in charge. I led the gossip, blackballed people, and thought my life was perfect." Ellison wrinkled her nose. "Looking back, I was rather unbearable."

Susan laughed. "I've never been an HBIC, as you say. I've always been too busy working to bother with petty school cliques, but Greenbriar is brutal. Morning drop-offs-" she shook her head.

"Fashion parade?"

"Exactly! I'm only up and dressed because I have to leave for work, but these stay-at-home moms with full hair and make-up kill me. Do they sleep like that?"

Ellison dragged a finger through some condensation on the table. "Trust me, it takes a lot of time to be like that. I used to wake up at five to hit the gym for an hour before coming home and getting the boys ready. Lunches were always organic and healthy. Nothing was out of place."

"Do you think it's an insecurity thing?" Susan asked.

"You know, it probably is. I never thought of it like that. But it's definitely a competition, even if no one admits it."

Susan shook her head and snorted. "Excellent. Guess I won't be making a lot of friends since I give my boys Goldfish every day."

"Oh you can't give them those!" Ellison exclaimed in mock-horror. "The dye alone may kill them; not to mention they're nothing but gluten. You should be in jail for child cruelty."

Dash and Max ran up to the table. "Mom, can we do a sleepover with Max?"

"Not tonight. It's a school night."

"Next weekend?" her son asked.

Ellison grimaced. "It's Dad's weekend."

Dash made a face and said to Max. "I guess I'm never going to see you."

"We'll do it the following weekend if Ms. Susan is okay with that."

Susan waved her hand. "I am. Your mom and I will work out details."

Max and Dash grinned. "Awesome," said Dash. "Max has all my old friends in his class – Charlie, James, and Andrew. How lucky is he?"

Ellison smiled. "Very."

The boys ran off, and Susan whispered, "Are those good boys? Or should I steer him away from them."

"Well, they're Eve and company's boys. So totally your call."

Susan settled back against the booth. "I think I'll see how it plays out."

"Good idea." No need for Susan to poke a hornet's nest unnecessarily. She was new and deserved to feel comfortable walking into Greenbriar and not like everyone was staring at her. Ellison knew that feeling all too well, and frankly, it sucked.

"Not to be rude, but how'd you end up here with the boys if you're from Arizona?"

Susan swished her beer and swigged. "My ex never really wanted kids, and the divorce was a way out of fatherhood for him."

"Oh my God. How awful," Ellison blurted before covering her mouth. "I'm so sorry."

"It's okay. He turned into a different person after the boys were born. He'd stay out until morning and come home reeking of alcohol. I'm not sure how he keeps his job."

Ellison leaned forward. "So he had no problem with you moving the boys out of state?"

"Nope. He didn't even ask for our address."

"That's terrible." For as horrible as dealing with Josh was, at least he was an involved father. He loved the boys just as much as Ellison. "Do your boys know?"

"Unfortunately, yes. He made a big scene and said some nasty things while we were packing the house. He left, and we haven't seen him since."

Ellison finished her beer. "Sounds like you're better off."

"Not everything about divorce is bad," Susan said.

Ellison lifted her empty mug and clinked Susan's. "Cheers to that, my friend. Cheers to that."

30

GET AWAY

Days without the boys had no meaning for Ellison. It was just one long expanse of time that had to be dealt with. At least she had them for part of Christmas, but not New Year's Eve. Which she was fine with since Andi was in town and promised to 'make this like no New Year's ever.' Which honestly, both scared and exhilarated Ellison.

Professionally, things were looking up. Meghan and her husband had accepted Susan's offer, but it was a sixty day close with a sixty day rent back. It would be Spring before Susan moved in, and more importantly, Ellison got her commission check.

Still, it was a deal, and Laurie had been pleased with the outcome, so Ellison's job was safe for a while longer. And when one deal closed, another usually followed. At least it did when Ellison had been on her A-game.

She sunk deeper into the soaking tub and turned the jets on. Her new house may be smaller than her old home, but the tub was better. Her old one didn't have jets, which Ellison found silly. Why build a house and put a substandard tub in?

Ellison sighed. Despite the professional wins, it had been two weeks since Luke came over to help Dash with his homework, and

Ellison had only seen him three times since: once when he took her to his very nice garden home and nothing happened; and twice in the classroom on Wednesdays. It was now the first weekend of Winter Break, and she had three weeks of not having an excuse to see him.

Not that she needed an excuse. Luke was into her, but they weren't exclusively dating, and she didn't want to appear clingy.

God, she hated all the uncertainty around dating.

Bubbles foamed around her, and she wiggled her toes just above the surface. When she had asked Luke what he had planned for break, he looked at her forlornly and said that every year, his family gathered at their Tahoe cabin and skied.

Ellison, not being a skier, thought that sounded terrible, but when Luke told her about the après ski part, she perked up. Hot chocolate by the fire, family sitting around playing games, and general laziness. Yup, it sounded like a good life to Ellison.

Her vacation options weren't so grand. She planned on drumming up some new business – even though the winter was the slowest time of year in real estate – and baking cookies with the boys. She had the boys for Christmas Eve and Christmas morning but had to hand them off to Josh at noon. At least she got to watch their wonder as they opened presents from Santa. Next year, and she really shouldn't be thinking that far in advance, she'd get them at noon.

Being divorced sucked. Being divorced with kids sucked more.

The water felt so good whooshing around her that she closed her eyes and let the steam open her pores. Once she was done with her bath, she was going to do a whole beauty routine: facial mask, cleansers, hot oil treatment, and maybe a pedicure.

This is what passed for a fun Friday night without the boys.

She wondered what Luke was doing. Was he off on the slopes right now? Had he even left?

Her cellphone buzzed, but it was up on the counter, and Ellison was too comfortable to retrieve it. Besides, with her luck, she'd drop it in the water and ruin it. No, better to let whoever was calling go to voicemail.

Her mind wandered back to that day when Josh said he missed

her, and Luke said there was something special between them. Two men, both vying for her attention. One she no longer wanted, and the other she shouldn't have. At least not for a year if she cared about him keeping his job.

Her phone buzzed again. And again.

Somebody was being persistent. Part of her worried it was Josh, calling about the boys. That something dreadful had happened. With that thought in her head, she stood up and stepped out of the tub. Her terrycloth robe hung on its hook, and she picked it up and wrapped herself in it before reaching for the phone.

Text after text from Luke filled the screen.

Are you home?

Are you available?

Check your voice mail.

Sure enough, there were two messages from Luke. She didn't listen to either, and instead, called him back.

He picked up on the first ring. "Hey," he said.

"Hey. What's so important?"

"Can you let me in? I'm at your front door."

Ellison quickly checked her reflection in the mirror. She had on no make-up, and her hair was twisted up in a towel. Her beloved bathrobe suddenly seemed grubby and old.

"I was in the tub. I hope you don't mind if I look less than optimal."

"Ellison, I could care less what you looked like as long as you are you."

Her heart melted in that hot lava way, spreading heat to every part of her body until she was sure she was on fire.

She looked down at the shabby robe, and for a moment, considered dressing quickly.

"Elle, it's kinda cold out here."

Bathrobe be damned. "I'll be right down."

She practically skipped down the stairs and to the front door.
Maybe this was a good old-fashioned booty call before he left town.
Not that she wanted to be a booty call, but she was dying for sex. It
had been a little too long.

Her heart thrummed when she threw open the front door. Luke
stood outside, holding a rolling suitcase.

"You moving in?" she joked.

Luke kissed her on the forehead. "Not exactly."

This was awkward.

"You look cute," he said. "Freshly scrubbed."

"Thanks." Ellison tightened the robe's sash.

"Can I come in?"

Ellison moved aside, and Luke and the suitcase entered the foyer.
He set the suitcase down. "So," he said. "I know this is crazy. And you'll
probably say no. But Andi said I should try-" He was rambling, and
Ellison found it adorable. He pulled the handle on the suitcase up.

"What's crazy?" Ellison was confused. Was he packed for an
overnight? Did he want to stay the night? She had no idea what was
going on.

"Would you like to come to Tahoe with me?" He pointed at the
suitcase.

Ellison's eyes grew wide, and she went slack jawed. "Is
that...for me?"

Luke nodded. "I bought it for you, as a Christmas gift, I guess. I
thought, maybe you'd like to come with me?"

"But we're not even serious. We're just friends, right?"

Luke placed his thumb under her chin and lifted Ellison's face to
meet his. "I think we both know that that isn't true."

Ellison's heart beat recklessly. She was sure Luke could hear it.

"Monica really wants you there, if that makes a difference."

Ellison laughed. Luke's twin sister was a force to be reckoned with.

She was determined to marry off her brother – that she'd made clear at the Gala. "Well by all means, if Monica wants me there, I should hurry upstairs and pack immediately," Ellison teased.

"*I* want you there. But only if you're sure you wouldn't feel awkward. I mean, my parents will be there, as will my younger brother and his wife and kids."

"And Monica."

"And Monica," Luke repeated with a smile on his face.

"When would we leave?"

Luke flicked his wrist and checked his oversized watch. "Now. If we don't want to miss our flight."

Ellison grabbed the suitcase and ran toward the stairs. "Make yourself comfortable. I'll be down in ten."

A deep, hearty laugh surrounded her. "So I take it that's a yes?"

"Yes," she said. "A hundred times yes."

"We're flying into Reno. It's closer, and the traffic isn't as bad as trying to drive up from the Bay Area," Luke said as they snuggled into their first class seats. He'd gone all out, and Ellison was impressed and a little embarrassed. All this from a guy she wasn't technically dating or in a serious relationship with.

"You know, I would have been fine with coach seats," Ellison said, wrapping her pashmina around herself. She hated using the onboard blankets. Who knew what nasty things lurked on them.

"I'm sure you would have been, but this is more comfortable, isn't it?" Luke smiled, the corners of his eyes crinkling.

"I'm going to sound crass, but this can't be cheap." Ellison touched Luke's arm, and heat flowed through her fingertips.

"I need to tell you something."

"What?" Ellison didn't like the sound of this.

"I don't normally travel like this."

Ellison nuzzled Luke's arm. "Hey, I've never been out of coach, so an upgrade to Economy Plus would feel like luxury to me."

Luke rubbed the back of Ellison's head. "I'll keep that in mind. But seriously, I need to tell you something."

Ellison braced herself. "What?"

"My family owns the largest vineyard and winery in Sonoma." The words tumbled out of Luke so fast that Ellison wasn't sure she heard him right.

"Your family owns the winery? The one where Monica works?" Ellison exclaimed as she tried to wrap her head around what Luke was saying. "Why would you hide that?"

"I wanted you to like me for me. Not my money. It's part of the reason I moved from San Francisco – I couldn't find a woman who just wanted me for me."

"Mr. Peterson," Ellison said, playing with the seat controls. "You never cease to surprise me."

"You're not mad?"

"Surprised and maybe a little hurt that you didn't trust me to like you for who you are, but I understand." She placed her hand over Luke's. "If any of the women at the Club knew, they'd circle like vultures."

"That's what usually happens."

"And I'm not a vulture?" Ellison asked playfully.

Luke grinned. "Not even close."

Ellison knotted her hands together. "I appreciate this. I really do. But do you think it's moving too fast? I mean, I'm meeting your parents. Is that weird?"

"No. My parents are very laid back. If you want, we can sleep in separate rooms. Although Monica may have something to say about that."

A deep, crimson blush worked its way into Ellison's cheeks. She hadn't thought of sleeping arrangements. In fact, she hadn't thought about much beyond how fun it would be to get away for the week.

Could she and Luke survive a week together, on vacation? And what were they? Friends, lovers, boyfriend and girlfriend? What?

"Hey, what's going on in that pretty head of yours?"

"Sorry," Ellison said. "Sometimes I get stuck in my brain."

"I noticed."

"If we had separate rooms, will I be putting anyone out?"

Luke tilted his head and stared at her. "Well," he drew the word out. "The kids will have to sleep on the great room floor, but that's okay. We'll make it work."

Shit, thought Ellison. She'd be inconveniencing his family.

"Elle, I'm kidding. We have plenty of rooms. In fact, we have a main house and a guesthouse. Don't worry about it. We'll find a place for you."

"A main house and a guest house?"

Luke dropped his head. "I know it sounds excessive, but we're a large family."

Ellison kept doing the math in her head. The first class tickets, the trip to Tahoe, the new designer luggage. All of that added up and surely, and Luke's teacher salary didn't cover the cost. She suddenly felt a bit like a leech. After all, he knew about her financial problems. Was that why he paid for everything, or was it really a treat?

"I hope you don't mind that I'm not flying back with you," Luke said, breaking her thoughts. "My family has a big Christmas tradition, and I can't miss it. Plus, I know it's your time with the boys. I wouldn't want to come between that."

Was this guy real? Ellison pinched herself on the thigh. Yup. It hurt. She wasn't dreaming.

"No, of course I don't mind."

The plane had now taken off and was climbing steadily. This was the part Ellison hated about flying – the ascent and descent. She reached for Luke's hand and squeezed it hard.

"Are you afraid of flying?" he said.

"No. Just take offs and landings," Ellison answered.

Luke's fingers interlaced with hers, and his hand felt warm and comforting. He leaned closer to Ellison, so that she could smell his aftershave. "I've got you, Elle. I've got you."

She settled back into her seat, but her fingers didn't leave Luke's. "Tell me about your family," she said. "Best prepare me before I get thrown to the wolves."

Luke laughed. "They're not that bad, Elle." He said her nickname with such ease, and unlike when Josh used it, it filled her with warmth. "My mom is a mom. She'll fuss and fawn over me non-stop. Just be ready. She hates that I'm living all the way across the country. And she'll tell you all about that too. How I broke her heart when I decided to up and leave. She can be dramatic."

"And your dad?"

"Pop is a wine guy. He's happiest when he's out working in the vineyard or doing tastings at the winery. He loves to talk product and work, so don't be surprised if you get a crash course in viniculture and enology."

"Enology?

"The science of winemaking." Luke winked. "See you're already on your way to fitting in."

"So your dad and Monica both work at the winery?"

Luke hesitated. "Yes. Dad's worked there his entire life. Monica didn't start doing PR until a few years ago. But don't worry, we talk about more than just wine. And no one will eat you alive."

Ellison snorted. "If Monica was an indication of what your family is like, I'm in for quite a week."

"Mo is unique. Don't let her enthusiasm put you off. She means well."

"I know. I just don't know if I can keep up with her."

Luke patted Ellison's hand. "Probably not on the slopes. She was a competitive skier when we were younger, but you can more than hold your own with her in every other category."

Ellison's heart sunk. "You know I can't ski, right?"

Luke nodded. "We're going to fix that problem, don't you worry. By the end of the week, you'll be on the black diamond runs."

For some reason, that sounded downright dangerous, and Ellison's hands shook a little. "Tell me more. About your younger brother and his wife."

"Mike is shy, if you can believe that. His wife, Sarah, is the outgoing one. She's a lot like Mo. That's why they butt heads so often, I think."

The flight attendant stopped next to them. "Would you like something to drink?"

"Champagne sounds nice, doesn't it Ellison?"

It did. And decadent too. "Yes, please."

While they waited for the champagne, another flight attendant handed them hot towels and small ceramic bowls of roasted nuts. Ellison, who had only ever traveled in coach, was struck by the lavishness of it all.

After the flight attendant handed them the champagne flutes, she laid menus down on their trays. "Just let me know what you want."

Ellison's eyes grew wide. "Steak, chicken, salmon?" She read aloud. "Is this how you always travel?"

Luke hung his head. "No."

"Oh, I hope you're not doing this all for me. I mean, I'd hate to think you'd wasted money on me for something like this. I really would be happy in coach."

Luke grabbed her hands between his. "Actually, Ellison," embarrassment crept into his voice, "my family has a private jet."

She blinked hard. Did he just say his family owned a private jet? Who was this man she was traveling across the country with? She was beginning to feel like she knew very little about Luke Peterson.

"They own a jet?" Ellison said in disbelief. What had she walked into?

"I hope you don't mind," Luke said. His eyes twinkled a little, and he was still holding Ellison's hand. "I'm going to kiss you, Ellison Brooks, if that's okay with you."

She nodded.

Luke's lips pressed against hers, and his hand worked up her back. He pulled away just when she stopped worrying what the other passengers might think and left her breathless.

"So," he said with a hint of wickedness in his voice. "Which room do you want?"

31

SLEIGH RIDE

Saturday had been a whirlwind. Between Monica trying to teach Ellison how to at least stand on her skis, and Mr. Peterson – John, please that's what everyone calls me – educating Ellison on the finer points of winemaking, she was exhausted.

All she wanted was a nice glass of Cab from the family winery. She tried some when they arrived late the night before, and it was heavenly. It also helped her understand why they were the premier vineyard and winery in Sonoma.

Ellison poked her head into the chef-grade kitchen, and Beth, Luke's mom, was at the cooktop stirring a huge pot of something. "That smells delicious," Ellison said.

Beth smiled warmly at her. "It's a Moroccan beef stew. One of Luke and Monica's favorites."

"Judging by the way it smells, I think it may soon be one of mine too."

"Now you're buttering me up," Beth said, laughing. So far, all of Luke's family had made Ellison feel right at home. It was as if they'd known each other for years. "How was skiing?"

"Sore." Ellison rubbed her backside. She had spent more time on her butt in the snow than skiing. Even the bunny hill wasn't safe from her wild careening. But Monica hadn't given up on her. In fact, she seemed to be a well of endless patience despite having such a hopeless student.

"You're in good hands, Ellison," Beth said, stepping away from the cooktop. "Monica has been teaching children how to ski for years. You'll get it."

Ellison laughed loudly. "I don't know. I may have taken out a toddler or two." Her gaze roamed around the kitchen. "Do you have any of that wonderful Cab left?"

Beth motioned to an area across the room where several bottles of unopened wine sat. "I'm afraid I polished off that bottle, but feel free to open a new one."

Never one to say no to wine, Ellison readily grabbed a bottle and the corkscrew. "Would you like some?" she asked Beth.

"No, I've had my fill. That's one thing you have to learn living among so much wine is when to quit. I'd never be able to finish making dinner if I had one more." She made a funny face that Ellison interpreted as Beth play-acting a tipsy person.

Ellison poured a nice, full glass for herself and re-corked the bottle. Part of her wanted to stay and chitchat with Beth, but she knew the rest of the family had gathered in the massive great room. When she walked in, she was again struck by how grand it was. The ceiling soared to eighteen feet easily, and exposed beams gave the room an upscale rustic look. Overstuffed leather chairs flanked the fireplace, and a long couch sat before it. Behind the couch and toward the back of the room, Mike's three children sat at the game table playing Pokémon. The two girls were roughly Dash and Alex's age, but the boy was closer to thirteen. Ellison hadn't spent much time talking to them, but they seemed like well-behaved children.

Across from them and nearest Ellison, was a full bar, stocked with the finest liquors.

She had never been in a home like this before. Yes, Waterford homes were upscale, but this was luxury living. Ellison was, to be honest, a little out of place despite the family's hospitality.

Ellison surveyed the room one more time, before crossing its expanse to one of the chairs. She was on her own because Luke was showering. Skiing, she'd discovered, was a sweaty sport.

"Hey, Ellison," Monica said, sitting up from the couch. Her blond hair was fuzzy from wearing a ski hat, and her cheeks were flushed. Ellison didn't know if it was from the cold or the wine. Either way, Monica was a stunning woman. "I'm surprised you haven't zonked out. You had a tiring day on the slopes, and you seem a little jet legged."

"I don't do well with time changes," Ellison said, slightly embarrassed. "But the Cab is so good, I can't possibly nap."

"It's my favorite, too. Our chardonnay wins all the awards, but the Cab is a family favorite. It's taken Dad and me years to perfect it." A smirk crossed Monica's face. "Speaking of being tired, how'd you find your accommodations last night? Satisfying?"

Ellison fought the blush staining her cheeks, but it was no use. Her face flamed hot. They'd arrived so late that the only spot left for her was Luke's bed. Not that she minded, but she liked to keep her sex life private. Luke, however, had barely touched her except to give her a goodnight kiss. A kiss Ellison had hoped would turn into more. But it didn't, and they both collapsed from exhaustion.

"Everything is amazing, and the bed is very comfortable."

Monica glowed. "You know, you're the first woman Luke has brought here in years. You must be very special to him."

The idea of Luke have brought someone else here disheartened Ellison. She knew Luke really liked her – at least enough to introduce her to his family, even if it was "This is my friend, Ellison."

Friend. Not girlfriend. Not significant other. Friends. Ellison was starting to hate the word.

All because he was Dash's teacher, and her reluctance to let it be more. Oh, and then there was her obsession with what others thought.

If there was an obstacle in this fledgling relationship, it was Ellison. She knew it, and so did Luke. So why was he wasting time and money on her? Did he really like her that much?

A large dog bounded into the great room and shook the snow off his coat. Water sprayed everywhere, and Sarah, Mike's wife, came running in behind the giant dog carrying a towel. "Wesley, you come back here," she said, trying to wrangle the drenched dog. "Wesley come."

The kids had stopped their game and watched. "Mom, this happens every time," said Caden, the oldest. "You need to shut the mudroom door before letting Wesley in."

"I know that, Caden. He's just so fast."

The dog shook again, and Sarah caught him this time. "Oh no, you don't," she said, gripping him between her legs and running the towel all over the dog. She lifted one paw and dried it before moving on to the rest. When Wesley was satisfactorily dried, Sarah wiped down the hardwood floor.

"Happens every time," Monica whispered. "You'd think she'd learn."

Ellison took a swig from her wine glass and stared into the fire. From what she had gathered, the family tolerated Sarah because Mike adored her. She wasn't stunningly beautiful – not like Monica – but she was sweet and seemed like a good mom, albeit a bit clueless.

Ellison hoped the family wasn't nice to her only because of Luke. She wanted them to really like her. After all, she thought they were great.

Wesley lopped over to the fireplace, yawned, and stretched out on the ground.

"In my next life, I'm coming back as Wesley. He has it made," Monica said.

Ellison nodded in agreement and took another sip of delicious wine. It danced over her tongue, leaving behind a full-bodied flavor with a hint of black pepper. John had explained the different notes to Ellison, and she was pleased to discover she could taste exactly what he described.

"Do you ski often?" Ellison asked Monica.

"Only every minute I get," Monica answered. "Nothing beats the feeling of flying downhill, the air whooshing past you, and knowing you could lose control at any moment. It's better than an orgasm, actually."

Ellison tried not to spit out her wine.

"What?" Monica said. "I know you haven't skied down a black diamond, but I assume you've had an orgasm."

Too embarrassed for words, Ellison merely nodded and checked to make sure the kids weren't listening. Fortunately, they were engrossed in their Pokémon game.

"Well, take the most earth-shattering orgasm you've had and multiply it by a hundred," Monica said. "That's what skiing is like for me."

"Must be nice." A male voice said from behind Ellison. She turned around and saw Luke standing at the edge of the couch.

"You're just jealous because I beat you every time today," Monica said with a devious smile.

"And you're jealous because I'm going to steal Ellison away before you can mortify her anymore."

Monica stuck out her bottom lip. "Who am I going to talk to?"

"Sarah? Mom? The kids, Mike, Dad? I don't know. It's not like you're lacking in options."

"But I like talking to Ellison so much better." Monica pouted out her lip.

"Mo, Ellison and I have some things to do."

At that, Ellison tensed up. What could they possibly have to do besides...oh God. Was he planning on making out or having sex right now?

He put his hand on Ellison's shoulder. "Do you want to finish your wine first?"

"Yes, if you don't mind." She needed liquid courage to get through whatever he had planned.

"Don't look so afraid, Elle. I don't bite." After she finished, he held out his hand to help her up. "My only request is that you leave your cellphone here."

What in the world? What was he up to?

"Dress warmly," Luke had said. "Ski clothes might be best."

She shuddered. Her wet ski clothes were the last thing she wanted to slide back into. Maybe a sexy negligee after everyone else had gone to bed, but not damp ski clothes.

"Don't worry. Mom dried everything," Luke said, as if reading her mind.

She followed Luke into the mudroom and lifted her white ski pants – the ones Monica had picked out for her before she even arrived – off the hook. The family was so confident she would agree to Luke's crazy plan that they had bought things specifically for her. It was both sweet and a little anxiety-inducing.

But who was she kidding? Only an idiot would say no to someone as sweet, thoughtful, and hot as Luke. And his family knew it. She wondered how much he'd told them about their non-relationship relationship.

After stepping back into the ski pants, she pulled on her matching jacket, gray ski hat, and gloves. "How do I look?" she asked Luke.

"Beautiful."

"Thank you." Ellison blushed despite herself.

Luke grinned. "You're getting better with taking compliments."

"Well when they come from you-" she teased.

"C'mon," Luke said taking her gloved hand in his. "We don't want to be late."

They trudged down the cleared path to the guesthouse where Mike and his family were staying. "This way," Luke said, guiding her around the building and toward a barn farther out. Here, the snow wasn't plowed, and they waded through calf-deep snow. Across the field, the barn doors were flung open, and the interior glowed a warm yellow. But she couldn't see inside.

Then she heard it. The jingle of sleigh bells.

Ellison tilted her head and looked up at Luke. A smile twitched at the corners of her mouth. She grasped Luke's arm. "What is this?"

"Shhh," Luke said excitedly. "It's a surprise."

As they neared the barn, he placed his hands over Ellison's eyes, and the two of them shuffled forward until Luke dropped his hands and whispered, "Go ahead, and open your eyes."

Four Clydesdale horses stood ready and hooked up to a sleigh. Ellison's face lit up in delight. "Is this for us?"

Luke wrapped his arms around her. "Yes. I thought a sleigh ride around the property would be fun."

Ellison threw her arms around Luke and kissed his cheek. It was like stepping into one of the Hallmark Christmas movies she loved: there was a hero, a gorgeous house, and now a sleigh ride.

Please don't let me wake up.

Luke helped Ellison into the sleigh. Thick fur blankets covered the seat, and she slid beneath them. Luke climbed in next to her, and his hand searched out hers beneath the blanket.

It all felt so surreal. Only a few days ago, she was wallowing and eating Ritz crackers with cream cheese and pepperoni slices by herself. All her worries had slipped away, and for the first time in over a year, Ellison felt relaxed enough to fully live in the moment.

"We're ready," Luke said to the driver, and away they went, jingle bells and all.

The cool, late afternoon sun struck Ellison's face, and she smiled beneath her scarf.

"So all this is your family's property?" Ellison asked.

Luke motioned with his free hand. "Three hundred acres. My great-grandfather bought it way back when. It's been in the family for generations."

Snow clung to the evergreen trees as the sled flew over the pristine snow, transporting them back a hundred years. She rested her head on Luke's shoulder, and his hand tightened around hers.

"Ellison?"

"Uh huh," she answered lazily.

"I know you have reservations, and I know it's socially and maybe professionally frowned upon, but I'd very much like for you to be my girlfriend."

If this is how he asked her out, imagine what he'd do if he were asking to marry her. *Oh stop it, Ellison. You're getting ahead of yourself.* A girlfriend was hardly the same as a fiancée. One step at a time.

She considered Dash and Alex, both of whom adored Luke. And then there was Dash's asking if Luke was her boyfriend. He'd been okay with it. Or was he just saying that because it's what he thought Ellison wanted to hear? And how would Josh react? He'd already threatened Luke's job once.

Ugh. And Eve and her crew.

Stop overthinking it. Everything is going to be fine. Luke makes you happy, and that's what matters most.

Ellison pulled down her scarf and smiled broadly. Luke bent forward until their lips touched. When they broke away from each other, she said, "Yes. I'd love to be your girlfriend."

Luke grinned, and his gray eyes twinkled in the dwindling daylight.

Ellison didn't let him grin for long. She pulled him into another kiss.

32

BE MINE

"She said 'yes'!" Luke announced to his entire family. They were gathered in the great room playing a board game when she and Luke walked in.

"That's wonderful," Beth said, beaming at her son.

Monica squealed and jumped up from the table. "I told you she would. I told you!"

So everyone knew about Luke's plan, except Ellison. She was impressed by how good they were at keeping his secret.

"Does this mean Uncle Luke is getting married?" asked the youngest of Mike and Sarah's children.

Mortification crossed Sarah's face. "No. It means they're boyfriend and girlfriend." Over the top of the child's head, she mouthed, "I'm so sorry."

There was nothing to feel sorry about. Luke and she were official. She needed to tell Andi a.s.a.p.

"If you'll excuse me, I want to go clean up before dinner," Ellison said.

Everyone spoke at once, and Ellison laughed. It was so easy being with these people. Not at all like being with her ex-in-laws. With them, she was always on edge, worried that she wasn't doing things exactly right. But Luke's family had embraced her so warmly that she felt as if she'd known them for years.

She climbed the stairs to the room she shared with Luke. Her stomach fluttered. Now that they were official, would they have sex tonight? Would it be awkward knowing that everyone else knew what they were probably doing?

She found her phone on the bedside table, and her heart sank. Six messages from Josh. She groaned.

Since she couldn't very well ignore the messages, she listened to the first one.

"Ellison, this is Josh. Alex is running a fever. You need to come get him so he doesn't make Jenn sick."

Are you freaking kidding me? Ellison thought as she dialed Josh back.

"Ellison." No hello. Just her name.

"Hi, Josh. What's the problem?"

"Alex has a fever, and you need to come pick him up. Dash, too. We can't risk Jenn getting sick in her condition."

"How high?" Ellison asked.

"Like 99.9 or something," Josh answered.

"That's barely a fever." Ellison inhaled deeply. He was making a big deal out of nothing. "I can't pick him up." She almost said she was sorry, but she was done apologizing to Josh for things that weren't her fault.

"What do you mean, you can't?" Josh snapped.

"I'm in Tahoe, on vacation, and won't be back until Thursday."

"You're in Tahoe?" Disbelief filled his words. "With who? That teacher?"

"I'm here with a friend. That's all you need to know."

"And what exactly am I supposed to do with a sick kid?" Josh was practically screaming, and Ellison had to force herself to remain calm.

"Give him some children's fever reducer and put him to bed." Josh was acting as if he'd never been around a sick boy before. Oh right, he hadn't. That had always been her job.

"Great. I get to do this while you gallivant around Tahoe." Anger seeped into his words. "What about Jenn? What if she catches what Alex has?"

"That's not my problem," she answered. "Besides, pregnant women are around sick kids all the time."

"Way to be sympathetic, Ellison."

Anger boiled inside her. "You know what, you can go screw. You're not going to mess up my vacation." Without saying good-bye, she hung up.

Josh hadn't managed to dampen her happiness, and that was fantastic. Normally, a conversation like that would have thrown Ellison into a tailspin.

By the time she called Andi, the anger had completely subsided.

"Hey, Ms. Tahoe," Andi said.

"So how much of the planning did you help with?"

"Just the kids' schedule. And maybe some of your favorite things." Andi laughed in her devious way. "Are you having fun?"

"We spent the day skiing, or in my case laying on my back trying to stand up. And this afternoon, he took me on a sleigh ride and asked me to be his girlfriend."

"I knew it!" Andi said. "I knew he was going to do that. Did you say 'yes'?"

"Of course I did."

"So no more worries about the school board, or Josh, or the boys?"

"No. I mean it's still there. I don't want him to lose his job, but how often does a man like this come along?" She paused. "As for Josh, he called me six times to say Alex had a fever, and I needed to come pick him up because heaven forbid, Jenn gets sick."

"What?"

"Right?" Ellison said. "He's being crazy isn't he?"

"What did you tell him?"

"That I was in Tahoe with a friend and wouldn't be back until Thursday night."

Andi let out a low whistle. "That must have gone over well."

"It didn't. But you know what? I'm done being Josh's childcare backup. He and Jenn need to step up and act like parents to our boys."

"That's my girl," Andi said. "I've been waiting for my ball-busting friend to return."

Ellison chuckled. "You know I was a bit of a bitch before."

"Yeah, but you were my bitch, and I loved you."

"Okay, I'm going to run. The family is in the great room waiting for me. It's nearly dinner time."

"Have fun, my love," Andi said, smooching loudly into the phone. "Do everything I would and more."

Ellison hung up the phone and debated calling Josh back to speak to Alex. But no. If Alex were with her, she wouldn't tell Josh. She'd deal with it. And he couldn't possibly be too sick, or Josh would take him to the doctor's office. She sighed. Josh was just trying to unload his parental responsibilities. She fought with the nagging feeling that she was a bad mother for a moment, before deciding to call Alex tomorrow and check on him.

She wanted to change out of her clothes and into something fresh. While she was gone, the maid had put her clothes in the closet. She wasn't sure how she felt about a stranger going through her belongings – especially her lingerie – but it seemed to be the norm around here.

Once she was changed, Ellison glanced in the mirror. She brushed out her hair and smudged on some lip gloss. She didn't want to look overdone, but she wanted to look presentable.

A smile tugged at the corners of her mouth. She had a boyfriend. A good, honest man.

Thank you, Santa.

Ellison felt like a shy schoolgirl. She had brushed her teeth twice -- just to make sure her breath wasn't funky, checked her reflection in the mirror, sucked in her gut, and worried that she might not live up to Luke's expectations.

The black lace nighty she wore showed off all her curves. Curves she had thought long gone until Josh cheated on her, and she dropped twenty pounds almost overnight. She ran her hand over her hips. For thirty-eight, she looked pretty damn good. Yes, there were stretch marks here and there, but she wasn't flabby. She wasn't ripped either. Just the right amount of softness.

At least she hoped so.

You're being ridiculous, Ellison, she thought. *Luke has already seen you naked, and he liked what he saw.* Or, so he said. Memories of that night at the hotel flooded her mind. She fast-forwarded to the day they made out at her house. Or when they made love on her couch. He'd seen her naked then.

So why was this so stressful?

"Ellison?" Luke called from the bedroom. "You okay?"

She cracked the door and peered through the slit. Luke was sitting on the bed in just his jeans. His muscular upper body made her wonder what he saw in her as a sex partner. Surely, he'd been with hotter women.

Push those thoughts from your head, Ellison Brooks.

Maybe what he said had been true. He adored her. She'd never had a man say that to her before, and it made her knees weak just thinking about it.

"Come out here," Luke said.

Ellison bit her bottom lip, and with a deep breath, opened the door fully.

Luke let out a whistle. "Damn," he said. "You look amazing."

With a little swagger in her step, Ellison crossed the room to where Luke sat. She stopped in front of him, her knees skimming his, and said, "Do you like this? I picked it out special for you."

Luke placed both of his hands on her hips. "I like it very much, but I like what's inside better – and I don't mean your body. I think you are beautiful in here." He tapped her forehead with his index finger.

She melted. A huge giant puddle of Ellison splashed across the floor.

"It appears, Mr. Peterson," Ellison said, once she pulled herself together. "That you only came half-dressed to this party." She ran her hands over his broad chest, allowing the heat of his body to fill her.

"And it appears, you're wearing too much, as usual." Luke said, sliding his hands down the sides of her body to the edge of her nighty. He tugged at it softly before falling back onto the bed.

Ellison climbed onto the bed and straddled Luke. She leaned forward and lightly kissed him on the lips. He responded like a starved animal. His mouth was on hers, his hands roaming up and down her sides. When she moaned, Luke flipped her over so he was on top of her. He pushed up her nighty and playfully slapped her thigh.

"Well, well, well. What do you have here? No panties?"

A warm blush colored Ellison's cheeks.

Luke jumped up and pulled off his jeans. When he was standing before her in just his boxer briefs, he said, "Now we're equally dressed. Unless, I can help you out of that hot nighty."

She lifted her arms and let him undress her. When she was naked, lying on the bed, Luke snuggled up beside her and gently kissed her neck.

Ellison's fears all disappeared.

"My girlfriend," he whispered in her ear. "Mine."

Ellison loved the sound of that. "And only yours."

With Luke, she had no fears that he would cheat on her or laugh at her mommy body. Her walls were down.

And she liked it that way.

Thursday came too soon. The days had been spent hitting the slopes – she made it off the bunny hill! – playing games with the family, drinking fabulous wine before the fireplace, and of course, making love to Luke. Her favorite part of the day was when he'd roll over in the morning and softly kiss her bare shoulder three times.

If she could have this life forever, she would. But that would mean giving up the boys, and she wasn't about to do that. Still, it was a nice dream.

This morning, after Luke's three kisses, Ellison slid from bed, walked over to her closet, and got dressed. She dug her new suitcase out of the corner and began filling it with her clothes. "I'm afraid the ski clothes won't fit," she said to Luke who lounged on the bed, propped up by several pillows.

"Leave them here. That's what I do. They'll be here when you come back."

Come back. "I like the sound of that."

He motioned her over to him and when she was about a foot away he jutted out his arm and pulled Ellison into an embrace. "It's been a gift having you here. Everyone loves you. Especially Monica. And she can be hard to please."

Ellison snuggled into his arms. They were so warm and inviting that she didn't want to leave, but she had a plane to catch and that was after the hour drive to Reno. "I have to get going," she said. "I can't miss my flight."

Luke released her, but not until giving her once last kiss. "Go, but know you're breaking my heart," he teased.

With little thought of wrinkling, Ellison shoved her clothes into the rolling bag. When everything was stuffed inside, she pulled Luke up by the arms. "C'mon. You're going to make me late."

"Would that be so bad?" He asked, running a finger down Ellison's arm and sending tingles along her spine.

"Not ordinarily, but I have two young boys who need their mom."

Luke jumped off the bed and pulled on his jeans. From his closet, he selected a pale blue cashmere sweater and yanked it over his head. Some of his hair stood up from static, and he ran his hand over them.

"How do I look?" he asked, grinning goofily.

"Like a movie star." And he did with his gray eyes, mussed up hair, and square jaw. He was perfection.

"C'mon," he said grabbing Ellison with one hand and her suitcase with his other. "I don't want to make you late."

Luke led Ellison through the maze of hallways until they reached the curved staircase. The rest of the family was already up and going.

"I'm taking Ellison to the airport now," Luke announced. Everyone stopped what they were doing and rushed over to her. She took a step back, unprepared for the onslaught. Beth caught her and pulled her into a bear hug. "You take care of yourself, Ellison. And make sure this boy eats, will you please? He's looking too skinny."

"I will," Ellison laughed.

One-by-one the family said goodbye to Ellison. Monica even teared up a bit. "It's been so good having you here. I haven't heard Luke laugh in a long time."

"You're exaggerating, Mo," Luke said.

Monica crossed her arms. "No, I'm not. You light up around Ellison in ways I haven't seen in years."

Luke caught Ellison's hand and dragged her toward the front door. "If this keeps going," he said over his shoulder to his family. "Ellison is going to move in with us."

"Would that be so bad?" Monica shouted as Luke and Ellison headed down the steps and toward the waiting car. Sunlight was just starting to hit the tops of the snow-drenched trees.

They climbed into their seats and sped away from the Peterson Ranch, as the family called it.

Soon, Ellison would be flying solo across the country, leaving Luke behind.

With a heavy sigh, she laid her head on his shoulder. The next week couldn't pass soon enough.

33

BESTIES

As soon as Ellison landed, she turned on her phone. There were angry texts from Josh, a sweet message from Luke, and a voice mail from Andi.

When the pilot turned off the seatbelt sign, she pressed her phone to her ear and listened to Andi's message.

"Hey babe, I'll meet you in baggage. Thought you needed a ride home. Love you!"

Ellison laughed softly. Andi was always so upbeat. So positive. Even when hit with a setback, she didn't fall into the kind of depression Ellison did, and Ellison admired that.

Some people rushed past Ellison as they hurried to their flights, and some meandered toward the exit. Ellison was somewhere in between – not in a hurry, but not killing time either.

She spied Andi leaning against a pillar chatting up some guy. Of course. The woman was a man magnet and naturally outgoing. Which meant she couldn't go anywhere without meeting someone new.

"Hey, Andi," Ellison said. "I see you've made a friend."

Andi threw her arms around Ellison, nearly knocking her over. She planted a huge kiss on Ellison's lips. "I've missed you so much! I was just telling Mark all about you."

Mark's eyes roamed up and down Ellison like he was making a decision about something. "You must be Andi's girlfriend?"

Ellison tried not to choke. Andi had done this before, but it still made her laugh. She decided to play along and laced her fingers through Andi's. "Yes, I am."

He nodded. "It was nice talking to you."

"You too," Andi said as he walked away.

When Mark was out of earshot, Ellison burst into laughter. "What was that?"

Andi rolled her eyes. "He was overly persistent. It was either that or knee him in the crotch, and I really don't feel like being arrested today."

"Have you been arrested before?"

A devious look crossed Andi's face. "Not in this country."

"Okay, Ms. International Woman of Mystery." They walked toward the parking garage. "What are your plans tonight?"

Andi shrugged. "Since it's the day before the day before Christmas, I figured eggnog and some seasonal movies. You?"

"I get the boys back tomorrow night, so I thought I'd wrap a few presents. Makes for less work on Christmas Eve."

"I wouldn't know."

"Tell me you're not working on Christmas." Ellison paused while Andi unlocked her car. "You know you're always welcome at my place. The boys would probably think it was a Christmas Miracle if Aunt Andi came over."

The two women climbed into Andi's car. "I'd love to, but this year, I really do have to work." She eyed the back-up camera before pulling out. "The boys' gifts are in the backseat."

Ellison turned around, and sure enough, two laundry baskets of presents sat on the seat. "Andi, you spoil them."

"Only so I'll have someone to visit me when I'm in a nursing home."

"Stop it. You have friends and family."

"They'll all be dead or my age."

"Then we'll have to be in the same nursing home, so we can keep each other company."

Andi laughed. "That's been my plan all along. Make a lifelong friend at age eight and sponge off her when we're elderly."

"Speaking of friends, I think I made a new one," Ellison said as she fiddled with the radio station. Andi liked country, Ellison liked pop, so the Taylor Swift song she found was appropriate. "Susan, that client I told you about who bought the house on the Waterford border, wants to get together again with the boys. I was thinking we should invite her out sometime for drinks. You'd like her. Very direct and has a dry sense of humor."

They pulled up to a stoplight. "Sure. If my calendar if free, I'm up for it."

"You around this week?" Ellison asked.

"Maybe."

"Do you mind hanging out with four little boys?"

Andi shook her head. "Not at all."

They took off again, and Ellison grabbed onto the door. "Oh my God, do you have to drive so fast?"

Andi laughed. "That wasn't even fast. But really, why have a car like this if you can't really drive it?"

One more turn and they were at Ellison's house. "Come in?" she asked.

"Sure," Andi replied. "But only if drinks are involved, and you tell me all about your sexy trip."

"It was fun, not sexy."

Andi's eyebrows shot up. "Right. There was absolutely no sex. Just skiing, sleigh rides, and games. I hear you. A lovely house in Tahoe doesn't invite romance at all."

Ellison dropped her bag next to the stairs. "You're mocking me."

"A little."

The two women moved to Ellison's kitchen, and Ellison took two glasses from the cabinet and poured some red wine she had left over from the last time Andi visited.

"Isn't it funny," Ellison said. "That we've been friends all this time, went to college together, moved across the country together, and were roommates, but you never once told me I was a bitch until recently."

"Why would I?" Andi asked. "You've always been nice to me."

"But you saw how I acted with Eve and company. You watched me turn into a stressed-out Stepford Wife and never said anything."

"I figured it was part of having kids. You know, you get the man, the house, the kids, and the attitude."

Ellison sat on a barstool. "Is that why you've never entertained getting married?"

"I really love my job, and I couldn't do it if I had kids."

"Do you want kids?"

"Sometimes. But then I have Dash and Alex, and it's good enough. I've gotten to watch them grow up without any of the headaches."

"Lucky you."

"Plus, you need me." Andi said, "If I had a husband, I would have to split my Ellison time in half. And I really wouldn't want that." The skin around Andi's eyes crinkled, and she laughed.

Ellison flicked her on the arm. "Tell me true. How unbearable was I during my marriage?"

"I love you, Elle. I do. But when you got around Eve, Kate, and Julia, you were...well, you weren't the nicest person."

"So I *was* a bitch."

"More or less."

Ellison frowned. "Awesome."

"Why are you asking this?" Andi poured some more wine into their glasses.

"Because my reputation might be mucking up my listing options."

Andi nodded. "People were afraid of you. No one wanted to upset you out of fear you'd make her life miserable. At least, at the club. I don't know about school."

Ellison sighed. "I'm sure it was the same." She swigged from her wine glass, and her lips turned a dark purple. "How do I get people to see I've changed?"

"Deeds, not words. You have to show them."

"And how do I do that?"

Andi shrugged. "Hell if I know. Everyone thinks I'm promiscuous. Which I am. A little." She slid off her barstool. "C'mon. Let's watch something trashy while you tell me all about your trip."

Just the thought of Luke made Ellison smile. "Where should I start?"

"With the suitcase," Andi said. "What do you think of that?"

"Did you pick it out?"

"No, but it was my idea. I've seen your ratty old bag, and Luke wanted to surprise you, so we thought it was a fun idea."

"The two of you plotting away isn't an idea I necessarily like."

Andi threw herself onto the couch while somehow not spilling a drop of her wine. How did she do that? "Oh, you only know the half of it."

"Oh? Then why don't you tell me your story first."

Ellison's phone rang. It was late. Close to ten. She flipped it over, eager to see if it was Luke, but it was a number she didn't recognize. She flipped it back over and let it go to voicemail.

"Not taking calls?"

"Unknown number. I hate those."

"We could reverse search it." Andi always had the answer.

"Of course we could," Ellison said. "Or we could get to the bottom of how you and Luke pulled off the most romantic week of my life."

"Oh that." Andi swished her hand as if it were nothing. "It was all Luke, actually. Monica and I just helped with the details."

"So you talked to Monica?"

"Well someone had to tell her your sizes and stuff."

That was true. Ellison had just assumed Monica guessed right, but this made more sense. "How long did you know?"

Andi pursed her lips and looked up at the ceiling. "Two weeks out, maybe. I can't remember."

Ellison shook her head. "And what other secrets are you keeping from me?"

"None now that you're officially a couple. You know everything I do."

"I better!"

"You know I wouldn't tell you even if you threatened to cut my toes off." Andi was like the Fort Knox of secret keepers. Unless it was blurting out Ellison's one-night stand info to Eve and company. She still hadn't forgotten that day at the pool, and the envy and surprise that her former friends had. Old Ellison would never have done such a thing. Ellison 2.0 was all about stepping outside her comfort zone and taking chances. At least, Ellison hoped she was.

After all, people can change.

34

SANTA NO

"Mom! Mom! Wake up!"

Some small creature, possibly Alex, pulled her eyelid back. Never mind that she was up until two in the morning wrapping presents and nibbling cookies. Alex didn't care about that, not that he knew. At eight, he still believed whole-heartedly in Santa.

Ellison eyed the blue numbers of the clock. Six a.m.

It was days like this that she wished she drank coffee. It would make getting out of bed so much easier. Or, so Andi told her.

"Mooom...get up! Get up! Santa came!"

There was such wonder in Alex's voice. Such innocence. Hopefully he'd keep it for a few more years. She and Josh had agreed that all of Santa's gifts would be at her house this year, and he could do the parent presents.

She had a feeling Josh's 'parent presents' were going to rival Santa's, and the boys were going to be presented-out by the end of the day.

She slid her feet into her fleece slippers and grabbed her robe from the floor. As tired as she was, Alex's excitement was catching.

They had a long-standing rule in the house that the boys could open their stockings before the parents got up, but Alex seemed to have forgotten that. All the lights were off downstairs. "Buddy, have you been downstairs yet?"

He nodded enthusiastically.

"Then why didn't you turn on the lights?"

"I did! I turned on the tree and the fireplace."

Sure enough, when they turned the corner, the Christmas tree was lit, and the gas fireplace glowed. Dash sat near the tree, eyeing the presents. A giant grin covered his face, and Ellison smiled. She hadn't seen her son this happy in ages.

"Looks like we've had some good boys this year," Ellison said.

Alex jumped up and down.

"Okay, on three. One, two, two-and-a-half, two and -"

"Mom!"

"Okay. Three!"

The boys started building piles of presents, and soon the wrapping paper that she had worked so hard on, lay in heaps on the floor.

Two glowing faces looked up at her.

This was all she needed for Christmas. Everything else was gravy.

———

The house phone rung, and Dash hurried to answer it. Ellison looked at the clock. It was a little past eleven. Luke couldn't possibly be calling now. Besides, he'd call on her cell.

"It's Dad," Dash said before handing the phone to Ellison.

Great. She'd been avoiding Josh all week. When he dropped off the boys on Friday, she politely but firmly refused to answer his questions about whom she'd been with. He said he knew that she wasn't with Andi because Jenn had seen her at the grocery store. So, whom, pray tell, was she running around Tahoe with?

The lack of knowing, it seemed, was driving Josh crazy.

"Hi, Josh," she said monotonously. He most likely called on her landline, so she couldn't caller-ID him.

"Elle, I know we said noon, but Jenn is feeling really sick again, and I don't know what to do."

Ellison rested her forehead on her palm. Was he really calling her about this? Really. "What do you want, Josh?"

A long silence followed. Finally, "I thought maybe I could bring the boys' presents over, and we could do Christmas at your place. Just the four of us. Like we used to."

"And let me guess, you won't be taking them tonight either?"

"Why, do you have plans with your mystery friend?" Josh sounded put out.

"No."

"Good then you should be happy. You get the kids all Christmas."

Ellison inhaled sharply. "No. What would make me happy is if you kept your promises to our sons. They look forward to spending time with you."

"Way to lay on the guilt, Elle."

"I'm not guilting you. I'm stating the obvious. They need both of us, equally."

"Can I come over or not?" Josh barked. When he was like this, Ellison hated caving to him. She glanced at her boys who sat on the floor surrounded by torn bits of wrapping paper. As much as she wanted to keep them all day, she knew Josh had to take them or shred their little hearts on his own. She wasn't going to be part of his promise breaking.

"Fine. Come over. But you explain why they can't come to your house."

Josh let out a whoosh of air. "Thanks, Elle. I owe you."

"Yes, you do."

"See you in twenty." Josh hung up.

Twenty minutes? Good lord. Ellison was still in her slippers and robe. She couldn't let Josh see her like this. "Boys?" she called. "I'm going upstairs to change. Dad is on his way over."

"Okay," Alex said. Dash looked at Ellison oddly. Like he knew something was up. She didn't have time to explain, so she ran upstairs to her room. From her dresser, she pulled out a pair of jeans; from her closet, she chose a loose, green sweater. Next up, hair and make-up.

Ellison rolled her hair into a slightly messy topknot and brushed on some mascara and lip gloss. Nothing too special for Josh.

Just as she was putting a last coat of mascara on, the doorbell rang.

She stopped what she was doing and walked to the top of the stairs where she could get a look at the front door.

To her surprise, Dash wasn't standing there with Josh. Instead, someone she had never seen before, dressed in a delivery uniform was waiting with pen in hand. "Miss," he said. "You're going to have to sign for all this."

All this?

Ellison flew down the stairs, and to her shock and horror, another delivery guy was carrying vases of roses toward her front door.

"What is all of that?" Ellison sputtered.

"Ten dozen red roses."

Luke. It had to be, but it seemed too extravagant for him.

She took the delivery form and signed. She paused. Something didn't seem right. She read the delivery slip, and her stomach flopped.

Josh.

Jenn probably felt fine. Josh just wanted Christmas as a family again. And he was trying to butter Ellison up with the flowers. No wonder he was in such a hurry to come over.

And sure enough, as the delivery guys carried the last vase to her front door, Josh pulled up with a huge smile on his face. Smug, like he'd won some competition.

"What?" Ellison demanded.

"Do you like your flowers? I thought it would bring some cheer to your Christmas." Josh leaned against the doorjamb, holding two giant sacks of presents. Figures. He had to outdo her. Just like always.

Anger simmered inside Ellison. She couldn't remember the last time he gave her flowers. No, she wouldn't give him the satisfaction of knowing she thought they were beautiful. Because beautiful or not, they were from Josh and therefore, tainted.

"You shouldn't be sending your ex-wife flowers," Ellison hissed softly. She didn't want the boys to hear.

Josh squished up his face. "Why not? You are the mother of my kids after all. We're stuck with each other for eternity."

When he said it like that, Ellison's stomach churned.

"Come in," Ellison said. "The boys are in the living room."

Josh followed her to the back of the townhouse. When the boys saw him, they jumped up in delight. "Dad!" Alex said, pointing at the bulging bags. "Are all those for us?"

"Yup. Every single one." Josh handed an overstuffed bag to Dash. "Go organize them while Mom and I have a talk."

Oh good Lord. Another famous Josh talk. What was he going to say now? That Jenn was having triplets? That they were moving? What?

She ushered him into the kitchen, away from the boys. "What is it?"

Josh gave her puppy eyes. "I miss you."

"You've said that before, and I've told you it's too late for that."

"What if I said I wanted to leave Jenn and come back to you? What if I told you I made the biggest mistake of my life?"

Ellison stared at him in disbelief. "Josh, you've got to be kidding me."

He plopped down on a barstool. "No. Nothing is the same without you. And Jenn isn't you. I thought she was the you you were when we first got married, but she's not. She's doesn't have your class, and she doesn't know how to parent the boys."

"Being a parent is a learned skill."

Josh tilted his head. "Well, yeah. Maybe so, but she still doesn't have it. She's not exactly maternal and is more concerned with going out than having the baby."

Ellison folded her arms. "So I'm your default?"

Josh shook his head, "It's not like that." He reached for Ellison's hand, but she yanked it away. "I miss this. All of this. Not just you, but our family. You, me, the boys. Think of all the good times we had. You could come home. Don't you miss it and your friends? Don't you miss me?"

It was a near copy of a speech she'd given him when she found out he'd been cheating. He was unmoved then, and she was unmoved now.

Ellison stood near the cooktop and poured herself another cup of tea. The water was lukewarm, but she didn't care. It gave her something to do while she mulled over Josh's words.

"I think you should go. Take the boys early and go." As much as she wanted to spend every minute of her time with the boys, she knew the longer Josh stayed, the harder it would be to get him to leave.

"Mom! Dad! C'mon. We want to open our presents!" Dash said from the living room.

"What do you say, Elle? We have one last Christmas as a family?"

She knew she wasn't winning this one, at least not without disappointing the boys. "Fine. They can open their presents, but then you need to take the boys and the toys back to your house."

"Have plans?" Josh said saltily.

"No. But it's your day, and the boys were looking forward to spending it with you."

Josh smirked. "And I'm choosing to spend it with you."

"Josh, stop. Just stop. This isn't going to go anywhere." *Because I have a boyfriend. Because you are a slime ball. Because I've finally found my backbone.*

"See, Ellison," he said her name harshly. "This is why I left you. You're too uptight."

She let Josh's insult settle over her. She wasn't going to react. Not today. Not on Christmas.

With purpose, Ellison walked out of the kitchen and over to the Christmas tree where the boys sat waiting. "Well, Josh. Do you want to get them started?"

Josh plopped down on the floor, just like he had in years past, and grabbed at the presents. "Dash," Josh exclaimed and tossed a gift football-style at their son. Dash grinned. "Alex," Josh announced and handed the present to the younger boy.

"Okay. Open them up." Ellison didn't care what was inside. She just wanted it done with.

The boys didn't hesitate and tore into the wrapping paper. It occurred to Ellison that Jenn must have wrapped the gifts because Josh had no idea how to do it. At least so he claimed – all the years Ellison spent meticulously wrapping presents while he watched SportsCenter.

Oh well. Not her problem anymore.

35

AIN'T NO PRESENT LIKE A CHRISTMAS PRESENT

At three o'clock, Josh was still sitting in her living room. Still unwilling to leave. "Ellison," he had said. "Look at the snow falling. I can't go right now. Not with the boys. It wouldn't be safe."

She had to admit, the snow looked like a blizzard, and anyone going out in it would have to be insane. Plus, she wasn't crazy about Josh driving the boys around in that mess, so she gave in and let him stay.

He hadn't, not once, looked at his phone or called Jenn, and Ellison wondered what she was doing all alone on Christmas Day while her husband was playing "Do you remember?" with Ellison and the boys.

While the boys ran around, testing out their new toys, Josh sat at one end of the couch and Ellison at the other. Both had hot cups of tea, and both were staying to their own areas.

"Why don't you stretch out on me? I can rub your feet," Josh said. He smiled in the Cheshire cat way he used when trying to get his way.

Ellison shot her eyebrows up. "I don't think that's a good idea."

"It's fine." Josh reached for her, but she was faster and tucked her feet under her.

She shook her head. "It will send the wrong message to the boys. And besides, I'm not interested."

Alex zoomed past holding a model airplane he and Josh had built. "Look at me, Mom!"

Ellison lifted her head and smiled at her youngest son. He was so sweet and caring. She hoped he stayed that way forever.

Off in the corner, near the tree, Dash sat on the ground working on his new electronics set. Every so often he'd scrunch up his face and move things around.

Life, Ellison had to admit, was pretty wonderful sometimes. Even if it meant having Josh sit at the end of her couch.

Ding Dong.

Everyone looked at Ellison, who in turn looked at Josh. "This better not be Jenn looking for you."

Panic filled Josh's face.

"You didn't tell her you were here, did you?" When he didn't answer, Ellison said, "She probably used Find My Friends on you and is standing outside waiting to skin you."

Josh blanched. "Elle, you've gotta understand, it's not the way you think it is." He sunk deeper into the sofa cushions. "She's-"

Ellison didn't have time for his excuses and was already on her way to the door. Her breath came fast, like she was on the verge of hyperventilating. She and Jenn rarely interacted with each other, and that was fine by Ellison, but now Jenn was on Ellison's doorstep looking for her wayward husband. Awesome.

Ding Dong.

Ellison closed her eyes to steady herself. She could feel Josh's looming presence behind her.

"Don't answer it, Elle," Josh begged.

She threw him a nasty look. "Seriously? Your car is in front. She knows you're here."

With a turn of the doorknob, Ellison swung the door open.

"Merry Christmas, Elle!"

She blinked her eyes hard. What in the world? Was Luke really standing on her doorstep? In this blizzard?

"How? Why?" she sputtered.

Luke laughed and tumbled into the house like an overgrown child.

In his hands, he held three presents and his suitcase.

"Is that Dash's teacher?" Josh said in a booming, angry voice.

From behind her, a small voice said, "Mr. Peterson? What are you doing here?"

What, indeed?

Luke's eyes scanned the crowd gathered before him. He looked at Ellison in puzzlement. "I thought," he shifted his stance. "I thought you'd be alone by now. I'm sorry to intrude." He took a step back toward the open door. "I'll go."

"No," Ellison said, reaching for his hand and pulling him back inside. "Stay. It's a mess out there."

"Are you sure?"

In a perfect world, it would be just her, or even her and the boys, but Josh was there which meant she had to explain why Dash's teacher was bringing her gifts.

"Is this your friend from Tahoe?" Josh sneered. "A fucking teacher? C'mon Ellison, you can do better than that."

Luke pulled himself up to his full height. His broad shoulders dwarfed Josh and made him seem smallish in comparison. She'd never noticed how much bigger Luke was than Josh until right now. Even when his muscular arms were wrapped around her, she still didn't fully grasp Luke's size.

"I may be a teacher, but at least I'm making a difference. Can you say that about your job, Josh?"

Ellison stepped between the two men and held out her hands, one on each of their chests. "Hey, cool it. The boys are here." She turned toward her ex-husband. "Josh, Luke is here as my guest, and you're here because we're snowed in for now."

The two men looked at her in disbelief. "You mean he's staying?" Josh whined.

"Yes. It's terrible outside, remember?" She ushered everyone into the kitchen. "Dash," she said looking down at her son. "Go, play. The grown-ups need to talk."

Relief washed over Dash's face, and he scurried away.

Ellison pointed at the bar stools. "Sit," she ordered, and neither man questioned her.

"Josh, I know this isn't what you want to hear, but there is no more us. You made that decision. You married Jenn. You can't come over and expect me to take you back because you made a poor decision. You need to live with that."

"As for Luke, yes, I went to Tahoe with him. We're dating. The boys don't know, and I don't plan on telling them until much later. When and if things become serious."

Josh scowled. "How long has this been going on?"

"That's none of your business," Ellison said.

Her ex shook his head. "How wrong you are. You're dating our son's teacher. Did you stop to think how that will play out if you break up? What kind of favoritism does he give Dash? What's his motive in all this?"

"I have no motive," Luke growled. "Except to get you out of this house as quickly as possible."

"Oh yeah?" Josh said. "You think you can kick me out of my wife's house?"

"Ex-wife," Luke corrected. "Your wife is at your house, probably wondering where the hell you are."

Josh knocked his barstool back and squared his shoulders. Ellison had seen him behave like this once before. He was gearing up for a fight.

Things were getting tense fast, and Ellison had no idea what to do. She couldn't kick Josh out because of the boys, but she couldn't let Luke leave either. The storm was too bad. So they were stuck. The three of them.

"Josh," she said. "Why don't you call Jenn and let her know you're okay. She'll appreciate it." Ellison stared down the two men, daring them to defy her. "Luke, why don't you come out to the living room with me." She turned and walked away. If they want to act like overgrown boys, then they could do it on their own time. Right now, she wanted to enjoy Christmas with her actual boys. The two little ones were waiting in the living room for the adults to start behaving.

Luke was close behind, carrying the three presents. When he saw the tree, he placed the presents under it.

"Who are those for?" Alex asked.

"Santa left them for your mom at my house." He winked at Ellison, and she felt the rage of earlier slip away.

Ellison looked over her shoulder. Josh was nowhere to be found.

"Why'd he do that?" Dash asked

"Because he wanted her to have something for being such a good volunteer in my classroom. Only the classroom is closed for break, so he delivered them to my house instead."

The explanation seemed to appease Dash, and he went back to playing his new video game.

"Are you going to open them, Mom?" Alex asked. He loved everything about opening presents, even if they weren't his own.

"Yeah, Ellison. You going to open them?" Josh leered at her from the doorway.

She raised her eyebrows at Luke, and he nodded.

"You can open them," he said.

Josh's face fell.

Alex brought the first gift over to Ellison. His tiny hands grasped the box, and he shook it before giving it to her. "It makes a swoosh, swoosh sound." Alex was a big believer in box shaking.

With trepidation, Ellison took the box and began to unwrap it. Surely, Luke wouldn't have her open unsuitable presents. Or would he?

"The wrapping is beautiful," Ellison said.

Luke hung his head. "Monica did it."

"Well, she has a knack for it."

Ellison pulled back the layers of tissue and inside was a Burberry scarf. Ellison ran her hands over its cashmere softness. "Thank you," she said. "It's lovely."

Josh scoffed. "How does a teacher come up with money like that?"

Ellison shot Josh a dirty look. "Mind your own business." Then noticing the boys watching them, she added, "They're from Santa, remember?"

The next box was bigger and heavier. She ran her finger under the tape so as not to tear the pretty wrapping paper. She wasn't one to save and reuse paper, but this was too pretty to trash. Underneath the wrapping was a medium box. She couldn't tell what it was from the top, so she took the paper off the sides.

It was oversized headphones.

Ellison looked up at Luke in surprise. "How did Santa know?"

"You work in cafés a lot, so he thought they'd be handy. Help block out the noise and all."

Ellison nodded. "They're perfect. My old ones are getting so ratty. Plus, I'm holding the microphone together with tape."

Josh cleared his throat. "Did you notice my gift?" he asked Luke. "All the flowers? Those are from me."

"Ah, I was wondering why it looked like a florist threw up in here."

Clearly, Luke was taunting Josh, but she didn't care. They could handle it themselves.

Alex handed Ellison the last box. It was considerably smaller than the other two. More like a jewelry box. Her heart sped up as she flipped the box over, looking for the seam.

"That one," Luke said, looking at the boys. "Is from my sister Monica. She really likes your mom."

Ellison's heart slowed a little. She pulled the paper away and lifted the lid. Instead of jewelry there was a small card. Ellison flipped it over and read. It was a membership to the Bliss Spa, good for one facial or massage every month for a year.

"Is she serious?" Ellison asked.

"Very. She thought you might enjoy that," Luke said.

Josh got up from his spot by the fire and yanked it from Ellison's hands. She didn't bother to correct him. Not in front of the kids. "Wow," he said sarcastically. "Your sister must really like Ellison."

Luke stood with his hands resting on the couch behind Ellison. "She does."

Outside, the snow had settled into a soft sprinkling. "Josh," Ellison said. "Maybe it's time for you and the boys to go? The snow has slowed, and Jenn must be worried about you."

Josh turned his head toward the window and then back at Ellison and Luke. "Yeah. Maybe it's time for me to go." He walked over to where the boys sat playing a video game. "C'mon boys."

Dash stood and turned toward Luke. "Mr. Peterson, are you coming too, or are you staying here?"

"I'm staying here for a little while, if that's okay with your mom."

"Are you dating?"

Silence hung over the group. Ellison didn't want to talk about it in front of Josh, and she didn't want Dash telling all the kids at school. But she and Luke had promised to tell him when the time was right.

She knelt down before her two boys. "Mr. Peterson and I are good friends. We've been on a few dates."

"So, he's like your boyfriend?" Alex said.

Ellison looked up at Luke, who smiled down at her. "Yes."

Dash nodded his head. "Thought so." A wide smile bloomed across his face, showing off his missing molar.

"You're okay with it?" Ellison asked.

"Yup." Dash grabbed at Josh's hand. "C'mon, Dad. Let's go."

Alex was already at the front door putting on his snow boots and jacket. "I'm going to make an igloo when we get to your house, Daddy."

Josh nodded absent-mindedly. He walked over to the boys as if in a daze.

"Thanks for the flowers," Ellison said. "It makes the house look more festive."

Her ex-husband narrowed his eyes. "This isn't the end of our conversation. Don't think I don't know my rights."

Ellison bit her tongue. *What rights?* She wanted to scream. *What fucking rights?* But Luke's calm, steady hand on her back kept her emotions in check.

As she waved goodbye to the boys, she couldn't help but feel like something dreadful was coming. Something she couldn't see, but was coming nonetheless.

For the first time in ages, Ellison was afraid of Josh.

Luke kicked off his shoes and sat down on the couch. "Come here," he ordered, and Ellison obliged. She crawled onto his lap. The boys had been gone for an hour or so, and she and Luke had just finished picking up from the Christmas cyclone that had hit her house.

"Something's bothering you," he said.

Ellison sighed and snuggled deeper into the crook of his arm. "It's Josh. He showed up with ten dozen roses." They had thrown them all away. Which was a pity since they were so pretty, but Ellison didn't want gifts from Josh. "Then he said he misses me and the way things used to be. Before you showed up, he was – and I kid you not – trying to get me to either be his mistress or tell him it was okay to leave Jenn."

Luke stroked her hair. "That's unbelievable."

"Right?" Ellison said. "I'm not being crazy that that's messed up?"

"Not at all. But that's not why you're scared of him, is it?"

Ellison shook her head. "He's going to cause problems for us. Either custody issues for me, or job problems for you."

With a shrug, Luke waived off Ellison's concerns. "So, let him. If it will make him go away, let him pretend to be Mr. Bad Ass."

She fluttered her lashes against the stubble of Luke's cheek. "I hope you're right."

A bottle of Cab from Luke's family winery sat on the coffee table. Ellison had opened it a few minutes earlier and still hadn't poured any into the glasses. "Wait here," she said, scampering away from Luke's warm embrace. "I'll be right back." She ran up the stairs and toward her bedroom. From the closet, she selected a short black and cream lace nighty, and after undressing, slipped it over her head. She ran downstairs and into the kitchen. Just for fun, she stopped by the cookie jar and took out two chocolate chip cookies. Something to munch on if they get hungry later.

Ellison paused outside the living room door and readjusted her walk. With one leg in front of the other and a swagger in her hips, she entered the room. Luke was stretched out, waiting for her. She knew her nighty barely covered her backside, and she probably gave Luke a peek of her still-perky ass when she leaned forward to put the cookies on the coffee table.

"Hey," she said in a low, gravelly voice.

Luke sat up. "You look beautiful."

"Thank you." She hesitated. "Can I ask you something?"

"Only if you come here first."

Ellison couldn't resist Luke. She folded into his arms and immediately felt his soft lips on the base of her neck. Her brain was cloudy with lust. All she could think about was this moment.

"What did you want to ask me?" Luke whispered against her bare skin.

"How did you get here? The blizzard was pretty bad." Ellison glanced out the window. Snow still swirled around, but not as bad as earlier.

Luke laid Ellison down on the couch and stretched out next to her. His hand wandered up her thigh and paused on her hip. "I flew on the family jet. That was the easy part. Finding a taxi to bring me here was another story. No one wanted to venture out into that mess. But I needed to get here. I needed to see my girl."

She shifted a little to give Luke better access to wherever he desired to go.

"Your girl," she said.

"Hopefully, *only* mine. Josh did sound rather convincing."

Ellison laughed. "I don't want him. I haven't since the day I met you." Her fingers slid under the edge of Luke's shirt and bunched the material up. She moved down and kissed the bare spot just under his navel.

Luke groaned and placed his hand in her hair, his fingertips massaging her temple.

"Oh Ellison, you don't know how good that feels."

"Tell me," she answered, licking him and chasing it with a breath of hot air. "How much do you like it?"

"Too much," Luke said, starting to sit up.

"Should I stop?" Ellison said, looking up at Luke and making her eyes as wide as possible. "I don't want to hurt you," she teased.

"Oh, God, woman. You're going to drive me crazy."

"We wouldn't want that, now would we?" Ellison kissed his chiseled stomach again. "Merry Christmas."

36

NOT YOU TOO

The first day back to school after a break was always hectic. This particular morning was no different. While Ellison stood in the kitchen making PB&Js, Dash ran around looking for his socks, and Alex moped over his breakfast. He had insisted on strawberry Pop Tarts, but when she gave them to him – because, after all, it was too early in the morning to be fighting over breakfast – he balked and said he wanted blueberry ones instead. Well, they didn't have blueberry, and besides, she'd already made the strawberry. Alex begrudgingly took the plate of offensive Pop Tarts and sat at the table, staring at them. So far, he'd managed to nibble off an edge.

"Hurry up, Alex. You're going to make us all late, or you're not going to get breakfast at all."

"Mommy," her son whined. "It's not fair."

Ellison dropped the sandwiches into baggies and the baggies into lunch boxes. "Life isn't fair," she said. "Now get moving." She walked over to the table and removed the plate of Pop Tarts. "There. Now you don't have to eat them." She bit off a huge piece and chewed dramatically.

"Mom!" Alex shouted.

"What? I'm not letting them go to waste."

Alex slid off his chair and slinked into the foyer. Dash was still running around trying to find his socks. Ellison went into the laundry room and pulled open the dryer door. Clothes sat unfolded and tumbled inside. In her past life, she would have been appalled by her laziness, but in this version of her life, she didn't care. She dug around quickly, looking for two socks that matched, and when that didn't go well, she just searched for two socks that would fit Dash. Once she retrieved the socks – one black and one blue – she hustled back to Dash and tossed them at him.

"They don't match," Dash said.

"I know," she answered. "But it's the best I can do."

Dash shrugged and put on the socks. At least one of her boys was cooperating this morning.

While the boys finished getting ready, Ellison hurried upstairs to brush her teeth and hair and generally make herself presentable. Drop-off was always such a fashion show. Turning up in flannel PJ bottoms and a fitted tee were a no-no. She yanked her skinny jeans up and pulled a soft wrap sweater over her head. With a swipe of lip gloss and mascara, she was done. Hopefully, she'd see Luke, but the chances were slim. Teachers didn't usually show up to drop-off.

"C'mon, boys," she yelled, running down the stairs. Both her sons were in the foyer waiting for her. "Looks like you beat me. Good job!"

They trudged out to the car like men on the way to the electric chair. Dash's head hung low, and Alex kept stopping and looking around. "Why can't we have a snow day?" Dash asked.

"You just had more than two weeks off, and you want more?"

Dash turned around. "I can't wait to be a grown up and do whatever I want."

"It's not that great, buddy. Trust me." Ellison held the Suburban door open, and the boys crawled inside. "I've been a grownup and a kid, and I largely prefer being a kid."

"Yeah, but you didn't have to live in two houses. You didn't have divorced parents and a wicked step-mother."

"Dashiel Garret Brooks, you stop that right now. Jenn isn't that bad." She was worse, but Ellison didn't say that out loud. It was important that she, Josh, and Jenn present a united front.

Josh. Ugh. Her stomach soured. So far, he hadn't made any problems for Ellison and Luke, but who knew what he had planned.

She hopped into the car and steered it down the street and around the corner. The line for parking was around the block, but moving fast. Not all parents stayed for morning announcements, but most of the stay-at-home/work-from-home moms did. It was, just like at their old school, a competition to see who was more of a superstar mom. Who could volunteer more, who could balance home life with kid activities better, and who could remain standing at the end of the day and still not have a hair out of place.

Ellison used to excel in all categories, but she'd learned over the course of the past year that those things didn't really matter. As long as she got the boys fed, dressed, and to school in one piece every day, she was doing her job.

She pulled into a parking spot and hopped out of the SUV. The boys did the same. The three of them made their way into the school gym, where the principal stood on the stage. Seeing their friends, the boys ran off without goodbye hugs or kisses. Ellison pressed her back into the wall and scanned the room for Luke. Of course, he wasn't there.

Oh well.

She'd stop by his classroom later, before she picked the boys up from their enrichment classes. Maybe give him a little surprise.

Ellison looked around one last time and waved goodbye to Alex. Dash had disappeared into a huddle of boys and didn't notice her.

She slinked along the back wall, hoping not to draw attention to herself. The principal had started announcements, and it was rude to leave in the middle of them.

As she stepped out of the gym door, she bumped straight into a familiar chest.

Luke.

"Hey, Ellison. Sneaking out early?" he teased.

"Long day of work ahead of me. I had a few offers come in despite it being the holidays. I'm hoping to close a deal today." She'd been working steadily since selling Susan her home.

Luke grinned. "I'm not surprised. How could anyone say no to you?"

Ellison blushed and swallowed hard. She forced her voice to sound confident. "I'll see you around four. When I pick up the boys."

"Oh will you?"

"Yes," she said, walking away and making sure there was a little extra bounce in her step. "Be ready for me. We're going to celebrate if my clients accept an offer."

Luke let out a hearty laugh. "I'll be ready for you, Ellison Brooks. I certainly will."

"Do you ever work?" Ellison asked Andi. The two women sat in Ellison's favorite café facing each other.

Andi tossed her hair back and laughed. "Oh, Elle. If you only knew a fraction of the bullshit I put up with each day. Have I ever told you, I'm the only woman on my team? It's all guy stuff, twenty-four seven. It's like living in a frat house."

"Which is why you being here at eleven in the morning is even more puzzling."

Andi shrugged. "Work break."

"Something doesn't smell right," Ellison said.

"Okay, fine," Andi exhaled loudly. "I took a mental health day."

"What's going on?" Ellison asked.

Andi closed her eyes. "You know how I was gone most of December?"

"Yeah."

"Well, I was on assignment – don't ask, I can't tell you – and the days were really long, Elle. Really long." Andi studied her nails. "Anyway, I slept with my boss."

Ellison's jaw dropped open. "Shit."

"Indeed." Andi wrung her hands together. "And now it's all awkward and uncomfortable."

"Andi," Ellison said, not really wanting to know the answer but needing to know. "Is he married?"

Her best friend buried her head in her hands. "Yes." She peeked up at Ellison. "Don't hate me."

Rage and hurt filled Ellison. How could Andi do something like that? How?

"Tell me it was only once," Ellison said, looking for some kind of silver lining. Like the number of times made any difference.

Andi shook her head. "It was the whole month we were gone." Tears filled her eyes. "I don't know what I was thinking."

"It's not still going on, is it?" Ellison fought the urge to shake Andi. How could she do something like this after knowing what Ellison had gone through with Josh?

Andi kept her head down. "No, I broke it off."

"So now you're here because..."

Andi looked panicked. "Because I can't face Steve. He's my boss. What am I supposed to do?"

"Suck it up and put on your big girl undies."

"Easy for you to say. Did you forget the part where I said I work in a frat house? All the guys on my team know."

Ellison huffed. "Oh, Andi. I'm so sorry, but you created this mess. You need to clean it up."

Her best friend blew into her coffee. "Just tell me you don't hate me."

"I don't hate you," Ellison said. "I hate what you did, but I don't hate you."

Relief filled Andi's eyes. "I'm swearing off my man-eating ways. No more one night stands. No more late-night booty calls. I'm done. I'm too old for that shit."

"How realistic is that?" Ellison asked.

Andi hung her head. "Not very."

"Just swear off married guys, and you'll be fine."

With a giant sigh, Ellison's friend rested her chin on her hand.

"Not to change the topic, but let's change the topic. How are things with Luke?"

Andi had been gone for most of December and had been mostly out of reach except for a few days before Christmas when she'd been home. She also missed New Year's despite promising Ellison a night she wouldn't forget. But more importantly, it meant she hadn't heard about the Luke-Josh debacle. As Ellison quickly filled her in, Andi's mouth kept getting lower and lower until she gaped at her.

"You've got to be kidding me," Andi said. "Josh actually stayed and was upset Luke showed up. What is wrong with that man?"

"Oh, I haven't told you the best part. Josh wants to get back together. I can't make out if he wants me as a mistress, or he wants me back as his wife, but he's on this serious memory lane kick."

"Screw him. He made his decision," Andi said, her voice full of force.

"That's what I said."

A devious smile danced across Andi's face. Her distraught demeanor from before had evaporated. "And what kind of Christmas present did you give Luke?"

Ellison wanted to tell Andi all the dirty details, but instead said, "Well, he was a very good boy this year."

Andi laughed and flailed her arms, nearly knocking her drink over. "Enough said." She grabbed her drink and sipped. "What we need is a night out. How about tonight?"

Part of Ellison was hoping to see Luke tonight, but she hadn't seen Andi in so long, she felt the need to catch up. "Sure. What time?"

"Seven?"

"Sounds like a plan," Ellison said.

Andi stood up. Concern touched the corners of her eyes. "Time to get back to work. I'm the team slut and might as well suck it up. Can't hide forever."

Ellison held up her hands. "Stop slut-shaming yourself. You did wrong. Go face the music. And for what it's worth, I still love you."

Andi nodded. "Thanks, Elle."

"No problem."

37

TEACHER'S PET

Andi's situation weighed heavily on Ellison when she knocked on Luke's classroom door. He threw the door open as if he were waiting for her, and his hands darted out and pulled her into the room. Then he slammed the door shut and pressed Ellison against it. She was supposed to be surprising him, but so far, he had the upper hand.

"You know what I've been dreaming about?" Luke said, nibbling on Ellison's ear. The classroom seemed bare without all the kids running around.

"Me, naked, on a beach somewhere?" she offered.

"That's one of those things that sounds better in theory than it is in practice. Too much sand in sensitive places."

Ellison laughed. "Then I don't know."

"You, me, and this desk," Luke said with a twinkle in his eye.

"That sounds like a recipe for getting in trouble." Ellison liked being a little dangerous, but this seemed like it could go south very quickly.

"I've locked the door."

Ellison glanced at said door and grinned. The idea of messing around in Luke's classroom did turn her on, and she seemed to lose all sense when around Luke.

"Let's do it," she said, surprising herself as she walked toward the desk.

When she turned around, Luke's gray eyes fixed on her, and she melted. Her hand reached out to the desk to keep from tipping over.

Luke crossed the room, and his gaze never left her. He was devouring her. "Did you close on that house?"

"I did," she brushed her hand up her leg, pulling her skirt a little higher. "We should celebrate."

"We should indeed," Luke growled.

He lifted Ellison by the waist and sat her on the desk, bunching her skirt up around her thighs. Luke pushed it higher and kneeled before her. He began running his hand up and down her inner thigh before slipping off her panties.

"What are you doing?" she said breathlessly.

"Enjoying you."

Ellison moaned and leaned back on the desk, knocking a stack of papers to the ground. She braced herself on her elbows so that she could watch Luke. His tongue trailed along her thigh, and she closed her eyes, enjoying the moment.

BANG.

Both Ellison and Luke jumped. Someone was knocking on Luke's door. Ellison hopped off the desk and pulled down her skirt while Luke crossed the room. She kicked her panties under the desk and hoped no one noticed them.

Bang, bang, bang. Luke threw the door open and was greeted by Dash and Alex. "My mom told us to meet her here," Dash said.

Oh shit. She'd forgotten about that.

"I'm here, honey," Ellison said, hurrying across the room, realizing too late that she didn't have her panties.

"I'm hungry," Alex said, and Ellison cast a sad glance at Luke.

"To be continued?" she asked.

"Absolutely." He grinned at her.

"What were you doing?" Dash asked.

Ellison felt her face turning red, and thankfully, Luke answered for her. "We were working on the reader's corner."

Dash's face fell. "Oh."

"Why?" Ellison chuckled. "Should we have been doing something else?"

Dash shook his head. "No."

Ellison stared at her son. Something was up. It wasn't like Dash to be visibly disappointed.

About halfway home, Ellison realized she hadn't told Luke about leaving her panties behind. Panicked, she pulled into her driveway and began texting him.

"I'll be right in," she told the boys. They scurried out of the Suburban and up the front stairs into the townhouse.

Her fingers flew over the keypad.

Still at school?

No. Why?

I left my panties under your desk.

The cleaning crew will have fun with that.

LUKE!!!

. . .

I'll go back and retrieve them. They were red lace with black bows, if I recall correctly.

How many panties do you have in your room???

More than I should.

She laughed out loud. Busted by her kids and possibly a cleaning crew. Such was the story of her life.

Ellison hustled into the house, dropped her keys on the counter, and removed her coat. Dash stood at the fridge.

"There's nothing to eat," he complained.

"I know. I have to go grocery shopping." It was a toss-up on what she hated more: laundry or grocery shopping. Since she hadn't had the boys last week, she had lived off Lean Cuisine on the nights she hadn't gone out to dinner with Luke.

"God, Mom," Dash said. "Can't you at least have food to feed us? Jenn always has food. Always."

Ellison gritted her teeth. She didn't know what was worse. Dash comparing her to Jenn or his mouthiness. "Dashiel Garrett Brooks don't you dare speak to me like that."

Her son looked down at his shoes. He mumbled something.

"What was that?"

"You were probably too busy with Mr. Peterson to remember Alex and me."

Okay, now he was guilt tripping her, plain and simple. "No. Mr. Peterson has nothing to do with this. I've been busy selling houses and didn't have time to grocery shop."

Alex skidded into the room on stocking feet. "Can we make cookies?"

"That sounds like a great idea." Ellison looked at Dash. "Can you wait that long?"

He sighed. "Forget it." He turned and ran up the stairs.

"What's with him?" Ellison said out loud, to herself.

"He's still mad about Jenn's baby. Dad said we need to help pick a name, but Dash doesn't want to."

Great. No wonder Dash was acting out.

"Sweetheart," she said to Alex. "Get the flour and sugar out. We're going to make cookies with or without Dash."

Her youngest son set about retrieving the items, and she found a bag of chocolate chips in the back of the cupboard. When all the ingredients were assembled, Ellison pulled out the stand mixer.

"Okay, Alex-bear, I'll turn on the oven. I want you to follow step two."

They often cooked together, and Ellison's friends – her old ones – were always amazed by how much she let Alex do on his own. Ellison's philosophy was that they'd never learn if they didn't have the opportunity to try and fail. Luckily for her, Alex was a good little baker. Chocolate chip cookies were a no brainer for him. Even if he was only eight.

Her phone pinged, and she dusted her flour-covered hands over her apron before reaching for it.

Found your panties. Want me to drop them off?

Her fingers flew over the keyboard.

Now isn't a good time. Dash is having a meltdown.

Okay. I'll keep them until next time.

Xoxo she typed, then erased it for being too presumptuous – they hadn't said the big "L" word yet. She looked at the screen and said, "Fuck it."

Xoxo – see you soon, she wrote. After all, what were a few kisses when you intimately knew someone's body?

"Mom?" A little voice called. She stuck her head around the corner, and Dash stood on the stairs. His eyes were red and puffy.

"Yes?"

"I'm sorry."

Ellison held out her arms, and Dash readily folded into her. His body shook with sobs. "What's going on with you, Buddy?"

Dash pulled away and wiped the back of his hand across his nose. Ellison didn't bother to tell him to get a tissue. "Dad and Jenn will forget about us once the baby comes."

"Daddy will never forget you."

"Yes he will."

Ellison closed her eyes and tried to pretend she was a ten-year-old boy. "Is that why you were so angry about Mr. Peterson?"

Dash nodded. "Kind of. I mean, what if you like him more than Alex and me?"

"Oh baby, I could never love anyone more than I love the two of you."

Dash softened. "Dad doesn't want you dating Mr. Peterson. I heard him and Jenn talking. He's going to tell on you."

Ellison scrunched her brows together. "Tell on us?"

"He's emailing the principal."

All the air rushed out of Ellison's lungs, and she made a weird strangling noise. *Why would Josh do that? Didn't she deserve to be happy? Was he really that jealous?*

"You heard him say this?"

"Uh huh. He and Jenn were saying that it's bad for me, and I need to be in another class. Why is it bad?"

Ellison hugged her boy closer. "It's not. It's just that some people might think you get treated differently because we're dating."

Dash shook his head. "That's stupid."

"I know."

She swatted him on the backside. "Now go help Alex with the cookies."

When Dash was fully engrossed in the activity, she picked up her phone again and called Luke.

"Hello, gorgeous."

"Hey," Ellison said. "I don't want to alarm you, but Josh is planning on emailing Ms. Sylvian about us."

Silence.

"Luke?"

"I think he already did. I have a meeting with her tomorrow before school."

Ellison's heart plummeted. "Are you okay?"

Luke breathed heavily into the phone. "Yeah. I just hope she's willing to hear what I have to say."

"Me, too," Ellison whispered. "Me, too."

38

OVER IT

The babysitter was late. Andi, Susan – who Andi loved – and Ellison sat in her living room, drinking Luke's family's chardonnay. "This is really good," Andi said.

Ellison nodded. "They grow their own grapes and make their own wine. That's unusual, but it gives them total control over the whole process."

"Look at you, Miss Wine."

"If you spent a week with Luke's family, you'd know a thing or two about the wine industry too." Ellison put her glass down. "How was the rest of your workday?"

Andi's normally I-don't-give-a-fuck attitude evaporated. "Tough, but I got through it. No one on the team is talking about it outright, which I guess is okay. But I know they are gossiping behind my back."

Susan leaned in. "Did something happen?"

"Nothing much. I was a dumb-ass." Andi gave Ellison a look that told her to drop it. Susan wasn't completely in the inner circle yet. She set her wine glass on the coffee table. "Enough about me. How was your day?"

"Well I forgot my-"

The doorbell rang, and Ellison jumped up to answer it. She checked her watch. Fifteen minutes late.

"Hi, Ms. Brooks," the sitter said. Her name was Annabelle, and she was seventeen even though she looked about fourteen.

"Hi, Annabelle. I've already put the boys to bed. Just remind Dash at eight that it's lights-out time, or he'll stay up all night drawing comics. Alex should be sound asleep by now."

Annabelle followed Ellison to the living room. "Feel free to eat whatever you want. There's Coke in the fridge and snacks in the pantry."

"Great," Annabelle said, fishing her phone out of her backpack. "I have a ton of homework tonight."

The poor girl's backpack was stuffed. Ellison couldn't imagine her boys having that much homework.

"Ready, ladies?" she asked.

Andi was already up and carrying two wine glasses. "Can't let this go to waste," she said, pounding the rest of her wine. She handed Ellison her glass. "Bottoms up," Andi said. Ellison eyed the wine before tipping her head back and letting the delicious liquid pour down her throat. "That's a girl!" Andi said, laughing. "A way to kick off our night."

Ellison's head swam with images of the last time they went out to a bar. That was when she met Luke, and she hoped Andi or Susan had such good luck tonight. One could hope, right? As they walked to Andi's car, she said, "What were you telling us? About forgetting something?"

Ellison stopped next to the car door and laughed. "My panties. I left them in Luke's classroom. Luckily, he went back and retrieved them."

Andi burst out laughing. "That. Is the best thing I've heard. All. Day."

"Well this isn't. Josh seemingly wrote a letter to the principal about my and Luke's relationship."

"Oh." Susan shook her head. "Why?"

Ellison gritted her teeth. "He's hell-bent on getting back at me for some unknown offense."

"Could be that he wants you back," Susan said.

Ellison climbed into the passenger side of Andi's car. "That boat has long since sailed. I mean, am I missing something? *He* divorced *me*."

"Josh wants what he can't have," Andi offered. "And from the sound of it, he sees Luke as the obstacle to having you."

Ellison knotted her hands together. "But why does he have to go to the principal? Why can't he leave it between the two of us?"

"A jealous ex is the worst. I see it all the time at work," Susan said from the backseat. "Completely irrational."

"Wonderful."

A car raced past them, and Andi sped up. She pulled up next to the car at the stoplight, and seeing that it was a cute man, blew him a kiss.

Had she really learned nothing from the boss debacle?

The parking lot of the lounge was packed for a Monday night. Andi circled the lot twice before sliding her sports car between an SUV and a BMW sedan.

"What is going on here?" Susan asked as they walked toward the building.

Andi shrugged. "Monday is the new Thursday?"

"Hopefully, we'll be able to get a booth." Ellison yanked the door open and pulled back the midnight blue curtain separating the entrance from the lounge area.

And she froze.

There, along the far wall, sat Eve, Kate, Julia...and Jenn. Along with a handful of other women Ellison recognized from the Club and Greenbriar Elementary.

But the four women – -her former friends and Jenn – had their bodies turned inward, toward one another like a closed-off box.

Is this how I used to look? she wondered. *Did we isolate ourselves from the rest of the world?* She watched the four women drink and laugh, and an ache pounded at her heart. Part of her wanted so badly to belong to their world again. To think of nothing but recipes, and playdates, and sex lives. To go out on girls' nights and girls' weekends without worrying who was going to watch the boys.

She wanted to live her life out loud again, not in constant fear of something going wrong.

"Ellison?" Andi had her by the arm. "Do you want to go?"

Waves of nausea washed over her. *Did she want to go?* Yes, her body screamed. But no. No. She didn't really want to leave. She wanted them – her former friends – to see her. To see how far she'd come. She wasn't scared, timid Ellison anymore, even if Josh was threatening her.

"I'm going over to say 'Hi,'" Ellison answered.

Andi swung around and blocked her path. "I don't think that's a good idea. They're having Jenn's baby shower."

All her life Andi had been there for her, and because of Ellison, Andi knew these women well. So when she told Ellison to stop, Ellison should have listened.

But she didn't.

She stepped around Andi and bee-lined for the group of four. Memories came crashing down on her. Was it really only a year ago that she sat with them, bad-mouthing Jenn as a home wrecker while downing vodka tonics? And these women, hadn't they promised to stand by her through thick and thin?

Jenn saw her first, and she paused mid-laugh. The resulting sound was a cross between a gurgle and a choke.

Three other sets of eyes turned on her. She could feel Andi at her back, as always, ready to leap in when necessary. Susan wasn't far behind. Was she committing social suicide by being seen with Ellison?

"Hey, you!" Eve exclaimed. Of the four, she seemed the least rattled by Ellison's appearance. "What are you doing here? Meeting that handsome teacher?"

Ah. So Jenn had been gossiping about her. Wonderful.

With fingernails pressing into her palms, Ellison said, "Andi, Susan, and I are having drinks and catching up."

Eve scanned Ellison from head-to-toe before turning her gaze on Andi and Susan. "Ah. I see. Your plus one is now a plus two." She glanced at her tablemates. "Why don't we scooch over and make some room for Andi and Ellison? And what's your name again? I've seen you at school, so we must have met."

"Susan. Susan Dembs."

Ellison's blood ran hot. She didn't want to sit with these traitors. And she most definitely didn't want to sit with Jenn. Her gaze fluttered down to Jenn's round, protruding stomach. It was covered in ribbons and bows. A bunch of presents sat on the table in front of her.

Pregnant before the divorce decree was even issued. *I guess that's one way to get the man*, Ellison thought. "Sorry I didn't bring a gift. I didn't know it was a requirement."

"Sit. Sit," Eve insisted. "We're all friends here, aren't we?"

No, Ellison thought. We're a bunch of traitors, a whore, and three friends.

Andi grabbed at Ellison's arm and said, "Don't mind if we do," before dragging Ellison behind her and into the circular booth. Susan flanked her other side.

No one uttered a sound. Shock flitted across Julia's face, while Kate fidgeted with her handbag, and Jenn shot death rays at the new arrivals. Which Ellison, for some reason, found quite funny.

"So," Andi said, oblivious to how much they weren't wanted – or she was playing dumb which was more likely. "What's been going on, ladies? I haven't seen you since...oh I don't know...the Gala?" She glanced at the table of gifts. "Looks like you're having a baby shower."

As she said the words, Ellison realized that by standing by her side, Andi had lost friendships too. If that's what you could call them. Real friends don't ditch you when you're down and then befriend the other woman.

"Oh my gosh," Kate said. "That's right. I mean, we barely got to talk at the Gala." She paused. "You know how it is, don't you, Ellison? Always running from one task to the next, never having a moment for yourself. Kids. Family. Sports. It's just so much, you know?"

Once upon a time, when Ellison was living what she thought was a fairytale, she would have agreed. Her life then existed of school meetings, volunteer work, drinks with friends, dinner parties to plan and attend, work, and of course, her boys. She was busy, busy, busy every moment of every day. Weekends were taken up by sports, errands, and open houses. Weekdays with work, committee meetings, home-work, and dinners.

She had had, she realized, no life. At least not one of her own.

Ellison looked around the table at her perfectly polished, perfectly kept frenemies, and she smiled.

That life was eons ago. Brushed aside and left for dead.

And honestly, she didn't want it back.

"So," Eve said. "The word on the street is that you're dating that hot teacher I saw you with. The one you denied kissing."

Ellison knotted her hands under the table. Josh had already sent the email. The damage was done. No use lying about it. "I am."

"And you went to Tahoe with him?" Eve's voice rose, like she couldn't believe someone would actually be interested in Ellison. Like she was a sad sack or something.

"I did."

"Was it romantic? I think being bundled up in a cute cabin with a fire roaring would be so romantic. Or did you have to stay at one of the hotels?" Eve was fishing for information. Well she wasn't going to get any. At least not what she wanted.

"It was incredibly romantic. We took a sleigh ride late one after-noon, and it was beautiful. The snow sparkled in the moonlight."

"He's Dash's teacher, isn't he?" asked Julia.

"Yes."

"Well that's convenient," said Eve. " Don't you work in the class-room or something?"

Ellison wasn't going to give them any details for Jenn to report back to Josh.

"I do work in the classroom on Wednesdays, but I keep it professional."

"You know," Andi said, bouncing around in her seat. "I did the most unprofessional, stupid thing, and I could really use all of your good advice."

Don't say it. Don't do it. Andi's mouth opened, and Ellison willed her to shut it. Don't do this for me.

"I slept with my boss."

BAM. All interest in Ellison and Luke evaporated.

"Oh my God. Tell me more," Eve said, leaning in and jumping up a little in her seat.

Susan shot Ellison an "Oh No She Didn't" look which she quickly erased and replaced with a blank façade. It was the perfect attorney reaction.

Andi touched Ellison's hand under the table, letting her know it was okay. These women already thought Andi was promiscuous. Still, Ellison didn't need her to fall on the sword for her, but she appreciated it.

As Andi launched into story after story of her wild sexcapades, the other four women sat in various degrees of shock.

"You mean he's married?" Kate said before clasping her hand over her mouth. Next to her, Jenn shifted uncomfortably.

"He is, but surely I'm not the first person to sleep with my married boss. Right, Jenn?"

Jenn's face flushed red with anger. "This is my baby shower with *my* friends. You three can leave now."

"Not a problem," Ellison said, waiting for Susan to stand up and let her out of the booth. "I wouldn't want to interrupt your time with *your* friends. Just make sure to check your back for stab marks. They're sure to be there."

Andi laughed. "Later ladies."

With that, Ellison Brooks, Andi McClaren, and Susan Dembs successfully ruined Jenn's baby shower. Which, to be honest, was merely an annoyance compared to the disruption she had caused in Ellison's life.

But whatever. It felt good.

39

LAW AND ORDER

Ellison's gut would not stop rolling. She'd barely slept, and her eyes burned. Luke was meeting with Ms. Sylvian right now. It took all she had to focus on making the boys' lunches and getting them out the door. She didn't bother to put on a cute outfit or brush her hair straight. Instead she tossed it into a messy topknot.

The drive to school was excruciating. After getting home from her night out with Andi and Susan, and paying the babysitter, Ellison called Luke. It was only ten, and she had hoped he was still awake.

He had been, and they talked until two in the morning. At one point, he asked if he could come over, and as tempting as it was, she wasn't ready for the boys to see that side of their relationship yet. So they'd stayed on the phone, working through all the different scenarios that could go down today.

Why, when every other area of her life was going great, did something have to go wrong?

She tried batting away her fears, but the worst, and the most realistic, was Luke losing his job – and him maybe deciding she wasn't worth it.

Would he do that? He once said he'd pick her over his job, but when push came to shove, would he really? And could she ask that of him?

Bile rose in Ellison's throat just thinking about it. Granted, it wouldn't impact him monetarily, but Luke was great with the kids and losing him would likely set the class back. He had to make an argument for that. He had to.

When she walked into the school, heads snapped up, and eyes followed her. "That's her," Ellison heard someone whisper. "That's the woman who's dating the teacher."

It was like living a nightmare all over again. When Josh left her, she showed up at school the next day, and eyes full of pity greeted her. Everyone had whispered as she approached, and she had heard a few moms say, "Poor thing." Like now, the parents then didn't know what to do with her. So they stared and whispered.

But unlike then, when she had a sneaking suspicion who told everyone – Eve, of course – she had no idea how the parents of this new school had found out. Who had told them about Luke and her?

"Mom," Dash said. "Why is everyone pretending they're not staring at us?"

Ah, so it wasn't her imagination. "I don't know, honey," she lied. "Maybe because we look like rock stars?"

Dash didn't laugh. In fact, he marched ahead of Ellison like he was embarrassed to be seen with her.

"Hi," said a woman Ellison vaguely recognized. She stepped in front her. "Are you Ellison?"

"Yes."

"Oh. So is it true? Have you been dating Mr. Peterson?"

Ellison's hands shook, and she pushed past the woman. How did all these people know? She kept walking and didn't know exactly where she was going until she arrived at the office. "Ms. Brooks!" the lady behind the front desk exclaimed. "What are you doing here?"

"I'm looking for Luke."

"I'm afraid he's been put on leave," the secretary answered.

"What?" Ellison said in disbelief. "Why?"

"Oh, I think you know why. We have strict policies and procedures."

Ellison blinked back tears. What had she and Luke done?

———

Luke wasn't picking up his cell which made Ellison even more frantic. What if he realized she wasn't worth losing his job over? What if he had changed his mind about her?

She redialed his number for the twentieth time. Finally, he answered.

"Hey, babe," he said, his voice calm. "How are you holding up?"

"Me?" she said. "I'm not the one placed on leave."

"Oh, that." He sighed. "I have to attend an emergency school board session this afternoon."

"What? Why?"

"My attorney feels my contract is unclear on whether dating a parent is rights for termination. It's not written particularly well."

"Then why are they doing this?" Ellison didn't hide her anger.

"Because Josh complained. And so did a few other parents."

Ellison swallowed the lump in her throat. "How did *they* find out?"

"Honestly, from what I can gather, Dash told some of the kids I was your boyfriend." He paused. "And they told their parents."

Ellison wanted to cry. "What are you going to do?"

"I'm going to go to that meeting with my attorney and point out that I technically have done nothing wrong. Or at least we believe so based on the ambiguous language of the contract."

Ellison sighed. "Can you meet me at Peet's for coffee?" Since she spent most of her time working in coffee shops, she knew which ones would be the least busy at this time of day. They needed some privacy, but not at her house. He couldn't be seen there. Not today, anyway.

"I don't think that's wise, Elle."

"But I'm worried about you. And your job. We can't lose you as a teacher. We can't."

"Awww," Luke said slowly. "Thanks for saying that. It's exactly what I needed to hear."

Ellison took a deep breath in. "What are we going to do about us? About all the judgmental parents?"

"Whoa." Luke said, his voice calm and steady. "Let's deal with one thing at a time. I need to prepare for my hearing."

"Who's going to be there?" she asked.

"It's an open hearing, so anyone can attend."

"What time?"

Luke hesitated. Maybe he didn't want her there? Maybe that wasn't a good idea? After all, she was part of the problem.

Finally, after a long moment, he said, "Four."

"I'll be there," Ellison said.

———

Anxiety coursed through Ellison as she pulled into the School Board's administrative building. She sat in her car, dabbing at the tears sitting the corners of her eyes. She couldn't very well go in with mascara streaming down her face or raccoon eyes. She needed to look polished and pulled together. So no tears.

She needed confidence, so she grabbed her phone from the bottom of her handbag and called Susan.

"Hello?"

"Hi, Susan, it's Ellison. Do you have a minute?"

"Of course. What's going on?"

"Luke has a hearing before the school board in a few minutes to determine whether he'll be fired for dating me or not."

"Oh," Susan said. "It's not in his contract?"

"Not specifically spelled out according to Luke."

"Then I wouldn't worry. It might get tied up in legalities for a while, but if it's unclear, he should be okay."

That's the reassurance Ellison needed. "Thanks, Susan. I'm a wreck. I have to get inside."

"Call me and let me know what happened, okay?"

"Will do. Thanks, again."

After they hung up, Ellison dialed Andi. She was supposed to pick the boys up from school, and Ellison wanted to make sure she had done so.

"Hey, Momma," Andi said. "We've got everything under control over here, if that's why you're calling."

"It is. Are they doing their homework?"

There were some funny noises in the background before Andi answered. "They are now. Snacks have been had, and homework is getting done."

"Good," said Ellison. She watched a group of well-dressed women enter the building.

Fabulous. This was going to be a spectator sport for the moms at school. And everyone was going to know who she was and the details of her relationship with Luke. No more flying under the radar.

"I've gotta go," Ellison said. "Make sure Alex doesn't OD on candy."

Andi laughed. "Aye aye, Captain."

With shaking hands, Ellison opened her car door and exited the vehicle. She stood there for a moment in the freezing cold, unable to move. The last thing she wanted was to make things worse for Luke, but she wanted to show him her support.

Fuck them all, she thought. *I'm not ashamed of my relationship.*

She slammed the SUV door shut and walked confidently up to the building, before climbing the short flight of stairs to the entrance.

The auditorium was a mad house. People were everywhere. Ellison scanned the crowd until she spotted Luke sitting with a man she assumed was his attorney at a lone table toward the front of the room. The whole set up reminded her of a courtroom. Which she guessed it was in a way.

Luke's attorney had his head down and was scribbling away on a legal pad. Hopefully, he'd come prepared.

Ellison slinked into a seat toward the back of the room. She pulled her knit hat lower on her brow and kept her arms crossed. Even like this, some of the parents who glanced in her direction pointed and whispered.

Was it going to be like this forever, or for as long as she and Luke dated?

There was a commotion near the doorway, and Ellison turned to see what was happening. Josh and a very pregnant Jenn had just entered the room. Josh spoke animatedly with another man while Jenn stood there, looking uncomfortable both physically and mentally.

One-by-one, the school board members filled into the room. They took their seats and a gavel banged on the heavy oak bench the members sat behind.

"Silence, please," a female member said. She had long, stringy, graying hair and the look of someone's spinster aunt. "These are official proceedings, and we ask that the audience remain quiet."

A few murmurs circulated, but almost everyone settled down. Josh and Jenn took seats up near the front, behind Luke. Josh surveyed the room a few times, like he was looking for someone. Probably Ellison. No doubt he'd seen her car in the parking lot.

"Luke Peterson, we asked you here today because there is concern that your impartiality toward the children in your class has been compromised by your involvement with one of the mothers." The stringy haired woman spoke, and Ellison hated the way she over-enunciated her words. Drawing them out. Making them hang in the air. "Your contract prohibits this."

Luke's lawyer spoke. "I'm afraid it doesn't. It's ambiguously written."

The woman leaned forward. "Do you have a copy of the contract?"

"We do."

"From section 4.2.1. 'Teachers and administrators should refrain from fraternizing with parents above and beyond what is deemed necessary.'"

Luke's lawyer nodded. "The problem is the language. It says 'should,' not must. Also, what is deemed necessary? Who defines that and how?"

The woman's gaze settled on Luke. "Are you, in fact, involved with a parent from your class."

Luke grasped the microphone. "I am."

"And you began dating when?"

Luke and his lawyer leaned into each other and whispered. Finally, Luke said, "We met in August, before school started, but we didn't begin dating until Christmas."

"So you met before you knew her son was in your class."

Luke cleared his throat. "That was a happy surprise."

The woman shifted. "Have you ever given preference to the boy? For example, help tutor him or raise his grade because of your relationship with his mother?"

"When he was suspended from school, I did visit him and went over what we'd learned that week. I also moved a science test so he wouldn't miss it."

The members of the board scribbled away on their notepads. "Would you have done this for any other student?" a man wearing a Duke sweatshirt asked. He was in his sixties, and probably had grandchildren in the school district.

Luke's shoulders rose and sunk. "I don't know. I haven't been put in that position."

"Well let's pretend you have been, shall we?" the woman said. "Would you do the same for another student."

"That's speculation," Luke's attorney said.

"It's okay." Luke leaned closer to the microphone. "I'd like to believe I would."

"You believe you haven't shown the student in question any preferential treatment?" the woman asked.

Luke and his attorney conferred again. Luke leaned forward, into the microphone. "I don't believe I have."

Duke man surveyed the crowd. "By all accounts, you are a wonderful teacher. Your quarterly review was outstanding, and parental feedback excellent. I'm not sure how I feel about your personal life crossing over into your professional life, but if there is nothing in our contracts expressly forbidding it, I don't understand why we're here."

The stringy-haired woman answered. "The contract clearly states-"

"Does it?" Duke man asked. "It sounds unclear if you ask me."

Principal Sylvian stood up. "If I may?"

The stringy-haired woman nodded. "Of course."

"The reason we are here is because of parent complaints and concerns. Namely from the student's father, but we have had others."

The Duke man shook his head. "I think this needs to be handled between the parents and not here, wasting our time. I call for a vote."

"Second," said a woman in a lime green top.

"All in favor of having Mr. Peterson return to the classroom," the stringy-haired woman said.

Five of the seven hands went up. Ms. Stringy Hair kept her hand down firmly on the table. "Motion passed. Mr. Peterson, you may return to your classroom tomorrow, but please remember to keep things professional at all times. You are a representative of this school district in and out of the classroom."

Luke stood up, but the woman stopped him. "And might I suggest this parent not work in the classroom."

"Is there a rule about that?" Luke's attorney asked.

The Duke guy said, "Not that I know of." He winked.

The room was abuzz as Ellison made her way down toward Luke. She was almost there when Josh stepped in front of her. Jenn stood at his side, like an obedient dog. She was grasping her stomach and clenching her jaw.

"Are you okay?" Ellison asked before Josh could say anything to her. "Are you having contractions?"

Jenn looked down at Ellison. "I think so. I don't really know. My back aches."

"Josh," Ellison said. "You need to get her to a hospital." She turned to Jenn. "When's your due date?"

"Last week."

"Good Lord!" Ellison exclaimed. "How do the two of you have time for all this bullshit?"

Two very strong hands grasped her shoulders. Luke. Ellison turned her head up and back to get a good look at him.

"Is everything okay?" Luke asked, as Jenn winced.

"I think Jenn is in labor," Ellison answered. "I'm trying to convince Josh to take her to the hospital."

Jenn groaned and rested her hand on Ellison's shoulder. "We need to go now," she gasped. "Please, Josh, let's go."

"This isn't over, Ellison. We're going to have conversation about this." Josh's eyes flashed with anger.

Luke bent down and kissed the top of Ellison's head as if to taunt Josh. But Ellison didn't care. She found it amusing.

"Looking forward to it," Ellison said as Josh ushered his wife toward the exit.

40

KARMA

The sheets tangled with Ellison's legs as she laid her head on Luke's bare chest. She traced her fingertips across his collarbone and planted a kiss on Luke's cheek.

"Thank you," she said.

Luke rolled over, propping up on one arm. "For what?"

"For a lot of things. Making me feel like a human again; for staying with me even though it could have cost you your job." Ellison batted her long lashes. "For loving me," she whispered.

"I do love you, Ellison. There's no reason to whisper it."

She snuggled deeper into Luke's warm arms. "This is where I belong."

"Yes, it is."

After she had fed the boys dinner – mac and cheese with a side of Brussels sprouts – and put them to bed, Ellison had called Luke and asked him over. There was no hesitation on his part. They hadn't really had a chance to talk after the hearing, and Ellison felt they had a lot to discuss.

While she had waited for him in a red and cream lace baby-doll nighty hidden under her ratty robe, Josh had called to say Jenn was in fact in labor. Ellison didn't want to wake the boys, so she sat on that information. Besides labor could last hours. No need to tell them until the baby was here.

"Ellison," Luke said, touching her forehead with his finger. "Where are you going in that brain of yours?"

"Just thinking about today."

"Did Josh and Jenn upset you?"

Had they? She wasn't sure. Granted, she was livid at Josh for taking things to Principal Sylvian to begin with, but she kind of felt bad for Jenn. The truth was, Jenn was decent to Ellison's boys when she could behave a lot worse.

Plus, how sad was it that while Jenn was in early labor, Josh was more interested in ruining Ellison's happiness with Luke? Was he really that desperate to win Ellison back that he couldn't see his own wife needed him?

"I'm fine," Ellison said. "I just can't believe Josh would do such a thing to you."

Luke kissed her lips softly before saying, "I don't think he was doing it to me. I've seen the way he looks at you. It's the look of a man who wants what he can't have."

"That's what Andi says, too."

Luke leaned back into the pillows. "It's true. He only wants you because he sees you through a different lens now. You're happy, healthy Ellison."

"I was broken and a mess when we met," she said softly. "Why were you interested?"

Luke tilted his head. "A long time ago, I told you not all broken things are ruined, and I meant it. Look at you. You're strong and resilient."

"Do you really think so?" Ellison asked.

"Absolutely. Josh couldn't see your real beauty before, and look what he ended up with," Luke said. "I'd be dying to have you back too, if I had a wife like Jenn after having you. You were faithful to your marriage. Can't say the same about Josh."

Ellison smiled. Luke always said the right things. "Do you want some wine?" Ellison asked. "I have a bottle of Cab dying to be opened."

"That sounds delicious."

Ellison unwound herself from Luke and the sheets and pulled on her robe that lay on the floor next to the bed. She tiptoed out of her room and downstairs toward the kitchen where she grabbed the bottle of Cab, the corkscrew, and two glasses and placed them on a pale blue serving tray. For good measure, she added some dark chocolate to the mix.

As she made her way upstairs, she heard little feet scampering away.

"Dash?" she said. "What are you doing out of bed?"

Her son turned around. "I thought I heard something in the kitchen. I was going to see what it was." He dropped his hand to the side, exposing the mini baseball bat he carried.

"Oh baby, you don't need to do that. Mom has everything under control."

"So it was you in the kitchen?" Dash asked.

Ellison glanced at the two wine glasses. "It was me." She didn't want Dash to know Luke was in her bedroom. "Just me, getting something to drink."

Dash cocked his head and studied the tray, but didn't say anything else.

"You need to go back to bed. You have school tomorrow."

"Will you tuck me in?"

"Go climb in bed, and I'll be there in a minute."

Dash scampered away, bat still firmly clasped in his hand. When Ellison was sure he was in his room, she slipped back into her bedroom with one finger over her lips, signaling Luke to be quiet. "Dash is up," she whispered.

Luke nodded his head and held out his hands. Ellison gave him the tray and backed out the door. She tightened her robe's sash as she walked toward Dash's room.

When she entered, she heard the faint hum of her son snoring. With a smile, Ellison kissed him softly. "Good night, my little love bug," she said. Dash's eyes fluttered open before closing again.

Once back in her room, she had just enough time to lock the door before Luke grabbed her around the waist and kissed her throat. "Oh God," Ellison whispered. Luke scooped her up and carried her to the bed where he laid her down gently.

"Ready for round two?" he growled.

"Yes," Ellison said. "Absolutely."

Jenn had a baby boy the next afternoon after nineteen hours of labor. Alex, of course, was delighted to have a new, younger sibling. Dash, not so much. Since coming home from school and hearing the news, he'd been sulking and refusing to talk about the baby. Anytime Alex would bring it up, Dash would scowl and leave the room.

But here they were, waiting for Josh to pick up the boys and take them to meet the new baby.

"Mom?" Dash said, sidling up next to her. "Are you and Mr. Peterson going to have a baby, too?"

Ellison sunk down so she was eye level with her son. "Mr. Peterson is my boyfriend. That's it. Sometimes boyfriends become husbands, and sometimes they don't."

"You're not answering my question."

"Well, Mr. Peterson and I aren't married, so no, we won't be having a baby."

Dash squished up his face. "Dad and Jenn weren't married when she was pregnant."

Ellison almost burst out laughing. All the talking around the issue, and Dash still knew Jenn was knocked up before the wedding.

"Well, Dad and I have different beliefs about that." *And about being loyal to your spouse. And not cheating. And not being a big, fat liar.*

"But Mr. Peterson was here last night. I saw his truck out my bedroom window."

Busted.

Ellison scrambled for something to say, but she kept coming up speechless. Finally, the words came to her. "Mr. Peterson and I were discussing classroom stuff."

"Andi said she hopes you get married."

Ellison's jaw dropped open. Leave it to Andi to say something like that. "Well, you know he's my boyfriend. As for the marrying part, I think that's Andi's wild imagination."

"But what if you do get married? What will happen to Alex and me?"

This is what his therapist warned her about. Feeling not wanted – especially with the new baby's arrival. She wished Josh would spend more time listening to the therapist and less time worrying about whom she was sleeping with. "You and Alex will always be my first priorities," Ellison said, looking her son in the eyes. "Always."

Dash's little body slumped, and he let out a sob. Ellison folded him into her arms, "It's alright, baby. I've got you."

"Why are you crying, Dash?" Alex asked. "We have a new brother. I'm not the baby anymore!"

"Shut up," Dash said, his voice soft and weak. Resigned almost. Like he'd given up on trying to pretend to be happy.

"Hey," Ellison said. "We don't talk like that to each other in this house."

"Dad tells Jenn to shut up all the time." Alex shrugged like it's no big deal.

"Well, in this house we don't behave like that."

A fist pounded against the door. Josh, who thought doorbells were merely door decorations, waited on the front porch when Ellison answered.

"Congratulations," she said, trying to keep her voice upbeat for the boys. Really, all she wanted to do was throttle him and laugh in his face about how he didn't get Luke fired. But that seemed childish, and Ellison wanted to appear better than that.

"Yeah. Thanks," Josh mumbled.

Ellison smiled. "You look exhausted."

"Well everything took longer than I remembered. I didn't get much sleep."

Ellison laughed. "Get used to it. Remember how our boys were up every hour when they were little."

Dark circles ringed Josh's eyes, and he ran his hand through his hair. "Please don't remind me, or I'll never get through this. Forty is too freaking old to be doing this again."

There was no excitement or love in his voice. He acted like a man on autopilot instead of a proud new father. The exact opposite of what he'd been when their boys were born.

Ellison motioned to the boys. "They're really excited to meet baby Max."

Dash scoffed at the floor while Alex excitedly grabbed at Josh's hand. "C'mon, Dad. Let's go!"

"I'll bring them back around eight. I figured we could grab dinner after seeing the baby."

"I want Fudrucker's," Dash said.

Josh tousled Dash's hair. "I think we can work with that, Buddy." He ushered the boys out the door and to his car. "So see you around eight, okay?"

"Sounds good." She leaned against the door, and tears rolled down her cheeks. She wasn't crying out of misery this time. Those days were gone. What she had now were tears of laughter.

Josh was so in over his head. He was in a marriage he didn't want – or so he said – and now had a new baby to keep him up all night.

Karma, Ellison thought, *is a bitch.*

41

YOU'RE MY GLUE

A few weeks later, Ellison stood in the middle of the mall, trying to decide which way to go first. Andi had surprised her with a few free hours by taking the boys. Since Max's birth, Josh had cancelled most of his days with the boys saying things were crazy, and the baby had colic. Neither boy minded, because as Alex soon found out, babies don't really do anything except cry, eat, and sleep. Ellison had the distinct impression Alex was disappointed in his new brother but didn't want to say so.

Anyway, Andi insisted Ellison needed time off from being a mom twenty-four seven and had offered to take the boys out for ice cream and a movie, and Ellison eagerly took her up on it.

Ellison turned left – toward Saks – when she saw Andi, the boys, and Luke walking ahead of her. At first, she was surprised and thought to run after them, but ultimately, Ellison ducked into the nearest store, desperate that they not see her.

What in the world were the four of them doing here? And together? What happened to the movie?

She half-heartedly looked through the racks of overpriced clothes that she could neither afford nor wear. *There was an age limit on mini-*

mini skirts, right?. When she peeked her head back out of the store, they were all gone.

Ellison decided not to go and find them even though she wanted to. She glanced at her watch. She had two hours to kill. Thankfully, she'd sold another house and had two more in the pipeline. She was getting her professional and personal mojo back, and at the moment, she had no responsibilities except to get a mani-pedi at her favorite nail salon.

Ellison hurried to her car, worried that Andi and Luke might see her. Whatever they were up to, she suspected it had to do with her, and she didn't want to ruin the surprise.

As she drove, her mind raced with ideas, each one more ridiculous than the next. There was nothing at that end of the mall except Anthropologie and Saks. Were they getting her a birthday present? It was a little early, a month to be exact, but maybe that was it.

While the nail tech worked, Ellison couldn't let it go of her wild theories, and she decided to interrogate the boys later. That was probably her best bet at getting to the bottom of the matter.

Her phone rang, and Ellison jumped. The nail tech firmly grabbed her ankle and placed her foot back on the spa bowl. "You're going to get polish everywhere," she admonished. "Don't move."

"Sorry." Ellison looked at her phone. It was Andi.

"Hey love," Andi said. "We're home now. The movie was a no-go, so we went to the mall instead and had mall food. The boys loved it."

No mention of running into Luke or seeing Luke. Interesting.

"I'm getting a mani-pedi," Ellison said. "I probably won't be home for another hour or so."

"Not a problem. I can put the boys to bed."

Ellison twirled a piece of her hair. Something was up. She just didn't know what.

"So how was the mall last night?" Ellison asked, as the boys shoveled cereal into their mouths.

"Good." Dash said, averting her gaze.

"It was fun. Andi and-"

Dash shot Alex a look of death, and Alex looked like he might burst.

"What did Andi do?" Ellison asked.

"Andi bought me a *large* sandwich and fries." Alex said this proudly. Ellison never let him get a large anything because he never finished it.

"Did you eat it all?"

Alex nodded. "I did."

She turned her attention to Dash. "Did you see anyone else?"

"Nope," he kept his eyes down as he lied.

What was going on? Andi and the boys both lied to her about what happened. Or more correctly, they omitted Luke being with them.

"Hurry up and eat," she said to the two boys. "We're going to be late."

She ran upstairs. From below, she heard the faint arguing of the boys. She could eavesdrop, but clearly, no one wanted her to know what was happening. She frowned.

Maybe it was time to go directly to Luke.

Since it was Wednesday, she had to work in his classroom, which would give her the perfect opportunity to interrogate him – after the students had gone to lunch, of course. Thankfully, Ms. Sylvian had decided to let Ellison continue to volunteer as long as she and Luke kept things professional in front of the kids.

From her closet, she selected a purple wrap sweater and paired it with a gray camisole. She slid into her skinny jeans and stepped into her gray ballerina flats. Next, she walked to the bathroom and checked her reflection. Her hair was pulled into a slick ponytail, which made her cheekbones look sharper. Ellison dabbed on berry-colored lip gloss and decided she looked pulled together enough to brave drop-off. Since the school board hearing, she'd become the talk of the school. Mr. Peterson's girlfriend – not Dash and Alex's mom as she'd grown accustomed to hearing.

"C'mon boys. Get your shoes on."

Dash and Alex were already standing by the door, with backpacks, shoes, and coats.

How strange. Normally, she had to wrangle them away from morning cartoons. But not today. No. Today, both boys stood smiling up at her as she walked downstairs and grabbed her coat and purse from the banister.

"Okay," she said. "What's going on?"

Dash shrugged, and Alex followed his lead. But try as they might, neither could wipe the giant smiles off their faces.

"Nothing," Alex said. "Nothing is going on. Right, Dash?"

Her eldest son raised his eyebrows and shoulders. "Not that I know of."

"Fine," Ellison said. "No one tell me what's going on."

Alex giggled. "Don't worry, Mom. You're going to find out soon."

Dash stomped his foot and hissed, "Alex. Don't spoil things!"

Ellison suddenly felt dizzy. She needed to sit down and promptly plopped on the stairs.

Whatever was going on, everyone but her seemed to know.

And that worried her.

Ellison stood in the middle of the classroom. She stared at her hands. Ink smudged them. Across the room, Luke helped a boy with his spelling.

So far, she hadn't had a chance to speak with him, and he'd avoided her gaze all morning. She let out a sigh.

"Are you okay, Ms. Brooks?" a little girl asked.

"I'm fine. I just need to wash my hands." The ballpoint pen she'd been using had exploded, leaving her fingers a dark blue color.

Luke glanced at her, and catching her eye, quickly looked away.

All these secrets and stealth glances were becoming maddening.

"Alright, friends." The school district had a policy about using the term boys and girls. Students were friends. Ellison thought it was ridiculous. "Time to pack up and get ready for lunch."

The classroom turned into a hive of activity. Students shoved papers and books into their desks. Some wandered around, talking to each other while they grabbed their lunch bags.

Once everyone was in line, Luke opened the door. The line leader walked the kids out into the hallway.

"Should I stay?" she asked, wanting a few minutes of alone time with Luke. After all, how was she going to get to the bottom of whatever was going on if she didn't interrogate him?

Luke shook his head. "I'm on lunch duty today. I'll see you at dinner tonight?"

Since the school board meeting, they'd become more public about their relationship. Tonight, they had plans to have dinner at the Club.

"Okay," she said, hiding her disappointment. "See you then."

The kids had all exited the room. Luke gestured toward the hallway. "I have to go."

Ellison watched him retreat toward the lunchroom with the kids. He was avoiding her; she was positive of that.

With her bag slung over her shoulder, she made her way out of school and to her SUV. Normally, she'd call Andi, but Ellison was convinced Andi had a hand in whatever was going on. Plus, getting Andi to talk was like breaking into Fort Knox – impossible.

No, she was on her own this time.

Andi had offered to watch the boys again. This time Ellison had pre-bought the movie tickets so there could be no excuses for them not to go.

"How do I look?" Ellison asked Andi, who sat on Ellison's bed.

"Gorgeous."

At Andi's prompting, Ellison had twisted her hair up and wore dangly earrings. Maybe a little much for the Club, but who cared. It would give Eve something to gossip about.

The doorbell rang, and there was a mad scramble downstairs as the boys raced to answer the door.

"Hi, guys!" Luke's voice boomed. "Is your mom ready?"

"Mom!" Alex called. "Luke is here." No more Mr. Peterson, except from Dash who sometimes forgot.

There was some serious whispering going on when Ellison arrived at the top of the stairs. Dash spotted her, and they all stopped speaking.

Curious and curiouser.

"Have fun, you two," Andi said, grabbing her coat. The boys did the same. "We don't want to be late for our movie."

After they left, Luke pulled Ellison into a bear hug and kissed her forehead. "You smell wonderful."

Her face lit up. She was getting more comfortable with Luke's compliments. "Thank you."

Luke held the door open for Ellison. When they were both on the porch, she stopped to lock the door. "You know," she said, the idea popping into her head. "I should give you your own key. You're here so much. It would be more convenient."

"Is that all it is?" Luke was grinning at her. "A convenience?"

She shot him a sly look. "For now?"

They walked down the path to Luke's waiting truck. He quickly opened the door, and Ellison climbed up on the running boards before settling into her seat.

Once they were both in the truck, Luke backed out of the driveway and started down the street – but in the wrong direction.

"Luke," Ellison said. "The Club is the other way."

"I know."

"But we're going to be late going this way." They had a seven-thirty reservation. She had made it herself.

"I thought we could try something different tonight." Luke's voice, normally so confident, sounded off.

Ellison tilted her head. She wasn't one for changes in plans. In fact, it threw her a little bit. "But I told Andi we'd be there, and what if something happens?"

"Elle, relax. Andi knows where we're going to be, okay?"

She inhaled and exhaled. She trusted Luke. That's all that

mattered.

"Okay," she said.

"Now, sit back and relax. We're driving into DC."

He rested his hand on hers, and her anxiety melted away. "DC?"

"Yes. I know it's a bit of a drive, but I heard this restaurant is amazing."

Ellison nodded. "If you say so."

"When have I led you wrong?" Luke teased.

"So far, never."

The truck sped down the freeway toward DC. Ellison's heart sped along with it. Her pulse thundered in her ears, and she felt woozy.

Ha! she thought. *I don't even need a drink to feel buzzed around Luke.*

She interlaced her fingers with Luke's and let herself enjoy the comfortable silence between the two of them.

"What in the world?" Ellison said, as Luke pulled up to Whiskey Blu. A valet opened the door for her, and she looked to Luke.

"Go on," he laughed. "Get out."

Ellison scrunched her brows in confusion.

"I thought we could get a drink before dinner, and this place has a special meaning for me."

Ellison smiled. How could she ever forget this place? But something seemed off. Then it hit her. There was no line to get in, and it was a Friday night.

"Where is everyone?" she asked.

Luke shrugged. "Maybe inside already?"

Ellison gave him an incredulous look. "What's going on?"

"You'll see Miss Impatient."

Ellison's heartbeat sped up as they stepped through the revolving doors. A heavy curtain separated Luke and her from the lounge. Music pulsed around them, and Ellison turned back to look at Luke. He scrambled around her and pulled the curtain back.

The lounge was empty. At least it looked that way at first as her eyes adjusted to the dim blue lights.

Then she saw them: Luke's parents and Monica. Monica wore a giant smile and rushed forward and hugged Ellison hard. From the corner of her eye, Ellison caught sight of Andi and the boys.

What in the world?

Then it dawned on her. The change of plans, the trip to Whiskey Blu, their friends, and family.

Was he...Dash and Alex rushed forward and stood at Luke's side. Behind them, Andi beamed.

The DJ stopped spinning, and Luke dropped to one knee as Monica squealed. A numbing heat spread through Ellison's body. She tottered slightly before steadying herself.

He couldn't be? Could he?

"Ellison," Luke said, his voice trembled slightly. "I know this is fast, but the moment I met you, I knew you were the one." She stared down at Luke. His hand shook as he held out a beautiful antique-looking ring. She swallowed hard, trying to wet her dry throat. "Will you do me the honor of becoming my wife?"

It was absolutely perfect. The boys, Andi, and Luke's family being here. The setting. Everything.

"I was broken." Ellison touched Luke's cheek. "You were my glue,"

He shook his head. "You fixed yourself. I'm just the beneficiary of the stronger version of Ellison." He held the sparkling ring up higher and gave her an uncertain smile. "I don't want to be pushy, but I really need to know, will you marry me?"

"Yes," she said softly as happy tears slipped down her cheeks. Dash and Alex surrounded her in hugs as the rest of the group cheered. She closed her eyes to envision the future and all the possibilities it held. The dark days were behind her, and she was excited to move forward with Luke and her boys by her side.

Luke took the ring from the box, and Ellison held out her hand. He slipped the ring over her finger. It, like Luke, fit perfectly.

The End

ACKNOWLEDGMENTS

First and foremost, I have to thank my husband for not only listening to me talk about my imaginary friends, but for also reading every single word of every single book I've ever written out loud to me. He's the superman of my writing career, and more often than not, pushes me up the hill when I want to give up.

Caroline Hedges is my trusty developmental editor and never fails to find plot holes and places where I can beef up the story. Her touch is all over my books, and I'm forever grateful for her investing so much of herself into my writing. She is also a mean Karaoke singer and has taught me how to not give as many fucks — whether it's when I have a microphone in my hand or dealing with larger life issues.

Karla Kratovil. This girl. Every Thursday, she sits and listens to me prattle on about everything non-writing related until finally cracking the whip and making me write all the words. Her friendship has not only made me a better person, but also a happier one. Love ya, girl!

The Writing Circle is a merry band of mismatched writers that I've come to love. Thank you for welcoming me into your group and helping me drill my pages down.

Over the past ten years, I've been able to surround myself with some of the finest writers and call them my critique partners. Our retreats, Slack convos, YAWN, and Google Hangouts have propelled me through this crazy career.

And lastly, thank you, my readers, for reading, reviewing, and recommending my books. Thank you for handing over some of your precious time and letting my words guide you to another place. Without you, my stories would be locked up in my head with no where to go.

xoxo ~mia

ABOUT THE AUTHOR

Mia lives in Northern Virginia with her husband, children, and cats. When she's not writing, she's practicing yoga, traveling, or drinking ridiculous amounts of green tea.

She's been known to eavesdrop a time or two.

Keep up with Mia and her books by joining her newsletter: http://eepurl.com/dsfaTL or by following her on one of the sites below.

[f] facebook.com/miahayesauthor

[twitter] twitter.com/novahousewife

[instagram] instagram.com/miahayesautor

ALSO BY MIA HAYES

The Secrets We Keep

Printed in the USA
CPSIA information can be obtained
at www.ICGtesting.com
CBHW062013090624
9801CB00014B/172